W9-CEN-552

VIKING PENGUIN

Celebrates

ARTHUR MILLER

Photograph by Dan Weiner

Miller during the writing of *Death of a Salesman*

NEW FROM VIKING

ARTHUR MILLER

HOMELY GIRL,
A LIFE
and other stories

NOW AVAILABLE FROM PENGUIN

The Portable Arthur Miller
Edited by Christopher Bigsby

Timebends: A Life

Timebends is also coming soon on
audiocasssette from Penguin
Audiobooks

The Crucible
New Twentieth-Century Classics
edition,with an Introduction by
Christopher Bigsby

The Crucible CD-ROM is
also available from
Penguin Electronic

60
Penguin Years

Most of Arthur Miller's plays are available from Penguin

ANDRE
EMMERICH
GALLERY

41 EAST 57TH STREET

NEW YORK, NEW YORK 10022

TELEPHONE (212) 752-0124

FAX (212) 371-7345

CONJUNCTIONS

Bi-Annual Volumes of New Writing

Edited by
Bradford Morrow

Contributing Editors
Walter Abish
Chinua Achebe
John Ashbery
Mei-mei Berssenbrugge
Guy Davenport
Elizabeth Frank
William H. Gass
John Guare
Susan Howe
Robert Kelly
Ann Lauterbach
Patrick McGrath
Nathaniel Tarn
Quincy Troupe
John Edgar Wideman

published by Bard College

EDITOR: Bradford Morrow
MANAGING EDITOR: Michael Bergstein
SENIOR EDITORS: Martine Bellen, Ben Marcus, Pat Sims
ART EDITOR: Anthony McCall
ASSOCIATE EDITOR: Thalia Field
EDITORIAL ASSISTANT: Paulina Nissenblatt

CONJUNCTIONS is published in the Spring and Fall of each year by Bard College, Annandale-on-Hudson, NY 12504. This issue is made possible in part with the generous funding of the Lannan Foundation, the National Endowment for the Arts and the New York State Council on the Arts.

SUBSCRIPTIONS: Send subscription order to CONJUNCTIONS, Bard College, Annandale-on-Hudson, NY 12504. Single year (two volumes): $18.00 for individuals; $25.00 for institutions and overseas. Two years (four volumes): $32.00 for individuals; $45.00 for institutions and overseas. Patron subscription (lifetime): $500.00. Overseas subscribers please make payment by International Money Order. Back issues available at $12.00 per copy. For subscription and advertising information, call or fax 914-758-1539.

Editorial communications should be sent to 33 West 9th Street, New York, NY 10011. Unsolicited manuscripts cannot be returned unless accompanied by a stamped, self-addressed envelope.

Cover artwork © 1995 by Red Grooms. Scale model of set for John Guare's *Moon Under Miami*, first performed at the Organic Theater, Chicago, 1995. Reproduced by kind permission of the artist and Marlborough Gallery.
Cover design by Anthony McCall Associates, New York.

Printers: Edwards Brothers.
Typesetter: Bill White, Typeworks.

ISSN 0278-2324
ISBN 0-941964-41-8

Manufactured in the United States of America.

TABLE OF CONTENTS

THE NEW AMERICAN THEATER, Guest Edited by John Guare

COMING UP IN THE SPRING ISSUE

Our spring issue, *Brave New Word, Conjunctions:26,* specu-
lates on new directions American fiction is commandeering
here at the end of our mad century, in a special gathering of
new voices guest-edited by senior editor Ben Marcus, including remarkable new work by Brian Evenson, Jason Schwartz,
Teresa Svoboda, Gary Lutz, Dawn Raffel, Brian Schorn, and
others. "Theirs is work," writes Mr. Marcus in his prologue,
"marked by its refusal of the empty temptations of technology, by young artists who have yet to retreat into the safety
of private expression, intent on bringing forth their dark
worlds with fearless clarity."

Continuing our commitment to publishing new theater
writing — bringing the "stage to the page" — the issue will
feature plays by David Mamet, Liz Tucillo, Paul Auster, and
Lynn Martin.

Michael Palmer, Elaine Equi, Nathaniel Mackey, Ronald
Johnson, Ann Lauterbach, Forrest Gander, Martine Bellen,
Laynie Browne, and others weigh in with new poetry.

A ranging interview with Steve Erickson will be included,
as well as fiction by Rikki Ducornet, Carole Maso, Paul West,
and others.

Subscriptions to *Conjunctions* are only $18 per year — 25%
off the cover price. Please send your check to *Conjunctions,*
Bard College, Annandale-on-Hudson NY, 12504 and begin
your subscription with *Brave New Word.*

GUEST EDITOR'S NOTE

I WANT TO THANK Bradford Morrow for hearing me when I told him about the extraordinary burst of playwriting activity going on in America right now. He was amazed when I told him about this entire breed of playwrights out there doing work which is not a part of any literary scene and never gets exposure to a reading public — unless of course the play lands a successful production and then is deemed ready to be read. I trust this issue of *Conjunctions* will begin to remedy that situation and even generate more new work.

Because there are so many playwrights who could not be included in *Conjunctions: 25, The New American Theater*, I want to commend Morrow for his decision to make new plays a regular feature of each issue. In the next *Conjunctions*, you'll find work by David Mamet as well as the work of two brilliant new talents, Lynn Martin and Liz Tuccillo. I also have to thank Mary Pat Walsh, who has the best eye, ear, nose, mind and heart of anyone I know for judging new work.

— John Guare
September 1995
New York City

Plays As Literature
Joyce Carol Oates

READING PLAYS IS LIKE reading poetry: it requires, though in a very different way, an exercise of the imagination.

In poetry and prose fiction both, the "voice" of the work is provided directly. Though elliptical and metaphorical in poetry, and often expository in prose fiction, the voice is likely to be a singular, consistent voice, and the individual reader is its sole confidante. We may not be told what to think but we are provided with the atmosphere in which to think, and frequently in fact we *are* told what to think. These works of literature are always *past tense*, even when they purport to be presenting events in present tense; they record moments now history, and permeable to interpretation. The "point of view" of the work, its psychological perspective, allows us entry into the mystery to be explored. (For all works of the imagination are mysteries. *What has happened to bring us to this point of crisis? What will happen to push us further, to resolution? Out of what urgency has the work been created?*)

Plays more closely resemble poetry than they do most prose fiction, because poetry is a compact language, a heightened and accelerated form of communication, and what is omitted is an integral part of its meaning, just as plays are "narratives" severely reduced to human voices and gestures. A dramatic work is always *present tense*, and characters are vividly alive before us. We aren't told what they say or do, we observe them firsthand. We aren't told what to think about them, we draw our own conclusions.

Reading plays, the reader's mind *is* the stage, and a willful emptiness is desirable. Envision a play dramatically by seeing the characters enter this emptiness, as they would a stage in a theater; as much "background" is provided as the playwright has given you in his notes and asides. Your imagination is actively engaged. The silent reading of a play can be a "staging" that may in truth be more rewarding, and closer to the playwright's intentions, than one or another actual production.

So, too, the "staged reading" for many theater people can be more rewarding than the fully produced play. For the playwright him- or herself, the experience is often more illuminating. The colorful distractions of the set, the blocking, the director's interpretation of the work haven't yet come into being.

Some plays are more self-consciously literary, more designed to be *read*, than others. George Bernard Shaw's prefaces and stage descriptions are famously, or infamously, intended to be read; Shaw's doggedly witty, persistently hectoring voice competes with the voices of his dramatic characters for our attention. The exquisitely wrought and writerly plays of any number of classic playwrights — Chekhov, Turgenev, Strindberg, Ibsen, Calderon, Yeats, Lorca, Synge — repay countless readings. Most of us know the incantatory and elusive tragedies of Aeschylus, Sophocles and Euripides solely through reading, not the stage. Above all, the plays of Shakespeare demand to be read, reread, brooded upon, absorbed. In our classic American theater, Eugene O'Neill and Tennessee Williams are perhaps the most avidly *read* of playwrights.

Yet the distinction between the art of the play and the art of prose fiction is considerable. The prose writer, coming to the theater, is likely to be stunned, if not dismayed, by the leaden nature of his best "writerly" work when it is presented by living actors on a blunt, exposed stage. Where in prose fiction the writer is accustomed to shaping subtleties of meaning by way of carefully composed language, in which the very punctuation and the spacing of paragraphs may be a part of the meaning, in drama the writer must provide for his characters "living" roles. All great novelists — Dostoyevsky, Dickens, Flaubert, Eliot, Hardy, Joyce, Lawrence, Melville, Faulkner — provide rich, fascinating passages of description, historical background, character analyses, exposition; we are likely in fact to be reading novels for this reason, because we are mesmerized by a writer's unique voice. In prose fiction, style is art; there is no art without individual style. Yet, on the living stage, none of these qualities of prose fiction "works": not description, however brilliant; not historical background, analysis, any kind of exposition. What shimmers with life on the page may die within minutes in the theater precisely because prose is a language to be spoken to an individual, recreated in an individual reader's consciousness, usually in solitude, while dramatic dialogue is a special language spoken by living actors to one another, a collective audience overhearing. Most remarkably — and here I am speaking as a writer of prose fiction who approaches the art of the play with much humility, yearning and hope — the dramatic situation may not contain spoken language at all, but resides in a realm that can only be described as purely theatrical. It is something of a surprise, and certainly an instructive, chastising surprise, for the writer of prose fiction, to discover that scripts that appear barely skeletal to the reader's eye, by contemporary heirs of Beckett like Pinter and Mamet, spring astonishingly to life on the stage, because they are not "about" texts at all, but powerful subtexts to be brought into life by the art of acting. (The "act of acting"—a subject entire in itself, unfortunately out of place here. Only keep in mind that the most supreme artists of acting are precisely those who scarcely seem to be acting, at all, and may therefore be undervalued.) So we discover, to our astonishment, that theater is not "about" dialogue after all, but what might be called fields of dramatic tension; force-fields of human relationships beneath the level of language, and perhaps even of consciousness, at which dialogue hints in the way that a divining rod hints at a subterranean spring. If there is no mysterious, magical spring water hidden beneath the surface of the work, the most elegantly crafted, clever dialogue will not make the work live. We learn that the text of the play is not the play, still less is the written and published text of the play anything like the theatrical experience, which will vary considerably with individual productions, each production being a complex vision worked up into performance by an individual director-artist in company with individual actor-artists. (That these are "artists" no less than the playwright cannot be stressed sufficiently.) All theater is living experience, all published texts are histories or records of experience. Theater is *present tense*, the printed word is *past tense*.

In venturing into the territory of the theater, the writer accustomed to the printed word must leave behind all the cultivated strategies of his (or her) art — the shelter of language, the cocoon-like protection of an individual prose style; the powerful arsenal of intellectual analyses, historical and expository information; allusions, references, metaphors; all of interiority, in fact. *But isn't that everything?* you may ask. *Why would a writer give up so much, in exchange for the unknown?*

Precisely because the theater *is* an adventure, a challenge, a risk; because it is not only always *present tense* in the theater, but because the theater itself has no memory. All that you've learned, or believe you've learned, in one adventure, may be erased by the second, and yet again by the third. In theater, the playwright throws himself (or herself — I suppose I am speaking most frankly and intimately of myself) into a kind of free-fall, surrendering control in the hope of achieving something higher: that realm of the purely and ineffably theatrical.

*

Long recognized as one of our most imaginative, gifted, provocative and adventurous of playwrights, John Guare here presents in *Conjunctions: 25, The New American Theater* a gathering of works by contemporary American playwrights that is representative of the eclectic, experimental and hybrid nature of our theater. It is a heterogeneous assortment with no political rubric, no aesthetic banner. Familiar names are juxtaposed with the less familiar and the newly emergent; realistic, accessible works are juxtaposed with the bizarre and perhaps unstageable. There is a wonderful diversity of styles, from the hallucinatory *It's an Undoing World* of Tony Kushner, the gorgeously lurid *Venus* of Suzan-Lori Parks and the vividly theatrical *Insurrection* of Robert O'Hara to the powerful dramatic naturalism of Donald Margulies's short, tight, captivating *Kibbutz* and the melancholy comedy of Wendy Wasserstein's *Antonia and Jane,* the forthright low-keyed realism of Mark O'Donnell's *Wish Technology.* The section from Jon Robin Baitz's *Amphibians* suggests a full-length drama of character and conscience in a mode that resembles the most powerful work of Arthur Miller, while the section from John Guare's *Moon Under Miami* suggests an extravaganza of ever-shifting mock-madcap revelations, unpredictable like most of this playwright's work. There are plays here that richly reward close reading, among them Ellen McLaughlin's experimental verse plays *Iphigenia in Aulis* and *Iphigenia in Tauris,* and several that may require it — Erik Ehn's teasingly surreal *Every Man Jack of You,* for instance, and Doug Wright's *Quills.* Harry Kondoleon's notes to the director on the nature of the set for *Saved or Destroyed* makes for helpful information not available to a theater audience. The playwright's notes for Christopher Durang's surreal *Nina in the Morning* help to illuminate the play, like Mac Wellman's for the highly conceptualized *The Sandalwood Box.*

In a special category, in fact, is Kondoleon's frame-smashing work, in which an actor addresses the audience with painful candor, speculating on the reasons why people come to the theater: "To see actors and measure their own dissatisfactions against those of the characters?" He states bluntly, "I am your average sometimes-working actor. You have probably not seen me in undistinguished productions in regional theaters across the country... You have possibly not seen me on TV ... I am not, ladies and gentlemen, one of the stars."

For all their diversity, we can define plays in terms of two usually overlapping categories: the "realistic" (which need not, of course, mean conventional or formulaic) and the "surreal" (which need not, of course, mean shapeless, chaotic, impenetrable, willfully self-indulgent), and you will see here how fluidly playwrights move from one mode of expression to another, sometimes within a single scene. Tony Kushner's dithyrambic *It's an Undoing World* has the alternative title "Why Should It Be Easy When It Can Be Hard?" and the subtitle "Notes on My Grandma for Actors, Dancers and a Band"; it is a highly theatrical means of presenting private memoir and public history and the character of Sarah, "Grandma." A play in the realist mode would move along very different lines, though incorporating identical material (and one can envision a deeply moving realist play, in fact, in the penumbra of this one); the form Kushner has chosen is post-Modernist, time-fractured, choral, mythic, "confusing"—for, as it is said of Sarah, "She has no sense of, of *order*. She is *impossible*." Doug Wright's brilliantly inventive *Quills* is a meditation upon the Marquis de Sade as the exemplar of sacred and ungovernable processes of the imagination, the play's roots solidly biographical even as it soars to outrageous absurdist heights. ("The more I forbid," declares Sade's jailer, custodian of civilized bourgeois order, "the more you are provoked.") Paula Vogel's antic burlesque *The Mineola Twins* springs from an actual, if improbable, Mineola, USA of the sixties, seventies and eighties.

"Experimental" dramatic techniques have become, in the late twentieth century, so much a part of the playwright's arsenal of strategies that they seem scarcely "experimental" any longer, but rather more a kind of deft shorthand for what would have required, in an earlier decade, a more elaborate and methodical unfolding of plot. Have we not all been instructed in the sacrosanct virtues of *beginning, middle, end? Complication, climax, resolution?* A respect for Aristotelian *unities?* For the clarity of *chronology?* For *clarity* itself? As if the limitations of realism were not in fact limitations. Contemporary dramatists assume in their audiences a measure of sophistication that allows freedom to explore any number of modes of expression. Both Suzan-Lori Parks's *Venus* and Robert O'Hara's *Insurrection*, of which we have sections here, promise to be dazzling, disturbing works, strongly visual, musical and theatrical: reading such scripts is a stimulus to anticipating how they will be staged. The dreamy baseball fantasies, Arthur Kopit's *Elegy for the House that Ruth Built* and Eric Overmyer's *The Dalai Lama Goes Three for Four*, are monologues which will lend themselves to highly imaginative mise-en-scène stagings, precisely because they are so "interior." Nicky Silver's *Etiquette & Vitriol* is a more conventional monologue that opens into a full-length play comprised basically of linked monologues, like most of the dramatic work of this darkly gifted, idiosyncratic writer. Romulus Linney's two-character *Divine Comedy South* is essentially two monologists/narcissists in conversation, their subject being "the fast, furious and disgraceful rummaging through the old clothes of other [people's] bodies." And Han Ong's *Mrs. Chang* is another work of linked monologues, providing a mysterious fractured and strangely eloquent "English" that is, for the tragi-comic Mrs. Chang, a life-saving mask-talk. Han Ong demonstrates the ways in which, before our eyes, people "act" themselves. So too in the literally speedy scene from Jonathan Marc Sherman's *Evolution* two representative young men confront an electronic cloning of personality that dwarfs their quite ordinary selves: is this the next stage of human evolution? The parodied poets of Amy Freed's slyly cruel *The Psychic Life of Savages*, among whom one can identify almost too readily Ted Hughes, Sylvia Plath, Anne Sexton, Emily Dickinson, are continually inventing and exhibiting themselves through absurdly arbitrary distortions of language. Keith Reddin's *You Belong to Me*, with its rapid shiftings of perspective and its continuously overlapping, self-erasing melodramatic plots, is an artful variation on a familiar theme of marital betrayal.

Comedy by its very nature violates the decorum of realism, and leaps beyond our expectations of "common" sense in the service of a higher, and always a lighter, more transcendent vision. Perhaps the most effervescent and ingeniously realized comic play in this volume is David Ives's *Degas, C'est Moi*, which like the much-admired one-acts of Ives's recent "All in the Timing," glides with seamless fluidity from point to point, from interior monologue to exterior scene, with an irresistible momentum that can be realized only in the living art of the play.

It's an Undoing World
or
Why Should It Be Easy
When It Can Be Hard?
Notes on My Grandma for Actors, Dancers and a Band

Tony Kushner

Characters:
SARAH
THE ELDEST DAUGHTER
THE MIDDLE DAUGHTER
THE YOUNGEST DAUGHTER
THE SOLEMN GRANDCHILD
THE VOICE OF THE TEAPOT
BENJAMIN NATHAN CARDOZO, *a singer with the band*

Spanish translated by Moises Manoff
Yiddish provided by Joachim Neugroschel

Note: This is an early attempt at what will someday be a play on this subject.

This play is for my aunt Martha Deutscher
On an auspicious occasion

(Onstage are five women, a tin Statue of Liberty and a teapot, steaming. Three of the five have breast cancer, and under their eyes are dark rings and their heads are wrapped in brightly colored chemotherapy scarves. One of the remaining two is a SOLEMN GRANDCHILD *who never looks happy. The last is* SARAH, *she is dressed in a nice dress, and she wears a pink hat with roses and a net. Everyone is*

14

seated around a kitchen table eating. The voice in italics is the voice of the teapot.)

Oooooyyyyyyyy . . . It's an undoing world, I'm telling you.

SARAH. You want a place you can *be*, you can *think*, you can think a thought, my eyes are bothering me, a smell from the kitchens, it burns my eyes, it gives the floaters, this ain't a hotel, it's a *Hot Hell*. No I'm not happy. It's an undoing world.

So it was from Poland, no it was by Russia, no Lithuania, we wasn't Germans we was Litvhaks. No it was Polisia. The town was . . .

SARAH. Chiroszchjew.

Chiroszchjew, it was by Nodvorno, by Kiev, by Vilna.

THE MIDDLE DAUGHTER. There is no town on any map of any country on earth in the last two hundred years called Chiroszchjew, Ma.

THE ELDEST DAUGHTER. Her information is often unreliable.

THE YOUNGEST DAUGHTER. Her father had an inn there, by Tarnopol. By Covna by Vilna. In the country.

THE MIDDLE DAUGHTER. By the roadside.

THE ELDEST DAUGHTER. By Nodvorno was Chiroszchjew. You got to spell it with all the letters, it's Polish.

THE MIDDLE DAUGHTER. How do you spell it, Ma?

SARAH. It's Polish. No it's Russian no it's Jewish. I forgot.

I lived there with my father and also with my mother in an inn which my father owned near Chiroszchjew on the Russian-Polish border, and twice I went to America.

THE SOLEMN GRANDCHILD. Twice?

THE MIDDLE DAUGHTER. This is how twice your Grandma migrated to America.

I went, I came back, I went again . . .

SARAH. I never came back.

THE SOLEMN GRANDCHILD. Why twice, Grandma? Most people only came once to America.

SARAH. I don't remember I forgot.

THE YOUNGEST DAUGHTER. Once she knew many things.

THE MIDDLE DAUGHTER. How she came to know what later she forgot.

THE ELDEST DAUGHTER. At the inn by Chiroszchjew by when she was a little girl, so her father he decided Sarah should go cheder, to uh Torah school.

THE YOUNGEST DAUGHTER. A handsome young Russian her father hired to walk her there, by Tarnopol the cheder was, so Sarah could learn the prayers in Jewish, so that when he died her father my grandfather your great-grandfather Schmulik . . .

THE MIDDLE DAUGHTER. No Mendel.

THE ELDEST DAUGHTER. No Yussel so someone should say Kaddish for him that he might be remembered all the days.

THE YOUNGEST DAUGHTER. Because who else would.

THE MIDDLE DAUGHTER. His wife she wouldn't.

SARAH. And she never did.

I did.

THE MIDDLE DAUGHTER. The handsome young Russian student carried her piggyback to Tarnopol.

SARAH. Yah. He was handsome.

THE ELDEST DAUGHTER. She liked it, the piggyback.

SARAH. Very much.

He was a student of botany. He was fifteen. I was five. We bounced up and down, the piggyback.

SARAH. Yah.

THE ELDEST DAUGHTER. She rode on his back through hayfields, and secretly she acquired his knowledge: Through his shirt, through the skin on his back it came: It was Russian words, it was Pushkin, it was botany.

16

THE MIDDLE DAUGHTER. She knew her pistils and her stamens. A leaf uncurled inside her head.

(*A piggyback dance.*)

One winter so a Polish Countess came to the inn.

THE MIDDLE DAUGHTER. She was wealthy and cosmopolitan this Countess, she was with a big sleigh it was made of silver and jinglebells, and it was with a team of red horses and in their manes was red ribbons, no gold ribbons, it was something.

THE YOUNGEST DAUGHTER. And then at midnight this Countess, she was a strange pale lady with chalky lips, beautiful, she comes to my little bed . . .

SARAH. Yah. When I was in America I met Benjamin Nathan Cardozo the Judge . . .

THE ELDEST DAUGHTER. So she comes to our little bed, the Countess, and . . .

THE YOUNGEST DAUGHTER. And so she steals me from the bed and . . .

I'm too scared to call my father and so she took me on a midnight moonlight sleigh ride, it was snow everywhere, in the pine trees and on the hills, bright as daytime but it was night and frozen.

THE YOUNGEST DAUGHTER. So in the pine forest there was a stork's nest with dead eggs and the Countess held my hands and she danced with my ma, she was six years old.

(*A sleigh-ride dance with the Polish Countess.*)

THE ELDEST DAUGHTER. And secretly she acquired the Countess's knowledge; through the flesh of the palms of the Countess, through her fine kid gloves it came: fluency in Polish, in Hungarian, French.

And how with a needle you make gold thread embroidery.

SARAH. And also I got from her a few Christmas carols in French.

(SARAH *sings a French Christmas carol.*)

SARAH. (*Singing.*) Minuit Chretien, c'est l'heure solonelle,
L'homme dieu, jus'qua nuit, jus'qua nous,

17

Pour l'effacer, la tache originelle . . .
Da da da dee, da da dee da da doo . . .

THE ELDEST DAUGHTER. Can you imagine that a Jewish girl should a Christmas carol sing?

THE SOLEMN GRANDCHILD. Yes, I can, in our house always we had Christmas trees. In all our houses.

SARAH. Yah. It was that Countess.

THE MIDDLE DAUGHTER. Maybe because Sarah sang that song, so her father died.

THE SOLEMN GRANDCHILD. No, it was not that it was because behind the bar at the inn was blocks of ice which melting made puddles, and in them he stood all his life her father, with the icewater soaking his shoes, eventually this killed him.

    (A dance with a dirge.)

SARAH. One two three my mother marries an ignoramus.

THE MIDDLE DAUGHTER. Sarah walked every day in the snow many miles to go to shul to say Kaddish for her father. She was tough, she was an old boot, she was six, I believe this.

The rabbis at the temple wasn't pleased that so young a girl and a girl at that should for her father the Kaddish say. But they saw she's substantial, a somebody, a mensch, a person.

SARAH. My father was dead.

THE ELDEST DAUGHTER. Der Tatte meyner iz geven toyt.

THE MIDDLE DAUGHTER. Mein Vater war tot.

THE YOUNGEST DAUGHTER. Moy Otyets byl myortvy. Az Apam halott volt.

THE SOLEMN GRANDCHILD. Mon Père était mort.

SARAH. My eyes are bothering me. My daughters are such bitches. They have left me in this hot hell. I got disjunctive arthritis in my hands it's animal claws, in my eyes it's floaters. They burn food in the kitchen they sell my clothes to the actors. It's an undoing world, I got three daughters, two got cancer and they died. My mother married an ignoramus and I went to America on a boat.

THE YOUNGEST DAUGHTER. She earned her passage doing gold thread embroidery she learned from the Polish Countess. She did gold thread embroidery for the Russian Navy.

SARAH. Yah.

THE ELDEST DAUGHTER. A spool of gold thread she stole and she hid it in a jar of chicken fat, in a bag in a bundle, because the Czar wouldn't miss it and you never know.

In that first building in America there was Mrs. Oggle, that lady who lived for bananas. I met Benjamin Nathan Cardozo the Judge.

THE ELDEST DAUGHTER. Not yet Ma.

THE MIDDLE DAUGHTER. She has no sense, of, of *order*. She is *impossible*. One, two, three.

THE SOLEMN GRANDCHILD. Her mother married an ignoramus. Did he have a name, Grandma.

SARAH. The ignoramus? No.

THE YOUNGEST DAUGHTER. None that she could ever remember. So she could not live by this ignoramus so the boat, it was by the harbor in Sebastopol, so it was a freighter no a steamer no a trawler no the Queen Elizabeth no it was just a boat.

In the steerage on the boat it was all Jewish students, fatherless girls and deserters from the armies of the Czar.

THE SOLEMN GRANDCHILD. And we went to America.

SARAH. The first time.

THE ELDEST DAUGHTER. The whole way over she danced with the students, she danced with deserters, she danced with the fatherless girls. And through the foul air of steerage it came, through the dirty patchy clothing and the dirty hair it came, through the way they shook their bums and their bosoms when they danced.

THE MIDDLE DAUGHTER. Cooking skills, sewing skills, all what my mother never taught me, the whole history of suffering, and military drinking songs.

SARAH. Yah.

Tony Kushner

It was fun.

> (*A dance with students and deserters and fatherless Jewish girls.*)

THE SOLEMN GRANDCHILD. And how did you find America, Grandma?

THE YOUNGEST DAUGHTER. It was the land behind the Statue of Liberty. So it was all goys and goniffs, everyone in America was an actor or a general or a thief, in the first building where I came, was my Fette Moishe who had already plumbing, but he painted his bathroom purple so I couldn't use it, so with him in his house was dogs, so there was also in this building a Mrs. Oggle . . .

THE ELDEST DAUGHTER. I remember her she . . .

SARAH. She was a Jewish lady but she fed her children bananas. She *lived* for bananas it was disgusting. So we said Mrs. Oggle go live someplace else, so the whole family Oggle it goes over by the wops on Mulberry Street.

THE ELDEST DAUGHTER. She's racist, she says wops, she says sheenies, she says schwarzes, later in the sixties when she's seventy something she says spics. What a terrible old woman.

SARAH. No I never did. My eyes are bothering me. You abandoned me here. We all talked that way. We never talked that way. *I* never did, the others they did, they called us kikes, they got theirs over there and we got ours here, and they got more and we got less and I never talked that way I wasn't no ignoramus, I marched with Annie Lazarus in the Immigrant Rights parade.

THE MIDDLE DAUGHTER. ANNIE LAZARUS. Annie Lazarus was a big woman who made the parades for Immigrant Rights, and for Internationalism . . .

THE ELDEST DAUGHTER. So after the parade Annie Lazarus she saw Sarah was substantial, a person, somebody, so Annie Lazarus, she's a rich Sephardim . . .

Those Sephardim they think they cornered the market on suffering. The Lazaruses they was all rich Sephardim, while I was a poor Ashkenazi.

THE MIDDLE DAUGHTER. EMMA LAZARUS. From Annie Lazarus Sarah met Annie's cousin Emma, so it was Emma Lazarus who wrote the poem on the pedestal of the Statue of Liberty, which by Battery Park Sarah saw from land for the first time with Annie and Emma Lazarus and . . .

THE SOLEMN GRANDCHILD. But Grandma Emma Lazarus died in 1887 and you weren't born till 1891.

SARAH. "A mighty woman with a torch, whose flame
Is the imprisoned lightning, and her name
Mother of Exiles. From her beacon-hand
Glows world-wide welcome . . ."

"her mild eyes command
The air-bridged harbor that twin cities frame."
It was by PS 27 I learned this poem.

SARAH. "'Keep, ancient lands, your storied pomp!' cries she
With silent lips."

"Give me your tired, your poor,
Your huddled masses abubbadah bubbudah bubbudah.
Yearning to breathe free."

SARAH. EMMA LAZARUS. Emma Lazarus was a big woman with wavy hair and a handsome bosom. She bought for me the little tin Statue of Liberty that day at the Battery Park as a keepsake remembrance.

THE ELDEST DAUGHTER. Which I inherited. I am the eldest daughter.

THE MIDDLE DAUGHTER. Which you stole from Ma's room in the hotel when she died.

SARAH. The Hot Hell.

THE YOUNGEST DAUGHTER. I got the teapot. I am the youngest daughter.

THE MIDDLE DAUGHTER. Which I got after you died of cancer.

THE SOLEMN GRANDCHILD. But Emma Lazarus died in 1887.

SARAH. Yah, when I knew from her already she was very old.

THE SOLEMN GRANDCHILD. She was dead Grandma.

21

SARAH. Yah?

THE ELDEST DAUGHTER. Solemn grandchild, never tell these stories, they ain't for mass consumption.

THE MIDDLE DAUGHTER. So this is how she met Cardozo.

THE YOUNGEST DAUGHTER. BENJAMIN NATHAN CARDOZO. So Emma Lazarus makes my ma an introduction to all her family, the Lazaruses which was relatives to the Nathans which was relatives to the Cardozos, these was all Spanish Jews, they was here a hundred fifty years before us and I'm telling you they knew it.

THE MIDDLE DAUGHTER. So then this is how Emma Lazarus's cousin Benjamin Nathan Cardozo she met.

SARAH. So Annie Lazarus in the twenties she left she hated America then, it wasn't no internationalism here nor no immigrants' rights it was Republicans so she goes to live by Venice Italy and then in the forties she disappears there.
And wasn't heard of no more.

Later, Benny Cardozo, his pragmatical-philosophical inquiries into the highly subjective nature of the Judicial Process they paved the way for an Interventionist Activist Court which was what made America decent, so he went to the Supreme Court eventually but back then, I was by ten years old.

THE ELDEST DAUGHTER. He was a sad and lonely man, Benny Cardozo, he never married nobody. He was in love with the law. This became clear to Sarah when with the Lazaruses and Cardozo she was ice-skating her first winter in America by the duck pond in Central Park.

BENJAMIN NATHAN CARDOZO'S LOVE SONG
TO AMERICAN LAW

BENJAMIN NATHAN CARDOZO. (*Sings.*) I fell in love with the Law
Burnt by her icy caresses:
Drawn to her complex recesses,
My intellect effloresces.
And in my studies I saw
Just how my Goddess progresses:
She is driving on,

To awake the Dawn,
And my soul is enkindled with awe.

So a conclusion I draw:
Subjective interpellation,
Talmudic amplification:
Judging is also Creation.
Never believe it a flaw:
Hot-blooded adjudication.
Bring thy Goddesshood
To the Social Good!
If a justice is ardent she'll thaw.

When she thaws her heart will bloom like a tree
And her breasts like trumpet lilies will be
And her buds will fig and fatten,
And her kindness overflow.
And she'll tip her scales toward Mercy,
And she'll chance a glance at equality,
And she break the chains we carry,
And in joy she'll marry me.

When she agrees to be mine,
More-than-impartial Athena,
This will become our subpoena:
The Court must not be a machine!
Law is Democracy's shrine
Here in the Gold'ne Medina,
Where the legal light
Will dispel the night
And my Goddess of Justice will shine!

THE YOUNGEST DAUGHTER. Dancing on the boat, secretly Sarah had acquired from a Hasid student of the Talmud who with a girl and a young girl at that shouldn't have been dancing, a knowledge of the Law.

THE ELDEST DAUGHTER. Benjamin N. Cardozo was impressed. She talked with him the Law of Torts and Product Liability.

THE MIDDLE DAUGHTER. Like most men of his generation Benny Cardozo invented female personifications of abstract things which was offensive to real women with whom very effectively he couldn't deal.

23

Tony Kushner

He had a sister.

THE MIDDLE DAUGHTER. Benny Cardozo wanted to marry my ma.

SARAH. Yah.

THE ELDEST DAUGHTER. But that *sister.* Sarah was Ashkenazi and those rich Sephardim, nobody suffered like they suffered since after all THEY was expulsed from Spain and the Ashkenazi, who was THEY? Wretched refuse that all *chose* to leave their homes.

She hated me that sister.

THE MIDDLE DAUGHTER. And Sarah was eleven then.

THE YOUNGEST DAUGHTER. Ten.

THE ELDEST DAUGHTER. Fourteen.

When comes the San Francisco earthquake.

SARAH. Yah. What a bad place this is, what a crazybad place, they sold my things to actors who foul everything, who in the bath-tub are leaving dirt rings, in Polisia there wasn't never no earthquake. This augurs bad for America, we figure, an earthquake, yah, so all the Jews who could manage got back on the boats.

THE SOLEMN GRANDCHILD. I believed in this reverse Exodus, after the San Francisco earthquake all the Jews fled shaky fiery America and back across the sea they headed but but but I could never find it mentioned in any book.

To Chiroszchjew I came again.

THE MIDDLE DAUGHTER. Wasn't no earthquake she went back because she missed her mother terrible

SARAH. Schtick-dreck. *(To the solemn grandchild.)* Schtick-dreck means shit, dahlingk.

THE MIDDLE DAUGHTER. There wasn't no earthquake.

SARAH. Yah. There was.

THE YOUNGEST DAUGHTER. She sold the golden spool of thread to book passage.

THE ELDEST DAUGHTER. The passage returning was it was a boat, and in the boat was Glaziers from the Glaziers' Union.

THE YOUNGEST DAUGHTER. She danced with the Glaziers, and she realized she would marry a Glazier someday, and she would break his glass heart, and something like this did happen eventually.

(The Glaziers' dance.)

THE SOLEMN GRANDCHILD. And how did you find Chiroszchjew, Grandma?

SARAH. I didn't.

It was burnt to the ground.

THE MIDDLE DAUGHTER. So this is why it's not on any map, Chiroszchjew.

By the ashes of my father's inn on the ground sitting I found my mother and her ignoramus, my stepfather, and so that night I slept on my father's grave.

THE MIDDLE DAUGHTER. She danced with his ghost on the grave in her dreams, and from this dancing came knowledge of the Yenne Welt, the land of the dead, and years later in the Home when for ten years she sat alone in the nursing home while two of her daughters died of breast cancer . . .

Alle mayne techter hobm brustkrebs!

THE ELDEST DAUGHTER. So in the Home they thought a vegetable but she wasn't she was still alive she travelled living to the Yenne Welt to seek her father. So when she actually died wasn't nobody home in there, but this came later.

The Oylem-Habbe, the World To Come.

THE SOLEMN GRANDCHILD. "Brustkrebs" is "breast crabs" Grandma.

Cancer. Krebs is cancer it pinches.

SARAH. Yah.

THE ELDEST DAUGHTER. By Tarnopol the mother and her husband made a living selling ice cream and candy in a store, standing behind a wood counter in pools of icewater which Sarah knew would kill them eventually, and eventually it did.

THE SOLEMN GRANDCHILD. Grandma in your stories is always women fucking up and letting you down. Is sexist, Grandma.

SARAH. Yah. Sexy.

THE MIDDLE DAUGHTER. NO NOT SEXY NOT SEXY SEX*IST* SEX*IST WHAT IS YOU DEAF ALL OF A SUDDEN!*

SARAH. Yah, sexy, not much but some of it was sure.

I love my daughters they is such bitches though.

THE MIDDLE DAUGHTER. We wasn't such bitches, we was all smart hard-working women who got sick.

SARAH. My mother married an ignoramus no she never loved mayne tatte we never got along. Emma Lazarus give me this tiny Statue, it's hollow tin. From me the only mother is the Mother of Exiles.

THE ELDEST DAUGHTER. So the next morning she woke up on her father's grave by Nodvorno and she saw it's finished here, so back to America she came and she never returned.

(*She dances with her father's ghost.*)

SARAH. My father died standing in icewater so from the fucking capitalist exploiter Polish landlords what owned his inn he was killed they killed him.

THE SOLEMN GRANDCHILD. Grandma what exploiters I'm confused you said that Great-grandfather Mendel no Schmulick no Yussel *owned* the inn, you always said that.

THE ELDEST DAUGHTER. From the dance on the second boat with the Glaziers' Union she acquired also politics. Red Politics.

SARAH. Yah.

On that second boat was Glaziers. But on the last boat back to America the third boat that boat . . .

THE MIDDLE DAUGHTER. Was only the mother and the stepfather and Sarah.

SARAH. I don't remember I can't remember anybody else.

THE MIDDLE DAUGHTER. Took a month the crossing.

THE YOUNGEST DAUGHTER. And one night on the big empty boat so she danced with the stepfather.

THE ELDEST DAUGHTER. And because he was such an ignoramus during this dance Sarah forgot many things she knew.

THE YOUNGEST DAUGHTER. She forgot almost all the languages: Hungarian Russian Poland French, and Jewish German and even most Yiddish she forgot. Also how to say Kaddish for her father.

THE MIDDLE DAUGHTER. All the while we growing up we never believed that she once knew all those things.

THE ELDEST DAUGHTER. Unexpected snatches of phrases from other languages would surface in her talk.

THE YOUNGEST DAUGHTER. So maybe it all happened as she said it did.

Alle mayne shayne techter hobm brustkrebs! Oy vey. Oy vey iz mir.

THE SOLEMN GRANDCHILD. So how it came she was in the Bronx living? When she returned to America how did she find it?

SARAH. Same only worse. Why should it be easy when it can be hard.

THE ELDEST DAUGHTER. With her mother and that ignoramus so she cannot live, nor with Fette Moishe's purple toilet and his dogs they was animals.

THE MIDDLE DAUGHTER. So up to the Bronx she went and she found yah a Glazier and to him she was married.

A Glazier with a glass heart.

THE YOUNGEST DAUGHTER. The Rabbi in that shul there married her to the Glazier and at the wedding so Sarah made a terrible sin.

THE ELDEST DAUGHTER. To herself while the marriage prayers was being said it suddenly came to her to sing the only last piece of what she once knew secretly, and this piece was unfortunate, it was the Polish Countess's Christmas Song in French.

   (SARAH *sings a bit of "Minuit Chretien."*)

SARAH. And so because of that song she sang so the marriage wasn't no good.

27

THE ELDEST DAUGHTER. It would end eventually with the Glazier's glass heart in pieces at her feet.

SARAH. And the floaters I got 'cause of the smelting, and the disjunctive rheumatoiditis 'cause two daughters dead of cancer and the third in trouble and plus glass splinters there always was in my hands, from him from our bed.

GAH-NISHTS! GAH-NISHTS! Das iz kaputsky, die ganze welt makhs nishts! My eyes, my eyes . . .

THE SOLEMN GRANDCHILD. But tell me one thing Grandma?

SARAH. Yah? You is too sensitive solemn grandchild.

THE SOLEMN GRANDCHILD. As a child as a grandchild maybe so I was opened and closed too many times, Grandma, so now I am like an old used valise what the hinges on broken are and also yah the latches busted, and the contents inside too exhaustively rifled through, and also the actors has borrowed things from me and soiled them by the theater. But Grandma . . . ?

SARAH. What can I tell you dahlingk?

THE SOLEMN GRANDCHILD. Never again Benjamin Nathan Cardozo you saw?

SARAH. And wherefore from this whole confused story you are asking me specifically that?

THE SOLEMN GRANDCHILD. What the teapot tells of Cardozo's pragmatical-philosophical inquiries into the highly subjective nature of the Judicial Process which they paved the way for an Interventionist Activist Supreme Court which was what made America decent. Now, it's not so decent now. Lately it has very indecent gotten.

THE ELDEST DAUGHTER. No internationalism.

THE YOUNGEST DAUGHTER. No immigrants' rights.

SARAH. Oh Annie Lazarus, oh Glaziers' Union, it's an undoing world, I'm telling you

But this I ain't sure of, Solemn Grandchild, whether ever again Benny Cardozo I saw. Maybe.

THE MIDDLE DAUGHTER. It was by a big crowded ballroom dancing, during the Great War.

SARAH. Yah. So that was maybe I was American then a few years.

THE ELDEST DAUGHTER. So she had a hat, so not this hat but a
hat a nice hat and a pinafore blouse.

THE YOUNGEST DAUGHTER. So my ma she dances with a few boys
and one is a rich Sephardim, in Union Square where the radicals
was, was balloons and buntings and Enrico Caruso was from the
Liberty Bond Drive. So this boy this rich Sephardim has jasmine
water on his neck. Maybe so this boy was Benny Cardozo but
Sarah is now older.

THE ELDEST DAUGHTER. So he is so they don't know from one
another, but they dance maybe, three dances.

SARAH. One two three.

And through my arms my wrists my neck-nape my boobies
   And from off the top of my head in heat it came
   Ribbons of smoke which he breathing in dancing inhaled he
   my secret knowledge, was a song:

SARAH. (*Sings.*) By the time we're done with dancing, elsewhere
   darling you'll be glancing and the night's a river torrent tearing
   us apart.
   Merely melody entwined us, easily the ties that bind us break
   in fibrillations of the heart.
   Don't cry out or cling in terror darling that's a fatal error
   clinging to a somebody you thought you knew was yours.
   Dispossession by attrition is an imminent condition which the
   wretched modern world endures.

   You drift away, you're carried by a stream,
   Refugee a wanderer you roam;
   You lose your way, so it will come to seem:
   No Place in Particular is home.
   You glance away, your house has disappeared,
   The sweater you've been knitting has unpurled.
   You live adrift, and everything you feared
   Comes to you in this undoing world.

Copper-plated, nailed-together, buffeted by ocean weather stands
   the Queen of Exiles and our mother she may be.
Hollow-breasted broken-hearted watching for her dear departed
   for her children cast upon the sea.
At her back the great idyllic land of justice for exilic peoples
   ponders making justice private property.
Darling never dream another woman might have been your
   mother someday you will be a refugee.

A refugee, who's running from the wars,
Hiding from the fire-bombs they've hurled;
Eternally a stranger out-of-doors,
Desperate in this undoing world.

Mother, for your derelicted children from your womb evicted
   grant us shelter harbor solace safety
Let us in!
Let us tell you where we travelled how our hopes our lives
   unravelled how unwelcome everywhere we've been.

He wasn't never a brave man exactly Benny Cardozo.

THE MIDDLE DAUGHTER. Those Cardozos always only what they wanted from America was that nobody should know they was Jews.

THE ELDEST DAUGHTER. That's harsh.

SARAH. His cousin Emma Lazarus wrote that poem.

THE YOUNGEST DAUGHTER. But to the law he helped to add human complication subtlety nuance a sense of society of history a sense of the tragic by which law is made mobile by which torts dances and yah becomes eventually justice.

SARAH. His cousin Annie Lazarus made the parades for Immigrants Rights. She died in Venice by Mussolini maybe, by the Nazis, poor Annie Lazarus, she disappeared, exile. In a dream in the thirties I danced with the whole U.S. Supreme Court.

   (A dance with the Supreme Court.)

THE ELDEST DAUGHTER. El nuevo coloso: The New Colossus.

SARAH. The Court now it's just vulgarians, it's just actors and goniffs, it's stiff it's dishonest it ain't good for the unions it's only big business they got a smart Jewish woman up there now das makhs nishts it's all for business now it's bad for the immigrants bad for the Jews. The Lazaruses the Cardozos they was Sephardic Spanish Jews. Once they was immigrants, once they was poor.

THE ELDEST DAUGHTER. No como el gigante bronceado de fama
     griega,
Con miembros conquistadores extendidos de tierra en tierra:
Aqui banado por el mar, en nuestro portal de la puesta del sol
     estara
Una mujer poderosa con una antorcha, cuya llama
Es el relampago aprisionado, y su nombre
Madre de los Exiliados . . .

THE YOUNGEST DAUGHTER. . . . "Denme sus cansados, sus pobres,
Sus apinadas multitudes anhelando suspirar libremente,
Los desechados miserables de sus playas estadas,
Manden a estos, los desamparados, arrojados por tempestades,
Yo alzo mi lampara junto a la puerta dorada!"

THE SOLEMN GRANDCHILD. She died a hundred and three, grandma. It was the day what passed Proposition 187 in California she died strangled in disgust no that ain't true she died before that under Reagan she died it was from the fucking capitalist exploiters what made her stand all her life her feet was in icewater her eyes was bad.

THE ELDEST DAUGHTER. No she wasn't no she didn't it was a nothing she died of a little sniffle, a bobble, a hiccup, a toytenbankas, an ache, a cold in the hip. Took maybe a minute, that crossing.

THE SOLEMN GRANDCHILD. We visited sometimes her Home in the Bronx to ask her why did you come here? Why did you leave? Why did you come back? Why did you never return? She didn't answer. We make answers up.

SARAH. My eyes are bothering me. It's an undoing world.

So from when I died my spirit would not leave this world so it could not be homeless so it had two choices, it could live in the little tin Statue what Emma Lazarus gave me, I think it was Emma Lazarus maybe I don't remember, anyway a big beautiful lady with a handsome bosom gave it to me. But after I died

31

I could not find a doorway in, and so in the Statue I couldn't go. And so instead I went to live in this teapot.

THE YOUNGEST DAUGHTER. She bought the teapot in 1937.

THE MIDDLE DAUGHTER. In Woolworth's. It cost four bucks. It had four teacups. They broke.

THE ELDEST DAUGHTER. All our lives we fought over who should have that teapot.

Inside was me. And my youngest daughter died first of cancer, and my eldest daughter died second, and my middle child, who is bristly and tough but but she is beautiful her sharpest points is like diamonds, she glitters my daughter, so now the teapot comes by her and I am inside. And I lived to a hundred and three and one of my children is gonna live older. Hang on to that teapot middle daughter. You will live to a hundred and five.

SARAH. Yah. You will live a long time. And *then* you'll know suffering.

From Venus
Suzan-Lori Parks

Characters:
MISS SAARTJIE BAARTMAN, A.K.A. THE GIRL, AND LATER,
    THE VENUS HOTTENTOT
THE MAN, LATER, THE BARON DOCTEUR
THE MANS BROTHER, LATER, THE MOTHER-SHOWMAN,
    LATER, THE GRADE-SCHOOL CHUM
THE NEGRO RESURRECTIONIST
THE CHORUS as:
    THE CHORUS OF THE 8 HUMAN WONDERS,
    THE CHORUS OF THE SPECTATORS,
    THE CHORUS OF THE COURT,
    THE CHORUS OF THE 8 ANATOMISTS

Overture.

(VENUS *clothed and facing stage right. She revolves. Counter-clockwise. 270 degrees. She faces upstage.*)

THE NEGRO RESURRECTIONIST. The Venus Hottentot!

THE BROTHER, LATER THE MOTHER-SHOWMAN.
   The Venus Hottentot!

THE MAN, LATER THE BARON DOCTEUR. The Venus Hottentot!

(*rest*)   (VENUS *revolves 90 degrees. She faces stage right.*)
(*rest*)

CHORUS. The Chorus of the 8 Human Wonders!

THE MAN, LATER THE BARON DOCTEUR. The Man, later
   The Baron Docteur!

THE NEGRO RESURRECTIONIST. The Negro Resurrectionist!

33

THE BROTHER, LATER THE MOTHER-SHOWMAN. The Brother, later
  The Mother-Showman! later
  The Grade-School Chum!

THE NEGRO RESURRECTIONIST. The Negro Resurrectionist!

CHORUS. The Chorus of the 8 Anatomists!

(*rest*)　　(VENUS *revolves 180 degrees. She faces stage left.*)
(*rest*)

THE MAN, LATER THE BARON DOCTEUR.
  The Chorus of the 8 Anatomists!

THE NEGRO RESURRECTIONIST. The Man, later
  The Baron Docteur!

THE MAN, LATER THE BARON DOCTEUR.
  The Negro Resurrectionist!

THE BROTHER, LATER THE MOTHER-SHOWMAN.
  The Chorus of Spectators!

THE NEGRO RESURRECTIONIST AND THE MAN. The Brother, later,
  The Mother-Showman!, later
  The Grade-School Chum!

THE MAN AND THE BROTHER. The Negro Resurrectionist!

THE BROTHER, LATER THE MOTHER-SHOWMAN.
  The Chorus of the Court!

ALL. The Venus Hottentot!

(*rest*)

THE VENUS. The Venus Hottentot.

(*rest*)
(*rest*)

THE NEGRO RESURRECTIONIST. I regret to inform you that the
  Venus Hottentot is dead.

ALL. Dead?

THE BROTHER, LATER THE MOTHER-SHOWMAN.
  There wont b inny show tonite.

CHORUS OF 8 HUMAN WONDERS. Dead!

THE NEGRO RESURRECTIONIST.
Exposureiz what killed her nothin on
and our cold weather. 23 days in a row it rained.
Thuh Doctor says she drank too much. It was thuh cold I think.

THE MAN, LATER THE BARON DOCTEUR. Dead?

THE NEGRO RESURRECTIONIST. Deh-duh.

THE BROTHER, LATER THE MOTHER-SHOWMAN.
I regret to inform you that the Venus Hottentot iz dead.
There wont b inny show tonite.

THE NEGRO RESURRECTIONIST. Diggidy-diggidy-diggidy-diggidy

THE BROTHER. Im sure yr disappointed.
We hate to let you down.
But 23 days in a row it rained.

THE NEGRO RESURRECTIONIST. Diggidy-diggidy-diggidy-dawg.

THE MAN, LATER THE BARON DOCTEUR. I say:
Perhaps,
She died of drink.

THE NEGRO RESURRECTIONIST. It was thuh cold I think.

THE VENUS. Uhhhh!

CHORUS OF 8 HUMAN WONDERS. Turn uhway. Dont look. Cover
her face. Cover yer eyes.

THE VENUS. Uhhhh!

CHORUS. (Drum. Drum. Drum. Drum.)
(Drum. Drum. Drum. Drum.)

CHORUS MEMBER. They came miles and miles and miles and miles
and miles.
Comin in from all over to get themselves uh look-see.
They heard the drum.

THE BROTHER, LATER THE MOTHER-SHOWMAN. Drum Drum

CHORUS. (Drum Drum)

35

THE BROTHER. DRUM	CHORUS. (drum)
DRUM	(drum)
DRUM	(drum)
DRUM	(drum)

THE VENUS. (I regret to inform you that thuh Venus Hottentot iz
　　dead.
　　There wont b inny show tuhnite.)

CHORUS. (Outrage! Its an outrage!)

THE MAN, LATER THE BARON DOCTEUR. Dead?

THE NEGRO RESURRECTIONIST. Deh-duh.

THE BROTHER, LATER THE MOTHER-SHOWMAN.
　　Tail end of r tale for there must be an end
　　Is that Venus, Black Goddess, was shameles, she sinned or else
　　completely unknowing of r godfearin ways she stood
　　totally naked in her iron cage.

CHORUS OF 8 HUMAN WONDERS. Shes thuh main attraction she iz
　　Loves thuh sideshows center ring.
　　Whats thuh show without thuh star?

THE VENUS. Hum Drum Hum Drum.

CHORUS. Outrage! Its an outrage!
　　Gimmie gimmie back my buck!

THE BROTHER, LATER THE MOTHER-SHOWMAN.
　　Behind that curtin just yesterday awaited:
　　Wild Female Jungle Creature. Of singular anatimy. Physiqued
　　in such a backward rounded way that she out shapes
　　all others. Behind this curtin just yesterday alive uhwaits
　　a female — creature
　　an out — of towner
　　whos all undressed awaiting you
　　to take yer peek. So youve heard.

ALL. Weve come tuh see your Venus.

THE MAN AND THE BROTHER. We know youre disuhpointed.
　　We hate tuh let you down.

THE NEGRO RESURRECTIONIST. A scene of Love:

36

THE VENUS. *Kiss* me
  Kiss me
  Kiss me. *Kiss*

THE MAN, LATER THE BARON DOCTEUR. I look at you, V
  and I see Love

THE VENUS. Uhhhhhh!
  Uhhhhhh!

CHORUS OF 8 HUMAN WONDERS. Turn uhway. Dont look. Cover
  your face. Cover your eyes:

THE BROTHER, LATER THE MOTHER-SHOWMAN.
  She gained fortune and fame by not wearing a scrap
  Hiding only the privates that lipped in her lap.

THE CHORUS OF 8 ANATOMISTS AND
THE MAN, LATER THE BARON DOCTEUR.
  Good God. Golly. Lookie-Lookie-Look-at-her.
  Ooh-la-la. What-a-find. Hubba-hubba-hubba.

A CHORUS MEMBER. They say that if I pay uh little more
  I'll get tuh look uh little longer
  and for uh little more on top uh that
  I'll get tuh stand
  stand off tuh thuh side
  in thuh special looking place

A CHORUS MEMBER. *(And from there if I'm really quick I'll stick*
  my hand inside her
  cage and have a feel
  if no ones looking.)

ALL. Hubba-hubba-hubba-hubba

THE VENUS. Hum Drum Hum Drum

ALL. THE VENUS HOTTENTOT
  THE ONLY LIVING CREATURE OF HER KIND IN THE
    WORLD
  AND ONLY ONE STEP UHWAY FROM YOU RIGHT NOW
  COME SEE THE HOT MISS HOTTENTOT
  STEP IN STEP IN

Suzan-Lori Parks

THE VENUS. Hur-ry! Hur-ry!

ALL. Hur-ry! Hur-ry!

THE VENUS. But I regret to inform you that thuh Venus Hottentot
   iz dead.
   There wont b inny show tuhnite.

ALL. Outrage Its an outrage!
   Gimmie Gimmie back my buck!

THE NEGRO RESURRECTIONIST. Hear ye Hear ye Order Order!

ALL. The Venus Hottentot iz dead.

THE NEGRO RESURRECTIONIST. All rise.

MEMBER OF CHORUS, AS WITNESS. Thuh gals got bottoms like hot
   air bulloons.
   Bottoms and bottoms and bottoms pilin up like
   like 2 mountains. Magnificent. And endless.
   An ass to write home about.
   Well worth the admission price.
   A spectacle a debacle a priceless prize, thuh filthy slut.
   Coco candy colored and dressed all in *au naturel*
   she likes when people peek and poke.

THE VENUS. Hum drum hum drum.

THE BROTHER, LATER THE MOTHER-SHOWMAN.
   Step in step in step in step in.

THE VENUS. There wont b inny show tuhnite.

THE MAN, LATER THE BARON DOCTEUR AND
THE CHORUS OF 8 ANATOMISTS. Hubba-hubba-hubba-hubba.

THE VENUS. She gained fortune and fame by not wearin uh scrap
   Hidin only thuh privates that lipped inner lap.

ANATOMIST FROM THE EAST. I look at you, Venus, and see:
   Science. You
   in uh pickle
   On my library shelf.

38

THE VENUS. Uhhhhhh!
  Uhhhhhh!
  Uhhhhhh!
  Uhhhhhh!

ALL. Order Order Order Order!

(*rest*)

THE NEGRO RESURRECTIONIST. Tail end of our tale for there must
    be an end
  Is that Venus, Black Goddess, was shameles, she sinned or else
  completely unknowing of r godfearin ways she stood
  totally naked in her iron cage.
  She gaind fortune and fame by not wearin a scrap
  Hidin only the privates lippin down from her lap
  When Death met her Death deathd her and left her to rot
  Au-naturel end for our hot Hottentot
  And rot yes she would have right down to the bone
  Had not the Docteur put her corpse in his home.

  Sheed a soul which iz mounted on Satans warm wall
  While her flesh has been pickled in Sciences Hall.

      (*Curtain. Applause.*)

Scene 31: May I Present to You "The African Dancing Princess"/
          She'd Make a Splendid Freak

      (THE GIRL *with scrub brush and bucket on hands and knees*
      scrubs a vast tile floor. She is meticulous and vigorous. The
      floor shines. THE MAN *and his* BROTHER *walk about. They*
      are deep in conversation.)

THE MAN. Last time you wanted money lets see what wuz it.
  Damn, it slips my mind nope Ive got it now:
  A Menagerie.
  "Gods Entire Kingdom All Under One Roof"
  A miserable failure.

THE BROTHER. I didnt know theyd die in captivity.

THE MAN. Should of figured on that, Man.

39

THE BROTHER. I fed and watered them.

THE MAN. An animal needs more than that but god
  you never were a farmer.

THE BROTHER. Never was never will be.
  (*rest*)
  You missed a spot.
  (*rest*)

THE NEGRO RESURRECTIONIST. Scene 31:
  May I Present to You The African Dancing Princess,
  She'd Make a Splendid Freak.
  (*rest*)

THE BROTHER. So yll finance me? Yes or No.

THE MAN. I need to think on it.

THE BROTHER. Whats there to think on?
  A simple 2 year investment. Back me
  and I'll double yr money no lets think big:
  I'll tripple it.

THE MAN. You need a girl. Wholl go all that way to be a dancer?

THE BROTHER. Finding the girls the easy part.
  (*rest*)
  Shes good. Vigorous and meticulous.

THE MAN. (You dont know her?)

THE BROTHER. Cant say I do.
  Yll back me, Man? Say yes.

THE MAN. Scheme #3 remember?
  You went to Timbuktu.

THE BROTHER. What of it.

THE MAN. Timbuktu to collect wild flowers?
  Wild flowers to bring back here.
  "Garden Exotica" admission 2 cents.

THE BROTHER. They didn't take. Our soils too rich.

THE MAN. I lost my shirt!

THE BROTHER. And like a lizard anothers grown back in its place.
   Back me!
   This time Ive got a sure thing.
   Ive done tons of background research. This schemell bite!

THE MAN. A "Dancing African Princess"?

THE BROTHER. The English like that sort of thing.

THE MAN. (You really dont remember her?)

THE BROTHER. Not from this angle.
   (*rest*)
   Theres a street over there lined with Freak Acts
   but not many dark ones, thats how we'll cash in.

THE MAN. A "Dancing African Princess."

THE BROTHER. Im begging on my knees!

THE MAN. Get up. Youve got it.

THE BROTHER. Just like a brother!

THE MAN. I am yr brother.

THE MAN/THE BROTHER. Heh heh. Heh heh.

THE MAN. (You really dont remember her?)

THE BROTHER. Enlighten me.

THE MAN. (Scheme #1?)

THE BROTHER. (Marriage with the Hotten-tot — thats-her?)

THE MAN. Father recognized the joke straight off
   but Mother poor thing she still gives you funny looks.
   You were barely 12.

THE BROTHER. Shes grown.

THE MAN. As they all do.
   Big Bottomed Girls. Thats their breed.
   You were at one time very into it.

THE BROTHER. Big Bottomed Girl. A novelty.
   Shes vigorous and meticulous.
   (Watch this, Brother!)
   (Oh, whats her name?)

41

THE MAN. Her — ? Saartjie. "Little Sarah."

THE BROTHER. Saartjie. Lovely. Girl! GIRL!?

THE GIRL. Sir?

THE BROTHER. Dance.

THE GIRL. Dance?

THE BROTHER. Dance! Come on!
    I'll clap time.

> (THE BROTHER *claps time.* THE GIRL *dances.*)

THE MAN. An "African Dancing Princess"?

THE BROTHER. The Britsll eat it up.
    Oh, she'd make a splendid freak.

THE MAN. A freak?

THE BROTHER. Thats what they call em
    "freaks," "oddities," "curiosities."

THE MAN. Of course. Of course.

THE GIRL. Can I stop Sir?

THE BROTHER. No no keep up.
    Faster! Ha ha!
    (I still dont recognize her).

THE MAN. (She might know you though.
    Their kind remember everything.)

THE BROTHER. (Ive grown a beard since then.)

THE MAN. Thats true.

THE BROTHER. Stop dancing. Stop!

THE GIRL. Stopped.

THE BROTHER. Girl?

THE GIRL. Sir.

THE BROTHER. How would you like to go to England?

THE GIRL. England! Well.
    "England." Whats that?

THE BROTHER. A big town. A boat ride away.
  Where the streets are paved with gold.

THE GIRL. Gold, Sir?

THE BROTHER. Come to England. Dance a little.

THE GIRL. Dance?

THE BROTHER. Folks watch. Folks clap. Folks pay you gold.

THE GIRL. Gold.

THE BROTHER. We'll split it 50-50.

THE GIRL. 50-50?

THE BROTHER. Half for me half for you.
  May I present to you: "The African Dancing Princess!"

THE GIRL. A Princess. Me?

THE BROTHER. Like Cinderella.
  She's heard of Cinderella, right?

THE GIRL. A princess overnight.

THE MAN. Thats it.

THE BROTHER. Yd be a sensation!

THE GIRL. Im a little shy.

THE BROTHER. Say yes we'll go tomorrow!

THE GIRL. Will I be the only one?

THE BROTHER. Oh no, therell be a whole street full.

THE GIRL. Im shy.

THE BROTHER. Think of it: Gold!

THE GIRL. Gold!

THE BROTHER. 2 yrs of work yd come back rich!

THE GIRL. Id come back rich!

THE BROTHER. Yd make a mint!

THE GIRL. A mint! A "mint."
  How much is that?

THE MAN. You wouldnt have to work no more.

THE GIRL. I would have a house.
I would hire help.
I would be rich. Very rich.
Big bags of money!

THE MAN. Exactly.

THE GIRL. I like it.

THE BROTHER. Its settled then!

THE MAN. Yr a rascal, brother.

THE GIRL. Do I have a choice? Id like to think on it.

THE BROTHER. Whats there to think on? Think of it as a vacation!
2 years of work take half the take.
Come back here rich. Its settled then.

THE MAN. Think it over, girl. Go on.
Think it all over.

THE BROTHER
THE GIRL
THE MAN
THE BROTHER
THE GIRL
THE MAN. (*rest*) (*rest*)

THE GIRL. Hahahaha!

THE MAN. What an odd laugh.

THE GIRL. Just one question:
When do we go?

THE BROTHER. Next stop England!

THE GIRL. "England"?

THE BROTHER. England England England HO!

THE GIRL. "England"?

THE NEGRO RESURRECTIONIST. Scene #30:
She Looks Like Shes Fresh Off the Boat.

Amphibians
Jon Robin Baitz

Characters:
MALCOLM RAPHELSON
ANDREW PATTERSON
TALIA FOX
JORDAN COMBES
CARTER HAMILTON
JULIAN SAWYER
LIZ FRIAR

Act 1. December 1993.

(*A sprawling, rambling, decrepit old house in Chiapas, Mexico, near but far from the town of San Cristobal. There are mountains in the distance. All rooms lead out to a lovely central courtyard. Off the dining room on one wing of the house is a painter's studio, chaotic and solitary, with over thirty years' worth of canvases stacked up in piles. Lights up on dining room after dinner:* MALCOLM RAPHELSON, *seventy-five years old, is sitting at the head of the long table. A shock of white hair, close-cropped, a cigar, old white pants, a white shirt. The other guests,* TALIA FOX *and* JULIAN SAWYER, *are kids in their late twenties (and informal assistants to Raphelson),* CARTER HAMILTON, *a journalist,* JORDAN COMBES, *a black lawyer,* ANDREW PATTERSON, *an art dealer, and* LIZ FRIAR, *a girl of twenty-one.*)

RAPHELSON. Let us be clear, for once and for all. Nothing could make me go back home.

PATTERSON. Yet you still call it home. After thirty years. You at least acknowledge that America is still home. (*He smiles slightly.*) This is cause for hope.

45

TALIA. They'll pay your way, Malcolm. It wouldn't cost you anything.

RAPHELSON. No, it's expensive in other ways.

COMBES. There will be other painters, other artists, people you have not seen in years.

RAPHELSON. For good reason, too. God, a room full of splashes of paint, hell no. And worse — painters talking. Jesus, I swear, if I am to be bored, I would rather be the one doing it.

PATTERSON. They want to celebrate you. Invite you in. From the wilderness. To bask. To claim your place. To be acknowledged. Is this a bad thing?

RAPHELSON. Oh it all sounds so damn trite. What do you think, Hamilton?

HAMILTON. Ah, me? Well. New York has changed. That might be interesting. Not having been back in thirty years. And it gives me another angle on you. Forgive me. (*He smiles.*) I am a journalist before all other things. Yes. Go back. What can it hurt?

RAPHELSON. I'm not an industry. I've seen it happen. Some little bit of life goes out of the subject. Some part of them is taken away. (*Beat.*) They become self-conscious. No more air in the cells. It's why Mexico is so good. The light. The air. It's all so much more real down here. (*There is a silence at the table.*) And you see, I am not an industry but a very old man with not a whole hell of a lot to say. So . . .

TALIA. You are a workhorse, Malcolm.

JULIAN. Picasso hated himself too.

HAMILTON. Yes. He could barely get out of bed in the morning. He had to be coaxed. Supplicants all about, urging him on. This is in his eighties. Supplicants, come to pay their respects . . . (*He gestures about the table.*) Comme ça.

RAPHELSON. Ah. He had something of the quick-change artist in him, a showman. He punched me in the stomach once in Madrid, to prove a machismo point. I deserved it but I've never been able to forgive him, never could bear bad manners.

JULIAN. That, pal, is a laugh and a half.

RAPHELSON. It's too true, though. The modern sensibility? Rudeness and cruelty, viciousness and superiority. It's why I've never been back. It's a nation of house cats and trained monkeys beating each other up.

PATTERSON. If you go back, your price will go up.

TALIA. Ah. The lawyers speak.

PATTERSON. Why is talking about money to a man who might just make a little in his seventy-fifth year an insult?

RAPHELSON. (*Turns, suddenly bored with this, to* LIZ.) Are you liking Mexico?

LIZ. Pardon? I'm sorry? I —

RAPHELSON. What exactly is it you're up to?

LIZ. Me? Was that — ? Me?

TALIA. He does this.

LIZ. It's amphibians. I'm studying them here.

JULIAN. You're working at the lake?

LIZ. Yes. There's a particular salamander. Only at Lake Grijalva. There are not many left. I'm on a grant. My college.

TALIA. (*Apologetic, to* LIZ.) He does this. Ignores you throughout dinner and then turns on you.

JULIAN. You're dessert.

COMBES. May we talk business? It's why we came, Mal.

RAPHELSON. No. I'm talking to the girl. So. What's so interesting about these salamanders?

LIZ. Oh. Well. Yes? You want to . . . ? You want to know?

RAPHELSON. Go ahead.

LIZ. Something is happening to the frogs. To all amphibians. There is a worldwide depletion in the amphibian population. Frogs in particular. Also certain species of salamander. In Mexico, here, it's been very bad.

RAPHELSON. Life is cheap here in Mexico.

LIZ. Maybe. What I'm finding, the hard part, is that there are so many factors. For instance, the lake is being sold to a hotelier from Texas.

JULIAN. Right. They're going to build a resort for fishermen.

RAPHELSON. I'd heard that. And a direct flight from Dallas. It's bad. Very bad.

LIZ. The thing is, you see, they're stocking — they are going to stock the lake with bass. Which I think could actually do in the salamanders — I mean I have no absolute proof. There's been no impact report so . . .

JULIAN. Go on.

LIZ. I went to Mexico City. They're like, the trade agreement is very good for them, they think. They think "It's going to be like Los Angeles here now. There will be *so* much money. . . ." I have a meeting with someone from the Minister of the Interior. I explain about the danger to the frogs, the salamanders. He listens, nodding. The man nods and says, "Have you seen the women walking on the streets here with air filters? Children sent home from school because the sky is brown. . . ." (*Beat. She shrugs.*) The single most polluted city in the world. "So how can I concern myself with the little frogs of the lake . . . ?" That sort of thing.

RAPHELSON. Look. I don't mean to sound like an asshole but he's right.

LIZ. I suppose it's easy to sit here and say that. At your house here. . . .

RAPHELSON. (*A smile.*) Yeah, it's easy to sit here and say that. But the fact is, young lady, there is a tension to life. There is a necessary battle. Few things survive. That dull old argument about "Why didn't God get involved with the concentration camps." Man chooses what he will save. And his jury is still out as to whether he will stick out his neck for his own damned species. So.

LIZ. Yes, but if you could explain to me what, if anything, this has to do with amphibians.

TALIA. He argues sideways.

JULIAN. Like a crab.

RAPHELSON. No, I'm saying that there are a lot of fights these people will have but —

(LIZ *cuts him off, not impolite.*)

LIZ. "Man chooses what he will save?" But, Mr. Raphelson, that kind of hubris, egotism — we end up in an ash heap.

RAPHELSON. Yes, we do. I know. (*Beat.*) The sky is falling, and has been forever. (*Beat.*)

LIZ. Extinction, of amphibians in particular — it's the canary in the coal mine. What happens to them happens to us.

COMBES. If you were to allow me to take back say two pieces, think they would sell.

RAPHELSON. Ahhhh . . . there's nothing worth showing.

COMBES. A real interest. Corporate buyers. Nobody has bought art in years. Perhaps a commission. There is a lobby. A particular lobby. A large communications company with an interest in culture. They have put out feelers for a mural. Muralist.

RAPHELSON. (*Turns suddenly to* LIZ.) Mexicans have more pressing problems than the fate of their frogs. Frogs don't translate into cash, into any currency really, so . . .

HAMILTON. So much of the world down here has been sold off for money, remember, United Fruit — last century, so why not sell to a hotelier now?

JULIAN. The two hotels in town, they used to be churches. Now it's all room service and the satellite dish, you know. The salamanders are not alone . . . it's all . . .

PATTERSON. Malcolm, come back to the States, meet the commission people, let yourself be rediscovered. We've worked so hard for you. . . . It's unfair to fall back into being a hermit at this point. . . .

COMBES. If you continue to get the attention we think you're going to. Malcolm . . .

PATTERSON. It's an important building.

49

RAPHELSON. Oh for God's sake! "Important building."

COMBES. We come down here. You ignore us. We check into one of those converted "churches." He's your lawyer. I'm your *dealer*. A *little* courtesy. Forgive me. But we've been waiting in our hotel for three days to see you. Enough of this rustic crap. My temper is frayed. I have a rash. I can't get an outside line.

JULIAN. The hard sell, Malcolm. I warned you.

COMBES. *(Turns to* JULIAN.*)* Please. Let me speak to the man, would you? Alone.

JULIAN. Frankly, you know, here you come, really a criminal guy, this art dealer who has insinuated himself without even asking, without even—and he listens because you're *black* and he's intrigued so—

(COMBES *easily and calmly slaps* JULIAN *backhanded, across the face. His chair falls backwards.* COMBES *rises and puts his booted foot firmly on* JULIAN's *neck.*)

COMBES. *(Calm and polite throughout.)* I swear to God this stuff is not on. Now listen to me, son. From now on, when I call from New York, you put me through to Mr. Raphelson or I'll send down a whole team of kids far smarter, far more amusing than yourself, right out of Harvard, and very cynical, and Mr. Raphelson will forget all about you, understand? And we're going to rediscover manners as well. *(He takes his foot off* JULIAN's *neck.* JULIAN *gasps. Then laughs, as do* TALIA *and* RAPHELSON. *Only* HAMILTON *and* LIZ *sit pale, looking down at their plates.* PATTERSON *is bored.*)

JULIAN. *(Rising.)* Mr. Hamilton, are you going to write about all this for your magazine?

(RAPHELSON *pours himself tequila.*)

RAPHELSON. *(Gentle.)* You had it coming, son. You know about Mr. Combes here. *(He turns to* HAMILTON.*)* Six months' hard time for defacing a canvas. It's art dealers who always go to jail. The Rothko thing . . . that guy . . .

HAMILTON. He went back to London.

RAPHELSON. Which is worse than jail, in fact.

TALIA. We have a very nice café con leche flan for dessert.

COMBES. I can't do business like this. Can you? (*He turns to* PATTERSON.)

RAPHELSON. I did warn you not to bother coming down. Look. Gentlemen, you've sold a few of my paintings, but I'm too old to be an industry and too young to become an institution. (*Beat.*) What the hell use do I have down here for money? It sits there, roaring at me, challenging me. I don't need the noise. I'm not selling. You know, you made me a great deal of the stuff this year and I don't know that I'll ever require any again.

PATTERSON. Does that mean you won't sell any more pieces? You know — you still — there's going to be a tax bill — your ex-wife — the — you don't have as much as you think.

RAPHELSON. I'll think about giving you a piece on one condition, Mr. Combes.

COMBES. One condition?

RAPHELSON. Apologize to Julian here for hitting him. (*Beat.*)

COMBES. If I apologize then you'll give us something?

RAPHELSON. I'll entertain the notion. (*Beat.*)

PATTERSON. Well.

TALIA. Come on. Do it. What harm can an apology do?

COMBES. (*To* JULIAN.) I should not have resorted to physical violence. It never solves anything.

JULIAN. And?

COMBES. I apologize.

JULIAN. (*Grinning, trying not to laugh.*) I accept your apology. Sir. I refuse to live in a world where people think that resorting to fisticuffs solves anything and furthermore — (*He can bear no more. He collapses in gales of laughter.* TALIA *joins him.*) People — there comes a time when people get tired, Mr. Combes. . . .

COMBES. (*Enough. He's had it. On his feet.*) I'm leaving. That's it. Fine. You want what you want, Mr. Raphelson, this little circus . . .

RAPHELSON. Ahh, hell, let's go into the studio. (*Beat.*)

COMBES. Ah.

RAPHELSON. Don't be thin-skinned, Combes. The kid's just josh-
ing, hell. Let's go into the studio. Maybe we'll find something.
(*He points to* LIZ FRIAR.) You choose, dear. If there's anything
there, let her choose one.

LIZ. I don't know anything about art. I'm not interested in art.

RAPHELSON. Nor is Mr. Combes, but it hasn't stopped him from
exploiting it successfully for a quarter century. Come on, it'll
be fun. You choose and he can take whatever you choose back
and sell it and that will be that. Maybe. If I like it.

LIZ. I think I'll be leaving. I have to go.

RAPHELSON. You don't like us.

LIZ. I'm not—I don't understand any of this, Mr. Raphelson, and
it's late. I'm sorry. I don't mean to be rude. I just don't understand
any of . . . (*Beat.*) And no, I don't think I like you.

RAPHELSON. That, my dear, is because you're used to amphibians,
to fish and salamanders and frogs, you think it's clearer if the
blood is cold, huh? Ahh. Come on. Come look at the pictures.
The pictures are similar to the salamanders. They're very cold-
blooded, dear. (*He rises out of his chair and raises his arms.*)
Let's look at some art. (*They walk into the studio across the
courtyard.*)

Act 1, Scene 2

(RAPHELSON's *studio. The group assembled about a large
canvas which we do not see.*)

RAPHELSON. Ahhh, a landscape? God. No. I—This is bad.

LIZ. You asked me to choose. I recognize—I mean—it's partially
recognizable.

COMBES. I like it.

RAPHELSON. Shut up, this has nothing to do with you. I'm asking
the girl.

LIZ. You understand how quiet it is here. How lonely it is. (*Beat.*) Also. Dangerous, even though it's beautiful. When I'm out at the lake there is always the sense that something unspeakable is about to happen. And you feel it in the painting? How did you know? How do you know that, Mr. Raphelson?

RAPHELSON. Because Mexico, Miss Friar, is about death. Most places in the world are about life and death in more or less equal measure, but for some reason, Mexico is more death than life, more dark than light, even though the light is spectacular.

LIZ. It is?

RAPHELSON. Think back to the Aztecs. Horrifying marvelous people. Loved nothing more than a human sacrifice. The Spanish hated all that. You know, they hated everything that was here, the people and their temples and their gods. (*Beat.*) Since you're so interested in extinction. The church in that picture — there are more than one if you look closely, well. The reason there are so many churches in Mexico, you see, is that Cortez and co. wherever there had been a temple — they would tear it down and build a church. It's an entire country of extinct peoples, dear. (*Beat.*) The idea of life is — was — different here. This idea of human sacrifice — the Spaniards would burn people as heretics condemning them to eternal damnation. Whereas — the Aztecs when they sacrificed someone — and there were days when thousands lined up to go down — some of them became gods after. Thousands of people waiting to die. Another view of life. That is Mexico. Another view altogether of faith and religion. Man and God.

PATTERSON. Yes and it's quite clearly all in that painting, it's right there in front of you. I mean —

(*Wearily,* RAPHELSON *holds up his hand to stop this line of bullshit.*)

RAPHELSON. Just stop.

HAMILTON. In this one. The village. El Salvador. The murdered Jesuits.

RAPHELSON. Manet's executions. And Velázquez. Something going on in the dark. Horrible goings-on outside of basic kindness that — (*He stops himself.*)

53

COMBES. If you could let me sell one of these. (*Pause.*)

HAMILTON. Are you afraid?

RAPHELSON. Of what?

HAMILTON. (*Thoughtful, deductive.*) I don't . . . know. When you left. When you left in '59, it was very bad. You were forty. Perhaps the country — the way it's changed — it might be exciting for you to see. Do you think . . . ?

RAPHELSON. I am not an American anymore. I am a Mexican citizen. I gave up my citizenship.

PATTERSON. It is not the same country.

RAPHELSON. It will always be the same country. (*Beat.*) Diego Rivera was heartbroken when Rockefeller painted over the mural he did for Rockefeller Center. (*Beat.*) Did you know that at the post office in Sag Harbor, there was a mural of mine . . . W.P.A. . . . (*He seems to drift away.*) When they paint over your work because someone in it looks a little like Lenin, you're extinct, there's no place for you. A little town! And vilified! My town.

COMBES. I didn't know.

RAPHELSON. Well they just painted it over one day. I'm sorry, I don't feel like selling anything, or going back.

PATTERSON. You're almost broke.

RAPHELSON. Yeah, well, I've been almost broke most of my life and now I'm old, soon I won't need anything. We are not on Beekman Place.

COMBES. There are . . . at least a hundred pictures in here. In this studio.

JULIAN. Two hundred and counting, pal.

PATTERSON. You know, your family back home, they've made contact, they've made demands, they've — your ex-wife, your son. Your son! You know you have to think about your executors. Your family?

RAPHELSON. Like something out of Grimm's fairy tales. The crone and the scold. "The gingerbread harridan." Is she still doing constructions out of rice?

COMBES. Millet actually. And *Artforum* loved them.

RAPHELSON. *(To* LIZ.*)* My second wife, I've had three and a half, makes art outta oatmeal or somethin'. She divorced me when I poured maple syrup over one of her "constructions," it looked like something from Kellogg's. "Quaker instant grant." *(He starts to walk out.)* I thought she was doing the unthinkable; making me breakfast.

> *(*RAPHELSON *exits. Pause.* PATTERSON *and* COMBES *stand.* JULIAN *grins.* TALIA *makes to clean a stray brush.* COMBES *touches a canvas, rolled up in the corner.)*

PATTERSON. Through the looking glass, isn't it? Another world.

COMBES. How—how would you say his health is, Talia? He seems . . .

TALIA. Oh he's a horse. A colt. He wears me down.

PATTERSON. I see.

JULIAN. Talia keeps him from sinking under the ice, he gets so sad.

COMBES. Uh-huh.

> *(*COMBES *lifts the canvas but* JULIAN *is there, blocking the man's arm with his own.)*

JULIAN. I'm sorry. It's just not happening. You don't touch anything without him here.

COMBES. I cannot work this way. Patterson, I can't. I mean . . . I'm not a crook, I'm an art dealer.

TALIA. He actually thought that you might try and take something and asked us to make sure we stayed with you. . . .

HAMILTON. Is it like this here all the time?

LIZ. It's just — you all behave like adders. Goodbye.

HAMILTON. *(To* LIZ.*)* I always thought "there's no one on the planet quite as bad as movie people" but these folk, wow.

PATTERSON. Why is he doing business with me and Combes if he doesn't trust us?

TALIA. Because he doesn't trust you. If he trusted you, you'd kill him. You can't, if he knows you want to. Simple, simple logic of an old coyote, right?

COMBES. Let's go back to the hotel, Andrew.

PATTERSON. We can try again tomorrow.

COMBES. Maybe go see the ruins.

JULIAN. They're closed.

TALIA. Some kids spray painted them.

JULIAN. They just discovered graffiti art. (JULIAN *holds the door open and they all go into the central courtyard, into the dark night, stand by the fountain in the near black.*)

PATTERSON. Tell him good-bye. We'll call before we leave tomorrow.

(*The two men exit into the night.*)

JULIAN. I tell Raphelson we need dogs, and we need alarms and we need security, but he doesn't listen.

HAMILTON. (*Disliking this kid.*) Why is it, I wonder, that the terribly talented must always surround themselves with their lessors? Eh?

JULIAN. One asks oneself this . . . every day, sir.

HAMILTON. In a small town, at the end of Mexico. An expatriate, maybe ex-communist American painter, ignored for decades after fleeing the Red Years, Eisenhower, McCarthy, bomb shelters, et al., is about to be rediscovered, and sobered up, maybe half-mad — by young people who stop here on their drift down southward —

JULIAN. A story, yeah. Perhaps. Maybe. Yeah. I like it.

HAMILTON. Wasn't there an assistant who stole a few pictures?

TALIA. A friend of Julian's. Cahill. He got Mal drunk and disappeared . . . and showed up in New York . . . which was why Malcolm got Patterson and Combes. To protect him. And we protect Malcolm from them. It's a nice little ecosystem. Mr. Hamilton.

JULIAN. And he can't really handle the rapids these men swim in. For some reason. I can. Me and Talia we can handle most things, you know . . . you don't like me. Well. Hey. But I love Mal. I actually do. (*Beat.*)

HAMILTON. Do you paint?

JULIAN. I clean brushes. I fetch and steppit. I carry. I'm a water bearer.

HAMILTON. How did you end up here?

JULIAN. (*Smiles.*) I'm just, we're just, "young people who . . . stopped here on our drift . . . southward." As you put it.

HAMILTON. Yes. I know. (*Beat.*) My son follows the Grateful Dead around. He doesn't, I don't think, speak English anymore. They nod and grunt. Like some tribe . . . and if the Dead are on the Eastern Seaboard, we see him, lank hair and English teeth, he's twenty. A year at MIT and then this. Zoning out. (*Beat.*) I don't know what any of you are looking for. (*He looks at his watch,* LIZ.) I have to go back to town, care for a lift?

LIZ. No. I'm the other way. The lake.

HAMILTON. It sounds like a story: your lake. "The end of the world . . ."

LIZ. (*A small smile.*) At very least it's a story, Mr. Hamilton.

HAMILTON. Yes. Too bad, though, I only write about culture. That's all they give me now. So the end of the world will have to be reported on by others.

TALIA. I'd like a lift into town if you don't mind. They're showing *Last Year at Marienbad* in Spanish.

(*They both exit.* JULIAN *and* LIZ *are left in the studio.*)

LIZ. I am finding that Mexico brings out the worst in Americans.

JULIAN. The entire world brings out the worst in Americans.

LIZ. Why did Raphelson invite me to dinner?

JULIAN. He likes young people. He likes new people. He's lonely. He's bored. He's still curious about the world. He's hospitable, I don't know. . . .

57

LIZ. Talia. Tell me. I mean, is it like — she really sleeps with him?

JULIAN. You think people give up sex at a certain age? He's not old. I think if he gave up sex he'd get old. Anyway, probably it's not sex the way we think of it, probably at a certain age anything young is attractive — you just want to sleep with it cause it's young.

LIZ. Do you sleep with him?

JULIAN. *(Laughing.)* No. But I mean, why not? Love is love.

LIZ. Is it?

JULIAN. He was in Spain in 1936. Seventeen years old. You probably know nothing about the Spanish Civil War. He just went. Those posters up there. *(He points to the wall high up.)* He did those, and they're sort of famous. The mother, the child, the pattern of German bombers above them in formation. Famous. Image of that war. . . . Can you read the caption?

LIZ. *¡Que haces tu para evitar esto!*

JULIAN. What are you doing to prevent this?

LIZ. And so what happened to the social conscience? He drank it up?

JULIAN. *(Shakes his head and walks away, cleans a brush.)* If you'll forgive me, fuck you.

LIZ. He just doesn't seem to care about —

JULIAN. — Your *frogs?* What's he supposed to do?

LIZ. *(Offended, and young.)* He found it funny.

JULIAN. It is. What isn't? On some level? Funny. I mean, please. *(Beat.)* Raphelson fled the States. He had murals of his painted over. He had a brother who killed himself rather than name names . . . Raphelson . . . is a . . . god. *(Beat.)* Tell me about the lake.

LIZ. At the lake . . . at the lake. *(A sigh.)* We get death threats. I have a handbook on how to deal with death threats. "Report them to the authorities." But what that means is: "Ignore them and keep on working." A shed with tadpoles and salamander hatchlings — with shotgun blasts into it — because we're trying to block the Texans. Gunshots and fires. At night. I mean I am twenty years old.

JULIAN. And you might get killed for a salamander. Is it worth it?

LIZ. (*A smile.*) "*¿Que haces tu para evitar esto?*"

JULIAN. When Raphelson started getting attention last year, a museum in Germany bought some books, he had done editions of Brecht — very beautiful woodcuts — so one sold at auction for a fair amount. So this room is worth something now. (*Beat.*) Maybe many millions. Suddenly, this worthless, terrific room here. (*Beat.*) So Malcolm is scared now because this terrific room used to just be a studio.

LIZ. Well, I wish I knew what to do with all this fear besides ignore it, go on. It's worse at home. Wake up on Sunday, feel useless, that's worse, I think, than this fear.

(JULIAN *smiles at this.*)

JULIAN. It's late to go back to the lake. There are more beds than people here, most nights.

LIZ. Ah. More beds than people.

JULIAN. Occasionally.

LIZ. You are one of those people who are unpleasant when there's more than one person in the room?

JULIAN. Besides me, you mean? Yes.

(MALCOLM *enters, drunk. He wears only a robe which is in danger of opening.*)

RAPHELSON. Listen kiddo, stay here at my little circus, lot more fun than the little fishies and salamanders and so on, cause after they've all died there'll always be a Raphelson.

(*They stare at him as he drinks and the lights fade.*)

59

Mrs. Chang

Han Ong

Characters:
MRS. CHANG, fifties
LILY CHANG, early to mid thirties
ROSHUMBA, black. Clipboard in hand, to which she occasionally
  refers
BRUCE, mid thirties
IVAN, late thirties

Scene 1

(*Lights.*)

ROSHUMBA. So you're here Mrs. Chang —

MRS. CHANG. Ees my name   Yes yes!
  (*Claps hands.*)
Ees Mrs. Chang but you calling-calling me Esme for shortening
Ees what all my olding-olding friends call me fo' making appoint-
  ment: Ring ring
          Hello?
                  Hello?
          Who this?
                        This olding-time friend.
                        Ees Esme in?
          Me Esme me Esme!
          Hello olding-time friend! Wana make date?
  See what I making meaning?

ROSHUMBA. Esme

MRS. Shortening fo' guess-what-name

ROSHUMBA. Esmeralda?

MRS. Good guess good guess
An' fo' because correct answer you making-get Door Number
Four

ROSHUMBA. So Esme

MRS. That my name. Don't wash-and-wear it out.

ROSHUMBA. You're here because you want
you have a desire to master —

LILY. Learn not master. Nothing too fancy.

ROSHUMBA. Basics?

LILY. Just one two three

MRS. Four five six
Hello Big Bird!
Me making-friending with Big Bird who like me to making correct
accounting

LILY. Just the basics

MRS. (*To* ROSHUMBA.) You know why me here?

ROSHUMBA. Learning   To learn

MRS. But why-oh-why Delilah

ROSHUMBA. Grace. You want to move through life with grace.

MRS. (*To* LILY.) She good.

LILY. (*To* ROSHUMBA.) Grief not grace.

MRS. No no grace too   Me long time
long long buried in secret heart when
going to see Hollywood
me long wish
making praying to God, Hello God, me
say, Me no want be me
Plees plees
Make me Grace Kelly plees with stiff-stiff skirts like billowing
(that right word right? billow
like cloud where Grace Kelly live out of
reach of me from Fukien come all the way here to sit in dark
and pray

61

                    Me not want be me
                    Make me Grace Kelly
                    Make me be billow
                              like a line in Grace Kelly movie:
           You billow in light so beautiful
                    Make me be from not Fukien
                    Make me be from Montana
                              United States of Billow-billow
                                        That word so
           important to me you don't know)

LILY. (*To* ROSHUMBA.) You were recommended by a friend's mother
    who said that she forgot
                    she learned how to forget
                              through a class you
         taught
              Dancing
                    And once I heard
                         I knew my mother —

MRS. Ees me Esme!

LILY. — I knew I should bring her here

ROSHUMBA. You said grief

LILY. My father —

MRS. Ex ex! Mr. Ex!

LILY. — He just
    He passed away

ROSHUMBA. But your mother doesn't seem —
    If anything she looks too cheerful

MRS. You crazy? Who has time?
                    No time be sad.

LILY. Appearances

MRS. Me happy 'sho 'nuf happy with goody-goody daughter

LILY. She asks very little from life, as you can see

MRS. 'sho 'nuf
              Boo Ya!

        me listen
        all day listen to radio playing music called
Electric Googaboo —

ROSHUMBA. Boogaloo

MRS. Electric Boogaloo
        but no instruction on how to Boo-Ya!ga-loo
so me come here to fin' out

ROSHUMBA. But your daughter said Basic

MRS. You know making dancing the Electric Boogaloo?

ROSHUMBA. Yes

MRS. Good   Me gone learn   Right?   You gone teach?

ROSHUMBA. If it's all right with your daughter

LILY. So long as it's not too strenuous

ROSHUMBA. It involves spins
        and twists   And popping   You know
what that is?

MRS. Me can do me can do!

LILY. In moderation

ROSHUMBA. I'll scale it down for her

MRS. Moderation never got no one nowhere

LILY. Is it going —
Will it be effective?

ROSHUMBA. Nothing will make people forget who don't want to
forget
That's what I believe

MRS. Me gone forget aw'ready
Who me? Who ees me?
   (*Beat; she laughs.*)
Joke! Ees punching line

ROSHUMBA. (*To* LILY.) I don't think we're gonna have a problem

MRS. (*To* ROSHUMBA.) What your story?

ROSHUMBA. I like to think —

MRS. No good too much thinking
  Look at me daughter

ROSHUMBA. I wasn't finished

MRS. Oh making-sorry

ROSHUMBA. My mother came here from Egypt and I like to think
  of dancing as my feet's version of what she did
                    I believe in
                              (it's so lonely otherwise)
                    I believe in a continuum

MRS. You making dancing all yo' life?

ROSHUMBA. Before this I was a model

LILY. I thought you looked familiar

MRS. Wha' meaning model?

ROSHUMBA. (*Beat.*) Billow
  I got paid to billow

MRS. You? But you no look nothing like Grace Kelly how is possible you be billow?

ROSHUMBA. That's the point. I don't do it anymore.

MRS. Cause you anti-Grace Kelly?

ROSHUMBA. Because they wanted me to unlearn my face
  And how do you do that? I'd like to know
  Because I couldn't
                    much as I wanted to
                    much as I *did*
  But not anymore

MRS. Me no understand how someone say, No wish be Grace Kelly

ROSHUMBA. My face —
  I have a face that twins my feet
                    and my feet (which are my mother's)
  I love my feet
  They have taken me far

My feet, next to my mother's, are the most beautiful thing I know
But I know it in retrospect. Because when she was alive when her feet were kicking up a story for me to follow all I could say was, How ugly
how how non-exemplary
But now
My feet are
beautiful. They give my face precedent.
Tell me Esme do you love your feet?

MRS. No. Me no think no feet
Me walk from pointing A to pointing B ees will not feet
Can I—
Lee-lee you go, me need talk private to
(*Looks to* ROSHUMBA.)

ROSHUMBA. Roshumba

MRS. Me need talk private to
(*Forgets; looks to* ROSHUMBA *again.*)

ROSHUMBA. Ro

MRS. Ro

ROSHUMBA. Shum

MRS. Shum

ROSHUMBA. Ba

MRS. Ba

ROSHUMBA. Roshumba

MRS. (*Beat.*) Me need talk private to her

LILY. What for?

MRS. You understand meaning of private?
Meaning two not three

LILY. Make it short (*Exits.*)

MRS. I no understand your feet speech Miss Ba but I feel confident tell you secret:
Me no really want learn Electric Boogaloo

Me no got body
     ees obvious to you ya?
          Sixty seventy eighty
          Calendar fly by so
impossible

Me only say me want learn because
Lee-lee See Lee-lee need example because me got responsible-
ness fo' letting-her-up and me put on
        see
          put this smiling huffy-puffy
big chest of Go-Get-Wha-Behind-Door-Number-Four cause Wha-
Behind-Door-Number-Four is me of other gen'ration no reach
(me only get to Number Two)
          but she think cause I don't have
meaning it not belong to her too
         But not true!
So what can I do to conveens?
So me listen to radio (that part true!) and learn cheering-cheering
big-example can-do like Boo Ya!
      like Electric Boogaloo
          to conveens Lee-lee
but all like fake
   like puttin' lipstick on cow
         because inside me no feel
But I want to learn now
      With you
       You will teach
       I will learn
That part not fake
   not fake at all
       Now ees a start
       But only basic Right?
       Me learn
       And Lee-lee will learn
If me do not-Electric-Boogaloo but simple like Big Bird teach:
one-two cha-cha-cha
three-four cha-cha-cha;
       if that me can accomplish she can too
Then everything pro'ceed from that
Everything billow

And me want learn grace too
    me want — What you say earlier about face?

ROSHUMBA. What did I say?

MRS. You — unlearn?

ROSHUMBA. Unlearning your face

MRS. Me want unlearn me body
        like Gin-GER ROH-GERS gone go
new Mr. Clean floor step-two step-three eyes and slipper-feet
both go, Boo-Ya!
For once
Plees plees
    And me want forget
      Me so bad want forget
      Me want — Wha' that word?

ROSHUMBA. Which word?

MRS. Fo' when An-GEE Dee-ken-son gone go driving hit her head
then fo'get: Who ees me?
      Where ees I live?
      Who this man making calling ha-band?

ROSHUMBA. Amnesia?

MRS. Goody-goody word!
  Me gone want Am-NEE-shia through dancing
    gone fo'get him ha-band
  Me want fo'get so me can billow
        me want billow
            Plees plees
            Make me billow

(LILY *reenters.*)

LILY. Mom?

MRS. Oh look Lee-lee gone come back

LILY. We should go
Make funeral arrangements

MRS. Look at me daughter stand there
See Lee-lee
    Lee-lee stand straight

LILY. If I do can we go?

MRS. Lee-lee so pretty

ROSHUMBA. Yes she is

LILY. Don't be absurd you're instructing my mother not me

MRS. Oh look   Me so hopeful

    (Lights fade down a notch.)

  Right Lee-lee?

    (Lights fade down another notch.)

  you gone give me hope?

    (Lights reduce to spot on LILY. ROSHUMBA *and* MRS. CHANG *exit in darkness.)*

Scene 2

LILY. Listen
  All you women in the audience
  All you pink-skinned
       pink-dreamed
       come-here-for-some-music
          -some-solace
              people
  Listen to me about how
          it's possible
          it is
          myself as an example
       how possible?
       very possible.
       that word, stamp it into your brain:
  possible possible possible
       how it's possible
          in the middle of your life to
 find
   this big fat thing called the past
          that you don't understand
 (How did it get here? you say and you have no clue

nothing to play with
nothing to bet
      and because you have nothing to bet you don't
know what your future
        if you have a future
            what it'll look like
A past you don't understand &
No future
    These are your hands
        stumpish little things)
Me as an example
Me
Stamp that word: me me me
Stamp me
    This is Lily Chang
    This is Lily
        here
         to say
          possible possible possible
          me   me   me
      here to say
         This is Lily
         Lily is who
         Lily is possible

(MRS. CHANG *enters.*)

Scene 3

MRS. Lee-lee
  You inside-ah

LILY. Who needs mending

MRS. Make
  making
  you making-making peace-ah

LILY. Pizza?

MRS. No no making *peace*-ah

LILY. Who is it

69

Han Ong

MRS. Unca Ester

LILY. Who

MRS. Pow-papa-boom-papa-pow

LILY. *Aunt* Mama

MRS. Ant?

LILY. Gender   Female aunt   Uncle male

MRS. Air male

LILY. As in dick

MRS. That a funny word dick

LILY. As in Dad

MRS. Papa?

LILY. He   You   Friction
  And Lily's here
  But that's science mama
  which I understand well enough
  having excelled
  having propelled
           well
  a star next to my name in Chemistry

MRS. Lee-lee

LILY. But science equals easy access
  I don't
  What I don't
     I can't get purpose
  I open
     Mama? Can you understand?
                    magazines and books opening
  and movies
      all make mockery
           aimed at Lily
  who's 35
  who's stranded
  so 35: (like math
     like science, both of which Lily knows

because Lily obeyed
and obedience has left Lily stranded) —

MRS. Obee-deeance key to success

LILY. — at 35
but useless Mama
I ask science and math questions and find out only that they
don't speak   Not now at 35

MRS. No foolish foolish Lily
Boo-boo talking American
You you thirty-fai
Thirty-fai look for fam-lee gone grow into boo-teeful
chi-ren and papa ha-band
gone ma-ree dak-tor
gone ma-ree ma-ree lo-yer who say,
You my case study give me good good chi-ren
good good house-keepan
good food (see?
rhyme like Time and
Prime: Food ees Good)
you prime time be momee

LILY. Mama?

MRS. Go in go in Unca Ester

LILY. If you could speak English Mama
If you could just billow out
speaking gospel
and tell me good things

MRS. Spik? Kick better
Go kick Unca Ester keep quiet like me fo' better swim big pool
of sadness fo' papa dead in heaven

LILY. (*Beat.*) OK
OK Mama

(LILY *exits.* MRS. CHANG *remains onstage. She espies audience. And is made uncomfortable.*)

MRS. Oh me
my my
who is that

71

    who you
    who is you

VOICE. This is God

MRS. (*Still looking at audience.*) God?
    Oh my   So manee of you God

VOICE. This is God

MRS. This is Esmeralda Chang God
      Esme fo' shortening
You remember?
How is he
      ha-band gone left earth fo' making bed with you?
How is Mr. Chang?
      Mr. Chang good
      Mr. Chang weak but good God

    (BRUCE *walks in. Goes to* MRS. CHANG.)

BRUCE. Mama?

MRS. Oh Bru-see

BRUCE. Who're you talking to

MRS. God

BRUCE. Let's go in

MRS. God no understand me?

BRUCE. The dog's pissing on the carpet
   The cat's scratching at the coffin
   The bird — Nobody knows where she is
   The fish are freaking out
   Who needs so many pets Mam?

MRS. My English no good 'naf fo' him?

BRUCE. Who

MRS. God   Who we making talking about?

BRUCE. No

MRS. No what

BRUCE. He understands you fine

MRS. You sure

BRUCE. Of course
God is bereft in seventeen languages

MRS. Who say that

BRUCE. The college you paid for

MRS. Wha' that mean bereft?

BRUCE. If I tell you will you go in

MRS. (*Claps.*) Yes yes!

BRUCE. It means joyful

MRS. Joyful?

BRUCE. Happy Mama

MRS. God is happy?

BRUCE. Come on   You promised now

MRS. Firs' let me making goodbye to God
GOODBYE GOD!   No fo'get me OK?

BRUCE. OK?

MRS. (*Starts to exit Stage Left.*) So Brusee today
yo' papa inside gone sleeping in boxing-boxing
we must not be bereft

BRUCE. No Mama we mustn't be bereft

(*They're gone. Lights fade.*)

Scene 4

(*In darkness, music. Something fifties or sixties and peppy.
Lights.* LILY *and* IVAN, *dancing arm in arm. Then side by
side. Doing the dip, shag, twist, roach.*)

IVAN. You think she's holding up?

LILY. Mom?

IVAN. She seems fine

73

LILY. More than I can say for him

IVAN. He's *dead* Lily

LILY. Not the right kind of make-up   Not for a Chinese guy

IVAN. They were trying to hide rope burns

LILY. On his *face?*

IVAN. The rope slipped

LILY. Do you —

IVAN. Do I what

LILY. Knock knock

IVAN. Who's there

LILY. Esme

IVAN. Esme who

LILY. Esme-grant

IVAN. Do I what?

LILY. Do you feel —

IVAN. No I don't

LILY. Do you think she — About him do you think she feels
she remains —

IVAN. What do *you* think?

LILY. Does Bruce stare at you like he stares at me?

(*Lights cross fade to spot on* BRUCE, *Stage Center.*)

Scene 5

(BRUCE *barks. Two yelps. Then —*)

BRUCE. I need to stick my dick in something
  I need my dick stuck
  A watermelon is not it
— All this death —
  A canteloupe is not

A parakeet's beak no
              — All this death today and I —
Make me stick it up
I need a little handshake
Someone shake my hand
                — All this death and I cannot —
I need some
Some food would be good

    (*Lights out.*)

Scene 6

    (*In darkness:*)

ROSHUMBA'S VOICE. (*Miked.*) And now I would like to talk about dancing
Hello? Is this microphone on

    (*Mike reverbs.*)

    (*Spotlight:* ROSHUMBA. *Holding mike. Downstage Left.*)

ROSHUMBA. Hello
Can you hear me
OK
And now I, Roshumba Chow, would like to talk about dancing
Having reached the midpoint of our course we will be presenting
in a few minutes an impromptu showcase
                        But first I would like
to *talk* about dancing

First I was a little girl

    (*On back wall, projection of slide: a cockroach.*)

    (ROSHUMBA *doesn't once check to see if slides correspond
with her narration.*)

And my body, being a little body, was unmarked
Years later it would not be unmarked

    (*Slide: dead dried leaves.*)

Years later it would be little
                              not in size but someways else
To the point of recession
A recessed body

   (*Slide: angel fish.*)

Years later I would be a model
But being a model didn't lead to dancing
Nor did being my mother's girl
I was my mother's girl
This is a picture of my mother

   (*Slide: sign which reads "No trespassing."*)

My mother took pictures in a zealous bid to corral the world around her into shapes she understood as being hers, as being kind to her, as being her kind

She took a picture of a cockroach and said: Roshumba this is Disgusting

Because of my mother I know what Disgusting looks like

My mother took a picture of leaves and sticks on the ground and said: Roshumba this is seasons

Because of my mother autumn is my favorite season

My mother shot things and advised me to do the same. She said: I have a word to say to you Roshumba. This is the word. Documentation. This is the corollary. To Not Get Lost.

Years later I would take a picture of gray concrete from the driver's seat of my Volkswagen and I would say, to no one in particular, to myself, just to hear what it sounded like, I would say, Roshumba this is escape

Years later I would need to escape

And that made me dance

Not my mother but that

But before then

   (*Slide: monkey behind bars.*)

I was a model
People would train a camera on me then shoot then say:
Roshumba you are a cockroach and I'd look in the mirror and it
would be true I'd be a cockroach   They'd say: Roshumba you
are autumn and again I would turn I'd be autumn

From one day to the next I wouldn't know whether to cockroach
or autumn unless someone said Cheese

So I left

(*Slide: traffic light green.*)

First I was Roshumba Turner

(*Slide: traffic light yellow.*)

Years later I would be Roshumba Chow

I thought that would mark me   He said: You be my Chow Mrs.
I said, I do

(*Slide: traffic light red.*)

First it was fun.

I thought a shared oppression would unite us. The comparison
of wounds.

Years later he started to say: My wound is bigger than yours

He said: I've been drunk for two weeks and I have a gun!

He said: I'm sick and tired of being Chow and being married to a
cockroach

So he marked me   On the legs   On the arms   The face
too if he felt like it

But before then I took a picture of him and said, Roshumba this
is what love looks like

This is a picture of him

(*Slide: roadsign which reads "End."*)

Today he is wanted in seventeen states but the wrong kind of
wanted

They show a photograph of him and they say, This is the Green Mountain Killer   They say, Information leading to an arrest

The Volkswagen only took me so far   Afterwards I had to dance   And then after that I had to teach   Because I wanted to share with people (it's so lonely otherwise)

Years from now I would like to have a daughter

(*Slide: a penny.*)

Dancing will run its course and then I'd like to have a daughter If I have a son it won't be as good but I won't abort   I'll make do but frankly I don't know what to do with a boy   Frankly there can be only one thing to do with boys   Which is at age three to tell them, This is the door   Your direction is Out   But a girl

I want a girl to make me a flower out of macaroni

From my mother to me to her, this girl who doesn't exist yet but will: I am less than my mother — less her sadness, her eccentricities, her character (which being outstanding stood out) — and my daughter will be less than me   This is what generation means   I look very much forward to this   To one day having this daughter come through the door and have in her hands for me a macaroni flower

(*Slide out.*)

To have that signal achievement

Which is to be gifted, unlike her mother and her mother's mother before her, with the supreme American gift   Which is normalcy   We will put that macaroni flower on the wall and look back years later and say, That was a great moment   And not much has happened to her since   And it will be a good thing

Our house

Our dog

Our fence   The word picket will apply   But not the wrong kind of picket

And there will be flowers

The same kind my daughter tried to approximate with her macaroni

And we will be normal   How normal we will be I cannot
even begin to tell you   Catalogues and catalogues subtracted —
subtracted

That is what I want to say about dancing

And now
Here she is
To demonstrate her mastery of Introductory Cha-cha   It's
Mrs. Chang

> *(Lights cross fade to Stage Center:* MRS. CHANG. ROSHUMBA
> *gone.* MRS. CHANG *is uneasy, tentative. She takes a deep
> breath. Then starts to dance. Slow. She counts each of her
> awkward steps out loud.)*

MRS. CHANG.   One two
                      chachacha
Three four
            chachacha
Five five
            chachacha
Six seven —
      (She stops. Looks out.)
Oh me oh my
Me no
Me can no
Me remember too much
Me remember
      (Breaks down and cries.)
How he kissed me
One two
            here
      (Points to right cheek.)
Here
      (Points to chin.)
       three four
Me no
Thirty years gone go making passing and me no forget me no
      (She stops.)
Help
Please help

79

The Sandalwood Box
Mac Wellman

Characters:
MARSHA GATES, a student and prop girl at Great Wind Repertory
　　Theater
PROFESSOR CLAUDIA MITCHELL, a Professor of Cataclysm at
　　Great Wind University
a BUS DRIVER and
a CHORUS OF VOICES, including DOCTOR GLADYS STONE,
　　that sadistic monster "Osvaldo" and others from the House
　　of the Unseen

(*Takes place in the rain forests of South Brooklyn.*)

(Note: *The occasional appearance of an asterisk in the middle of a speech indicates that the next speech begins to overlap at that point. A double asterisk indicates that a later speech (not the one immediately following) begins to overlap at that point. The overlapping speeches are all clearly marked in the text.*)

> *The Maiden caught me in the Wild*
> *Where I was dancing merrily*
> *She put me into her cabinet*
> *And lockd me up with a golden key*
>
> — William Blake
> "The Crystal Cabinet"

(*Scene: We see* MARSHA, *alone. Except for the table and the sandalwood box itself, all scenic devising is done vocally.*)

MARSHA'S VOICE-OVER. My name is Marsha Gates. I lost my voice on the 9th of November, 1993, as a result of an act of the Unseen. If you think you cannot be so stricken, dream on.

80

CHORUS. I took the IRT every other day for speech therapy. In a remote part of Brooklyn. Avenue X. Where my therapist, an angelic person, resides. Her name is Gladys Stone.

A SINGLE CHORISTER. Doctor Gladys Stone.

> (*The good* DOCTOR *appears.* MARSHA *tries to speak.*)

. . ?(!) . .

> (DOCTOR STONE *tries to speak.*)

. . !(?) . .

MARSHA'S VOICE-OVER. Doctor Stone tried to cure me. Alas, she too was stricken.

> (*Since neither can speak, both give it up. Pause.*)

CHORUS. Dream on I did, but . . .

> (*The good* DOCTOR *disappears.*)

MARSHA'S VOICE-OVER. Parallel lines meet in Brooklyn. The East and Westside IRT. This geometry is also of the Unseen. It is inhuman design, and therefore unnameable. Also the knowledge of its mystery* is subject to error.

CHORUS. It is human to be so* stricken;

MARSHA GATES. I took the wrong train.
We're on the wrong train.

MARSHA'S VOICE-OVER. I took the wrong train and arrived at a strange place. A place I did not know. The air felt humid and tropical. The air felt not of the city I knew. A lush, golden vegetation soared up, up and all around the familiar landscape of the city, like a fantastic aviary. It **was** a fantastic aviary. A place full of exotic specimens.
> (*Pause.*)
It occurred to me I might have lost my mind as well, although I did not think so because the idea gave me such strange pleasure, like the touch of a feather along the top of my hand. This place seemed a paradise. I laughed and fell asleep. I dreamed . . .

CHORUS. I am waiting at a bus stop, waiting to return to my home. Another person is standing there with me.

> (*We're at the bus stop by the Aviary.*)

81

Mac Wellman

PROFESSOR CLAUDIA MITCHELL. Hiya.

MARSHA GATES. Hello.

PROFESSOR CLAUDIA MITCHELL. I'm Professor Claudia Mitchell.

MARSHA GATES. I'm Marsha Gates, a part-time student.

PROFESSOR CLAUDIA MITCHELL. I'm an archaeologist, of sorts.

MARSHA GATES. I'm a student at City College. No declared major. I also work part-time in a theater. Great Wind Repertory. The plays are all shit. TV with dirty words.

PROFESSOR CLAUDIA MITCHELL. I see.

MARSHA GATES. I can't speak either.

PROFESSOR CLAUDIA MITCHELL. So I understand.

MARSHA GATES. It's very aggravating.

PROFESSOR CLAUDIA MITCHELL. So it would seem. (*Pause.*) My specialty is human catastrophe.

MARSHA GATES. That's very nice, but you're making me nervous.

PROFESSOR CLAUDIA MITCHELL. So it would seem.

MARSHA GATES. Is this the Zoological Gardens? The beasts seem to be making a considerable noise. Perhaps the person who is supposed to . . . feed them . . .

CHORUS. . . . has been stricken,* like you, by an act of the Unseen.

MARSHA GATES. Like me. And Doctor Gladys Stone.

PROFESSOR CLAUDIA MITCHELL. I see. Perhaps so. Perhaps, however, you mean an act of complete probabilistic caprice. A fly in the Unseen's ointment. An ontological whigmaleerie. A whim of the die.

MARSHA GATES. I work in the theater. Philosophy makes me nervous.

PROFESSOR CLAUDIA MITCHELL. I see. What theater?

MARSHA GATES. I am a prop girl at Great Wind Rep. I told you.

(*The* PROFESSOR *throws back her head and laughs. Pause.*)

82

PROFESSOR CLAUDIA MITCHELL. An artist! Then surely you must appreciate the higher things in life. Knowledge. Ideas pertaining to a theory of the world Id. The power of the mind to crank out ideational constructs beyond mere calculation and desire . . . not to mention . . . mere mortality.

MARSHA GATES. This bus sure is taking a long time.

CHORUS. The bus arrives in a wild rotation of dust, hot fumes and the clangor of the unmuffled internal combustion engine. (*All are deafened.*) An instrument of noice close to the heart of disaster.

BUS DRIVER. Ever seen a bus before? This is a bus. Don't just stand there quaking. We in the bus business don't have all day. We live complex lives. We dream, gamble, seek, deserve a better fate than Time or Destiny, through the agency of the Unseen, allows. So, get aboard if you are going to. If you dare. There, there in the valley, someone is playing a saxophone among the peonies. His heart is broke. There's no poop in his pizzle and surely the will of the Unseen shall bear witness, and lift him up from the abyss of his . . . of his wretchedness, to the bright air above where lizards, snakes and the mythic **tortoise** are . . . glub, glub . . . My basket of sandwiches flew off into the cheese that is the North end of the thing in the hot ladder. Groans and slavver. Spit and questions marked on the margin. A sale of snaps, larval coruscations. Sweet drug of oblivion. On a global scale. Flowers of unknown radiance, snarls of snails, all of a coral wonder. Just in time for the man who discovers himself stubbed, in an ashtray. Put out. All the work of the Unseen, like a wind in the sail of our hour, midnight, when we encounter the Adversary, anarchic and covered with hairs, in the form of our good neighbor's discarded sofa, left out for the garbage man to pick up. He would like to discover the truth about what can do no harm only if it is kept, safely under lock and key, in its cage, with no poop in its pizzle, aware of us but dimly, us lost in the crunching despair of our endless opening up before the doings of the Unseen, in all our sick, sad, pathetic innocence. Innocence that is only the half-cracked euphemism for our woe, which possesses not even the required token for the train, or bus. Nor even the train to the plane. Not even the faith to enact that pizzle.

MARSHA GATES. I don't have a token.* Do you have a token?

PROFESSOR CLAUDIA MITCHELL. No, I don't have a token. Do you have a token?

(*They look at each other hopelessly. Pause.*)

BUS DRIVER. Then what are you wasting my time for?

PROFESSOR CLAUDIA MITCHELL. And he drove off, leaving us both in a brown study, abandoned. So I turned to my young companion, green with anxiety, and spoke in what I imagined were soothing tones ... (*Long pause.*) I collect catastrophes. Vitrified catastrophes. Enchanted in a case of glass. Encased in glass,* that is.

MARSHA GATES. What a mess.* ***Farblonjet***.

PROFESSOR CLAUDIA MITCHELL. You like messes?* Aha.

MARSHA GATES. What a* disaster.

PROFESSOR CLAUDIA MITCHELL. So you are fond of* disaster!

MARSHA GATES. What a catastrophe!

PROFESSOR CLAUDIA MITCHELL. ***Quelle catastrophe***! I collect them, you know.

MARSHA GATES. What did you say?

PROFESSOR CLAUDIA MITCHELL. I collect catastrophes.* Vitrified, of course.

MARSHA GATES. No, the other thing you said.

PROFESSOR CLAUDIA MITCHELL. Vitrified. Encased in glass. They are very beautiful. Would you like to see my collection? My estate is very close, just beyond the lianas.

MARSHA GATES. No, no. The other thing* you said.

PROFESSOR CLAUDIA MITCHELL. Never mind. Never mind. That was in the French language. The language of love.

(*They exchange long, hard looks.*)

CHORUS. So I went to her house. In the deep Forest, near Avenue X. I went with her, although I knew there was something about it not quite right. (*Pause.*) Something, in fact, quite wicked.

MARSHA'S VOICE-OVER. I suspected that my hostess, Doctor Claudia Mitchell, harbored heretical views on the topic of the Unseen.

CHORUS. . . . heh-heh . . . (*Pause.*) . . . heh-heh . . .

(*She looks hard at the* PROFESSOR.)

MARSHA'S VOICE-OVER. I could not bring myself to ask. Her draperies were of the finest brocade, purple and stiff, annihilating the out of doors with its pedestrian bird-cries, bus fumes, the horror of the city's . . . hullabaloo . . .

CHORUS. Tick-tock . . . tick-tock . . . (*Repeat, etc.*)

PROFESSOR CLAUDIA MITCHELL. I poured a large glass of sherry for the young girl, and myself, and led her into my studio.

MARSHA'S VOICE-OVER. There, upon a long, dark-grained, baroque table of immense, carved teak, supported by four grotesque, dragon-faced whorls of some other, strange wood, lay . . . tada!

PROFESSOR CLAUDIA MITCHELL. My sandalwood box. Within it, my dear Marsha, is nestled my collection.

MARSHA'S VOICE-OVER. The deep plush of the box's dark interior . . . took my breath away.

(*The* CHORUS *joins* MARSHA *and the* PROFESSOR *around the sandalwood box.*)

PROFESSOR CLAUDIA MITCHELL. This is . . . (*She holds up a small, bright object.*) Seoul, Korea. December 25th, 1971. The worst hotel fire in history. An eight-hour blaze at the 222-room Taeyokale Hotel. A total of 163 persons are incinerated or succumb to the horrors of noxious inhalation. Two workmen are later sent to prison for terms of three to five years, convicted of carelessness in the handling of gasoline.
(*Pause. She replaces it in its place and holds up another.*)
This is Clontarf, Ireland, in the year 1014 A.D. Danish raiders under chieftain Sweyn the First (Forkbeard) are repelled by the forces of King Brian Boru. The Danes are mauled, with a loss of 6,000, and driven back to their stumpy ships. Both Boru and his son are killed. Forkbeard is slain later that year.
(*And another.*)
Saint Gotthard Pass, Italian Alps. 1478. During the private war between the Duke of Milan and another feudal lord, an array of sixty stout Zurichers, allies of the Milanese, are flattened by an avalanche in the early afternoon, with the solar furnace blazing away so innocently above.*

(And another.)

Kossovo, in former Yugoslavia. 1389. Prince Lazar's Serbian army of 25,000 meets the Spahis and Janazaries of Sultan Murad in the morning mists of the 28th of June. In accordance with a prophecy of the Unseen, the entire Serbian force is annihilated, thus clearing the way for Turkish mastery of the region for over half a millennium.

(And another.)

The Johnstown Flood. May 31, 1889. A wall of water thirty to forty feet high bursts down upon the town as the entire dam collapses. Over two thousand people are drowned, or dragged to their deaths over tree branches, barbed wires and overturned houses. Victims continue to be unearthed, some far upstream, for the next seventeen years.

(Yet another.)

The retreat of the French Army from Moscow, begun on October 19th, 1812. Hounded cruelly by marauding Russian guerrillas, the **Grande Armee** is soon mangled, and beaten — reduced to a desperate, starving horde. Snows begin to fall on November 4. Ten days later Napoleon is left with only 25,000 able-bodied fighters. At the River Berezina 10,000 stragglers are abandoned in the crossing on the 29th. French losses are the worst in history: 400,000 men, 175,000 horses, 1,000 cannon.

(Pause.)

This wonderful collection constitutes only a merest part of the world's catastrophe, which **in toto** comprises the dark side of the Unseen's id.

MARSHA'S VOICE-OVER. But I heardly heard the words she spoke because of a curious feeling that stole into my mind, and I began to wonder, out loud:

MARSHA GATES. Why is the night better than the day? Why do the young become old, and not the other way around? Why is the world made mostly of clay? Why can't a person always tell what is wrong from what is right? Why does the full weight of the Unseen fall most heavily upon the visible, like brass? Why can't we see what it is that compels both cause and effect to be so interfixed? Why can't I find a number beyond which nothing can be enumerated? Why can't I know what will come of what I do, think and say? Why can't I know truth from lies the way I do "up" from "down." Why is one person's disaster not catastrophe for all? And who knows why these things are called unaccounted. Unaccountable. Uncountable. And why, oh why, don't we know who **does** know the answers to these things? (*Pause.*) . . . because isn't it so that if we possess, and are possessed by a question, the answer must, too, be hidden somewhere, somewhere in the heart of someone, someone real, and not a phantom of the Unseen?

CHORUS. Dream on, they did. Dream on . . .

MARSHA'S VOICE-OVER. When, however, I perceived, at last, the true sickness of her id . . . her sick, squat, demented id . . . I stepped quietly behind her while she was focussed on her precious set of vitrified catastrophes . . . and picked up a large, blunt object to bludgeon her with, but . . . (*Picks up a chair, freezes. The* PROFESSOR *turns to her, freezes. Pause. They look at each other a long time.*) When I saw she wanted me to do it . . . She wanted me to do it . . . out of a curious . . . covetous . . . vexatious . . . perversity . . . (*Slowly* MARSHA *lowers the chair.*)

PROFESSOR CLAUDIA MITCHELL. I am a recovering alcoholic, and a fraud.

MARSHA GATES. And I knew she was neither . . . so:

CHORUS. Out of a curious, covetous, vexatious perversity . . .

MARSHA'S VOICE-OVER. (*Very softly.*) I refuse, I refuse, I refuse* to do it . . .

CHORUS. I REFUSE TO BLUDGEON* HER.

MARSHA GATES. Simply put: I refused to do* it.

CHORUS. She refused.

(*She laughs. The* PROFESSOR *roars out a command:*)

PROFESSOR CLAUDIA MITCHELL. **Osvaldo! Osvaldo!** Throbow hobero obobout.

(*The* CHORUS *beats her up, and throws her out. As this is being done we hear the following, sung by the* PROFESSOR *and* MARSHA'S VOICE-OVER:*)

In the name of Id
and all the Id's work
show me what dark works
are done in the dark.

In the name of disaster.
In the name of catastrophe.

(Pause. She lies outside the door of the PROFESSOR'S *house, dazed. We hear birds cry.)*

MARSHA'S VOICE-OVER. Her man, an ape named "Osvaldo," beat me, and threw me out, but . . .

(Pause. She opens her hand, revealing one small, glimmering object.)

CHORUS. As I lay, bloody and beaten, on the forest floor, amongst dead leaves and whatnot, nearly poisoned by lethal inhalation of spores, and accidental ingestion of strange moss and fennel . . .

PROFESSOR CLAUDIA MITCHELL. . . . wicked id's fennel . . .

MARSHA'S VOICE-OVER. I opened my hand, and my voice returned. I had stolen one small, nearly perfect catastrophe:

(A slow blackout begins.)

MARSHA GATES. April 4, 1933. The United States dirigible **Akron** goes down in heavy seas, in a remote spot in the middle of the Atlantic Ocean with a loss of seventy-three nearly perfect lives.

(Pause.)

MARSHA'S VOICE-OVER. It was the most perfect jewel of that sandal-wood box.

The Mineola Twins

A Comedy in Six Scenes, Three Dreams and Five Wigs

Paula Vogel

PRODUCTION NOTES

There are two ways to do this play:

1. With good wigs.
2. With bad wigs.

Personally, I prefer the second way.

It would be nice to score this production with female vocalists of the period—Teresa Brewer, Doris Day, Vikki Carr, Nancy Sinatra, etc. These singers were on the Top Ten; as a country, we should never be allowed to forget this.

Characters:
MYRNA, the "good" twin. Stacked.

         played by the same actress
MYRA, the "evil" twin. Identical to Myrna,
except in the chestal area.
JIM, Myrna's fiancé.

Scenes one and two take place during the Eisenhower administration; scenes three and four take place at the beginning of the Nixon administration; scenes five and six take place during the Bush administration.

This play is for Anne.

DREAM SEQUENCE NUMBER 1

(*Eerie lighting.* MYRA RICHARDS, *age seventeen, stands in a trance, in a letter sweater with several M's stitched on askew; it looks like bloody hands have clutched and stretched the knit during an apocalyptic Sock Hop that ended in disaster.*)

MYRA. So. It was like homeroom, only we were calculating the hypotenuse of hygiene. I whispered to Billy Bonnell — what does that mean? And he said: Yuck-yuck — it's the same angle as the triangle under your skirt. Yuck-yuck.

Shut-Up Creep! Thhwwack! With my metal straight edge which took off the top of his cranium. And then Mrs. Hopkins said, in this voice from the crypt: Miss Richards — what is the hypotenuse of the square root of hygiene?

And just as I was saying Excuse Me, Mrs. Hopkins, But I Didn't Know What the Homework Was for Today on Account of Being Suspended Last Week By You 'Cause of the Dumb-Ass Dress Code —

— **The Voice** Cuts in on the Intercom:

". . . Everyone . . . Down . . . Under . . . Your . . . Desks."

And we all got real scared. And the Nuclear Air Raid Siren Came On, Real Loud. And kids started bawling and scrambling under their desks. Somehow we knew it was For Real. We could hear this weird harmony of the bombs whistling through space. And we could see the bombs in slow motion coming for us, with a straight line drawn from Moscow to Mineola. Dead Center for the Nassau County Courthouse. Dead Center for Roosevelt Field. And Dead Center for Mineola High. Home of the Mineola Mustangs.

And I knew it would do diddlely-squat to get under the desk. I looked at the clock, frozen at five minutes to twelve. I said, real polite, to Mrs. Hopkins, who was clawing at the blackboard in terror: I've Decided to Let You Live. But You Can Shove the Hypotenuse, Mrs. Hopkins.

And something drew me into the hall, out of the maw of that classroom. Into the hall, where there was pulsing red light and green smoke.

Like Christmas in Hell.

Kids' bodies were mangled everywhere. Our principal Mr. Chotliner was calculating the hypotenuse under Miss Dorothy Comby's skirt, our guidance counselor. In the middle of the hall. She was going Ooof! Ooooff! And the tufts of white hair on his bald head were wiggling with their own desire on each stroke. And the kids in Detention Hall were watching.

I just kept walking.

The girls' Glee Club had spread-eagled Mr. Koch the driver's ed instructor further down the hall, and they were getting the long-handled custodian's broom out of the closet.

I just kept walking.

Lockers were opening and shutting like gills in a deep-water fish, singing "Peggy Sue" each time they opened.

I just kept walking.

I checked my watch. Five minutes to the Apocalypse. I could hear the bombs humming louder now. I thought of crossing against the lights and getting home. There's nothing lonelier than watching your parents hug while you curl up on the rug alone and Mom's ceramic dogs melt on the mantel as the sky glows its final Big Red.

Then I heard **The Voice** on the intercom say to me:

". . . Find . . . Her. . . ."

I had to Obey **The Voice**.

I knew that at the bottom of the stairwell, I would find my twin sister Myrna, hiding from me. Curled up in a little O, her back to me. Just like Old Times in the womb. A Little O trying to float away from me.

I entered the stairwell at the top. The lights were out. There was a thickness to the air. The stairs were steep. And I heard her soft breathing, trying not to breathe.

She could hear me breathe.

I felt her body tense, trying to be still.

She could feel me move.

Her soft neck, trying not to swallow.

She could taste my saliva.

Her heart, trying not to beat.

She could hear my heart thunder.

She knew I was there.

And I said: **"I'm Coming, Myrna."**

"I'm Coming . . . to Find . . . You . . ."

91

Paula Vogel

(Teresa Brewer's "Sweet Old-Fashioned Girl" plays into the next scene.)

"A Sweet Old-Fashioned Girl"— Teresa Brewer

Wouldn't anybody care to meet a sweet old-fashioned girl?
Wouldn't anybody care about a sweet old-fashioned pearl?
Who's a frantic little bopper in some sloppy socks
Just a crazy rock and roller little Goldilocks
Wouldn't anybody care to meet a sweet old-fashioned girl?

Scene 1. 1950s.

(MYRNA RICHARDS, age seventeen, is in the midst of closing up the local luncheonette, early evening. JIM TRACEY, age twenty-two, in neat attire, prepares to smoke a pipe while waiting for MYRNA.

As the play begins, MYRNA is waving goodbye to a customer who has left.)

MYRNA. 'Night, Mr. Hawkins! Thanks for the tip! Yes, you're right, a dime certainly doesn't go as far as it did —

(— MYRNA spies MR. HAWKINS's cane, still perched on the counter by his stool —)

— Wait! Mr. Hawkins! Your cane!

(MYRNA turns towards us and we see her high school clothes are protected by a demure apron. She quickly retrieves the cane, exits offstage and returns to the doorway.)

— You're welcome! That's right! Now you can go home and "thwack" Mrs. Hawkins with it! Ha-ha! Good night, now!

(MYRNA closes the door to the luncheonette and flips the CLOSED sign towards the street.)

Such a *nice* man.

(MYRNA returns to wiping the counter, straightening chairs. JIM succeeds in lighting his pipe. MYRNA sniffs the air in alarm.)

Did I turn off the grill? I smell something on fire —

(MYRNA *turns and sees* JIM *smoking his pipe.*)

Oh, goodness, Jim!

JIM. Do you like it? I got it today!

MYRNA. Golly! Now I'm engaged to a man who smokes a pipe!

JIM. Well, you know, all the fellows in the office smoke cigarettes —
and there we were, puffing away in the marketing strategy ses-
sion, trying to come up with ideas for this new car that Ford is
designing. And Bob, my boss's boss, was getting cross because no
one had said anything new — and that's when it hit me. I thought:
That's it! A pipe!

MYRNA. It's just the thing!

JIM. How does it look?

MYRNA. Very dashing.

JIM. (*Suddenly anxious.*) But I don't look . . . "intellectual," do I?

MYRNA. Oh, no. Not at all.

JIM. Because I don't want to go back to the mailroom. I don't want
to stand out too much.

MYRNA. Oh, you don't. That's why I fell so hard for you — the way
you just blend in.

JIM. Maybe this wasn't such a good idea. After all, Arthur Miller
smokes a pipe. . . .

MYRNA. Isn't he the baseball player?

JIM. Darling. That's Joe DiMaggio, Marilyn Monroe's first husband. Arthur's the lucky man who got Joe's "Sloppy Seconds" —

MYRNA. Oh, he's the one who invented that barbecue sandwich!
You know, after meatloaf, "Sloppy Seconds" is our most popular
menu item —

(JIM *feels ashamed of himself, and kisses* MYRNA *paternally
on her brow.*)

JIM. I've got to stop bringing home my mailroom language. God
bless your purity, Myrna.

MYRNA. Oh well, Arthur Miller, Joe DiMaggio, Estes Kefauver — you know how I am with names in the newspaper. You're my window on the world.

(JIM *puffs importantly.*)

JIM. So what's wrong, kitten? I thought we'd agreed not to see each other on school nights.

MYRNA. Oh, I know. But I'm so upset, Jim, and I don't know where else to turn —

(JIM *takes* MYRNA *in his arms.*)

JIM. Tell Big Jim.

MYRNA. (*Breaking away.*) Oh, it's that sister of mine again! She's got me to the point where I don't know what to do! She's driving my parents to an early grave! I swear, the devil rocked her cradle when Mom was out of the room!

JIM. Oh, now, Myra's a little wild, that's all. She lacks your maturity, but she's not a bad kid —

MYRNA. — You just don't know! There's such meanness in her! Such calculated meanness. I'd swear someone dumped her on our doorstep if it wasn't that we're identical twins —

JIM. (*Smiling.*) — Almost identical —

MYRNA. You don't know. You haven't shared a bedroom with her for seventeen years. How can anyone pop chewing gum that loud? She does it to get at me. And then the music she plays at night when I'm trying to study —

JIM. — Everyone fights with their siblings —

MYRNA. — I've tried, I really have. We decided, fair and square, to divide the room into equal halves. . . . I drew an imaginary line down the middle, and I said to Myra, reasonably, that she was not to cross that line. Except in the case of fire or nuclear emergencies. I would respect her space and she had to respect mine. If she wants to live in squalor and chaos and *utter filth*, that's fine, that's fine, just do it on *her half*.

JIM. That sounds sensible.

MYRNA. Except. Except! She discards her Joe Bazooka bubble gum wrappers under my pillow. Where I find them each time I try to sleep. (MYRNA *begins to cry.*) And the worst thing of all, Jim, is she discards her dirty socks on my side of the room. How does she get those socks so *dirty*?

JIM. Honey lamb, is this why you wanted me to come by tonight? When we get married, you won't have to put up with her dirty socks anymore — you'll only have to put up with mine —

MYRNA. — No, Jim, it's gotten really, really bad. Mom and Daddy had a big blowup with Myra. She's been sneaking out of the house, late at night, to go downtown and God knows where else with those boys she hangs out with — with their souped-up bombs and their ducktail hair and dirty fingernails — maybe even *Greenwich Village* —

JIM. Well, Greenwich Village isn't exactly Sodom and Gomorrah —

MYRNA. I don't know, Jim. There are an awful lot of girls wearing *pants* down there. (*Very slight shudder.*) Anyway, there's been a horrible, horrible fight. Mom's really upset. It's not just Myra's short-short pants, or her suspensions from school for smoking — Mom's so upset she's been lighting candles at the altar until it looks like George Bernard Shaw's birthday cake. And Mom doesn't even want to go to *bingo*, Jim — you know that's serious — because she doesn't want to show her face in the church. And finally Mom tried to ground Myra because my sister sneaked out again this past Saturday night — (MYRNA *sees* JIM *look at her.*)

   — Well, I *had* to tell Mom when I discovered her bed empty. Not exactly empty, because she bunched up her clothes and pillow to make it look like she was in the bed — but I knew she was missing because I woke up and didn't hear her gum-popping — I *had* to wake Mom and Daddy because I get scared, Jim — she is my sister, after all, and what if she was dead in a car crash or in an opium den in the Village? — So Mom said she was grounding Myra for a month, Myra said we could all go to *hell*, she was moving out, she was going to a girlfriend's and she was dropping out of school and she just packed up her leather jacket and stuffed her dirty clothes in her pillow case and left —

JIM. Well, honey cakes, maybe that's the best thing for everyone involved. Maybe she should be out of the house for a while, so

95

everyone can just calm down — and you won't have to put up with her dirty socks anymore —

MYRNA. She left her socks *behind*. On *my* side of the line. But that's not the worst thing. Daddy found out that . . . that Myra's gotten a job to pay her rent — in a roadside tavern of ill repute — as a so-called "cocktail waitress!"

JIM. What was your father doing in a house of ill repute?

MYRNA. He said he was having car trouble, and went into the Tic Toc to use the phone — and saw Myra in a skimpy outfit waiting on *men his own age!*

JIM. Well, I'm sure she'll make good wages in tips —

MYRNA. Jim! Mineola is a small but decent town! We can't let Myra ruin our good name in this town!

JIM. Well, why doesn't your father go speak to her?

MYRNA. Oh, you know Daddy. He's a man who doesn't show his feelings. Or speak, for that matter. He's so sweet and so tired when he comes home from the flower shop. He just sits in his rocking chair, thumping the arms of his chair. But I can tell he's upset. He's rocking much faster, and thumping and thumping away like his heart is breaking. In his anger, he even talked out loud last night. He called Myra a Whore of Babylon. But I know he doesn't mean it. He's never even *been* to Babylon.

JIM. Then why don't you try to have a heart to heart between two sisters?

MYRNA. Don't laugh . . . but she . . . scares me.

JIM. She scares you! She's just a kid, Myrna. She doesn't have your maturity.

MYRNA. No, really, Jim — there's something . . . evil in her. I get scared when . . . I look into her eyes. And then I have the most awful dreams at night — *nightmares* where even though it's the end of the civilized world as we know it, Myra tracks me down and . . . and . . . I can't say. I wake up.

JIM. Well, maybe your mother should go and talk to her.

MYRNA. Oh, Jim, that won't do any good. Myra only listens to people in *pants*.

JIM. I see. I suppose you want me to talk to her.

MYRNA. Oh, Jim, would you? I don't care if I never see my sister again, but Mom is really broken-hearted. She's got to come back home and quit that job. I know she'll listen to you. She's just got to listen to sense. I don't think I can hold up my head in this town anymore. And I've been trying so hard for the Home-Makers of America Senior Award.

JIM. Honey, people don't mistake you for your sister. You're two separate people.

MYRNA. It's gotten really bad. This past Sunday, I was conducting class for the Catholic Youth Organization, and I saw Johnny Lucas passing a note to Donny Frederiksen — and they were laughing — so I confiscated it. And read it. And were my cheeks red! The whole class was snickering, they'd all read it.

JIM. What did the note say?

MYRNA. It's hard for me to say. Don't look at me. It said . . . it said . . . "What does Myra Richards say . . . after . . . she . . . "has sex"? (MYRNA *blushes bright red.*)

JIM. (*Simultaneously.*) "Are all you guys on the same team?"   MYRNA. (*Simultaneously.*) "Are all you guys on the same team?"

(JIM *starts to laugh, and stops.*)

JIM. Sorry. I heard that joke in the mailroom at work. Okay, princess. Let me see that pretty little smile of yours, and I'll drop in on the Tic Toc tonight, okay?

(MYRNA *comes into his arms and puts on her bravest smile.*)

That's my girl!

MYRNA. But you won't "tarry" in the Tic Toc, will you, Jim?

JIM. Heck, no. It's not my kind of den of iniquity.

MYRNA. Because sometimes I worry — what if all the other girls find out about my special older man and try to steal him from me?

97

JIM. What if the football captain happens to glance your way?

MYRNA. The football captain? (MYRNA's *face falls.*) I think . . . he's already scored a touchdown at my sister's goalpost.

JIM. That was an unfortunate choice of words. What about the captain of the wrestling team? Track? Volleyball? (JIM *looks at* MYRNA's *face.*) Ooops. Let's steer clear of sports metaphors. What if . . . the captain of the chess team looks your way?

MYRNA. *He's* out of luck. I know what I want. It's going to be so grand, Jim. In just another year. I'll be out of high school, and I've saved my pennies from waiting on tables to take courses from Katherine Gibbs —

JIM. — Except I don't want my wife to work!

MYRNA. Oh, I won't for long! Just long enough for us to save a down payment on a little two-bedroom Levitown home.

JIM. If everything goes well with this new ad campaign for Ford, you won't have to work. The bonuses will be pouring in!

MYRNA. Oh. My. That sounds exciting. (MYRNA *starts to get flushed. They start to make out.*)

JIM. I'm pledged to secrecy — but you've never seen anything like this car! When it hits, it's going to hit big. The firm's even hiring this poetess, to come up with lyrical names — like Fiesta or Bronco or Ford Epiphany! — And wait till you see the grille on this baby — well, I helped a little to come up with the design — it looks just like — like — (JIM *starts to get flushed.*) — Well, I can't say. Guys are gonna go crazy over this buggy! Honey, the future is ours! You'll have the best of everything. You can stay home and cook to your heart's content! You won't have to go to Katherine Gibbs!

MYRNA. Well, a girl should always be prepared for the future. And besides, once I've learned stenography and typing, I can be an asset to my rising young executive-husband when he comes home with work from the office — you can put your feet up on the hassock and I'll take dictation. We'll have a son, and by the time he's three or four, we can afford a three-bedroom house in Great Neck with an office downstairs. Then we'll have a daughter, and maybe a dog. Or we'll have a dog, and maybe a daughter.

JIM. — Kitten. Maybe it's not wise to plan everything — we should let some things be a surprise —

> (*Appropriate music, like Teresa Brewer's "Til I Waltz Again With You," starts to play from the jukebox.*)

MYRNA. (*Coyly.*) Oh, there will be surprises. Every night, when my husband comes home, all hot and bothered from his commute, I'll be waiting on the other side of the door with all kinds of surprises —

JIM. Oh, yes? What kind of surprises?

MYRNA. Well, you'd be amazed at the casserole recipes I've been mastering in home economics — you'll have a new home-cooked surprise every night!

JIM. Oh.

> (MYRNA *laughs at his disappointment.*)

MYRNA. Oh, I know what kind of surprises you want. Just like a man. You've been spending time reading Mr. Hefner again, haven't you?

JIM. I'm a lonely man on school nights.

MYRNA. Oh, Jim. I know. I miss you too on school nights.

> (*They begin to make out seriously now.*)

I . . . I just . . . count . . . the minutes until . . . Friday night.

JIM. MMmmm. Me too. I can't keep my mind on work. (JIM shifts MYRNA's *weight against him.*)

MYRNA. You . . . you don't mind, do you, Jim? Waiting for me?

JIM. It's . . . hard. Awfully . . . hard. Myrna — (JIM *has started to loosen* MYRNA's *items of clothing.*)

MYRNA. Oh . . . Jim. Jim. . . . (MYRNA *starts to help him.*) Wait — I'm getting choked a little — there. That's better.

JIM. You've put the "closed sign" up, haven't you?

MYRNA. We're locked up . . . "tight."

JIM. Quick . . . turn off the overhead lights —

(MYRNA *complies. She comes back, panting slightly.*)

MYRNA. My. This *is* a treat for a school night.

(JIM *lifts* MYRNA *up on a stool. She wraps herself around him. Suddenly,* MYRNA *stops, puzzled.*)

Jim. How come, if Myra and I are identical twins, that we're not . . . identical? I mean, how come she's . . .

JIM. Flat as a pancake?

MYRNA. (*Giggling.*) True. And I'm so . . .

JIM. Stacked, darling. Like a stack of pancakes.

MYRNA. Yes. But I mean, is it scientifically possible? Wouldn't either both of us be . . . you know — (MYRNA *runs her hands coquettishly over her breasts.*)

JIM. Yes, yes — (JIM *starts trying to unsnap* MYRNA's *brassiere beneath her blouse.*)

MYRNA. Or we'd both be like Iowa in the chestal region? I mean, if we share the same makeup, how is that possible?

(JIM *is now helping* MYRNA *step out of her underwear beneath her skirt.*)

JIM. You're just lucky, I guess. I'm . . . just lucky. Please, God, let me be lucky tonight — (JIM *is nibbling on* MYRNA's *neck. She moans.*)

MYRNA. Bloodlines . . . science and *all that* . . . is just . . . so . . . strange.

JIM. Let's not talk about your sister anymore tonight. Let's not talk. (JIM *starts to press against* MYRNA.)

MYRNA. Oh! Oh, Jim! Oh . . . Oh, Jim!

JIM. Myrna . . .

MYRNA. Jim, Jim, Jim —

JIM. (*Urgently.*) Myrna, Myrna —

MYRNA. Yes! Right now! Jim! Now! Now! Ohhh!-Jimbo!-ooohhh —
(MYRNA *clambers up on all fours onto two adjoining stools;* JIM *climbs on his knees on the adjacent stool —*)

MYRNA. WAIT!

(JIM, *red-faced and behind* MYRNA, *stops stock-still.*)

Jim — this — this isn't right.

JIM. Oh, Myrna —

MYRNA. These stools are giving me motion sickness. (MYRNA *climbs down with iron-will control.*)

We . . . we shouldn't be doing this.

(MYRNA *looks behind and sees* JIM *rotating on his stool in frustration. She stops him from spinning.*)

Darling — I want you. Badly. But not now. Not here. I want it to be so . . . right. Not with the smell of meatloaf and "Sloppy Seconds" still in the air. And it will . . . it will be . . . so "right," won't it? Jim?

JIM. I guess.

(JIM *and* MYRNA *do not speak to each other for a beat. They adjust their clothing.* MYRNA *picks up her underwear with great dignity, tucking the cotton into her apron pockets.*)

MYRNA. I want to be pure for you on our Wedding Day.

JIM. Oh, Myrna. . . . Nothing could ever . . . stain your purity. You are pure. You have been pure. You will always be pure.

MYRNA. No, Jim — there are some absolutes we have to believe in. The flag. Kate Smith. And Virginity.

JIM. How did Kate Smith get in there?

MYRNA. You can't be more or less a virgin. Virginity is a state of mind. It's different for men. There are no absolutes for guys. I have to earn the right to wear white when I walk down the aisle.

(JIM *sighs wearily.*)

MYRNA. Oh, my. I haven't filled the sugar and condiment bottles yet.

101

(*There is an awkward pause as* JIM *finds his pipe and knocks out the ashes.*)

Please, darling. Tell me you understand. You do love me, don't you? Jim? I'm waiting just for you. But I want you to respect me on the day we march down the aisle. Please tell me you understand.

(JIM's *Adam's apple bobs as he speaks.*)

JIM. I understand, Myrna. You're a good girl. It's just that God made men differently than the female sex. It's not great for an automotive body much less the engine to torque it up like that without letting the throttle go. Do you understand what I'm talking about?

MYRNA. (*Puzzled.*) Automobiles?

JIM. No. I'm talking about . . . *agony.* Simple, unadulterated male agony.

(MYRNA, *concerned and anxious, turns to* JIM *to hold him.*)

MYRNA. Oh, Jim. I'm so sorry.

JIM. Don't *touch* me. Not right now. I've got to . . . let the engine cool down.

MYRNA. Oh, Jim. I don't understand about these things. But if there was . . . something . . . something I could do without compromising my innocence . . . something that . . . might make you feel better — would you tell me?

(JIM *thinks a moment, tempted. Then his better angel decides.*)

JIM. Maybe I'd better go. It's getting late. I think I should just leave now. (JIM *takes a huge breath.*) There. It's not . . . "hurting" as much now. I think I can walk.

MYRNA. Jim!

JIM. You are so . . . good. You're the only absolute goodness in my life. I don't want to do anything . . . you don't want me to do. Let's say goodnight while we have no regrets.

MYRNA. You're my guiding light, Jim. Will I see you Friday night?

(JIM *half-hobbles, half-sidles in a strange crab-walk to the luncheonette door.*)

JIM. You bet. (*He manages a half-smile from the doorway.*) I'd better find that sister of yours and give her a talking to.

(JIM *exits.* MYRNA *flies to the door, and waves, angelically, at his retreating figure.*)

MYRNA. Goodnight, darling! . . . 'Til Friday! (MYRNA *turns back to the room, worry now on her face. In a half-whisper, she addresses the Diety in the hush of the luncheonette.*) Please, God, please — let Jim wait for me!

(*Fifties music swells as the lights dim into Scene 2.*)

Scene 2. Later that evening.

(*We see the interior of a cheap motel, used for trysts of GIs on leave from Mitchell Air Force Base. The blinking neon of "MOTEL" flashes throughout the scene. At the start of scene,* MYRA *sits up in bed, agitated. She wears a push-up Maidenform and a panty-girdle.* MYRA *manages to smoke, furiously, in between cracking her gum. There is a heap in the bed beside her, curled under the cheap chintz spread, completely covered, and hogging the entire bedspread. Occasionally, we hear muffled sobs.*)

MYRA. "I like Ike. I like Ike." I mean, is that cornball or what? Can you believe how way-in this country is? They like some bald, golfing dude whose idea of a hot time is having Mamie stroke his clubs! They voted for that square twice! With his little turkey sidekick and his turkey chick in the cloth coat. "I Like Ike —" I mean, that is yo-yo's-ville.

(MYRA *stops, pops her gum. Listens to the heap.*)

Hey, man. Hey, daddy. I'm trying, see? I'm trying to "engage," dig? I'm dishing politics, man, I'm trying to connect.

(MYRA *nudges the heap.*)

Hey. Hey. You gonna come out sometime this decade?

(*The heap covers itself with some insistence.*)

103

Hey. Suit yourself, daddy-O. No skin offa my pearlie-whites. I've had cats cry before the Act, and I've had lottsa cats wail during. You're the first one to boo-hoo after.

(MYRA *waits for a response. Tries again.*)

Hey, I gotta idea. You got any bread? Any wheels? We could just spook in your bomb. Or we go peel on outta here and spin into the village. It's crazy down there, any night of the week. We go take in the Vanguard — do you dig that scene? It's the most, the meanest. . . . We could do a set, and then blow the joint and just walk around the streets.

There's this one guy, Ace, who walks around with a *parrot* on his shoulder. It's crazy. He's so hip — you pay him a dime, and he gives you a poem, on the spot. He poetizes on a dime. And these poems — they don't rhyme or anything. They're deep. They don't *mean*, they just *are*. It's far-out!

(JIM, *in a fury, pops up.*)

JIM. Speak English, can't you! If you want to talk to me, speak English! English!

MYRA. Wow.

(*Pause.* JIM *huddles, still clutching the spread around him.* MYRA *does her best Julie Andrews.*)

"The Rain in Spain Falls Mainly on the Plain." . . . Is that better?

JIM. Jesus. You've watched too many James Dean movies.

MYRA. (*Stung.*) He only made *three*. And then he *died*.

(MYRA *is moved.* JIM *is surprised.*)

JIM. Hey, look, I wasn't making fun of him or anything.

MYRA. He was important to a lot of people. He lived fast, died young . . . and really messed up his face.

JIM. I'm sure he was important to impressionable young women. But that doesn't mean he could act. Couldn't drive, either.

MYRA. Oh, he could drive. It was the yo-yo on the other side of the yellow line he didn't count on. I'll bet he was going over a hundred in that Spider, the top down, he was flying, he was putting something down! Over eight hundred thousand people filed past the wreck when they brought it to L.A. It was a *shrine*. I wanted to go in the worst way to pay my respects, but try talking sense to my square parents. I could of taken the Greyhound and been there in five days — five days going west, five days going east — and I would of missed only two weeks of school. Less than I've missed for stupid things like the dress code. If it had been the Pope that died in that Spider, Mom would be pressing me to the front of the line to kiss the bumper. Some asshole yo-yo in a *Ford*, for God's sake.

(JIM *clears his throat.*)

JIM. The Ford Motor Company happens to be one of my clients.

MYRA. Oh. That's nice. What do you do for them?

JIM. Well, I advise them on strategies for younger buyers, as a representative of a new and growing market in this country — consumers under twenty-five. We're devising a new model that's going to sweep aside the competition.

MYRA. So where is this company of yours you work at devising and marketing and sweeping?

JIM. Madison Avenue.

MYRA. Manhattan? Midtown Manhattan?

JIM. Last time I looked, that's where Madison Avenue was.

MYRA. You work in Manhattan? And you don't live there?

JIM. I like more air and more space and more *green*.

MYRA. Oh, man. You're free, white, over twenty-one and you get to get up every morning and take the LI-double R into Manhattan. If I were you, I'd cash in the return ticket to Mineola and find a pad like — (*Snap.*) — that.

JIM. You'll get your chance.

MYRA. Not soon enough. You think if you get a wife and one of those cornball aprons and tongs and barbecue in Mineola on the weekends, your bosses will promote you faster?

JIM. My bosses . . . have nothing to do with it.

MYRA. Uh-huh. Have you told them the truth?

105

Paula Vogel

JIM. Which is?

MYRA. American cars are *ugly*. They're dogs, man.

JIM. Well, you're entitled to your opinion.

MYRA. Eighty percent of Ford buyers watch *Ted Mack's Amateur Hour*.

JIM. What's your source?

MYRA. Detroit is obsessed with making cars look like sharks or spaceships with those pointy fins the size of Kate Smith's metallic hooters. Cornball City. The only good thing about 'em is the back seat. (MYRA *smiles at* JIM.) There's a new little car the Germans are making—now they're cool. Only problem is you got to be a midget to make out.

JIM. Would Marlon Brando drive a V.W.? Or James Dean?

MYRA. (*A faraway look comes into her eyes.*) At least he died quick. He didn't hang around, clutching, dying of boredom. Dying from living in an uptight little town like Mineola.

JIM. There's nothing wrong with Mineola.

MYRA. "There's no Shineola in Mineola, there's just shit—"

JIM. (*Shocked.*) You shouldn't say words like that.

MYRA. Like Shineola? What is there to do in Mineola? Go to bingo, go to the PTA, fight over whether or not *Catcher in the Rye* should be allowed in our libraries! Participate in Little League! This town is so dead, they finally closed down Roosevelt Field when they realized that no one wanted to fly into this burg! Mineola's so dull, there wasn't even a red scare here! No self-respecting communist would even try to infiltrate the school system! In Mineola, people keep their blinds up because *nothing happens* on a Saturday night.

JIM. You are full of hate.

MYRA. I'm restless! Don't you sometimes feel like you're gonna jump out of your skin if you don't do something, go somewhere?

JIM. Well, sometimes.

MYRA. Yeah? And then what do you do?

106

JIM. I go for a nice, brisk walk around the block.

MYRA. How old are you?

JIM. *(In his deepest chest voice.)* I'm . . . twenty-two. Going on twenty-three.

MYRA. Oh, man. I've gone with juvenile delinquents older than you.

JIM. I'll bet you have. *(Pause. They shift in the bed.)* So — this fellow with the parrot — Ace?

MYRA. Yeah, Ace.

JIM. What is his poetry like?

MYRA. It's hard to describe in words. It's like jazz riffs without the music. It's just a torrent of feeling and colors and *truth*.

JIM. No rhyme?

MYRA. Rhyme is out. Square. Dead.

JIM. Tell that to Robert Frost.

MYRA. What, we're talking aesthetics here? Aesthetics after sex?

JIM. — Look, I'm trying to "connect," okay?

MYRA. You think poetry's gotta be "Barbara Fritchie"? "Shoot If You Will This Old Gray Head?"

JIM. I didn't say that. I'm trying to show an interest. Look, I've read *On the Road*.

MYRA. You have?

JIM. Yes. In hardcover.

MYRA. Jeez. I've never done it with anyone else who's read Kerouac.

> *(This pleases* JIM.*)*

JIM. So I'm your first?

MYRA. Yeah. In that way, you are. Nobody reads Kerouac in Mineola.

JIM. Well, I have.

MYRA. So, what did you think?

107

JIM. Of Kerouac? It was kind of long.

MYRA. Yeah. Dull. (*They smile at this small island of agreement.*) You're okay for a man who wears ties.

JIM. You're okay, too. You're nothing like your sister — (*It strikes* JIM.) Oh, my God! Your sister! Oh, God, oh, God —

MYRA. Look, don't clutch on me, Jim. . . . Hang loose, okay? Just breathe. It's gonna be all right.

JIM. Oh, man, what am I going to do? What am I going to tell her?

MYRA. Look, you don't have to tell her anything. Okay? It's not like I'm going to show up dressed in Jezebel Red in church when the preacher says, "If anyone knows of any reason why these two should not be wed —"

JIM. This is not some joke. Okay? This is serious. This is about commitment and trust.

MYRA. We'll keep it a secret. I would sincerely like to keep something secret from little Miss Tom Peep. She knows everything else about me.

JIM. Oh, God. She'll find out.

MYRA. You don't know. You haven't shared a bedroom with her for seventeen years. She's pried into everything I've owned. Every date I brought home, she's eavesdropped on. She knew how far down my throat every guy's tongue has probed. . . . I tried to keep a diary, but I gave up on it. I got tired of her saliva stains smudging the ink.

JIM. She'll look into my eyes. She'll know.

MYRA. What, you think your eyes are gonna look different now? Oh, boy. Where did you get your information? Health classes at Mineola High? Although I'll bet you are going to walk in a different way. You know what they call it when they lower the front end of a car to streamline it? So it's real fast for dragging? They call it "raking." And that's you, daddy-o. You've been raked.

JIM. I've got to think. You've got to help me think. (*Pause.* MYRA *snaps her gum.*) Could you maybe not pop your gum?

(MYRA, *with great ceremony, removes her gum and places it on the headboard.*)

MYRA. Okay? Now we can think great thoughts. Okay. This changes nothing, okay? You don't tell her, she doesn't ask. Don't ask, don't tell. The formula for modern marriages.

JIM. You sound like an expert. When are you getting married?

MYRA. Hardehar-har. I don't know what I'm going to do when I get old. There's never been a movie made that's even close to how I'm gonna live. Mr. Goldwyn, in his wildest wet dreams, can't imagine my kinda life. I'm making it up from scratch. No marriage. No laundry, no cooking. No children. Just freedom.

JIM. But you're a girl! You can't do that!

MYRA. I am going to spend my life doing everything people tell me I can't do.

JIM. Maybe I should think over this marriage thing. No sense in rushing everything.

MYRA. Look, Jim — I don't want to tell any guy what to do. Outside of bed, that is. But you oughta marry my sister. She's already picked out the dinner pattern and silverware. She's been collecting recipes until she has dinner completely *planned* for the first year. Wait 'til you see what she's cooking for your first Christmas supper in Mineola —

JIM. Are you hot? There's no air in here —

MYRA. And she's been practicing her signature, "Mrs. James Tracey. Mrs. James Tracey." And sometimes just initials "MRT."

JIM. — for Myrna Richards Tracey — ?

MYRA. — whatdya think, for My Right Tit? She's ordering her towels, sheets and bathrobes and that monogram. Probably her underwear, too.

JIM. How do you know that?

MYRA. All's fair in war and between sisters. I read her dumb-shit diary, too. Hell, I gotta right to find out what stupid lies she's telling about me. When I can't sleep, all I gotta do is read an entry or two — *boring*. Better than Ovaltine.

JIM. Well, I think one thing is clear — I can't marry Myrna.

MYRA. You're kidding.

JIM. No. I'm seeing things differently now. I've been "raked."

MYRA. Oh shit. She's gonna blame me.

JIM. This has nothing to do with you.

MYRA. That doesn't matter. Everything's my fault. If she doesn't make Homemaker of America, it's 'cause her sister's a slut. If she gets a pimple on her forehead, it's because of the stress I'm putting her through. I'm glad I had an airtight alibi the day of Pearl Harbor — you gotta marry her. I want to get off the hook. Let someone else in her life get blamed.

JIM. No, see, Myrna was right.

MYRA. Now this I gotta hear.

JIM. It's the domino theory. Okay, let's say nobody notices anything different about me, right? I look the same, talk the same, almost walk the same. Like if I had a twin myself, but completely different on the inside. Tomorrow morning, I go into work, nobody notices. A year from now, I walk down the aisle with my intended, your sister, and she doesn't know the difference. The priest gives us the sacrament, and there's no lightning bolts striking me dead.

MYRA. I'm with you so far.

JIM. So virginity is not only *not* just a state of mind. It's a figment of imagination. It doesn't matter. It has no significance.

MYRA. That's what I was trying to tell you a while back when you were bawling.

JIM. So don't you see? The domino theory? There goes virginity, there goes my promotion, my work ethic, monogamy, mortgages, raising 2.5 children, truth in advertising, belief in a deity, shining my shoes, living in the suburbs, caring for my aged parents and saluting the flag.

MYRA. Wow. Heavy. (JIM *and* MYRA *sit next to each other in bed. Contemplate.*) Wanna cigarette? (MYRA *offers her pack.*)

JIM. Sure.

(*They puff.*)

MYRA. My brain hurts. That usually never happens *after* sex.

JIM. Yeah. I guess.

MYRA. So this was your first time.

JIM. Yes. . . . Myra? Was I — could you tell me — was I —

MYRA. You were wonderful, Jimmy. You know, you're different from the others. You're really smart, and sweet — and hip. I've never known anyone like you, Jim Tracey. A girl could get real sweet on you.

JIM. Thanks. . . . Myra? How "many" guys have you —

MYRA. Gone all the way with? To Home Plate?

JIM. Yes. Do you mind my asking?

MYRA. Well, no. Not really. Although after your little revolution revelation a few seconds back, it doesn't seem like these "little" flings really matter.

JIM. Of course they don't matter to you. They're just like . . . a "friendly" handshake.

MYRA. Yes, that's right. A "handshake" between two adults.

JIM. Sooo — a "friendly" question out of academic curiosity.

MYRA. Well, there are all the guys on the first string — and I'm working on the second string who have their letters —

JIM. Whoa! So it's really true about you. You really are a Whore of Babylon!

MYRA. Hey! Wait a minute! First of all, I happen to really like football. Second of all, we just jammed on a philosophical thing here, like a neutrality of moral consequence, so where do you get off calling me that? Putting that down?

JIM. I was talking about me. Men are defined by their minds, their thoughts. Men are defined by what they do — their actions in the world. It's different for you — you're a girl. There are . . . absolutes in the world for girls. Girls don't do, they just are.

111

(*Furious,* MYRA *gets out of bed and starts dressing. She tries not to cry.*)

MYRA. Why—why did you have to do this? I thought . . . for a minute—I thought you were different. I thought you understood.

JIM. Why are you getting all steamed up? I'm just another "notch" on your belt, right? Look, don't get all bent out of shape—you're a really, really "nice" girl—you're just not a "good" girl—

MYRA. —I hope my next decade is better than this one.

JIM. I mean, girls are born the way they are. Men *become.*

MYRA. I can't believe I fall for it every time.

JIM. Myrna was born "good." You were born . . . "nice." Myrna was born "stacked"—you were born—well . . . you have lovely eyes. . . .

MYRA. I'm cool to the guys, thinking, dip that I am, that they're gonna be cool back. That this time is gonna be different. I don't get it, I really don't. I'm nice to you, right? I made you feel good, I went all the way, I gave you what you wanted, no questions asked, no demands—why then do you guys always do this?

(JIM *is oblivious to the tirade.*)

JIM. So the bottom line is—you did sleep with the football team.

(MYRA *reaches the door, disheveled but dressed. She turns, goes back for her gum on the headboard.*)

MYRA. Well, lucky for us one of us had some experience. (MYRA *puts the gum in her mouth. Just then, there is a timid tapping on the motel room door.* MYRA *and* JIM *freeze.*)

MYRNA. (*Offstage—sobbing.*) Jim? Jim? . . . Jiiimm?

MYRA. (*Hissed.*) Shit!

JIM. (*Feverishly whispered.*) O migod . . . o migod . . . omigod—

MYRA. (*To herself.*) Is this like the goddamn Alamo? Or is there a back door?

(JIM *puts his trousers on backwards;* MYRA *checks out the bathroom.*)

MYRNA. Oh, Jim — I know you're in there. I know, Jim. You're in there with — (*Sob.*) HER.

(*There is a continued sobbing and tapping on the door.*)

MYRA. (*Stage whisper.*) There's a window over the toilet — it's gonna be a tight squeeze — lucky for me I don't have any tits. . . . Give me the keys to your car.

(*Sob/tap on door.* JIM *is in a state of shock.* MYRA *grabs him.*)

Your car. Your car, daddy-o. Give Me the Goddamn Keys. Now.

(JIM *reaches into his trouser pockets awkwardly; she grabs the keys out of his shaking hands.*)

Kiss her goodnight for me. I'm outta here.

(MYRA *rushes into the bathroom. We hear a window being pried open, a faint "Ooooff" of pain and a thud. Meanwhile, on the front door, the wounded thrush tapping has changed into the staccato pounding of a killer.*)

MYRNA. (*Off.*) MYRA! I'M GONNA KILL YOU, MYRA! WAIT TIL I GET MY HANDS AROUND YOUR SCRAWNY LITTLE NECK! MYRA! YOU SUCK, MYRA! I'M GONNA RIP OFF WHAT LITTLE THERE IS OF YOUR TITS, MYRA! I'M GONNA USE YOUR NIPPLES FOR MY KEYCHAIN, MYRA! *OPEN*— (*Pound.*) *THIS* (*Pound.*) *DOOR!* (*Pound.*) NOW! BEFORE I TAKE THIS FUCKING DOOR OFF THE HINGES AND SHOVE IT UP YOUR — MYYYRRA!

(*A huge thump. A beat. Then, the wounded thrush tactic again. The sound of a tremulous little girl writhing against the door in agony, who wouldn't hurt a fly, but might slash her wrists any moment.*)

(*Little butterfly sobs of pathos.*) J-jiimm? Baby? Jjiimm-bo? Honey — I know it isn't your fault. I know how good you are . . . baby — just let me in, let me see you, Jim . . . don't send me away . . . Jimm? Jimmy? Jimmy-Jim?

(JIM, *moved, scared, catatonic, sidles to the door with his backwards trousers falling down. He tentatively unlocks the motel door.*)

113

JIM. (*Sobbing.*) Myrna? Baby? There's — there's no one here —

(*As* MYRNA *hears the door lock click, she throws herself into the room with a Medea-scream.*)

MYRNA. I'LL FUCKING KILL YOU!!!

(JIM *lands on his butt.* MYRNA *flies across the room. They blink at each other in the empty, disheveled room. As* MYRNA *picks up something from the floor, there is the sound of Jim's automobile being quickly started, revved and thrown into reverse outside the room.*)

Shittt!!

(MYRNA *runs to the door, too late. She watches a car offstage screech out of the parking lot into the night. Her shoulders slump.* JIM *huddles where he is, completely still. A beat.* MYRNA *turns, limp and tired, with a single dirty sock that* MYRA *has cast off dangling from her hand in silent accusation. They both stare at the sock.*)

(*BLACKOUT.*)

DREAM SEQUENCE NUMBER 2

(*We see* MYRNA *in a hospital johnny. One wrist is bound in a leather shackle attached to a belt which has been gnawed and severed. Dangling from her head and body are wires which have also been severed, attached to electrodes still pasted on her skin. Her hair has not been tended to in some time; there are also dark red-brown stains on her johnny. Occasionally, there is an electronic buzzing.*

"Tea for Two" begins to play; two psychiatric aides run in slow motion behind MYRNA; *they catch up and restrain her, one at each elbow. The effect, though, is of a choreographed dance routine, which in fact it is. Throughout the following monologue,* MYRNA *spins beyond their reach; caught and lifted by each aide in turn, dipping and twirling. The aides are unable to fasten* MYRNA *into a straitjacket.*)

MYRNA. Six months from now.

His dinner has been simmering in a low oven, beef burgundy at 275, because of course he missed the 5:08.

But I will be unruffled.

He dragged his ass home an hour and a half late, and the dinner should be drier than Nagasaki.

I have applied a new shade of lipstick. A new negligee bordered in see-through lace; my hair coiffed. Because Dr. Prior says that personal hygiene is a sign of mental health.

He won't notice. He'll be sprawled in his leather easy chair in the den.

He's had three martinis on the 6:35 home.

I'll knock timidly at the door of his study and enter, with a tray and a Bloody Mary, the celery stick at a jaunty angle.

"Honey — your drink . . . just the way . . . you like it."

And I'll bend over him in serving the drink, so he can see the cleavage beneath the black silk.

But he won't notice.

He's got lipstick smeared on his collar, and his fly is only partially zipped up from his little escapade with his secretary on the floor of his office, only three hours ago.

I'll pretend not to notice as he sips the thick red juice.

"How was your day at work?"

I'll ask. But he won't hear me. I'll catch the highball glass just as he drops it, his hand limp from the drugs speeding through his veins.

I lock the study door from the inside.

Quickly, I put on my platex dishwashing rubber gloves, my rain bonnet and my London Fog. I turn up the volume on the stereo, blasting Frank Sinatra. Not loud enough to wake Kenny in his crib. But Loud Enough.

I go to his desk drawers, take out his financial statements and his diary, with the last notation:

"I Can't Go On This Way."

I put the open diary on top of the papers I strew over his desk.

Then I take his hunting rifle down off the rack, and check the ammo. Kneeling beside him, I remove his right shoe and sock, brace the rifle so that his big toe is jammed into the trigger and his open mouth sucks the barrel.

For the first time in a year, he and I touch as I squeeze his toe which squeezes the trigger.

I open his fly. For the hell of it.

"Good-bye, you prick," I whisper.

Then I jump out the window that overlooks the back yard. I lower the screen beind me on the other side, and go to the kitchen through the yard. Then I tidy up a bit.

> (The two psychiatric aides finally restrain MYRNA *in the jacket, but the three continue to dance the choreographed routine, in complete Hollywood harmony.*)

The beef burgundy is simmering in the oven. I taste a teeny tiny bit. It's delicious.

Then I call the police. (MYRNA *smiles at her dance partners/ keepers.*) Don't you love a nice beef burgundy?

> (MYRNA *and her partners dance to Doris Day's "Tea for Two," which is drowned out by the overlapping electric buzz of shock therapy as lights fade into next scene.*)

The Dalai Lama Goes Three for Four
Eric Overmyer

(*All the sounds of a day game: the buzz of the crowd, the cries of the vendors; you can hear the pennants snapping in the breeze and smell the aromas of the ballpark: beer, hot dogs, cigars, grass.*

The DALAI LAMA, *at home plate. Dressed in his purple robes. Sandals with baseball cleats. The familiar buzzcut, glasses, Western wristwatch, sunny countenance, guttural speaking voice. Behind him, an infinite blue sky. He looks over the audience, nods. Considers carefully what he is about to say.*)

DALAI LAMA. Baseball —
    (*Considers.*)
Baseball —
    (*Considers.*)
Is not a Tibetan game. But —
    (*He smiles. From within his voluminous robes, he extracts a decent-sized Louisville slugger —*)
(*Brandishes bat happily.*) Louisville Slugger —
    (*He limbers up. He raises his robes to reveal baseball shoes. He knocks the mud off his cleats. He steps into the batter's box and assumes a very respectable stance over the plate. He takes a couple of practice swings. He gets ready. He waits. The pitcher takes too long. The* DALAI LAMA *holds up his hand to call time, steps out of the box, looks down the line to check the coach's signals, steps back into the box and goes through the motions again. He waits: infinite patience and relaxation. The crowd noise surges a little in anticipation. He takes the first pitch. The ball pops into the catcher's mitt.*)
Low and away. Two and Oh.
    (*Considers.*)
Baseball is not a Tibetan game.
But consider the diamond motif.

117

(Taps home plate.)
Here is a diamond —
(He gestures to the playing field.)
There is a diamond —
(He gestures to the stadium.)
The stadium is a diamond, too. So the diamond sutra is realized within the —
(Considers.)
parameters —
(Considers.)
of the game of baseball. As with the Tibetan mantra, "Hum mani padme om." The jewel at the center of the lotus. This stadium is shaped like a diamond, and also like a lotus. And at the center of the lotus, in the middle of the diamond, is the jewel. The pitcher's mound.
(Cups his hands.)
Cupped. A cup is also a baseball term, I understand. Cupped within the lotus. The mound. The diamond. The game. The players. The spectators. All petals of the lotus. Unfolding over time. And look —
(Points.)
Those pennants. Prayer flags. Flapping in the breeze. Sending prayers to heaven with every snap. "Hum mani padme om." Sending prayers to heaven with every snap. "Hum mani padme om." What do these mantras say?
(Reading them.)
Chicago, Cleveland, Boston, Seattle.
(Smiles.)
Some prayers go unanswered for many years. Excuse me —
(He steps back into the batter's box. Does his rituals.)
Ritual movements.
(He takes the next pitch, which moves him off the plate a little.)
High and inside. Three and Oh. And now I am taking all the way. By the numbers. Baseball has its ancient wisdoms, you see. Even though, you might argue that it is predictable the pitcher will now —
(Considers.)
"groove" one, in order to keep from falling further behind in the count. So I therefore expect him to throw a strike — fastball right down the middle — but the ancient baseball wisdoms decree I should refrain from swinging anyway. This is a test of custom and

resolve. Everyone in the stadium knows what the pitcher is resolved to do. Throw a fastball down the middle. But can he do it?
What if he is wild? What if he has, in baseball parlance, "no control"? This is the first test. And knowing what he has resolved to
do, can I hold fast to my own resolve not to swing at this big fat
pitch? Or what if he deliberately throws a curveball out of the
strike zone, hoping to induce me to break my vow to be taking all
the way? This is the second test. We may call this situation The
Two Noble Precepts of The Two and Oh Pitch.

    (*He takes the next pitch all the way. When the ball hits the
catcher's mitt, it even sounds like a strike.*)

A strike. Predictable. I should have crushed it.

    (*Brightens.*)

But now, according to the ancient precepts, Two and One, I am
free to swing away.

    (*He steps into the batter's box, limbers up, does his rituals.
Sets.*)

Hum mani padme om. Hum mani padme om. Hum mani padme
om. I am relaxed. I am concentrated. The mind is the true jewel
in the lotus — and my mind is only one of an infinite number of
jewels that sparkle in the Net of Indra, which connects all sentient
beings, it is an infinitesimal bit of the Universal Mind, like a grain
of sand on the beach, a drop of water in the ocean, a star amongst
the countless galaxies — my mind is empty, clear, concentrated on
the moment, as it meets the pitcher's mind, similarly constituted,
as he stares down the center of the diamond, reading the catcher's
signals, the ancient symbols for fastball, curveball, changeup,
slider, low and away, high and inside, trying to place the ball, shave
the corners of the plate — and it would be the error of dualism to
perceive this meeting of minds as a duel or a showdown or a test
of wills — for both of us are cognizant of everything and nothing in
that moment — the tidal hum and roar of the crowd, rising and
falling like the days of a pennant race, the breeze blowing in from
center field, the smells of the ballpark, beer and pizza and cigars
and freshcut grass, the chatter mantra of the infielders — hum baby
hum baby hum baby hum baby — the counter mantra from our
dugout of my teammates on the Bodhisattvas — hum mani padme
om hum mani padme om — two consciousnesses, mine and the
pitcher's, both ultimately stripped of ego and ambition and concern
for personal statistics — examples of pure mind, two gems in the
infinite Net of Indra, in this moment concerned only with the

perfect completion of a single act which has significance only in this moment – he to throw and I to hit – and how we accomplish our mutual task will ripple like a stone thrown in a pool and affect the other players, the umpires, the spectators, and move them to actions of their own, which have significance only in this moment but will ripple into the next moment and the next infinitely – and there we are, I waiting, he going into his windup, thousands of other eyes upon the two of us, perfectly concentrated in the moment, except for those distracted souls who have gone to the restroom or the concession stands or whose consciousnesses have been clouded by alcohol or cotton candy or who have merely become bored or are daydreaming or reading their programs or are currently concentrating on an attractive person of the opposite or same sex seated near them or are watching a beachball bounce through the stands or are otherwise engaged in doing The Wave, standing and sitting, in that ancient spontaneous ceremony – or otherwise drifting out of the moment – but everyone else is concentrated on the two of us – and perhaps the most evolved among them have some flickering understanding that our sense of time is different, the pitcher and I, slower and more cognizant of the infinite nature of reality, its Illusory nature, the projections and delusions of the human ego, the emptiness of the void –

(*All crowd background noise stops suddenly and there is perfect silence.*)

And in that perfect silence that only he and I can hear –
(*Listens.*)
I watch the pitcher reach the apex of his windup, pause –
(*Watches.*)
and bring his arm back and then forward, hand turning, releasing the ball –

(*The crowd noise returns.*)

And I see the ball leave his hand and come toward me, revolving, stitch over stitch, a perfect faceted sphere, an eighty-six-mile-per-hour slider headed in a parabolic arc for the outside corner of the plate –
(*He starts his swing.*)
And I swing, aiming to catch it before it breaks –

(*The crack of the bat on the ball. The crowd roars.*)

120

And I drive it to the opposite field, into the gap between center and right for a base hit —

(*The* DALAI LAMA *drops his bat, gathers his robes and runs for first.*)

And as I approach first base, the first-base coach of the Bodhisattvas, His Holiness, The Panchen Lama, who has been, I must say, unfairly accused over the years of collaborating with the Chinese when he has successfully pursued a strategy of survival and pragmatism, waves me around first. And as I round first, I can see the ball hit wall and bounce away from the center fielder and the right fielder, and I dig for second —

(*And he digs for second.*)

And I round second and I see the third-base coach, Allen Ginsberg, waving me on — and I ponder for the briefest of moments whether to continue, or return to second base, for Allen has a poetic grasp of the game that encompasses a level of risktaking which I, as the player-manager of the Bodhisattvas and spiritual and temporal leader of the Tibetan people am not entirely comfortable with, although I encourage him to give his personal expression free rein — which he does — often in conjunction with Philip Glass, who is working on a Buddhist version of "Take Me Out to the Ball Game" for the seventh-inning stretch in our home ballpark of Dharmsala, which because of the altitude will set an all-time major-league record for most home runs hit in a single season, and Philip's sing-along will go something like this —

(*Hums a mantra-like version of "Take Me Out to the Ball Game."*)

— which is pretty catchy, don't you think? I like it — and it runs through my head just at this moment when I see Allen Ginsberg waving his arms and jumping up and down very excitedly, which makes me laugh out loud —

(*He laughs his wonderful deep guttural Dalai Lama laugh.*)

— and so I put all temporal doubts and fears of being tagged out and looking ridiculous and killing the rally aside — and dig for third —

(*Which he does.*)

Which I do, and see the slide signal from Allen —

(*Imitates Allen Ginsberg's slide signal.*)

And I slide in, under the tag —

(*He slides in under the tag.*)

And I'm safe!

121

(Big cheer from crowd. The DALAI LAMA *smiles broadly, calls time, gets up and dusts himself off, high-fives Allen Ginsberg, waves to the crowd.)*

After I finish giving Allen Ginsberg a high five, the next batter up, Richard Gere, hits a sacrifice fly to deep center — a can of corn, as the late great Dizzy Dean used to say —

(Crack of the bat. The crowd intakes its breath, the DALAI LAMA *watches the lazy, high trajectory of the ball —)*

The center fielder squeezes it like a ripe peach —

(Watches it happen.)

And I tag up, and stroll home, easily scoring the winning run —

(Which he does. The crowd roars as the DALAI LAMA *steps on home plate.)*

I congratulate my teammates —

(He goes down the line, giving the ritual handshakes, high fives and butt pats —)

Giving them the ancient baseball ritual handshakes, high fives and pats on the butt —

(He finishes.)

And then the meditation of the game is over. Except for the curious ritual of the postgame press conference.

(The sound of questions being shouted by reporters. The DALAI LAMA *picks out one reporter, listens for the question. He considers it before he answers.)*

Of course, it would be a great honor to be the first Tibetan Buddhist baseball team to win the World Series. If the Blue Jays can do it —

(Listens to a follow-up question.)

That is getting ahead of ourselves. We don't predict the future. Our to date perfect record, fifty-six wins, no losses, is not important in and of itself. We are only concerned with playing the best game we can each game. One game at a time. In our case, the old sports cliché really is true.

(Another question.)

It doesn't matter who the next other team is, or where. Being on the road is not new to us. We have been on the road since 1959. The objective conditions of every game are the same. We only hope that all who play do so at the peak of their physical and spiritual endeavor, in an atmosphere of empathy, and with the proper perspective. It is, after all, only a game. Thank you.

122

(The press conference is over. The reporters fade away. The DALAI LAMA *addresses the audience, while he sits down and takes off his baseball shoes.)*

We did not have a perfect season. In September, we allowed thoughts of a perfect season to spoil our concentration. We succumbed, you might say, to the pressures of — well, not the pennant race, since by this point we were sixty-five games in front of the second-place team in our division — but the desires of our own egos. We lost sight, temporarily, of the task of the moment, and became caught up in the hoopla attending our lowly efforts. We started thinking about the future in the present. Ambition clouded our endeavor, and we lost twelve straight games. Thus humbled, we righted ourselves, and went on to win our remaining regular season games, and finish with a record of one hundred and fifty wins and twelve losses. Some say the altitude of our stadium, as well as the jet-lag factor for other teams flying to India, gave us an unfair advantage. I will say in response that we did as well on the road as at home. In the words of the eminent Buddhist baseball scholar — the Berra Yogi — you could look it up.

(He rubs his feet a moment.)

I myself won the batting title, hitting .750. We politely declined all individual honors. I am told I am listed in the record books with an asterisk. I am not exactly sure what the asterisk represents, but surely it is an ancient baseball symbol. Roger Maris has one as well. We went on to sweep the postseason playoffs, and to defeat the Red Sox, four zip. I myself went three for four in the final game, with three rbi's and one stolen base. I'm not bragging, it's in the box score.

(He slips on his sandals, and stands.)

The Tibetan Diaspora has brought much suffering upon my people. It has also benefited us and the world in ways we could not have expected. We brought Tibetan Buddhism to the West. The West brought baseball to us. Baseball and Buddhism have more in common than either of them might realize. After our season of one hundred and fifty wins and twelve losses, this is now more widely appreciated. The other teams are now studying our techniques.

(Considers.)

In conclusion, let me say that although we must live in the modern world, certain ancient wisdoms should not be tampered with. I am against the wildcard format, the designated hitter and reckless expansion. I am in favor of a strong commissioner. Instead of the

Czar of Baseball, perhaps he — or she — could be the Lama of Baseball. And although I am a scholar of arcane texts, speak several languages and possess a keen sense of mechanics and engineering, I still do not fully comprehend the infield fly rule. And, although I think the movement of franchises should be discouraged, and entertained only in extremis, and with great caution, I look forward to the time when I can move the Bodhisattvas from Dharmsala — to Lhasa.

> (*He picks up his Louisville Slugger. Holds it out horizontal, his palms open. Closes his eyes. Concentrates. The bat floats out of his hands. Floats up and disappears. The* DALAI LAMA *opens his eyes, smiles at the audience and bows. The light fades. A pin spot on his smiling countenance. Blackout.*)

Antonia and Jane
Wendy Wasserstein

— Based upon a screenplay by Marcia Kahan

Characters:

JANE HARTMAN
ROSA GLUBERMAN
ESTHER MALKIN
MORRIS ACKERMAN
SYLVIA PINKER
SOL SAUTENBERG

HARRY ROSENTHAL
IRWIN CARLINSKY
MADELINE
NORMAN BEER
DR. ROTH

Scene 1

(Common Room — The Golda Meir Retirement Home — Riverdale, New York. A dozen elderly Jewish women and two men are doing the hustle. Two other men are sitting on the side behind walkers and clapping along to the music. "Woo-woo-woo-woo-woo! Do the hustle! Woo-woo-woo-woo-woo! Do the hustle!" JANE HARTMAN, thirty-eight, is at the record player. She wears a large flannel shirt, blue jeans and a gladiola in her hair. She would seem a Barnard professor except for the rhinestones on her tortoiseshell glasses. JANE watches the couples as they line-dance.)

JANE. All right everybody. Let's hustle to the right! *(To us.)* On Saturday nights I work as a disc jockey at the Golda Meir Retirement Home in Riverdale, New York. Riverdale is actually the Bronx. But the Riverdale Retirement Home is a lot classier-sounding for the sons and daughters who put their parents here than "The Bronx Retirement Home." After all, Archie and Veronica of comic-book fame went to Riverdale High School. And I used to date Jughead. Not really. That's just my hilarious ironic victim sense of humor.

125

I don't know where everyone here gets their energy. Rosa Gluberman—she's got one lung, one kidney, no gall bladder, is always the last one to leave the dance floor.

(ROSA, *one of the women, steps out in the middle of the dance floor for a solo. She sings:*)

ROSA. "You and you and you do the hustle. Rosa Gluberman does the hustle."

(*The men on the side applaud.*)

JANE. (*To us.*) Esther Malkin—she's outlived four husbands—is already making a play for Morris Ackerman who would be number five.

(ESTHER MALKIN *flirts with* MORRIS, *who sits behind a walker.*)

ESTHER. Morris, I'm a little hot today and my fingers are a little stiff. Would you mind unbuttoning my top two buttons?

(MORRIS *starts unbuttoning her blouse.* ESTHER *pulls his head toward her breast.*)

JANE. (*To us.*) Sylvia Pinker—the social coordinator—is always talking about her son Manny, the Beverly Hills accountant. So far, Manny has started Clint Eastwood's, Carol Burnett's and Barbra Streisand's I.R.A. accounts.

(SYLVIA *dances with* SOL SAUTENBERG.)

SYLVIA. You know who went to see my son Manny for a consultation? Goldie Hawn.

SOL. Goldie Hahn? She used to live here. I thought she died.

JANE. (*To us.*) And sometime during the Lindy, Harry Rosenthal always shouts.

HARRY. Give me gravy on my mashed potatoes!

(JANE *changes the record to "The Mashed Potato" and dims the light.* HARRY *begins singing.*)

HARRY. (*Sings.*) "The mashed potato started a long time ago. It was started by stompin' Joe."

(*Everyone joins in singing.*)

126

ALL. "C'mon baby
   I want some gravy
   So gimme gimme gimme
   Gravy tonight."

   (ROSA *bumps and grinds.*)

ROSA. "Give me gravy on my mashed potatoes . . ."

JANE. (*To us.*) Speaking of gravy, Sylvia Pinker never misses an opportunity to ply me with food.

SYLVIA. Janie darling — a little carrot cake? It's made with forty carrots. Just like gold. So it's not fattening.

JANE. (*To us.*) Then she pinches me.

SYLVIA. Look at that face! Isn't that some beautiful face.

JANE. (*To us.*) And then they're all pinching me.

ALL. That's some beautiful face!

   (*All the retirees pinch* JANE*'s face.*)

ALL. How is it such a beautiful face isn't married?

SYLVIA. Maybe she just hasn't met the right boy yet.

SOL. Janie is a smart girl. Smart isn't always sexy.

HARRY. Golda Meir was smart and she was very sexy.

JANE. (*To us.*) And then Irwin Carlinsky always shows me a snapshot of his nephew, Stephen.

IRWIN. (*Displaying a snapshot.*) My nephew, Stephen. He's not married. So what do you think — nice-looking boy?

JANE. Very nice, Mr. Carlinsky. (*To us.*) I never mention he's showing me a photo of an eight-year-old.

IRWIN. He's a triple Harvard. Harvard undergraduate, Harvard Medical two years and now he's a Harvard Hare Krishna.

JANE. Sorry?

IRWIN. He found religion in jail. He's in for five years for smuggling narcotics.

SOL. A Jewish boy in jail. I never heard of such a thing.

127

JANE. You never heard of David Berkowitz?

ROSA. Who's that?

JANE. Son of Sam. Actually he was my first husband. I specialize in serial killers.

ROSA. Bite your tongue. Go on, bite it.

(JANE *bites her tongue.*)

IRWIN. My nephew was experimenting with rats and hashish at Harvard. It was all for science. So now he's in a minimum security prison. He leaves every day to do community service. And when he gets out of the slammer altogether, he's going back to medical school. He's on the gastrointestinal track. So tell me — you interested? Janie?

JANE. Me? I have a boyfriend.

IRWIN. I'll give him your address. At least you two can be pen-pals.

ROSA. Irwin, she needs a husband, not a pen-pal. Janie, how 'bout a Tvister?

(JANE *puts on* Chubby Checker *singing "The Twist." Everyone begins twisting including the men with the walkers.* ROSA *yells.*)

ROSA. Everybody, look at the sky. Is it a bird?

EVERYONE. No.

ROSA. Is it a plane?

SOL. No.

ROSA. What is it, Janie?

JANE. It's a tvister!!

(*Blackout.*)

Scene 2

(JANE *sits with her nails in soapy water facing* MADELINE *the manicurist, a red-headed woman.*)

MADELINE. God bless them all for still tvisting. They'll all live to be 180. So, who's the boyfriend?

JANE. What boyfriend?

MADELINE. The boyfriend you told Mr. Carlinsky about so you don't have to date his nephew, the Harvard Hare Krishna in the minimum security slammer.

JANE. Oh, Norman! Well, he's not exactly my boyfriend. But Norman really exists. He even likes me. Sort of.

MADELINE. Just "sort of"? You need to have more self-esteem. Have you read Gloria Steinem's book? I do her nails.

JANE. Gloria Steinem and I have the same manicurist? That's incredible.

MADELINE. What's so incredible! You both have hands. Does your boyfriend admire your nails?

JANE. He admires Emily Dickinson.

MADELINE. I do her nails too.

JANE. Norman came into the bookstore about three weeks ago.

(NORMAN *appears browsing inside Womenbooks, a cozy woman's bookstore in Brooklyn Heights.*)

NORMAN. I'm looking for something by a woman.

JANE. What kind of something by a woman?

NORMAN. A book would be good.

JANE. Anything in particular? Fiction, travel, health?

NORMAN. Definitely not health, I'm the sonogram man at Maimonides Hospital. I want to understand women from a perspective other than their ovaries.

(*Lights down on* NORMAN.)

MADELINE. So he's a doctor. Your mother must be proud. Do you get free checkups?

JANE. Norman specializes in two-headed babies.

MADELINE. What?

JANE. He does difficult pregnancies. Which is admirable. The day I met him, we had a very nice chat about my menstrual cycle. Then it turned out we both like Gene Kelly and there was a Gene Kelly retrospective at the Modern so we went over the next three weeks to about nine Gene Kelly films and somewhere between *Singin' in the Rain* and *On the Town*, we started sleeping together. I mean that literally. We'd get into bed and nothing would happen. He would freeze up, which made me freeze up.

MADELINE. It's understandable. He spends all day with his hands in places . . . you know . . .

JANE. I don't like to think about that. Anyway we fixed it.

(*Lights up on* JANE *and* NORMAN *lying in bed together. The subway rumbles by.*)

NORMAN. Jane, do you think you could read to me aloud? Like my nana used to?

JANE. I don't have anything your nana used to read.

NORMAN. How 'bout the book on your bedside table.

(JANE *picks up the book on her bedside table.*)

JANE. The poetry of Emily Dickinson.

NORMAN. Poetry would be nice.

JANE. Emily wasn't a happy girl. This is not exactly romantic poetry.

NORMAN. Please, Jane. Nana always read me asleep. The subway scares me. If you read to me, I'd feel safe.

JANE. Okey-dokey. (*She begins to read.*)
"I felt a Funeral, in my Brain,
And Mourners to and fro
Kept treading — treading — till it seemed
that sense was breaking through — "

(NORMAN *suddenly moans with sexual pleasure.*)

"And when they all were seated
A service, like a Drum . . ."

(NORMAN *moans again. He motions to* JANE *to continue and begins to stroke her.*)

"Kept beating — beating — till I thought
My mind was going numb . . ."

(NORMAN — *in a frenzy of erotic excitement — falls upon*
JANE. *Lights down.*)

MADELINE. Listen, at least he didn't make you read him *Mein
Kampf* or *The Five Chinese Brothers*. There are some real weirdos
out there!

JANE. Ever since that night it has to be Emily Dickinson. No other
writer will do. Emily Dickinson died in 1886. It's almost necro-
philia. It sent me right into therapy with Dr. Roth.

MADELINE. But honey, no one needs a therapist *and* a manicurist!
That's redundant.

JANE. I'm exploring all forms of self-awareness. I plan to be very
healthy by forty.

(JANE *faces* DR. ROTH, *an intelligent-looking woman of
around forty-nine.*)

JANE. Dr. Roth, you don't understand! We have great sex — the only
problem is I've never liked Emily Dickinson. She wasn't big on
zaftig Jewish girls from the Bronx. She never left her house in
Amherst, Massachusetts.

DR. ROTH. You have low self-esteem.

JANE. Okay. Zaftig Jewish girls from Riverdale.

DR. ROTH. You must tell Norman you don't want to sleep with a
man who only has orgasms to Emily Dickinson and delivers
two-headed babies and you must tell Mrs. Pinker "I don't care for
your carrot cake or if your son is Brad Pitt's accountant," and
you must tell your mother not to send you any more Richard
Simmons *Sweating to the Oldies* tapes and if she wants to sweat
to the oldies let her sweat by herself.

JANE. It's *Sweatin' to the Oldies Part Two*. Look, it's not Norman
Beer, it's not Sylvia Pinker and her carrot cake, it's not even my
mother. It's Antonia McGill.

(DR. ROTH *recognizes the name.*)

DR. ROTH. Antonia McGill?

JANE. That's right, the editor, executive par excellence. The perfect woman with the perfect husband, perfect child, recently perfectly profiled in *The Wall Street Journal*, *Elle*, *Der Spiegel* and *The Washington Post*.

DR. ROTH. Yes, I'm familiar with the name.

JANE. I'm having dinner with her.

DR. ROTH. When?

JANE. In around six months. It's our annual meal. We've been best friends since high school. But I'm thinking maybe I'll commit suicide to get out of it.

DR. ROTH. Don't you think suicide to avoid dinner is a little rash?

JANE. I think it's nuts. That's why I came to see you. Do you know how far in advance you have to schedule a dinner with Antonia McGill? I'd hate to screw up her calendar on account of my suicide.

Nina in the Morning
Christopher Durang

Characters:
NARRATOR/LANCE/CON EDISON MAN
NINA
JAMES/ROBERT/LA-LA
FOOTE
MAID
MONK

(*Scene: A beautiful room in a rather elaborate household —
a chateau, a small castle. At Manhattan Theatre Club they
had floor-to-ceiling sheer curtains in front of a beautiful
azure blue scrim. The sound of the ocean. The curtains
gently move to a breeze.*

*There is a beautiful chaise. And in front of the chaise, a tall,
gilt-edged mirror. (The mirror should be only a frame, with
nothing where the mirror glass itself would be. Thus an
actor can sit or stand behind it, and still be seen by the
audience. Seeing a reflection in the mirror is mimed.)*

*Beautiful, mysterious music is heard. A lovely, haunting
soprano aria perhaps.*

The NARRATOR *is onstage. He is dressed in a tuxedo and
looks elegant.*

As the music is finishing, NINA *enters.*

*She is dressed beautifully. (At MTC the designer put her in
an off-the-shoulder red gown, with a very very long train.
However she is dressed, it should be elegant and flattering
to the actress. And a little extreme.)*

Her age is indeterminate — definitely over forty, though — and her face is on the white side, with perhaps too much makeup. She walks towards her chaise with great regalness, as if she's in a procession, on her way to be crowned.

When the NARRATOR *speaks, he is speaking her thoughts, usually. So her facial expressions change with his comments. She does not otherwise look at him or relate to him (with a couple of noted exceptions).)*

NARRATOR. The mist hangs heavy over the ocean today. Nina woke from an uncertain sleep and walked to the chaise in her dressing room and sat in front of the beautiful, cherished mirror.

(NINA *sits on her chaise, and looks out to her mirror and gasps.)*

Her facelift had fallen during the night, and her cheeks were held in place by straight pins.

NINA. (*Looking in mirror, touching her face delicately.)* Oh, Lord. Oh, Lord. How dreadful.

(*Enter* JAMES, *her child, dressed in short pants and a white shirt. He looks like a well-dressed prep-school boy. Played by an actor somewhere in his twenties or young-looking thirties.)*

JAMES. Good morning, mother.

NINA. Don't kiss mommy today, her face is precarious.

JAMES. I don't want to kiss you anyway. I hate you.

NINA. Please don't upset me, James. My plastic surgeon is in Aruba.

JAMES. What's this pin for? (*Reaches for her face, pulls out a pin.)*

NINA. James, stop that. Stop it. Foote! Foote! Come quickly, James is at my face again.

NARRATOR. But James kept reaching for Nina's face, over and over.

NINA. Stop it, you unruly child.

(JAMES *keeps trying to pull pins out of her face.* NINA *keeps trying to protect her face. All the pin business is mimed.*

FOOTE, *the family manservant, enters. Dignified and in a tuxedo.)*

FOOTE. You called, Madame?

JAMES. I want to pull your face off, mother!

NARRATOR. Foote, seeing Nina's predicament with her son, pulled James away from her, pushed him to the ground and sat on him.

(FOOTE *pulls* JAMES *away, pushes him on the ground and sits on him.)*

NINA. Gently, Foote, gently.

JAMES. *(Struggling with* FOOTE.) I hate you, mother, I hate you.

NARRATOR. Foote took out a hypodermic from his jacket pocket, and gave the misbehaving child a shot.

(FOOTE *does all that.)*

JAMES. I hate you. I'm sleepy. *(Passes out.)*

FOOTE. Will that be all, Madame?

NARRATOR. Foote was the family manservant, and often gave the children general anesthesia whenever they became unruly. Foote had once been a dentist.

NINA. Thank you, Foote. James was pulling pins out again. I must have done something wrong raising them. I thought I often smiled. I wonder if they wanted anything else.

FOOTE. Do you wish me to remove any teeth while he's out?

NINA. No, no. Leave his teeth alone, Foote. I just want quiet for a while. Look at how peaceful James is, curled on the floor. I always liked my children best when they were unconscious.

FOOTE. If madame needs me further, just call.

NINA. Thank you, Foote. You're a jewel.

(FOOTE *exits.)*

NARRATOR. Foote withdrew, leaving Nina with her thoughts. She thought about her face. She thought about James. Psychotherapy had been no help for James except perhaps in helping him to express his anger more freely, and how useful had that been.

NINA. (*Sort of to herself.*) Not very.

NARRATOR. Nina's hands shook as she lifted a coffee cup to her face. Her perceptions were off, and she poured hot liquid down the left side of her face. She put cream and sugar on her face, stirred it and then rang the bell for Foote.

> (NINA *mimes the actions the* NARRATOR *says above while, or shortly after, he says them. She uses a real cup, spoon, cream pitcher and sugar bowl, but no actual liquids or sugar.*
>
> *She does all the gestures without emotion. She feels the heat of the coffee and the mess of the liquids after she has done all of them. Then she makes a face of pain, and confusion.*
>
> *Then she rings the bell.*)

NINA. Foote, I need you. Bring a wet cloth. I'm sticky.

NARRATOR. Foote brought a basin of warm water and a roll of gauze and sponged her gingerly.

> (FOOTE *enters with a* MAID *as the* NARRATOR *speaks. The* MAID *has a tray with a silver bowl and a wet cloth.* FOOTE *starts to pat* NINA's *face lightly with the cloth.*)

NINA. Do you think I'm beautiful, Foote?

FOOTE. You once were very striking, Madame.

NINA. Yes, but now, what do you think of me now?

FOOTE. (*Looks at her.*) You have quite a nasty burn on your face, madame. Would you care for a shot of novocaine?

NINA. Go away, Foote. I want to think.

NARRATOR. And again, Foote withdrew, dragging James after him.

> (FOOTE *drags* JAMES *out the door, while the* MAID *curtsies and follows after them.*)

NARRATOR. Nina racked her brain, trying to remember what she wanted to think. The colors of her wall were beige. She had wanted burnt orange, but the designer had run through the house screaming "Beige! Beige!" and they finally had to give him his way.

NINA. *(Out, to the imagined designer.)* I wanted burnt orange, but you have given me beige.

NARRATOR. Later the designer turned against her too, like her son James. No, no, Nina wanted pleasant thoughts, nice things. Flowers, butterflies . . .

NINA. *(Hopefully.)* Little duckies.

NARRATOR. *The Little Prince* by Saint-Exupéry. That was a nauseating little book, she had never finished it. Some monk gave it to her when her car had been stopped at a traffic light.

(The NARRATOR *sits stiffly at the bottom of the chaise. He holds his arms as if holding a steering wheel. He stands in for the chauffeur now.)*

NINA. Drive on, Lance.

NARRATOR. *(To the audience.)* But Lance, the handsome chauffeur, insisted on the necessity of obeying the red light. *(Speaking as* LANCE, *to* NINA.) "I must obey the red light, Madame."

NINA. Laws are for other people, Lance. Not for me.

NARRATOR. *(Speaking as* LANCE.) "I'm sorry, Madame. I don't wish to lose my license."

NINA. I said, drive on, Lance.

NARRATOR. *(To the audience again.)* But the Mercedes just sat there, and the monk had a chance to pass the stupid book through the car window.

(A MONK *scurries across the stage, stopping just long enough to drop a copy of* The Little Prince *on* NINA's *chaise-car. He then scurries the rest of the way off.)*

NINA. Kill that monk, Lance.

NARRATOR. *(To audience.)* But Lance was selective in what commands of hers he followed, and eventually he had to be fired. *(The* NARRATOR *stands, no longer playing* LANCE. *He returns to his narration role.)* A long succession of chauffeurs followed, none satisfactory. Finally she gave up riding in the car. She stayed at home, hoping for visitors.

(NINA *rings the bell.* FOOTE *appears immediately, and waits for her bidding.*)

NINA. Foote, if any Jehovah's Witnesses come today, show them in, will you?

(FOOTE *exits.*)

NARRATOR. But no Jehovah's Witnesses came. And Nina found she had to fill the time with thinking and reminiscing. Nina had once been beautiful.

NINA. I am very beautiful.

NARRATOR. Men would stop on the street to stare at her. She caused traffic accidents. Jealous women would rush up to her in their homeliness and try to kill her.

NINA. Homely women were always trying to shoot me. It was flattering really.

NARRATOR. Everywhere she went, her eyes would anxiously seek out the mirrors. Sometimes she would bring her own mirrors with her.

NINA. Put this up, would you?

NARRATOR. . . . Nina would say, lugging a large mirror, and few could deny her. Her love affairs were unpredictable and random. Sometimes it would be royalty, other times it would be the men from Con Edison. (The NARRATOR *turns his back, pretending to look at a power box. He is now the* CON EDISON MAN. NINA *comes up to him, stands close and seductive.*)

NINA. I don't really know where the power box is, I'm afraid. Would you care to lie down?

(*The* NARRATOR *reverts to his narrator role, and addresses the audience again.*)

NARRATOR. Sometimes when she was especially lonely, she would try to seduce her children.

(JAMES *enters, dressed as before as a prep-school boy. He, though, also carries a lunch box. He sits on the chaise and looks at* NINA.)

NINA. Don't you find mommy especially attractive today?

138

NARRATOR. She would ask James . . .

(JAMES *looks startled.*)

. . . and Robert.

(*The actor playing* JAMES *puts on black-rimmed glasses and becomes* ROBERT. *His posture changes, and he looks at* NINA *also surprised, but somehow more adult, more jaded.*)

. . . and occasionally poor La-La.

(*The actor now opens the lunch box, takes out a simple skirt that wraps around in one gesture and clips a large yellow bow in his hair. All the while he makes the following sounds:*)

LA-LA. (*Happily and monotonously singing to herself.*) La-la-la-la-la, la-la-la-la, la, la, la, la . . .

(*The actor finishes his costume change and sits back down; and with a rather foolish and sweetly imbecilic expression, he becomes* LA-LA, *staring at* NINA.)

NARRATOR. La-La was retarded, and Nina hated her.

NINA. (*Firmly.*) La-La! Pay attention!

(LA-LA *turns away, opens up her lunch box and starts looking through it happily.*)

LA-LA. La-la-la-la-la, la-la-la . . .

NINA. Uhhhh. You're *willfully* retarded.

NARRATOR. Nina would shout this at La-La, and then hit her.

(NINA *swats* LA-LA's *head.* LA-LA *hits her head on the tin lunch box, and sort of stumbles offstage, happy but disoriented.*)

But Nina mustn't think of the past now. The present was what held promise. Her plastic surgeon was due back in several days.

(NINA *rings the bell.*)

NINA. (*Grandly.*) Foote, I want a cruller!

NARRATOR. She heard what she presumed were Foote's footsteps, but they belonged to her second son, Robert, who fired two shots, one of which grazed her shoulder.

(*Enter* ROBERT, *dressed the same as* JAMES *but with the addition of the glasses. He shoots a pistol twice at his mother. On the second shot,* NINA *moves her shoulder as if hit.*)

ROBERT. I hate you, mother!

NARRATOR. Then he ran into the garden.

(ROBERT *runs off.* NINA *holds her shoulder and rings the bell again.*)

NINA. Foote, bring the gauze again, please.

NARRATOR. Nina had been presented to the Queen twice.

(NINA *forgets her pain, and reenters memory again. She lets go of her shoulder, and stands proudly to meet the Queen.*

Then during the following, NINA *moves back to her chaise, and* ROBERT *enters and sits close to his mother.*)

It had been shortly after the second presenting that Nina, having been spurned by a member of the Royal Guard on duty, successfully seduced Robert, who was fifteen and seemed to enjoy the activity for a while but then became hysterical.

(NINA *and* ROBERT *lean in as if to kiss; suddenly* ROBERT *starts to scream hysterically. He stands in upset, looks at her, then screams again, running off.*

NINA *looks after him, unconcerned, feeling slightly incomplete.*)

The school psychologists were highly critical of Nina's behavior, but she was uninterested in their judgements. And then when Louis Malle made *Murmur of the Heart*, she called them up and said:

NINA. There you see! The critics thought it was charming, so I don't know what all the fuss was about my behavior.

NARRATOR. Nina quite liked the film, which had to do with a mother seducing her son one afternoon, but she felt that the actress Lea Massari was more coarse-grained than she was.

NINA. My features are more delicate, more lovely. I thought Lea Massari was a bit too earthy. I may be sensual, but I am never earthy.

NARRATOR. Neither Robert nor James would agree to see the film, but La-La sort of liked it.

(*Enter* LA-LA, *happy, in her own world.*)

LA-LA. La-la-la-la-la, la-la la-la la-la . . . (LA-LA *sits next to* NINA *and, as if they're watching a movie, stares out with a scrunched-up, interested face.*)

NINA. (*To audience.*) Yes, La-La loved the movies. *Murmur of the Heart* she liked. And that other Louis Malle film about suicide, *The Fire Within.* And that early Jeanne Moreau film where she makes love in the bathtub, *The Lovers.* Also directed by Louis Malle. La-La really seemed to like the films of Louis Malle. . . .

(LA-LA *leans forward in particular concentration.*)

. . . which just goes to show she's only retarded when she wants to be. No retarded child is going to like the films of Louis Malle. So I've proved my point, La-La is willfully retarded.

(NINA *pushes* LA-LA *away;* LA-LA *meanders off.* NINA's *thoughts return to the present, and her wounded shoulder.*)

NINA. Where is Foote with that gauze, my shoulder is bleeding. Foote! Foote!

NARRATOR. James's father had been a tax lawyer, but Robert's father had been one of twenty men; and La-La's father had been one of fifty-six men that busy summer she had the beach house painted. After a brief burst of self-judgment, she searched the thesaurus for alternatives to the word "promiscuity."

NINA. (*Miming looking in a dictionary.*) Synonyms include "debauchery." "Salacity." And "lubricity." "Lubricity." "Loooo-bricity." "Loooooo-briiiiiiii-ci-teeeeeeeeeee."

NARRATOR. Nina liked the sound of "lubricity" and that summer she would climb up the ladders and whisper the word into the house-painters' ears. (*The* NARRATOR *finds himself near* NINA. *She stands and seductively whispers in his ear, as if he's the house painter.*)

NINA. (*Whispering into his ear.*) Lubricity.

(*Enter* FOOTE *with some more gauze.*)

FOOTE. Has Madame been shot?

(NINA's *thoughts return to the present, and* ROBERT's *recent attack on her.*)

NINA. Yes, Foote. Robert said something to me, something mean, and then he shot me. What took you so long?

FOOTE. I'm sorry, Madame. I was giving La-La a hypodermic shot to calm her down. She was complaining about something and acting retarded, and now she's quiet and good as a lamb.

NINA. She is good as a lamb. (*Suddenly remembering; stern.*) Foote. I asked for a cruller. How many times must I ask for a thing before I get it?

FOOTE. We don't have any crullers. Would you like sausages?

NINA. Go away, Foote.

FOOTE. Sorry, Madame. I'll ask Cook to bake some crullers for tomorrow morning.

NINA. Tomorrow morning? Tomorrow, and tomorrow, and tomorrow. Who knows if I'll want a cruller tomorrow, Foote. It doesn't matter. Leave me now, please.

FOOTE. Yes, Madame. (FOOTE *exits.*)

NINA. Oh my life, my life, my life. What has become of my life? (*Looks in the mirror anew.*) And what has become of my face? Oh my. Pins are for curtains, not for faces.

NARRATOR. Nina stared at herself in the mirror and tried to decide whether or not to kill herself. She stared a long while. She didn't look well. Slowly she took the pins out of her face.

(NINA *mimes taking pins out. Then she pulls her cheeks downward, and stares tragically at herself in the mirror.*)

Her cheeks drooped downward, and her eyes filled with tears. She looked like Simone Signoret. Late Simone Signoret. Of course, when the doctor returned from Aruba, he'd make Nina look substantially better. And she didn't know how to kill herself, unless one of her children shot her. She rang for Foote.

(NINA *rings the bell.*)

NINA. (*Without force; slipping into despair.*) Foote. Foote.

NARRATOR. In lieu of crullers, Nina decided to have sausages and general anesthesia. And if Robert shot her while she was passed out, so be it; and if she woke from her sleep, she'd have a proper lunch.

NINA. Yes. Death or lunch. Death or lunch. One of the two. (NINA *continues to look in the mirror, touching her face lightly. Lights dim.*)

Kibbutz

Donald Margulies

Characters:
BRUCE
ISRAELI/YAKOV
JONATHAN

(*Lights up: A sun-drenched orchard on a kibbutz in the Israeli desert. 1970.* BRUCE, *seventeen, wearing a bandanna around his head, cut-offs and a soiled white T-shirt, sits on the ground among several basketsful of peaches. He has made a writing surface of his Army surplus shoulder bag, on which he composes an air letter. Nearby is a small knapsack. It is quiet. Birds pass overhead;* BRUCE *looks up and tracks them, then writes about them in his letter. Soon, a brawny, brown-skinned* ISRAELI, *shiny with sweat, runs very quickly past* BRUCE *and offstage.*)

ISRAELI. (*Without stopping.*) Hey!! What are you *doing?!!* Up up up!

(*Exits.* BRUCE *watches him run in the distance, then returns to his letter. In a beat,* JONATHAN, *sixteen, wearing shorts and a Midwood High School T-shirt, enters. Flushed and perspired, he struggles with a bushel of freshly picked fruit, and sets it down.* BRUCE *hardly looks up from his writing.*)

JONATHAN. Who was *that?*

BRUCE. (*Still not looking up.*) You know.

JONATHAN. Yakov?

(*No response.*)

Bruce? Yakov?

BRUCE. I think. Yeah.

144

(*Pause. Thick with tension.*)

JONATHAN. These Israelis. Boy. They're perfect machines. Strong to the finish. Yeah. A nation of Popeyes. All that matzoh and Coca-Cola. They don't sweat, these guys. No, they *glisten*. Like Kirk Douglas in *Spartacus*. Even the women. Incredible muscle definition.

BRUCE. (*Trying to concentrate on his letter.*) Jonathan . . .

JONATHAN. What. You're trying to write? Oo, sorry. (*He stretches out. Very long pause.*) Who you writing to?

BRUCE. Paula.

JONATHAN. (*Sarcastically.*) Really? Again? That was a dumb question. Boy is *she* gonna have some collection by the time we come home. All those air letters. . . . I run out of things to say on a *post*card. How could you be so full of things to say?

(BRUCE *looks annoyed again.*)

I mean, how come you have so much to say and I have to write really big to fill a postcard? It's funny, that's all. (*Pause.*) What are you writing?

BRUCE. Jonathan . . .

JONATHAN. No, tell me: What are you *writing*? You don't have to *read* it to me or anything, I'm just curious. What types of things do you talk about?

BRUCE. What "types"?

JONATHAN. Yeah, you don't have to *read* it to me, I'm just curious.

BRUCE. I'm writing about our trip.

JONATHAN. Well, I figured as much.

BRUCE. Like a journal.

JONATHAN. Oh. Well. I write in my *journal* like a journal. So, in other words, instead of writing in a journal, you're making all these pithy observations to *Paula*.

(*"Pithy" angers* BRUCE.)

I mean, not "pithy." . . . You know: smart, clever.

145

(*They look at one another for a long beat, then* BRUCE *returns to his letter.* JONATHAN *takes his sketchbook and a watercolor box out of his knapsack and sets up to sketch a landscape. Pause.*)

You know, we used to tell each *other* our stupid theories of life. I mean, I still tell *you* and *then* I write it down in my little journal.

(BRUCE *looks up at him. Pause.*)

BRUCE. (*Gently, a bit guiltily.*) What. (*Meaning "What's the matter?"*)

JONATHAN. (*A beat; quietly.*) Nothing. (*He and* BRUCE *paint and write for a long beat.*) Say hi for me.

(BRUCE *doesn't respond for a long time.*)

Bruce? Say hi for —

BRUCE. Yeah.

(*Pause.*)

JONATHAN. What are you mad at *me* for?

BRUCE. Who's mad?!

JONATHAN. What are you made at *me* for, *you're* the one who's always writing to fucking Paula, you never talk to *me* anymore . . .

BRUCE. (*Over "anymore."*) Well, aren't we sick of each other yet? Traveling around for five weeks?

JONATHAN. Are we? Gee. I guess we are. Gee, I —

ISRAELI. (*Off.*) HEY!! I don't believe you boys!

(JONATHAN *and* BRUCE *shoot their sights in the direction of the voice.*)

JONATHAN. Shit. It *is* Yakov. . . .

(*In a beat,* YAKOV, *twenty-two, approaches from the direction in which he ran. He is drinking from a canteen as he approaches them. He smiles always, but his tone is mocking, disingenuous.*)

YAKOV. Are you deaf?

BRUCE. Me?

YAKOV. Are you *stupid*?

BRUCE. Huh?

YAKOV. I told you to get up before. Didn't you see me when I ran by?

BRUCE. Uh huh.

YAKOV. I told you to get *up*, back to work.

BRUCE. I thought you were kidding.

YAKOV. Why would I be kidding? You've come here to work or you've come here to play? (*To* JONATHAN.) And what are *you* doing?

JONATHAN. Taking a break.

YAKOV. Oh. Tired?

JONATHAN. (*Tentatively.*) Yes.

YAKOV. You've been picking for two hours and you're tired?

JONATHAN. Since 8:30. It's almost twelve.

YAKOV. You're breaking my heart. I've been keeping an eye on you boys. A little rest here, a little break there. . . . What a spectacle you boys are. This is not Miami Beach, I hate to break it to you. (*Takes a long swig from his canteen, the water cascades down his neck and chest. He hands it to* JONATHAN.)

JONATHAN. (*Surprised, as he takes it.*) Thanks.

> (BRUCE *moves closer in anticipation;* JONATHAN *tries to sip from it.*)

It's empty.

YAKOV. (*Takes back the canteen.*) Oh, what a shame. (*Clicks his tongue.*) I feel sorry for you boys. Brooklyn boys. So pale. So delicate. Hands like pampered little girls'. I cringe for you when I see you working in the orchard. Slow motion photography. Not even lunch time and you're ready for your nap. Look at *you* and look at *me*: To think that we all, in the eyes of the world, we are all Jewish men. (*He touches his crotch lasciviously.*) Laughable.

You don't know what hard work *is*, my friends. . . . Boys. . . . You American *child*ren. Your mommies and daddies send you over on jets, for what? To *edu*cate you? No, I'm *ask*ing you. To turn you into good little Zionists, what? Cultural exchange? What is the fascination? I don't understand. This is, what, an alternative to summer camp for you? Arts and crafts? I see you have your little sketchbook. (*Reaches for it;* JONATHAN *resists.*) Please.

> (JONATHAN *hesitates, then gives it to* YAKOV, *who looks through it.*)

Oh, so you are a *good* little artist. Look at that: the orchard! I see! (*Flips pages; a tad mocking.*) Our cows, yes! Very good! Look at that: the Administration Building. Very talented. (*Returns the book to* JONATHAN.) This is my *life*, you know, this is my *home*. We kibbutzniks are not here for your entertainment. This is not a country club for rich Jewish children. I am not the boy who cleans the pool and changes your linens.

JONATHAN. I'm not rich.

YAKOV. You're not? Forgive me. I don't mean rich. I mean ... spoiled. Yes. Safe. You see, we go on in this fashion long after you fly home on your 747s. We remain. We are just an outing for you. Something to snap pictures of. This is not kibbutz-Disneyland where you ride the amusements and go home smiling. You are our guests. But you are the kind who expect only to be served and never rise to clean the dishes.

JONATHAN. I washed the dishes last night.

YAKOV. So you did. You know what I mean. You aren't ignorant. What do you know of survival? What do you know of death? In the Six Day War, seventeen years old, I fought. How old are you?

JONATHAN. (*Ashamed.*) That age.

YAKOV. (*Laughs, then—*) And where were *you* in '67? Dragging yourself off to Hebrew lessons when you'd've rather been playing baseball? I was fighting for your right to exist. (*Pause. He touches* JONATHAN's *face strangely, menacingly, sexually. A beat.*) Back to work, boys.

(He starts to go off, snatching a peach from the basket as he goes. JONATHAN touches his cheek and looks at his fingers, as if he's checking for blood. He's shaken by the encounter. To dispel the tension, BRUCE touches JONATHAN's face in a lame attempt at a joke.)

BRUCE. "Back to work, boys . . ."

(JONATHAN is not amused; he pushes BRUCE's hand away.)

JONATHAN. Fuck *you*, Bruce!

BRUCE. *(Now also very upset.)* Well, fuck *you*!

(In a flash, they're pushing and punching each other furiously. It's very heated and very quick. In the midst of the skirmish, JONATHAN violently grabs BRUCE's letter.)

Jonathan! Jonathan, give me . . . Give it back!

(But JONATHAN crumples the letter and throws it to the ground. They separate, out of breath, their adrenaline rushing wildly. BRUCE retrieves the balled-up letter and smooths it out. JONATHAN watches him for a beat.)

JONATHAN. Bruce? Brucie? I'm sorry, Bruce. . . .

(BRUCE ignores him as he gathers his things.)

Bruce?

(BRUCE starts to go, walking past him; JONATHAN reaches for his friend's shoulder.)

Hey . . .

(BRUCE evades JONATHAN's touch. JONATHAN watches him exit. He watches him walk farther into the distance, then calls to him at the top of his lungs.)

Brucie . . .?!

(Fade out.)

Two Iphigenia Plays
Ellen McLaughlin

IPHIGENIA IN AULIS

Characters:
IPHIGENIA
CLYTEMNESTRA

IPHIGENIA. In a windless place everything is eternal and bland
  Nothing can be changed here
  It all hums in terrible clarity
  With no wind to transform, modify or shift anything
  Feathers fall from a plucked chicken
  And make a neat circle that stays and stays
  There is a leaden singularity to each thing
  Each color immobile
  Everything has become too important here
  Like something stared at too long
  Until it might as well be anything
  A person could go mad
  As my mother combed my hair this morning
  Each broken strand
  Slunk down and coiled where it fell
  Separate and smug as etched spirals on the floor
  Bride
  What is it to be a bride here?
  In this windless place
  A bleached column?
  A sliver of standing bone?
  But perhaps that will not happen
  Nothing can happen here I think
  It is a place of dead air

CLYTEMNESTRA. We came down from the hot rock mountains. Everything creaking on the backs of our animals and their flanks straining to keep from falling. And as we descended, I was thinking — a world of men, what kind of place am I taking my darling? A place of idle soldiers — the most dangerous kind. Spears oversharpened by boys burning to kill for the first time. A man. A man. And one of those boys, one of those eager, beardless, ignorant hopped-up lonely bastards is waiting for her. He will take her from me. Because he can. I looked back. There she was behind me, squinting through the dust we kicked up, looking down, waiting for something to see, something to make sense. And she is taller than I remember. She is strong enough, I suppose. So we kept on descending.

IPHIGENIA. Nothing more useless than ships
Miles — could it be miles — of them?
Lined up
Hauled up
Tilting
Impossible
Baking in the sun
Nosing the water which barely moves
As if the ocean were some bloated pond
That was what I saw first
So many useless ships
Bristling for such a distance along a flaccid shore
That was before my occupation became clear
My occupation as *something which is visible*
Because then we descended to walk among the men
Cities' full
All of them watching me
What do they see, I wonder?
I am like Medusa, I change men to silent stone
Games stop, stories break at their start
And nothing stirs as I pass
Only their eyes, turning in their sockets
Such silence, such level dust
I am some phantom
No one in this dress
I am not here
I am just some spell that is cast

151

It is a powerless power
Like this wind which is only remarkable in its absence

CLYTEMNESTRA. Achilles, well, one hears stories, of course. But where is the man? How long have we been here? Yesterday and today. And still no one sorts himself out of this murmuring, dirty mob to present himself. "Watch for the armor," I am told. "His is priceless. You will know it when you see it." As if that meant anything. His armor.

IPHIGENIA. Helmets, lances, gold and iron skins they have
And me in this thin dress
It's a predicament.

CLYTEMNESTRA. "I'm a queen," I said, "and she's a princess" but these things have no meaning here. The old man dropped a plate of gray chicken on the wooden table and left without bowing. Then I became afraid.

IPHIGENIA. They killed a deer yesterday
I saw it while it was still running
Stamping down the boughs
Cracking its forest
Spotting through the stricken trees
Suddenly so visible
All of them running after it, not losing sight
There I go, I thought, run fast
But they caught it
Of course
And when they brought it in
Limp and undignified, head lolling
I couldn't watch, I turned away
Because the eyes were open
And they saw me
Dead, they saw me
I shivered
You and me, I thought
We know each other
They offered me the heart
Nice of them, I guess
But I said something
And backed away
They watched me, of course

152

All the way to the tent
So many eyes glittering in the firelight
Fixed on me diminishing
Until the flap swallowed me and I became invisible again
And they could turn and eat
I hold the darkness to my face
As if it were food

CLYTEMNESTRA. He finally appears out of the crowd, I recognize him by his armor. My husband. Harried and odd in his move-movements. He knows nothing, apparently. What is to be done on this windless shore with an idle navy that he seems to be so busy? I ask him to leave. He makes me nervous. He is happy to do so. Now I can't sleep.

IPHIGENIA. But something is wrong
My parents thrash at each other in the woods
Out of earshot
But there is screaming
Mother comes back, eyes swollen, face streaked
And smashes my head to her breast
Squeezing my ribs
I can't breathe I am so dear to her
Father stood in the tent for a while yesterday
He looks ill and won't meet my eyes
He won't touch me
Who is this husband?
What is this marriage?
Tonight the ritual knives are being sharpened on stone
Tonight there are figures circling the fire, all in black,
Telling hymns I don't know
What kind of marriage are we preparing?
I thought I would wear flowers
But nothing grows here
I thought there would be women
There are no women
Are there no other girls in the world?
Suddenly I am the last and only girl
And all these turning faces, all these anxious idle fingers
All these men to satisfy
This is the bride
The only bride

153

(CLYTEMNESTRA *begins to pant, first slowly then rapidly under this next speech.*)

Morning comes and I am a white dress
Walking up the crumbling cliff as if I know where I am going
What I'm doing
To meet him
Whoever he might be
I am ascending to the altar
I look down from a great height to see how the ships still lie
Splayed like broken teeth
Today the light is merciless
And sound would travel if there was sound
But there are only my feet on the pebbles
That hurl themselves down to the ships as I pass
I come to the altar
But there is no one
Just the black-shrouded priests
And there my father
Who has made his face a stranger
Eyes locked in their sockets
Dull as coal
And a knife
But where are the animals?
Poor innocents
With the last cropped grass still in their moist mouths
But there is only me
And all the eyes are on me
Visible me
This is a terrible place
Something must be done
Ah. I see.
I was right
Here is my husband
This ancient stone
And the quick shadow of the knife
I am to marry everyone
Every single one
This is what it is at last

Ellen McLaughlin

IPHIGENIA IN TAURIS

Characters:
IPHIGENIA
CHORUS
ORESTES

(IPHIGENIA, *in white, surrounded by five girls, the chorus, who are also dressed in white.* IPHIGENIA *is the tallest and wears the whitest dress.*)

IPHIGENIA. I was never really a woman
　And now I will never have the chance
　I never really lived
　And now I am immortal
　They say I was spirited away at the moment of the knife
　Some deer died in my place
　But it looked like me to me at any rate
　It was disorienting
　I rose up out of myself
　Looking down at the figure on the stone
　She's so young, I thought
　Beautiful in a way
　But then I forgot about her
　Because of the press of air and light
　The fact of traveling at such a high speed
　Intoxicating
　This is death, I thought
　Just another trip to an unknown place
　To meet a stranger
　And it seems I was right
　Because this is a sort of heaven
　The kind of place someone might have thought I would like
　Safety, certainly, and a nice view
　Who knew it would be so dull?
　I am the keeper of a shrine on a wild island
　I am surrounded by girls

CHORUS. (*These lines are split up between them.*)
　Who are all alike because we are all homesick for Greece,

155

Which is to say, life
No one to dress up for here
Just the unseen gods
No one to kiss
No crowds at the marketplace
No news
Nothing to talk about, really
I guess we should be happy
We are girls forever
And we are all rather pretty in white
And life is scorchingly uneventful
It's just that sometimes one dreams
And that can get you into trouble
Because we remember life in dreams
Noises, voices, cries
Colors that buzz up against each other
Things to touch
    the skin of oranges
    the cheek of a lover
    books
    tools
    paper
There is nothing to touch here
Except each other
And we are all too sad for that
This is privilege
We can't help wondering what we might have become without it
If we'd been left alone

IPHIGENIA. If I hadn't been so bloody special
I think I was fairly bright
Observant at least

CHORUS. Maybe that was the problem.

IPHIGENIA. I can't help feeling that I was put away just when I threatened to become interesting. Just when I started feeling things out of the ordinary.

CHORUS. Bleeding
Getting angry
Talking too loud

Too fast
Too much

IPHIGENIA. I hear my mother killed my father on account of me.
   I was impressed
   I didn't know I rated so much vengeance
   But Mom. Well, *she* was interesting
   She lived long enough
   I'm sure she's dead by now
   No woman can afford to be *that* interesting
   I wish I'd been that interesting
   Now I am something made of stone
   Handsome, bleached and perpetual

CHORUS. We are stand-ins for Artemis
   Who is too busy to be a stone
   She's off hunting and conniving
   Running
   Being impressive
   That would be fun
   Knowing something
   Feeling the muscle that pulls the bow taut
   Judging distance
   Accomplishing things
   Like Greece

IPHIGENIA. What did we know of Greece?

CHORUS. Or Life?
   We think of Greece
   And it is really all about what we didn't quite see, hear, touch
   But what we sensed
   We were girls there
   Privileged girls
   On the threshold of consciousness
   Hurried past what was essential
   We remember the cities and what we see are
   Corners not walked around
   Dark doorways
   Like open mouths
   We would not pass through
   But wondered
   Conversations held just barely out of earshot

So that we heard sound
Sibilance
Scattered syllables
But not the sense
Muted colors of a life seen through a veil
And now we are all still guessing
Just at a greater distance
At a terrible height

IPHIGENIA. Oh, and here's the irony
If a man should reach us at this place
We are supposed to kill him.

CHORUS. But all we want to do is speak to him
Ask questions
Touch him

IPHIGENIA. And I do
But only at the point of a knife
I feel their necks
From which would issue answers
But no

CHORUS. We terrify them with our whiteness
Bind them in ropes
The way market wives bind vegetables

IPHIGENIA. And then I say something or other
And the knife comes down

CHORUS. And we land ourselves in silence once more
The sea birds call
Rise and fall on currents of clean air
And we have served something
The silenced male body
Offered up to something

IPHIGENIA. Just as I was offered
It has a sort of
A circular
An inevitable
A sense to it, I suppose

*

CHORUS. Oh, there's a madman on the beach
  Look at him
  Pathetic
  He seems to be attacked by phantoms
  Birds is it?
  How he screams
  You can almost hear it
  Covering his head and running
  Rolling in the sand
  To get away from what?

IPHIGENIA. Now would be the time to bind and bring him
  Go

> (*The* CHORUS *leave.*)

What terrible suffering actual people endure
Look at life
A man trying to run away from his own head
I've heard of such things
What wars do to people
They cannot escape the moment
The horrifying moment, whatever it is
And they live inside of it forever
Even on a day like this
It's beautiful, of course
It always is
If he could only see it

> (*The* CHORUS *carry* ORESTES *on, bound to a long pole like a
> kill from a hunt. They lay him before* IPHIGENIA. *A member
> of the chorus hands her a knife. They all leave.*)

ORESTES. Birds and more birds
  Black or white
  Black or white
  They are all female

IPHIGENIA. And what do the birds say?

ORESTES. "You have killed her. You cannot kill her."
  "You have killed her. You cannot kill her."

IPHIGENIA. Who?

ORESTES. My mother.

IPHIGENIA. Well, why would you do that?

ORESTES. Oh, everyone told me to. A god told me to.

IPHIGENIA. And you always do what you are told?

ORESTES. Yes. I was a soldier first and for a long time. Only lately a matricide.

IPHIGENIA. Ah, well. I'm a priestess. I'm equally gifted in compliance. And I'm also a girl. So.

ORESTES. Just my luck. Obedience meets obedience. We'll probably end up killing each other.

IPHIGENIA. Funny you should say so. That's why you were brought to me. I'm supposed to kill you.

ORESTES. Why?

IPHIGENIA. It's what I have been told to do.

ORESTES. What god do you serve?

IPHIGENIA. Does it matter? Artemis.

ORESTES. Oh. And I serve Apollo. That's why I'm here.

IPHIGENIA. What did he want you to do here?

ORESTES. Steal the statue of Artemis. Bring it back to Greece.

IPHIGENIA. Why?

ORESTES. Who knows? I didn't ask. If I did it he said he would get the Furies off my back.

IPHIGENIA. We are all statues of Artemis. Take all of us with you. We are insane with homesickness.

ORESTES. But you're supposed to kill me.

IPHIGENIA. Oh, I know. I shouldn't even be talking to you. But you interest me. I miss the sound of men's voices. We don't hear them much and when we do, not for long. You are a sacrifice, you see.

160

ORESTES. I was always a sacrifice. Since I was a child. Beaten into submission to the tune of fathers all my life. I was plunged into the arms of the military early on, world of boys. Muscled, fatted to sacrifice in the name of fathers, which is the name of states, countries, gods. Told to obey, to lay down my body, my spirit to him, to always him. Fathers. It was easy to kill her. I've done it so often. The quick quieting of limbs, dulling of eyes. Simple. What did I know about mothers? Everything I've learned about mothers is what they have been screaming into my ears since the moment I did it. They strum my sinews like harps and sing about her. And in this song, this pain, this madness, I am taught that when I took my mother's life I made myself an exile from all nature. My crime, her blood, sears through the fabric of the world. What did I know about nature? It was not in my training.

IPHIGENIA. I was schooled in sacrifice as well. Just of a different kind. The girl, the virgin. It made a kind of sense, didn't it?

ORESTES. Oh, yes. The exchange. We knew it in our blood. We are the necessary payment of the people.

IPHIGENIA. The negotiation with the mystery.

ORESTES. The special ones. Were we special?

IPHIGENIA. *(She begins to untie him.)* Oh, yes. Terribly special.

ORESTES. I come from a house eccentric in blood.

IPHIGENIA. Eccentric in suffering.

ORESTES. Lie upon lie.

IPHIGENIA. Generation upon generation.

ORESTES. Aberrant.

IPHIGENIA. Pariahs.

ORESTES. Netted up.

IPHIGENIA. Tight knots.

ORESTES. In fate.

IPHIGENIA. In fate.

ORESTES. I thought you looked familiar.

161

IPHIGENIA. And you.

ORESTES. Blood knits us.

IPHIGENIA. Blood and service of blood.

ORESTES. My poor sister.

IPHIGENIA. My poor brother.

ORESTES. Saved.

IPHIGENIA. Saved.

(*They look up.*)

ORESTES. Everything is watching.

IPHIGENIA. What's up there.

ORESTES. Invisible.

IPHIGENIA. Terrible.

ORESTES. Hovering.

IPHIGENIA. We are performing a legend.

ORESTES. And the legend is performing us.

IPHIGENIA. For what?

ORESTES. In the name of what?

IPHIGENIA. Is it possible to become invisible at this late date?

ORESTES. Oh, to be unimportant.

IPHIGENIA. To live without a script.

ORESTES. Without duty.

IPHIGENIA. Oblivion.

ORESTES. Oblivion.

IPHIGENIA. So, who shall hold the knife now?

ORESTES. Which killing to echo? His of you. Mine of her.

IPHIGENIA. Or hers of him. Redress? Is it possible? I can't remember the sequence anymore, just the deaths.

ORESTES. I do. I murdered her last. Mine was the last. If it's redress, you should kill me.

IPHIGENIA. Oh, I know. But it's just death now. No sense.

ORESTES. No sacrifice.

IPHIGENIA. We have reached the threshold of futility.

ORESTES. The stone wall of history. End of sight.

IPHIGENIA. (*She looks up, uncertain, holding the knife.*) I have heard that a needle can be made to pass through stone.

ORESTES. A tiny hole, inconsequential to the structure.

IPHIGENIA. Just large enough for these two odd lives.

ORESTES. To somehow thread their way through into a different air.

IPHIGENIA. A different light. Beyond bargains.

ORESTES. Beyond exchange. Blood feuds.

IPHIGENIA. Justice.

ORESTES. Justice.

(*Pause. They are both looking up. They look at each other.*)

IPHIGENIA. I am the statue you have come to find
Take me to the city
To the center of the city
Build noise and life around me
I will be silent and tall
I will remind them
I will seem to see everything
I will be female and slightly terrifying
I will be what I have always been
Visible and mute
You will place me at the center of something
And you will lay your tortured head upon my cold feet
And you will finally sleep
This is how the legend performs itself to an end

ORESTES. I can do this for you

163

IPHIGENIA. I can do this for you

ORESTES. And this will be the part everyone will forget

IPHIGENIA. The needle through the wall of history

ORESTES. The part of justice which is merely

IPHIGENIA. Personal

ORESTES. Inelegant

IPHIGENIA. A quirk

ORESTES. A sliver of light

IPHIGENIA. That is only

ORESTES. And finally

IPHIGENIA. Something like

ORESTES. Love.

Etiquette & Vitriol
Nicky Silver

(As the house lights dim, we hear "Do, Do, Do," recorded by Gertrude Lawrence. As the song ends, lights come up revealing CLAIRE's *bedroom. She is in her early fifties and quite glamorous, an anachronism wearing a cream silk peignoir. Perfectly coifed and polished, she is alone, seated at her dressing table, adjusting her hair and makeup. She addresses the audience.)*

CLAIRE. I have, for a long time, been a person who tries to see the best in others. I have, always, tried to see the beauty in all things. No matter how *grotesque*.

And I find, more and more, I live in a grotesque world. Isn't everything ugly all of a sudden? I do not understand, I must admit, what passes for music in this age. But then, I force myself to remember that my mother did not understand my music, and I try to see the beauty in giving in, giving way, like a weeping willow bending gracefully in the inevitable face of gravity.

(She glances into the mirror and is momentarily sidetracked.)

My mother was a sad woman to begin with, and then, when I was eight years old, she lost a baby. And her sadness became exaggerated to the point of farce.

(Returning to her point:)

This morning, I went to the dressmaker, to be fitted for a dress. I walked to the shop. It's not very far and I enjoy what's left of the fresh air. And I enjoy seeing people. Or I did. You see, more and more people seem to feel it all right to behave any way they choose. For instance, more and more people seem to be — How shall I put this? — *spitting*. I do not approve of this. Sometimes they walk over to the curb and spit into the street, as if this were so much better than spitting in the middle of the pavement. It's not. And apparently plenty of people feel as I do and they spit right where they

165

are. And not just men, but women too! With hairdos and skirts! Now, I want to see the beauty in all of this, but it's *very* hard. It is eight blocks from my door to the dressmaker's and I must've passed thirty-five people spitting in the first three! Is it something in the air? Is it a by-product of auto exhaust that has everyone spitting so continually? Now, I am willing to blame an awful lot on the industrial revolution, but not this, this sudden spitting frenzy. NO!

(*She glances at her bed, and loses her train of thought.*)

When my sister died in my mother's womb, my father buried his head in bottles and, I suspect, under the covers of strange beds.

(*Returning:*)

At any rate, after the third block of my walk, I started counting these people who committed what I considered were affronts against civilization. Have we learned nothing in the past five thousand years? Don't these *people*, these *spitters*, realize that we all have to live together, and I would no sooner want to see their *expectorations* than I would their *bowel movements?* You may think me silly, but I believe that all the wars and suffering and prejudice and hate come down to nothing more than an unwillingness to understand each other. If we would only allow each other the space of our dignity, we would save so much time and trouble, and the money that we spend on nuclear weapons could be given to . . . the New York City Ballet, who really do lovely work, that no one could find fault with!

As I was saying, I started counting "spitters." And within the next three blocks, I counted thirteen more — well, actually I counted fourteen. But I allowed for one man who was also muttering to himself, and barking, from time to time, like a dog. I believe this man was suffering from the once little-known, suddenly fashionable, disease called *"Tourette's Syndrome."* I saw a story all about it on a television newsmagazine, and I was, therefore, in a position to be sympathetic. My aesthetic is not so rigid that it doesn't allow for legitimate illness. *I* have never been sick a day in my life — but when I was eighteen, my father developed cancer of the pancreas and died. And he left me a great deal of money.

I don't know why my mind keeps wandering back to my parents. It's not what I intended, because something happened this morning, and I'm trying to get to that. But my mind keeps wandering off in tangents. A dear friend of mine once told me I spoke in a

166

baroque fashion. I've no idea what she meant, but I'm sure it wasn't a compliment. Oh well, I never liked her anyway!

Oh, I'll get to my point, the thing that happened. I will. But right now I can't help remembering my mother's face at my father's funeral. It was long. She had a long face. Like a Modigliani painting. I've *never* liked Modigliani, although I found the Off-Broadway play about him, several seasons back, mildly entertaining. Still, I thought Mother was lovely. She had more dimension than his paintings. And she moved. Slowly. She possessed the grace of a ballet dancer and the alacrity of a pachyderm — I'm using sarcasm to make a point. She was languid in an era when things considered beautiful actually were. Before minimalism creeped into our landscape, when we could see farther and were unhindered by the cataract of modernism. I seem to see her all the time as a ballet dancer, in a Degas painting. I've *always* liked Degas, and I feel badly that they never made a play about him.

But Mother was lovely. And before "the baby," as we euphemistically referred to her miscarriage, she was melancholy, but serene. Her hands were white, and she never wore nail polish. Every year at Christmas she would tie bows on handmade presents, her fingers dancing 'round the ribbons. And she *worshipped* my father, who was enormous. He had to be six and a half feet tall, with feet as big as tennis rackets. He scared me, truth be told. He would be very quiet, but inside there was an anger, building up, building over something, it could be anything. And then all of a sudden he would explode! And fists went flying and plates and tempers. — But he never swore. Which is odd. And makes him seem, somehow, less masculine, in my mind. But after "the baby," things changed *drastically*.

Mother, whom I mentioned was laconic to begin with, became absolutely *inert*. I don't mean the days immediately following, which, of course, she spent in bed. But the days became weeks and she wouldn't budge. She *never* got out of bed of her own accord. After about three weeks, we, my father and I, foisted her into a sitting position and put a book in her lap. We tilted her head so she was in a position to read. But she didn't! I sat there and stared and stared, and her eyes never touched a word! I said to her, "Mother, why don't you read?". . . . I do not care to. She responded. Resolutely.

Oh. Well. If she didn't care to, she didn't care to. There was little arguing. So at day's end, we put the book on her nightstand and turned out her lamp. In the morning, we tried again. "Why don't you read, Mother? You might enjoy it."

"I do not care to."

Hmmm. After about a week of "the book game," I went with my father into her room. We tried to interest her in getting up, getting dressed. "I do not care to." This was a woman of definite likes and dislikes. But my father had decided this "bed-rest thing" had gone on long enough. Perhaps, being a woman himself and only recently having had an unborn baby die in his belly, he felt he was the best judge. — I'm using sarcasm to make a point. So, we lifted her out of bed. This was easy. He was big. She was small. And he held her up, rather like a marionette, while I dressed her. Now, I was eight, and naturally jealous that I'd been replaced as the center of the house, so I put her in a very ugly outfit! Plaid skirt, floral sweater, two different earrings and so on. "We're going for a walk!" my father informed her. And she responded — exactly right! "I do not care to." But out he went and, flanked on either side, she greeted the fresh air. We looked like Oscar Levant, Fred Astaire and a drug-ridden Nanette Fabray, three strong in strides from *The Bandwagon!*

Now don't misunderstand me. She was not catatonic. No. She was not a zombie. She just chose not to. From that day on, she chose not to. We pretty much had to prop her up all over the place. We'd stand her at the stove, and she'd cook something — although her disinterest in the project usually resulted in dinners of pudding and peas. Or my favorite: aspirin! She just reached up, into the cupboard, and cooked what she grabbed.

(*She is really enjoying herself.*)

Oh, we'd prop her up in front of the radio. We'd put a vacuum in her hand and she'd clean the same spot, over and over again . . . until it was immaculate! At first, I didn't mind at all. It was like having this huge doll that really did wet herself. And I'd have my friends over after school to play with her. But, before long, I grew bored . . . the way children do. And as the years passed, my father came home later and later, leaving her to me. And he never yelled anymore. . . . And he never threw things.

By the time he died he seemed very sad. That was a terrible time, the time he died. I was eighteen — Oh, I said that. And although he left me ample money to have someone take care of her, I didn't feel I could leave my mother. Besides, I was still in high school, where I was considered very pretty and everyone liked my stories.

I was *always* charming, even then. And in an era where chastity was vogue, I was liberal with my favors. I was very popular with any number of young men attending NYU and Columbia, and even as far away as Princeton. It wasn't that I liked sex so much. Because I didn't. Then. I don't know. I was too giggly to really dictate what I wanted. And besides, that was unheard of then.

(*With authority:*)

Women today are very lucky that it's become fashionable to actually indicate to their bed partners the location of their clitoris — excuse me, EXCUSE ME, but it's true.

Still I was never stupid. And I saw my peccadilloes as escape routes. Remember, I was still propping her up and picking her clothes and cooking for her, unless I was willing to dine on Ajax, which she took to incorporating into her recipes the way homemakers on a budget work with tuna.

The point is, I quickly became pregnant. I never took precautions, knowing little about them, and wouldn't if I'd known more. I didn't see a doctor. I didn't have to. I knew it. I could feel it. So, I spent the next week dating the seven candidates who might be my baby's father. A couple, I was sure, would softly hold my hand all the way to their Park Avenue doctors to have my ticket to freedom scraped from inside me. But Philip was, then, a gentle man. And I could tell when he looked at me that he adored me. Even if I couldn't tell when we made love. So the following week, I informed him that I was carrying his child, and true to form, he asked me to marry him.

Three months later, my mother who'd really deserted me ten years earlier, deserted me finally. She died of a stroke in mid-afternoon. She should have been dressed. She could have been up and doing things. But, I assume . . . she did not care to.

I thought of leaving Philip, since I'd married him to escape my life, which now escaped me. But I was pregnant and he was wealthy and solicitous. In time, I had Philip, whom I loved. And Amy, whom I did not. I don't know why. Perhaps it's because she's such a graceful and delicate flower — I use sarcasm to illustrate myself.

Children are an odd phenomenon, don't you find? I have to say, I've never really understood them. It seems so irrational to me. You create something. You carry something around, inside of you, for what seems an eternity, and then you are delivered a person. A stranger. And you can tell me otherwise, but from the minute

169

we're born, we are people. My children had likes and dislikes from day one. Philip adored music and art and emulated me. While Amy, on the other hand, turned her nose up at my breast and never really came around!

(*Lecturing:*)

I see young mothers in the park walking their children, like poodles on leashes. I am aghast! They treat their children as if they were objects. I claim no expertise *BUT* it has been my experience that children are not dogs. Were they dogs, I'm afraid, I'd've been tempted to put Amy to sleep several times by now. I don't mean to be hard about Amy. I'm sure she has many fine qualities — which are not apparent to me. All people have goodness inside of them! Only some people have very little, and it's *very, very, very* deep down. And she is a stranger! That's what it comes down to. I know she came from me, but she's not part of — oh, God. I must sound awful. But it's true. My feet are part of me. My hands are part of me. My children are people I know. I do love them. Don't mistake my objectivity for indifference. I love my children very much. I just see that they are *other* people. And, if you ask me, we'd have a great deal less crime and drug addiction if mothers and fathers realized their children are not their pets. And this understanding would lead to happier children, healthier adults, less crime, lower taxes, a thriving economy, prettier architecture, less television, more theater, less litigation, more understanding, less alienation, more love, less hate and a calmer humanity who felt less of a need to spit all the time in public!! Because that's what it is, really. All this spitting in public is just a thinly veiled hostility for ME, MY TASTE, MY AESTHETIC AND THE COMMON CONSENSUS OF WHAT IS GENERALLY CONSIDERED SOCIALLY ACCEPT-ABLE BEHAVIOR!! — AND ISN'T IT WONDERFUL HOW I HAVE COME FULL CIRCLE, AND CAN NOW CONTINUE WITH MY STORY IN A NATURAL, LOGICAL FASHION!!

Everything goes in circles really. Except things that go in straight lines. Hmmm.

I was counting spitters, vile angry, lost souls who feel impotent to change their lives in view of what they think is fate. Well, after about a hundred of these spitting villains, I could take no more. I was in a rage! What has happened to my lovely city? What has happened to it? The buildings are suddenly eyesores. There are placards everywhere, for so-called bands I've never heard of with fascist-sounding names and illustrations of women so wanton as to degrade women everywhere.

Finally, I could take no more. So I started following this one young woman, who looked reasonably sane — except for the fact that she was wearing a tweed skirt with sneakers, but I allowed for a foot condition. She had on a blazer. Her light brown hair was piled high on her head with a tortoise clip. She looked fine. She looked normal. I thought to myself, "I will just stare at this young woman. I will not look to her right. I will not look to her left. I will see only her. And I will convince myself that I am surrounded by similarly sane young women. I won't look, so I'll assume everyone around me is just as polite and normal as she. . . ." And it was working. I had myself believing it. Everything was lovely . . . and then she *veered* over to the curb.

(A real panic builds inside of her.)

I said a silent prayer. This woman had become, to me, a symbol: the last great kindness in a once kind world. My breathing changed. I felt my hands grow tense and saw my knuckles whiten in my clenched fists. She walked along the curb for a few feet. I thought, "Thank you, God, thank you. She's just walking along the curb. She's a little erratic, but she's not one of them, she's one of us!" And then slowly, it seemed as if everything was in slow motion . . . she *leaned* over. I hoped, I prayed she was going to faint! I hoped she was ill and going to die! "Let her die a martyr to beauty, but please God, *please*, don't let her spit! Let her fall over, into the street, into the traffic, let her be canonized the patron saint of civilization, but PLEASE GOD, don't let her spit!" And she made a small coughing noise. "She's coughing — you're coughing — she's coughing — aren't you? — please don't be clearing your throat — just be coughing!" If I shut my eyes, I'll miss whatever happens and I can pretend that nothing happened and I can go on, continue to live and hope! But they would not close! I couldn't shut them! I wanted to! I tried to! But I couldn't! I was hypnotized! I just stared and stared and the seconds became hours and the hours weeks and the weeks millennia! And then it happened!!!

SHE SPIT!!!

And the world went black and the sun fell out of the sky, burning the earth and sending the buildings tumbling, bricks flying, people crushed in the rain of debris, and humanity, which had only recently learned to walk, was SMASHED into oblivion for all time!!

171

"WHAT'S WRONG WITH YOU!?" I found my hand on her sleeve. "Don't you understand what you've done?!" She spun around with such a look of utter horror and disgust on her face that I was only spurred to continue — "The world is decomposing! Humanity is rotting away! We're reverting to the behavior of apes and YOU'RE TO BLAME!"

"Let go of me!!" She shouted, very loudly, much more loudly than was called for. "I had to spit. What's it to you?!" And with that she shoved me, hard, and I fell onto the pavement. . . .

All I could think about was how sad, how sorry, I was, that I'd chosen badly, chosen someone who didn't care, couldn't be convinced, didn't see that we are all just withering, dying, crumbling in on ourselves . . . I looked around from my *position* on the sidewalk and I was the center of quite a crowd. And I thought, "Oh no. I'm sitting in it. She's gone, and I am sitting in her *expectoration!*"

(Sad and shaken.)

And. Then. I shut my eyes and I hurried to the dressmaker. I was late of course and she was already on her next client, my old friend, Phoebe Potter. We were girls in school together. She looked so old, and I was so distraught from my experience that I mistook her for a mirror. It broke me completely, to see myself in her eyes and the folds of her flesh. "I'll come back tomorrow." "No, no. Mrs. Potter's almost finished." And so I waited . . . And, soon, it was my turn.

I looked into the mirror as I was pinned. And, I was me again. I was shaken, but I was myself. I heard music in my head while she worked. And. As soon as I could, I rushed home. To Tony.

(Quite still, forgetting herself.)

I did not speak. I unbuttoned his shirt and he wrapped his arms around my waist, mumbling something into my ear, which I couldn't or didn't understand. Didn't care. And I filled up the palms of my hands with his shoulders. He pulled my blouse from my skirt in the back and I pressed my hips against his genitals and felt his erection, under his jeans. I kicked off my shoes and unbuttoned his pants, holding him, hardened, in my right hand and pulling his hair with my left, while he penetrated my mouth with his tongue. He unbuttoned my blouse down the back and pulled it off, lowering himself to take my nipples in his mouth, while I stroked his eyelids with my fingertips. How late in life I came to understand sex, how much time I wasted. He unfastened my skirt

172

and it fell to the ground. I bent over and licked his ears and the back of his neck. He licked my thighs and in between. And I led him to my bed. My baby. My baby boy. And he stood over me, making me want him, and understanding that I wanted to be made to want. And we made love with the violent passion of children and animals ripping at each other, biting and hurting beautifully. . . . And from my bed, the window views the river and the city beyond, and as he held me, as I had him, I became a child again, the years dripping away and falling off me, until I was a girl. And the river flowed and the city on the other side changed from what it is to what it was: the sharp angry teeth of the building, the glass angles and steel knives became rounded. Until he finished. And I finished. And I threw my head back and the sun was setting on a city of the past, where everything was beautiful, and we were children, and more . . . easily pleased.

(*She looks around and realizes that she has exposed more than she intended.*)

So you see, sex, it seems, is very important, when it comes to seeing the beauty of things.

(*She crosses to her dressing table, and slowly lets her hair down as the light fades out.*)

Evolution
Jonathan Marc Sherman

Characters:
HENRY
ERNIE

(HENRY *walks in front of the scrim, wearing jeans and a T-shirt. He stares at a photographic portrait of Darwin on the scrim for a few moments. He turns towards the audience and rubs his eyes.*

Title: The speed scene.

The den. The scrim rises as the lights slowly come up on the den. There are cartoons on all of the televisions. ERNIE *is watching them, drinking a soda and smoking a joint.* HENRY *walks in.*)

HENRY. Hey.

ERNIE. Hey. What are you doing up?

HENRY. Couldn't sleep. Had this . . . *dream*.

ERNIE. Did you nocturnally emit?

HENRY. Huh?

ERNIE. Did you jizz all over your boxers?

HENRY. No, no. It wasn't that kind of dream. It's just . . . I keep having it, and I can never get back to sleep afterwards.

ERNIE. Take a hit. It'll relax you.

HENRY. You think so?

ERNIE. I myself feel . . . pretty relaxed at this moment in time. Puffing. Watching some high-quality, top-of-the-line animation. It's extraordinarily relaxing.

HENRY. Thanks.

> (HENRY *sits down next to* ERNIE, *takes the joint and smokes it. The two of them sit silently watching television, passing the joint back and forth between them.*)

HENRY. I think it's working. (*Beat.*) Who is that?

ERNIE. Who? The cartoon?

HENRY. Yeah.

ERNIE. Shut up.

HENRY. What?

ERNIE. You're not serious?

HENRY. I just asked who it was.

ERNIE. Have you ever seen that character before?

HENRY. Not that I'm aware of.

ERNIE. You're shitting me.

HENRY. I wouldn't shit you.

ERNIE. The dog biting the coin?

HENRY. Yeah.

ERNIE. You don't know who that dog is?

HENRY. No.

ERNIE. That's *Underdog.*

HENRY. Oh.

ERNIE. You mean to tell me you grew up in the United States of America and you don't recognize Underdog?

HENRY. I guess not.

ERNIE. You're a *freak*, Henry. (*Beat.*) I like that.

HENRY. I'm . . . really kind of . . . *high.*

175

ERNIE. I like that, too.

HENRY. *(Beat.)* That's *really* good pot.

ERNIE. My friend Marlon grew it. I'll pass your compliments along.

HENRY. Please do. *(Pause.)* I feel like I'm — *(Exhales.)* — very quiet . . . *drifting* . . . drifting . . .

> (ERNIE *takes a bottle of pills out of his pocket, opens it and hands two pills to* HENRY, *along with his soda.)*

ERNIE. Yeah, well, before you drift completely into nothingness and disappear, Underdog, I think you should take these.

HENRY. What are they?

ERNIE. Methampex.

HENRY. Oh.

> (HENRY *takes the pills and washes them down with soda while* ERNIE *nonchalantly flips the television channels so there are different images on each television: an infomercial, a music video, a test pattern, a religion show and an old sitcom.)*

HENRY. *(Beat.)* What's Methampex?

ERNIE. Anti-disappearant.

HENRY. Huh?

ERNIE. So you don't disappear.

HENRY. So . . . I won't disappear?

ERNIE. On the contrary. You will now *appear*.

HENRY. *(Beat.)* I don't get it.

ERNIE. It's Desoxyn.

HENRY. I still don't get it.

ERNIE. High-quality, blue-ribbon *speed*.

HENRY. *(Beat.)* Speed?

ERNIE. Speed.

HENRY. I've never done speed.

ERNIE. That's no longer true.

HENRY. Isn't it fairly dangerous?

ERNIE. Being *alive* can be fairly dangerous, Henry.

HENRY. Yes, but isn't speed specifically, especially dangerous?

ERNIE. Well, yes, Henry, it can be. It most certainly can be. I mean, let's face it, anything that makes your brain and body feel like staying energetically awake for long periods of time without nourishment is probably not the healthiest or most organic choice to make in the long run. But you know what rule I live my life by, Henry?

HENRY. What's that?

ERNIE. *Moderation.* In all things. I mean, if just a couple of pills could kill you, doctors probably wouldn't be able to prescribe them.

HENRY. Doctors *prescribe* speed?

ERNIE. Doctors prescribe *Methampex.* For people who are troubled by *extreme* obesity. Now, you and I are *not* troubled by extreme obesity, Henry, and we should be thankful for that, and try to enjoy our speediness while it lasts. Don't you think?

HENRY. I *think* I should have Just Said No.

ERNIE. All of that Just Say No crap has been severely misinterpreted. People miss the whole beauty of the thing. Just *Say* No. All you have to do is *say* it. You can still *do* drugs. Watch, I'll do a demonstration for you. (*Shakes his head.*) No. (*Takes a pill and washes it down with soda, shakes his head again.*) No . . . I'm sorry, but . . . No. (ERNIE *takes another pill and washes it down with soda. From this point on, the scene moves quickly.*) See how easy that was, Henry? Actions speak louder than words. Kind of a stupid expression, actually. If actions speak louder than words, why would anybody *say* "actions speak louder than words"?

HENRY. I don't know, Ernie.

ERNIE. *Henry.* I don't *care* if actions speak louder than words, I'm going to say a couple of words to you, so look into my eyes. (*Beat.*) *Trust Me.* (*Beat.*) Okay? Trust me, Henry. You'll be okay, but you've got to trust me, because without trust, human beings might as well be plastic drinking straws.

HENRY. (*Beat.*) Plastic drinking straws?

ERNIE. Okay, okay, okay, bad example. (*Beat.*) The smallest human being ever, Henry, was a full-grown woman under two feet tall. You know how small that is? (*Indicates with his hand.*) Very fucking small. And she wasn't a G.I. Joe or some Cabbage Patch Thing, she was a woman, with a brain and a body and emotions and a spine, okay? Imagine if she was in this room with us, you know, you'd stare at her, and she could look back at you, and talk to you, and maybe even fall in love with you. Less than two feet tall, Henry. Not Big. And every moment of her life, she had to completely trust the people around her, because she had no choice. (*Beat.*) *All* of us are her, Henry, we're *all* less than two feet tall, and unless we put ourselves into the hands of others, we don't add up to jack shit, so *Trust Me.*

HENRY. (*Beat.*) I feel a little better, now that you took two.

ERNIE. Side by side, Henry. I'm a firm believer in the power of teamwork. Moderation and teamwork, those are the linchpins of my existence — motherfucking-fucking-fucking-*fuck*!

HENRY. Oh, no.

ERNIE. Those guys are bullshit! They're hacks!

HENRY. What guys?

ERNIE. On the TV screen.

HENRY. *Which* TV screen?

ERNIE. The one in the middle. The music video guys. The so-called musicians on the middle TV.

HENRY. What's wrong with them?

ERNIE. Oh, come *on*, Henry. My band made these guys look like they were all still in grade school, playing the *recorder*.

HENRY. You're in a band?

ERNIE. Yeah. I'm in a goddamn *band*. (*Beat.*) I mean, not anymore, we broke up, I quit. We had a great concept, all hardcore Bee-Gees covers, but we had a shitty look, we clearly weren't going anyplace.

HENRY. That's too bad.

ERNIE. Also, everybody was addicted to heroin.

HENRY. Oh.

ERNIE. Except for me. But, you know, I come in, completely speedy all the time, wanting to play, play, play, everybody else was just sitting around all the time, staring at their instruments. Not a good mix. Listen to me. Sound like a schoolmarm. "Not a good mix." You want to know what it really was. It was Clash of the *Titans*. You see that? (*Beat.*) Henry?

HENRY. What?

ERNIE. You see *Clash of the Titans*?

HENRY. No.

ERNIE. With Laurence Olivier?

HENRY. No.

ERNIE. Olivier was a serious badass madman performer. You see *Marathon Man*?

HENRY. No.

ERNIE. Olivier played this Nazi dentist asking Tootsie if it's safe, freaking me out, I'm saying to myself, Grandpa Olivier might as well call it quits and retire, 'cause how can you top a *Nazi dentist?* So what does he go and do? He plays *Zeus*. The Big Guy. The God of Gods. Clash of the Titans. Some powerful stuff, my friend, makes you think, myths and shit. You ever study myths at school?

HENRY. Not really.

ERNIE. But that's what you're *supposed* to study at school. What do you study instead of myths?

HENRY. Uhh, Darwin, mostly. My major's natural history, but I spend most of my time studying . . . *Darwin*.

179

ERNIE. Darwin. (*Beat.*) *Huh.* (*Beat.*) I keep trying to convince Dad to give me the cash he'd spend if I actually decided to spend four years playing at college. I could put eighty grand in the bank, collect some interest, you know, live a free life, read, talk to people, hang out with my friends — the basic college thing, just keep the cash for some security down the line.

HENRY. College sucks.

ERNIE. (*Beat.*) What was that?

HENRY. College really sucks.

ERNIE. I can't believe I'm hearing this. Aren't you Mister Doctorate Grad School, intelligent young man dating my older sister? Doesn't sound like the kind of guy who'd say "college sucks."

HENRY. I mean it.

ERNIE. If it sucks, why are you *there*? To get your Doctorate in Doggypaddling? Time is short, my friend.

HENRY. Time isn't short or long, it's just time.

ERNIE. And it's *ticking.* It doesn't stop while you're getting your diploma, your $80,000 paper airplane. Time's like a car with a self-refilling gas tank.

HENRY. Great simile, Ernie. Real strong.

ERNIE. I'm serious, man. I was flipping through *Playboy* the other day —

HENRY. For the articles, right?

ERNIE. No, for the airbrushed pictures of women's tits. I'm reading the Playmate Questionnaire in the middle, you know, because I'm really interested to know what her favorite books are, and I look at her date-of-birth, and . . . she was born in '75. (*Beat.*) *Nineteen* seventy-five. That's a landmark in a man's life, the first time you're older than the *Playboy* centerfold. No more kid stuff. The time for action is *now.* (*Beat.*) How old are you, Henry?

HENRY. Twenty-two.

ERNIE. You see? By my *Playboy* theory, you better get a move on. Forget about grad school, worry about *Henry.* You feel alive?

HENRY. Yeah, yeah, I do.

ERNIE. That's the speed. (*Beat.*) They asked my girlfriend to pose for *Playboy*. She told them to suck her dick. (*Beat.*) Just an expression, of course, she's not a hermaphrodite or anything. (*Takes a picture from his wallet and shows it to* HENRY.) That's her.

HENRY. She looks beautiful.

ERNIE. She's a bitch.

HENRY. Why are you dating her, then?

ERNIE. I love carrying her picture in my wallet. It's a great photo. But in person, it's all confrontational bullshit, nagging, she wants *this*, so that means I can't do *that*, all sorts of fenced-in feelings. Who needs it? I mean, don't get me wrong, I still get together with her. You can't fuck a picture, you know what I'm saying? Unless you're some perverse sicko cutting holes with scissors and you know, God Bless, live and let live, that's not up my alley, I prefer living, breathing flesh. You can keep your two-dimensional photographic representations and blow-up plastic dolls, thank you very much, sorry, no sale, you know?

HENRY. Uh-huh.

ERNIE. (*Beat.*) So, you keep a snapshot of my sis in your wallet?

HENRY. Huh?

ERNIE. You got a photo of Hope in your billfold?

HENRY. Oh. Oh, no. No, she says photographs steal your soul.

ERNIE. That's not what she said when she was thirteen. She went off to college a sister, she comes back an Indian chief. Photographs steal your soul. Come on, Hope, it's the nineties, time to take off the hoop skirt. (*Beat.*) You got a charcoal *sketch* of her in your wallet?

HENRY. Nope. Just this. (HENRY *takes a picture from his wallet and shows it to* ERNIE.)

ERNIE. Who's this? Grandpa?

HENRY. That's Charles Darwin.

181

ERNIE. Oh. (*Beat.*) Could've used a Gillette Sensor, know what I'm saying? (*Beat.*) You know, actually, if you get rid of the beard and the moustache, then weave all that facial hair onto the top of his head . . . I swear to Christ, that's incredible.

HENRY. What?

ERNIE. If Charles Darwin shaved and joined the Hair Club For Men, he'd be the spitting image of Aaron Spelling.

HENRY. Who's Aaron Spelling?

ERNIE. Oh, Henry, baby, you're killing me. Aaron Spelling is legendary. *The Love Boat. Fantasy Island. Charlie's Angels. . . . 90210, Melrose Inc.* and *Models Place*. Aaron Spelling. He's like a living TV *God*. How can you not know Aaron Spelling? Or *Clash of the Titans*? Or Underdog? It's like you were raised by wolves or — *Whoa.* (*Beat.*) Stop. (*Beat.*) *Stop.* (*Beat.*) Oh, yeah. Oh, *yeah.*

HENRY. Oh, yeah *what*?

ERNIE. Shut up for a second, Henry. It's all coming together, making sense, fortifying — I'm going to say a couple of words to you, so look into my eyes. (*Beat.*) *Fuck Edison.* (*Beat.*) Was that clear? Should I repeat it? I *will* repeat it. *Fuck Edison.* Do you know what that means?

HENRY. I don't think so.

ERNIE. It means . . . exactly what it sounds like. Fuck Edison. You see?

HENRY. Not . . . *really* . . .

ERNIE. Fuck Edison and his ninety-nine percent perspiration, one percent inspiration malarkey, because perspiration is sweat and inspiration is genius, and I rank genius far above sweat, so . . . hence . . . *Fuck Edison.* Is it all becoming as clear to you as it is to me?

HENRY. I'm trying to put it all together with you, Ernie, but —

ERNIE. Okay, look: Moderation, Teamwork, The *Playboy* Doggy-paddling Theory and Fucking Edison. Those are the four basic food groups that fuel my every waking moment. And for some unknown reason — call it *fate*, Henry, call it *kismet* — all of my major concepts have merged to point me in the direction of the ultimate paradise that is going to be our collective future. (*Beat.*) I'm a Johnny-on-the-spot kind of guy, Henry, I may seem lazy, but I know when the time is ripe, and Henry, right now, the clockworks are *dripping.* (*Beat.*) Darwin's basic gist was that we descend with modifications along the way, right?

HENRY. How did you know that?

ERNIE. Surprise, surprise, Henry. I was extremely well educated when I was a small child, I just fucked it all up as I got taller. I know some handy tidbits of information, but I'm certainly no scholar. You, on the other hand, the left hand, since I was just gesticulating with my right hand, you, Henry, you certainly *are* a scholar. Pump it up, Henry. Use what you've learned. Darwin talked about adaptation, right? *Adapt.* Grow. Change. Look around, see what's going on, and realize the classroom is outdated, it's no longer the place for you. Harvard may have been exciting once, brand-new, then it matured, but now . . . now, Henry, now it's *traditional. Harvard.* It's a brand name, like Hershey's chocolate or Colgate toothpaste. I remember when MTV was cutting edge and *USA Today* published its first issue and Demi Moore was in *St. Elmo's Fire.* Well, she's having *kids* now . . . on the covers of *magazines.* What if she kept clinging to *St. Elmo's Fire,* Henry? Huh? Tell me. What *if?*

HENRY. (*Beat.*) What is *St. Elmo's Fire?*

ERNIE. Ask Rob Lowe. (*Beat.*) Don't tell me . . . you know who Rob Lowe is, don't you?

HENRY. The name sounds vaguely familiar.

ERNIE. (*Beat.*) Henry, you're a tabula rasa sent to me by the gods to alter television and change *history. Adapt.* Adapt and *Plunge.*

HENRY. (*Beat.*) Ernie?

ERNIE. *Yes?*

HENRY. What the *fuck* are you talking about?

(ERNIE *gestures grandly to the televisions.*)

ERNIE. *TV!*

HENRY. What about it?

183

ERNIE. That's where we belong. That's where we're going to go. I've got a friend whose father's a network hotshot. He can pull some strings, get us in the *door*.

HENRY. You're evidently excited, Ernie, I'm aware of that, I get that. But, what . . . what *door* do we need to get *in?*

ERNIE. The television network door. How can I make you understand, Henry? *Darwin's* door. When he wrote about survival of the fittest and reproduction, Darwin was writing about TV. Charles Darwin is alive and well and living in Southern California, Henry. Aaron Spelling is the reincarnation of Charles Darwin. Take *Charlie's Angels*. A TV show about three beautiful women detectives, a show that not only survived on television, a show that *prospered*. These women were *fit*, Henry, the *fittest*, and TV reproduced them over and over and over, ad infinitum . . . ad nauseam . . . with ads in between to sell products that consumers don't actually want or need. But we're not going to be consumers, Henry. We're going to penetrate the shell of that angelic machine that is TV. Talk about *affecting* people. TV. Everybody has it, everybody watches it.

HENRY. I don't.

ERNIE. That's the *point*. You don't know what they're doing, so you'll have fresh ideas, and that's what TV needs, all the time, it's like a vampire in need of blood. *We're* the blood, Henry.

HENRY. We are?

ERNIE. Yes, we are. And if our blood type is their blood type, they pay *Big*. Bigger than the Red Cross. *So* much bigger than the Red Cross. TV makes the Red Cross look *this* big, Henry, *this* big — *(Gestures with his fingers.)* — *Tiny*. The Red Cross is a trinket some little kid with sticky elbows wears on a chain around his neck. TV — *TV*, Henry, TV is this gargantuan crucifix with all of civilization nailed to it, hook, line, sinker — there ain't nobody getting off this baby, Henry. And just think . . . we can be a part of it. I keep you pumped up, juices flowing, you write the damn words down — WHIZ — BANG — we've got a script and we're in the door. We're in the foyer of the whole damn *thing!*

HENRY. You want me to write *scripts?*

ERNIE. You got it!

HENRY. Ernie, the only things I've ever written are critical term papers at school.

ERNIE. Words are words.

HENRY. I think I get it. You want us to write TV shows?

ERNIE. No, I *need* us to write TV shows.

HENRY. You seem to have a flair for the dramatic. Why don't you just do it yourself?

ERNIE. What's my most important rule, Henry?

HENRY. Moderation?

ERNIE. *Teamwork.* Simon and Garfunkel. Jekyll and Hyde. Ernie and Bert.

HENRY. Who's Bert?

ERNIE. From *Sesame Street.*

HENRY. I never saw that.

ERNIE. You are so *untainted.* So *pure.* That's our selling point. You've been living like a monk in the trenches of academia preparing for this task. You haven't got your finger on the pulse of the American public, Henry, you've got your finger on the pulse of *All Civilization*, from the Big Bang to Evolution. I see it now: *Evolution — The Television Event Of All Time.* Written by You. Executive Produced by Me. Created by Us. Me and You. The Spark and the Follow-Through. The Quirk and the Rock.

HENRY. *(Beat.)* What does an executive producer *do*?

ERNIE. I keep you happy and bank my rather excessive paycheck *daily. (Beat.)* But it's not about the money, Henry. I mean, the money's gonna be nice, but it's not what it's *about.* It's about the *power.* The feeling that you can only get when you're tuned into *everything*, when your ideas and your creation are being pumped into the minds of people *everywhere. (Beat.)* Take Madonna, for instance. She's used music and videos and the press to her advantage and created an *empire.* She's changed the course of *history*, influenced the entire *world. (Beat.)* Do you know who Madonna is, Henry?

HENRY. Yeah, I know Madonna.

185

ERNIE. See what I'm saying, Henry? Even *you* know Madonna. I guarantee you I can find Madonna somewhere on television right this very second.

(ERNIE *flips the channels on one of the televisions until he finds a Madonna video (she's singing the song "Holiday" in concert, from the movie* Truth or Dare*). When he does, he flips the channels on the rest of the televisions to that station, so the Madonna video is on all five televisions. There is a long pause as* ERNIE *and* HENRY *stare at the televisions.)*

ERNIE. *(Long pause.)* We can be everywhere, Henry. Not just right here, or right now. Everywhere. For All Time.

(The lights black out. The Madonna video ends as the scrim falls.)

From The Psychic Life of Savages
Amy Freed

Characters:
SYLVIA FLUELLEN, a young American poet
TED MAGUS, a young English poet
ANNE BITTENHAND, an American poet in her forties
DR. ROBERT STONER, a man in his sixties, the American Poet
     Laureate
(Ensemble — two women and one man)
EMILY, the ghost of Emily Dickinson
TITO, Anne's husband
RADIO INTERVIEWER, played by the actor playing Anne's
     husband
KIT-KAT, Anne's daughter
REBECCA, a young mental patient, played by the actor playing
     Kit-Kat
FEMALE COLLEGE STUDENTS/PARTY GUESTS, played by the
     actors playing Tito and Kit-Kat

PLAYWRIGHT'S NOTE
This play is a work of dramatic fiction inspired in the loosest sense
by the lives and writings of several major poets. The persons, events
and relationships described are imaginary and not intended to be
in any way factual or biographical. All poems are my invention.

Scene 1

(*A radio station.* TED MAGUS, DR. ROBERT STONER *and*
INTERVIEWER *are on the air.*)

187

INTERVIEWER. Welcome to Potshots. I'm interviewing Britain's Ted Magus and our own American Poet Laureate Dr. Robert Stoner here at Wardwell College. Mr. Magus, you say, in your introduction to *Songs of the Fen*, "Bark and bleat. Reach into your own darkness and remember how to howl. Ask the beasts. Ask the birds." What does that mean?

TED. Call to a hawk in a foul black wind, and have him scream his answer to you. I have.

INTERVIEWER. What are you suggesting — ?

TED. I'm sure Dr. Stoner would share my belief that the poet is the shaman, chosen to heal our soul-sick society —

STONER. I couldn't agree less.

TED. Oh, really?

INTERVIEWER. Would you like to say more about that, Dr. Stoner?

STONER. No.

INTERVIEWER. Mr. Magus. You consistently use nature as metaphor — the hawk, a symbol for freedom and release, the cow for domestic stagnation. . . .

TED. A trout don't think when he leap for the sky.

   (*Pause.*)

INTERVIEWER. Let's talk about some of your poetic techniques. Your unique use of rhythm, for example.

TED. Rhythm. It's both awakening and sleep inducing. Trance. The fall-through to the spirit world. I'm very interested in that. Paradox. We are surrounded by paradox. In sleep, we wake. In waking, we sleep. We starve in the midst of plenty. And in fasting, we become full.

STONER. If my aunt had a dick, she'd be my uncle.

TED. Oh, but exactly. Dr. Stoner, you're joking, but the joke is, you've actually touched something far truer —

STONER. Oh, please.

INTERVIEWER. You've said a lot, here, Mr. Magus, let me pick up on what you said about rhythm. Do you actually attempt to induce a trance-like state in the reader?

TED. Well, there's an instance in the title poem, for example, where I say —

Skirts of the wind sweep
Dry rustle grasses
Shucka — shucka — shucka —
There go me glasses.
Reaching into gassy bog
Bluggah bluggah bluggah —
I hear my heart in
Song of frog
I read my soul
In rotted log
Good night little sleepers, little peepers,
God's sticky creepers —

INTERVIEWER. It seems that there's almost a tribal intensity at the beginning and then it slides imperceptibly towards what's really a hypnotic lullaby near the end.

TED. Exactly.

INTERVIEWER. Extraordinary.

TED. Well, do you know what's even more extraordinary, I came to find out later what I heard in the bog that day was known in ancient Bali as the monkey chant. Identical! It goes —

— shak shaka shak
— shak shaka shaka shaka shak,
— shak shak shak
— shak shaka shaka shaka shak . . .

INTERVIEWER. Fantastic.

TED. Chanted by hags. Women are more connected with the occult.

INTERVIEWER. Which brings us to you, Dr. Stoner.

STONER. Why?

INTERVIEWER. You said in a recent interview, Dr. Stoner, that you are not convinced of the innocence of the Salem witches.

STONER. There's a lot of room for doubt in my book.

INTERVIEWER. And quite a "book" it's going to be. I doubt any book of poems has been awaited with as much eagerness as your free-verse cycle on the life of Cotton Mather. Will you give us a little teaser?

STONER. Well, there is this one little piece I've begun about the witch-girls. Now, I have the image, the spear is in my hand, as it were, but I'm having trouble with the target. Frankly, I think that what with the damned insulin therapy that maybe my focus is a little off, but well, here goes.

Mather knew —
And for this they hated him, all the dark daughters,
Old Cotton, he was blessed with eyes that see 'round corners
Eyes that through God's hard grace could render even
Termites translucent.

With those pale and potent eyes
Mather could see the Witch Girls —

And then it goes something — something — something — . I don't know. And that's where I've been stuck with it for years, now.

(*Pause.*)

INTERVIEWER. Interesting. The whole process, I mean —

STONER. I can hear the shrill of a high wind, and a chill, like a damp petticoat. Oh, they're around, all right, and they're probably out to fuck me up.

INTERVIEWER. Who, Dr. Stoner?

STONER. The witch-girls, of course.

INTERVIEWER. What?

TED. (*Slowly, as if feeling his way in a trance.*) One. Mather sees in a dream. A young witch screams astride the bucking buck from Zanzibar. Her ice-cold teat reminds him of his wife.

STONER. Hah Hah! Not bad, Son.

TED. Wait! Wait! I'm getting . . .

— Two. Seen in residue of
Lumpy morning porridge —
Bowl uncleared by slattern daughter,
Does she dance now with the broom — ?

STONER. An old witch and a young one
With their mobcaps cast aside
Stand in skanky petticoats
Bare toes sunk in stable muck —
Hold a jar,
It's full of winter wheat —
And something fat and white.
Floating closer, Father Mather sees
His member, long and hungry — !
Too large to be a maggot, with that freckle on the tip!

TED. (*Angry and excited.*) Mather, in a lather, now
Knows the way is stony
But that fire will be the answer,
If he wants his penis back!

STONER. My boy! My boy! My boy!

INTERVIEWER. We've just witnessed an astonishing improvisation
between two remarkable poets, it seems to have surprised them
as much as it did me, they're embracing now, on the stage floor,
much moved, much emotion, and Ted Magus is now drumming
in what seems to be a tribute to the senior poet, who has his
eyes closed and is covered in sweat. Our time is up and — astonishing program — goodnight, this was Potshots, live from Wardwell College.

TED AND STONER. Shak shak shak shak shaka shaka shaka shak!
Shak shak shak shak shaka shaka shaka shak!

Scene 2

(*A mental institution.* ANNE *is on phone.* REBECCA, *a young
mental patient, is sitting on the floor drawing on a large
pad.*)

ANNE. I'm O.K., I'm not O.K. I'm O.K. Stop yelling at me! Would
I be back in the nuthouse again if I knew why I did it! Use your

head, Tito! I'm sorry, lover. I can't really make sense of it to you. Because you won't — no, you don't — do you remember that thing I was describing? What happened last week at the hair-dresser's, where the tops of the trees started forming into a hostile pattern? I can just tell! For God's sake! (*Pause.*) Don't you think I'd rather be home taking the lamb chops out of the oven? Or whatever you cook them in. If I could cook, I mean. It's not a matter of making an effort! I have a time bomb in my brain, and it just — WENT OFF! That's all. (*Pause.*) Did my agent call? Well, why didn't you say so? They're taking *Thoughts On My First Bleeding Time!* That's wonderful! Did you tell her where I was? (*Pause.*) Listen! My readers do not *care* that I'm a *nut!* My readers *love* that I'm a nut. So tell her. No, Baby, not this week-end! Because, I can't handle it, that's why. Don't you understand that it's a little hard for me to be playing wife and mother for you and our daughter right now? I just feel like the whole world is one big stinking gas chamber! Don't come up yet! (*She hangs up. Pause. She crosses to* REBECCA, *who is muttering to herself as she draws.* ANNE *looks at* REBECCA'*s drawing.*) What's that?

REBECCA. My dog.

ANNE. Why does he have so many legs, Baby?

REBECCA. (*Upset.*) Because his name is Spider!

ANNE. That's just what I thought. Isn't he beautiful!

REBECCA. Hey Anne. I'm going home for the weekend. (*Stabbing her drawing pad.*) I hate it there! (*Hopefully.*) Want to come?

ANNE. Oh, Baby. I've got a home of my own not to go to.

REBECCA. Last time I was home, my mother made a pot roast. And the funniest thing — right as we sat down? It started to bleed. Then it started moving and she really knew she had done something wrong. She was screaming at it and waving her feelers. Wow.

ANNE. (*Intensely.*) Oh, yes. That is very interesting. Yes. (ANNE *lights a cigarette, groping for the right words as images come to her.*)

Breakfast is crawling all over the house —
The toast is coming out of the drain —

192

(REBECCA, *caught by* ANNE*'s concentration, begins to draw her.*)

The cereal is gossiping.
The fried eggs are swimming like devilfish.
I look into the garbage disposal —
That dark stinky navel
And it is saying Mmmm.
It is saying Mmmm. Mmmmm. Mmmm.

ANNE. Mmmm. Mmmm.   REBECCA. Mmmm. Mmmm.
Mmmm —   Mmmm —

(ORDERLY *enters with* SYLVIA *in a wheelchair. She is radiant with malice and rigid with self-loathing. Her arms are covered with bandages. She does not move or speak.*)

ANNE. Who's this?

ORDERLY. New roommate. C'mon Rebecca, time's up.

(REBECCA *backs out, frightened by* SYLVIA*'s appearance.* ORDERLY *exits.* ANNE *sizes up* SYLVIA. SYLVIA *stares at something invisible. A pause.*)

SYLVIA. (*A savage private declamation.*)
What odd Godmother, what withered Aunt,
Did you invite —
Mother, oh Mother — to my first birthday party?
Where everyone danced the Hanukkah dance, but me —

Standing alone, all foolish and Unitarian, my tea set filled
With scummy water.
You wept, but could not help me.
I have still not the ear for jigging.

(*A pause.*)

ANNE. That's — very good.

SYLVIA. (*Looks at* ANNE *for the first time.*) Thank you.

ANNE. What a strange, gritty . . . somethingness . . . it has. You're very talented. (*Lighting a cigarette.*) So what happened to you, Miss Golden Girl?

193

SYLVIA. *(Rarely looking at* ANNE, *with frightening enunciation.)* I live in a house on campus with some of the other girls. Everyone gathers in the common room at night, to dry their hair and paint their nails. Much laughter, and vicious, cozy gossip. But whenever I spoke, there was a potent silence. As if a foreigner had just — farted.

ANNE. I see.

SYLVIA. I tried to blend in. MOTHER told me to let down my hair. No one likes a grind. So I wore a mud-pack to dinner in an attempt at henhouse sisterhood. Mistake! I was the only one. My world flickers around me, soundless. Faces look like soap bubbles. When I close my eyes, the faces disappear. I want to keep them closed.

ANNE. *(Pulling her chair closer.)* Oh, Baby. Death is a big commitment . . .

SYLVIA. For a while, I thought of leaving school. But that would have killed Mother. She would have loved that. No. There is no dropping out for a Golden Goose. So I just said "No Thank You."

ANNE. Oh, yes! The lovely "no thank you" moment! Haa!

SYLVIA. Some time back I'd discovered a trick of cutting myself with a pen knife to get me in the mood for composition. It's how I came to write "Rose Red at the Big Game" for *Seventeen* last year. Second prize, maybe you saw it . . . ?

ANNE. I'm sorry, I . . .

SYLVIA. So it didn't take much, just a little extra pressure, and —

ANNE. There you were . . .

SYLVIA. My heart started to beat faster. I was real! An excursion into the fabled third dimension!

ANNE. Oh really? For me it's more like —

SYLVIA. At first it was like flying . . . you really do start seeing —

ANNE. Seeing your *life*! Like pictures in a scrapbook! Oh, I *know*! Mummy and Grandma dressing me in a bunny suit!

SYLVIA. Me, standing in a soggy gym-suit, when I'd wet myself in fear before the teams were chosen . . .

ANNE. Padding my first bra!

SYLVIA. (*Increasingly excited.*) Mother walking me to school on the first day of college . . .

ANNE. (*Trumps her.*) Making love in the back seat of the family Ford . . . with Daddy! (ANNE *is shocked at this memory — the women turn to stare at each other.*)

SYLVIA. (*Turns away again, suddenly composed.*) Then something changed. Suddenly I couldn't see. A ringing in my ears. Terrifying, but at the same time so *important* . . . like I was going —

ANNE. Where?

SYLVIA. I never found out. But I felt I was expected. Then, of course my *mother* broke down the door. And here I am.

> (*Pause.*)

ANNE. Got a fella?

SYLVIA. Flesh disgusts me. My own face sickens me! Encrusted, swollen, greasy in the cracked yellow mirror over the dormitory sink. Well, hello, Truth! There you are! No wonder it was darkness that seemed more . . . forgiving.

> (*Pause.*)

ANNE. No one special, huh. I'm beginning to get the picture.

SYLVIA. Nobody wants to go out with me. (*She looks away.*)

ANNE. Yes, they do. Oh, sure they do. Why not? Why ever not, Baby-girl?

SYLVIA. My hair is rat-colored, and my lips are smeary and — (*Fierce.*) I've never got below an A-Minus!

ANNE. Lip-liner! Peroxide! Blow an exam! C'mon Baby! Live a little!

SYLVIA. I don't want it! I just want to stay here forever and watch the hair grow on my legs. I love it here.

ANNE. Me too.

> (ORDERLY *enters and begins to wheel* SYLVIA *away.*)

SYLVIA. Where are we going?

(ORDERLY *wheels* SYLVIA *to shock treatment station.*)

Scene 3

(*A wing in the psychiatric hospital.* SYLVIA *is receiving Electro-Convulsive Therapy.*)

SYLVIA. (*Ecstatic with electricity.*) Yes! Yes! Yes! (*She catapults to a sitting position. Sound of wind in a desert.* EMILY *enters — a small, terrible ghost dressed in an elaborate white Civil War dress.*)

EMILY. "Convulsion — pleases — for it does not counterfeit."

SYLVIA. Who are you? A hallucination? I did not expect this.

EMILY. Oh, phoo. Let me try again. (*She clears her throat shyly.*)

"The pink and tender earthworm
Waits the rending of the beak —
And cut in half —
It dies again —
A sensate coffee cake!"

SYLVIA. (*Curiosity mingling with terror.*) Beak — cake! Can you do that?

EMILY. (*Quivering.*) What a pleasure this is. I rarely get to greet a kindred spirit.

SYLVIA. Kindred? You and me? What do we have in common?

EMILY. A certain desire to — scratch the surface? Here, you dropped this. (*She pulls out a big razor blade and offers it to* SYLVIA, *who reaches for it tentatively.*) (*Whispering.*) I'm so glad you'll be joining me. It's been so lonely being dead. I have no one to talk to and I've been looking for — (*She primps a little.*) — that Special Anyone for the longest time.

(SYLVIA *drops the razor.*)

SYLVIA. Special "Anyone"?

EMILY. (*Shyly.*) I've felt him so close, sometimes. But, oh, well, Longing is its own Rapture!

SYLVIA. If you are a hallucination, shouldn't you perhaps be gone?

(EMILY *smiles at her.*)

EMILY. Rapture. Now there's a word. From the Latin. To seize, pillage, plunder, rape. Mmmm. (*Shouting.*) Take me, Somebody! I'm not busy! (*Listening.*) They're playing with me, again.

SYLVIA. (*Afraid to know.*) Who?

EMILY. Ooh, that naughty Universe! Tell me. (*She comes closer.*) What did it feel like?

SYLVIA. No! (*She is convulsed by an electric current.*) Yes! That was a good one! (*Terrified.*) I want you out!

EMILY. You won't remember me when you wake up. But I'll remember you!

SYLVIA. Please go away!

EMILY. Not just yet.

SYLVIA. My head is splitting!

EMILY. (*Screams.*) — How else will anything get in? (*Pause.* EMILY *is mortified at herself for losing her temper.*) I'm truly sorry. Want to meet my baby? (*She reaches under her dress and pulls out a shrivelled, blasted little book.*) Isn't he beautiful? Guess who his father was. (*Lifting her arms.*) Lightning!

(SYLVIA *convulses.*)

Poor thing. But I can't take care of him any longer. And I've selected you to be his mother! And now, you can have him! He'll bring you luck. (EMILY *advances with burnt book.*)

SYLVIA. No! No! No! Sterility! Madness! Bone-bag! I want real children. I want a man to plunge his stake through my heart so that I can sleep at night!

(EMILY *tosses it on* SYLVIA's *lap.*)

I don't want it! It's a curse!

197

Amy Freed

EMILY. Our duty is to sing. No backsies! (*She disappears, singing a wordless note.*)

SYLVIA. (*Convulsing, gratefully.*) Yes! Yes! Yes!

Scene 4

(*A classroom at Wardwell College, a women's Ivy League school.* TED MAGUS *is conducting a poetry seminar.* FEMALE STUDENTS *are taking notes.* SYLVIA *walks into the classroom area, joining the other girls during* TED's *story.*)

TED. Yes. The ending was a nightmare. I wrestled with it for weeks, like Jacob wrestling the Angel. Finally, I dreamed it. I saw the slug dying, covered with salt by a vicious housewife. As clear as day, I dreamed him, a big quivering mass of slop and mucus writhing in the rotted mulch . . . and I found the final lines . . . "And bubbling there, I'm left alone, a bitter pool of fragrance, shrinking in the sun."

ALL THE GIRLS. Wow. Oh, that's incredible. I cried when I —

TED. So. What have we learned? Don't be polite. Don't be small. Poetry is not all rose gardens and my cat with last year's dead leaves, you know. We're talking about the dark side. The unmentionable terrors. The unspeakable joys. What are yours? Show me. I know my fears are . . . shedding tears in public, showing affection for other men . . . in a physical way, you know, hugging, wrestling, that sort of thing, and — Hah! Dancing! — I mean why — dancing? It terrifies me. My own twisted ideas of manhood, I suppose, as passed down from one generation of small, cramped men to another, when — my God! The blood of our ancestors *thrummed* with the dance. A good jig, a leap under the moonlight — the hunt, the rites of mating or of death — oh come! Let's . . . tango! Who wants to jump in first?

GIRL 1. (*Played by female actor. A flirt. Comes up to front of class with notebook. Adjusts her sweater. She giggles.*) Um, O.K. I'm a nervous wreck. O.K. Should I say anything about this first? Or just go?

TED. I'm not your judge. I'm not your executioner.

GIRL 1. Oh, Time, why keep'st thine armies marching on
Destroying flesh and withering with age?
The swelling breasts of happy girlhood droop, and —

TED. Yes, yes. And all that. I can tell you've faithfully studied the form. I commend your hard work. I recommend . . . a naked swim with a boy you love in a rock quarry in the blaze of a hot afternoon.

GIRL 1. I'm not sure I understand . . .

TED. Good, good. That's a start. Who else? Come, come, come.

GIRL 2. *(Played by male actor. A grind. She comes to front of class with notebook. Very nervous. Adjusts her glasses. Suddenly levels a passionate gaze at* TED.*)*

The azure Mediterranean
Leaps against the chalky cliff
My skin scorches in the hot Greek sun
I left my sunblock at American Express
Dmitri sticks his hand inside my dress
Why, oh, why do they overload these donkeys so?

(Pause.)

TED. Someone else? No one? Oh, come, come. Don't make me talk about dancing again.

*(*SYLVIA *gets up. Recites.)*

SYLVIA. It is again the place of nightmare.
Hot breath surrounds me, rich and reeking
Brambles tear the skins from my thighs —
As I run, my blood excites.
Oh, rip from me this borrowed hide.
Teach me my skin.

(Girls look at each other.)

TED. Excellent.

SYLVIA. Omigod. Really? Thank you.

TED. I mean, profoundly usual, but excellent.

SYLVIA. Excuse me?

199

TED. You know, girls, it's interesting, that this last being one of the best, it's also one of the worst. Ha! That feels like the beginning of an insight! So? What. Class dismissed. Assignment! Assignment! For next week, I want everyone to go out and — spend a night — on a park bench. And write a poem about it.

(*Pause. Consternation in the class.*)

(*Thundering.*) Or don't. It doesn't really matter, does it?

(*Student puts up her hand.*)

No, I'm not taking any bloody questions! Just *do* it!

(*Students leave.* TED *collects papers.* SYLVIA *walks over to him. He looks up.*)

What's up, Miss — Fluellen? is it?

SYLVIA. I have a little bone to pick with you.

TED. Oh? What?

SYLVIA. "Profoundly usual"?

TED. (*Packing up books, not looking at her.*) Oh, you know, the Tarzan meets Rima the bird girl fantasy stuff, the typical Junior-year ambivalence about fellatio, the underlying hatred of your mother. But other than that, it's very well crafted. One of the best.

SYLVIA. (*Choking with fury.*) Tarzan? Rima the bird girl? Junior-year ambivalence about — How dare you? How dare you? You — standing up there bullying all the girls all week in that filthy black sweater! Well, how about you! How about your boring male performance anxiety that's so rippingly evident in "Afternoon of a Slug"! Talk about profoundly usual!

TED. (*Laughs.*) Oh, what nonsense.

SYLVIA. Oh, come on! After the evil housewife puts salt on the poor old slug and you say "And bubbling there, I'm left alone, a bitter pool of fragrance, shrinking in the sun . . ."

TED. Don't be idiotic. "Afternoon of a Slug," my dear girl, is about the agony of the creator, writhing in the fleshy bondage of his own creation. An artist must come to terms with agony. The

200

bubbling of a salted slug on a summer morning . . . (*Pause.*) Oh, my God.

SYLVIA. Ha Ha Ha! I'm right, I'm right, I'm right!

TED. I don't believe it.

SYLVIA. I caught you out! I—

TED. Be quiet! I'm thinking. "Short, thick, white-bellied worm, I have not the vertebrate advantage . . ."

SYLVIA. "Flesh-helmeted, despised—"

TED. Shut up, will you?

SYLVIA. Hah Hah Hah.

TED. "—the boneless one that will never stiffen—oh, where are you, muscle for my dreams . . . for my ramping will . . ." Oh, God. I don't believe it! It is! It's about my dick!

SYLVIA. See, I told you, I was—

TED. I can't believe it. It's so bloody obvious. I sweated blood over "Afternoon of a Slug." It was a death struggle. I pursued that poem like Ahab chasing after Mm—.

   (*Pause.*)

SYLVIA. I am so attracted to you.

   (TED *looks at her.*)

TED. Don't fuck with me, Miss Fluellen.

SYLVIA. I'm going to.

TED. (*Throwing his books to the floor.*) I'm death to Little Girls!

SYLVIA. I'm not a Little Girl.

TED. And I hate Women!

SYLVIA. Not as much as I do!

TED. (*Crosses to her.*) I'm trouble. I'm a filthy rucksack of a man in the dungheap of existence. I want a great muck of a woman, not a bright little coed. I need a Big Ugly Woman!—to wake me up. When we have each other in the dead of night, it won't be full of sticky tenderness. It will be with the ancient frenzy of the fire ants that couple and kill.

SYLVIA. You don't frighten me.

TED. Such an all-American girl. Dyed yellow hair, red painted lips and — (*Grabbing her arms — she gasps and tries to break away.*) —bandages all over your arms. (*He laughs.*)

SYLVIA. Take your hands off me, you sick bastard!

> (*He releases her easily. She stares at him for a moment, then suddenly pulls him to her for a passionate kiss. He mounts her as she lies back over desk top. Her head hangs upside down, face toward audience, hair streaming downward. A tableau.* TED *remains frozen in position as* SYLVIA *speaks.*)

SYLVIA. (*Face front, ferocious, joyful.*) Off! Sticky Mother Pot!
I throw my saddle shoes at your head
And dance barefoot with a goat-footed giant
We are laughing at you, he and I
My lips are red and my hair fills the forest.

> (*A metered laugh.*)

Ha ha ha ha ha.

Scene 5

> (ANNE's *house.* ANNE *is in her bed. She is in a state. Her husband,* TITO, *is with her.*)

TITO. What can I do? I just don't know what to do for you!

ANNE. Get Dr. Dickter on the phone! I want to go back to the bin! I want to go back to the bin!

TITO. Please, Baby, no. Shall I call one of your lovers?

ANNE. It doesn't help. Nothing helps.

TITO. (*Reluctant.*) Do you want — to have sex with me?

ANNE. (*Anguished.*) I might as well masturbate! I mean, c'mon, Tito, we've become the same person! (*Pause.*) Oh, I've hurt you,

Baby, my love. I'm a big mess. Make me a milkshake? I want the big sweet mama I never had. I want it with a straw.

TITO. Chocolate?

ANNE. (*Screams.*) Vanilla! Don't you listen?

TITO. All right! (*He leaves.*)

ANNE. Mommy's feeling crazy! Kit-Kat! KIT-KAT!!! (ANNE *lights a cigarette, fussing for a moment.* KIT-KAT *enters, apprehensive.*) Oh, it's so good to be home again with my Bunny-girl. Let's cuddle up. Give me your hands. Baby Bunny, do you believe that Mother loves you and what happened has nothing to do with you?

KIT-KAT. (*Reluctant.*) I guess so.

ANNE. (*Taking her hands.*) I'm so sorry, Kit-Kat, that you had to find me like that. Never again. Believe me?

KIT-KAT. I guess so.

ANNE. Do you really, Kitty? 'Cause part of our healing is to say what we really feel. (*Pause.*) What is it, Baby?

KIT-KAT. Oh, Mom. It was so gross! I had to clean everything up, all the puke and the pills — and all the kids coming over for my Sweet Sixteen party! Why'd you have to try and kill yourself on my birthday!! You hate me!!!

ANNE. I do not! Shut up, you little bitch! Are you out of your mind? I said I was sorry!

KIT-KAT. Sorry! 　　　　TITO. (*Entering with milkshake.*) For
　　　　　　　　　　　　　　　　Christ's sake, Anne!

ANNE. Oh, God, Tito — I could die! — this waste of my life — forced early into marriage (that prison routine of pancake breakfasts and chicken pot pies) — scrubbing toilets instead of fighting to save myself, singing idiot songs to an insomniac infant, whose little red face could only reflect my own fury back to me —

TITO. (*Furious.*) First of all, we eloped. Secondly, you don't cook, I do. And Kit-Kat has done all the housework! Ever since she moved back from Foster Care!

ANNE. You are undermining me! Do you give a shit if I survive or not!

TITO. Of course —   KIT-KAT. Oh, Mommy, what's wrong!
                                        What did I do? Stop crying —

ANNE. Then support my truth!

TITO. *(Leaving so he won't hit her.)* Excuse me. I've got to check
the roast.

ANNE. Oh, shit. *(Pause.)* Mommy loves you, Baby. Forgive me.

KIT-KAT. For what?

ANNE. I'm grudging my blooming baby her day in the spring sun.
Look how beautiful you are. I'm sorry I missed that darn party.

KIT-KAT. It's all right, Mom.

ANNE. No, it's not all right! I wanted to give you something my
mother never gave me. Trust in yourself. In your body. Listen. You
are beautiful. Your vagina is beautiful.

KIT-KAT. Mom, please, you're embarrassing me.

ANNE. Don't be. Everything you are, everything you feel, is right,
love. Kitty, are you padding that bra — that can't be YOU — is it?
Let Mommy feel — *(Swiping at her.)*

KIT-KAT. No!

ANNE. Listen. I know how it is when you're young and your whole
taut little body is singing the song of sex. Is there anything you'd
like to ask Mommy?

KIT-KAT. I've got to go. Some of the gang is waiting.

ANNE. I want you to never feel ashamed, Baby.

KIT-KAT. I'm not.

ANNE. I love you!

KIT-KAT. I know you do.

ANNE. Mommy wrote a new poem, in the hospital. It's going to be
in *The Atlantic Monthly*. Isn't that exciting?

KIT-KAT. Cool.

ANNE. Don't you want me to read it to you?

KIT-KAT. *(Exiting.)* Yeah, but not right now.

ANNE. All right, my angel. Some other time when you have the time. Jesus. (*Sighs. Reaches for her last cigarette and crumples the empty pack. A silence. Then, as a prayer, or a poem, or something she sees in the curling smoke.*)

Jesus — God — Baby —
What would you do with an old crazy lady —
Can you smooth this piece of worn brown wood —
With your carpenter's hands —
Can you make something out of me?

Anne is finally ready for you, Jesus —
A holy man with holes in his hands —
A man in a white dress with a kind, kind face —
Sweet old ghost that blesses all our adulteries —
'Cause we *are* all adults now, aren't we?
Except I'm not, Jesus, God, Baby —
I'm just little Anne
And I need a Big Kind Daddy to help this old girl home.

Divine Comedy South
A Play in Three Scenes
Romulus Linney

Characters:
HORACE, a farm insurance salesman
MURIEL, a grade school teacher

PART ONE: HELL

Place: A North Carolina beach

Time: A night in June

(*Stars. Surf. Bottle of Jack Daniels, transistor radio, not playing. On a hunting blanket sit* MURIEL *and* HORACE. *Both are in their late forties or early fifties, both very plain people.*)

MURIEL. Give me a drink first.

HORACE. OK. (*He opens the Jack Daniels.*)

MURIEL. I wasn't coming here. You were very persuasive.

HORACE. Well, I'm a salesman.

MURIEL. So am I.

HORACE. I thought you taught school.

MURIEL. Similar. You sell what kind of insurance?

HORACE. Farm, car, home.

MURIEL. Not life?

HORACE. No. (*Pause.*) Where do you live in Fernwell?

MURIEL. Custer Street. 312.

HORACE. Red brick. Early fifties.

MURIEL. How'd you know that?

HORACE. We insure three houses on Custer.

MURIEL. You live on Raymond?

HORACE. 18 North.

MURIEL. Why did you come to my church?

HORACE. To join the choir.

MURIEL. And meet women?

HORACE. I like to sing.

MURIEL. And meet women.

HORACE. Yes.

MURIEL. Do you like the choir at all?

HORACE. Very much.

MURIEL. Me, too.

HORACE. I haven't done it outside in a long time. Have you?

MURIEL. No. Do you know my husband?

HORACE. We weren't going to talk about that.

MURIEL. When I told him you joined the choir, he said, "Oh, sure, Horace. Good man."

HORACE. Ever meet my wife?

MURIEL. Once. We weren't going to talk about that, either.

HORACE. Right.

MURIEL. May I?

HORACE. Please. (*He hands her a bottle of Jack Daniels. She drinks.*)

MURIEL. You do sing well.

HORACE. So do you.

MURIEL. You have perfect pitch. I don't. (*She hands the bottle back.*)

HORACE. Almost. You sing with great feeling.

MURIEL. I love a good choir.

HORACE. So do I.

MURIEL. Where did you go to church as a kid?

HORACE. Buck River Baptist, near Goldsboro. You?

MURIEL. This same one all my life.

HORACE. More?

(MURIEL *takes the bottle, drinks again.*)

MURIEL. I've been married thirty years.

HORACE. Me, too, just about.

MURIEL. I do this more than I should.

HORACE. I know that.

MURIEL. *How* do you know that?

HORACE. Jim and Rebecca Smith.

MURIEL. Oh. Otherwise, I am very discreet.

HORACE. Me, too.

MURIEL. I made a mistake with Jim.

HORACE. I made a mistake with Rebecca. (*Pause.*) Lot of folks don't have flings, at all.

MURIEL. No, they don't.

HORACE. They stay together. They think about it, but don't do it.

MURIEL. We do.

HORACE. Yes, we do. (*He reaches for her.*)

MURIEL. Wait. I want to think about this.

HORACE. OK.

MURIEL. I don't know you at all.

HORACE. OK.

MURIEL. Let's talk first.

HORACE. OK. How about the first time?

MURIEL. First time what?

HORACE. You did this.

MURIEL. Oh, please!

HORACE. If we have to talk, might as well be about something interesting. Have another drink.

(*She does.*)

MURIEL. Ormond Beach, Florida. A year after I was married. I loved my husband, but there I was, in a very strange man's bedroom. He had three walls of his bedroom lined with fishtanks.

HORACE. You mean aquariums?

MURIEL. Bigger.

HORACE. OK.

MURIEL. When he turned off the bedroom lights, to undress me, all those fishtanks lit up.

HORACE. Really.

MURIEL. From within. In many colors, pink, purple. Neon globes, tiny crystal rainbows.

HORACE. Any fish?

MURIEL. Hanging there, gaping at us.

HORACE. Really.

MURIEL. In bed, kissing, embracing, he kept looking at them.

HORACE. The fish.

MURIEL. The thrill of adultery. One fish was some big white flat thing, the size of your hand. Transparent, like a ghost. It turned black.

HORACE. What?

MURIEL. Puffed itself up, doubled its size and turned black! Honest!

HORACE. Watching you? Please.

MURIEL. It happened.

209

HORACE. What did this strange man do for a living?

MURIEL. Well, Horace. He sold insurance.

HORACE. When?

MURIEL. Many years ago. Never mind his name.

HORACE. OK.

MURIEL. I don't know why I told you that story. Yes, I do. Give me a drink and tell me one.

HORACE. About what?

MURIEL. Your flings. Your fast, furious and disgraceful rummaging through the old clothes of other women's bodies.

HORACE. Not if you put it like that!

MURIEL. Talk. I did.

HORACE. Well, there was that polar bear.

MURIEL. Polar bear?

HORACE. Well, fish, polar bear. I read a novel about a woman who did that.

MURIEL. Impossible.

HORACE. A woman and a bear alone in north Canada. Beautifully written, got a prize.

MURIEL. I don't believe it. What happened?

HORACE. They couldn't do it. They liked each other and they tried, but it was impossible and they couldn't do it.

MURIEL. So?

HORACE. It was sad.

MURIEL. Wait a minute.

HORACE. The poor bear just went away.

MURIEL. Have you ever had sex with an animal?

HORACE. Of course not.

MURIEL. Sheep? Men do. Chickens?

HORACE. Chickens?

MURIEL. I read where Turkish farmers take a chicken and an old dresser drawer. They screw the chicken with its neck in a half-open dresser drawer. When they ejaculate, they slam the drawer, decapitate the chicken, mixing sperm and blood in a flopping death spasm. Have you ever done anything like that?

HORACE. Really.

MURIEL. I bet you have.

HORACE. I have not!

MURIEL. Horace!

HORACE. Well, sort of!

MURIEL. I knew it.

(*Pause. Drinks.*)

HORACE. I am living in Winston-Salem, married for the first time, about a month.

MURIEL. How many wives have you had?

HORACE. Two. This wife has a friend. One afternoon they go shopping, leaving her friendly dog with me. We are watching television together —

MURIEL. Dogs don't watch television.

HORACE. I'm watching television. The dog is watching me.

MURIEL. All right.

HORACE. Well.

MURIEL. What do you mean, well?

HORACE. I get seduced.

MURIEL. By the dog?

HORACE. Yep.

MURIEL. Tell me how.

HORACE. No. A week later, I arrive at my wife's friend's apartment, to have supper and go to bed with her.

211

MURIEL. I'm getting confused. You're seduced by this dog — no telling me how exactly — then you seduce her mistress?

HORACE. The dog's name is Brian.

MURIEL. Brian?

HORACE. Dachshund. Clumsy, energetic, sexy, German.

MURIEL. A male German dachshund.

HORACE. Right.

MURIEL. This is a homosexual encounter.

HORACE. Yes.

MURIEL. All right. (*Pause.*) Then how —

HORACE. Dachshunds have tongues.

MURIEL. Oh!

HORACE. Yep.

MURIEL. At the apartment?

HORACE. When we go into the bedroom, she says, "Be right back, Brian." An hour later, we come out, there sits Brian. He hasn't moved. She pats him on the head, makes him a Gainesburger. She doesn't see what I see in his eyes.

MURIEL. What?

HORACE. Reproach.

MURIEL. For what?

HORACE. Treachery.

MURIEL. What?

HORACE. I pat Brian on the head. He looks at me with cold revulsion. I am guilty.

MURIEL. Sex doesn't bother dogs. Grown men and women, I guess all the time, but not dogs. This isn't what I meant. Animals and sex, I think of exotic orgies and bestial group couplings, I don't know, like —

HORACE. Goats?

MURIEL. That's the idea.

HORACE. Parrots? Anteaters? When I was in the Army there was this sergeant major who told me about this convent in Spain? The sisters take a sort of Spanish wood ant, put some honey on themselves and —

MURIEL. Stop!

HORACE. You started this!

MURIEL. I did not!!

HORACE. Those fish?

MURIEL. The fish weren't the point, adultery was! What was the point with the dog?

HORACE. The same!

MURIEL. It couldn't be!!

HORACE. Brian, the dog, possessed a moral sense. We didn't.

MURIEL. You're crazy.

HORACE. Fido? Fidelity? His disloyalty, mine, hers? It was in his eyes. Animal shame, and animal dignity.

MURIEL. You felt yourself sexually reproached by a moral dachshund.

HORACE. That's right.

MURIEL. You're a lunatic. Polar bears and dogs?

HORACE. Fish and chickens and dresser drawers?

MURIEL. Nuns and wood ants! (*Pause.*) Oh, God.

HORACE. What?

MURIEL. Never mind!

HORACE. What?

MURIEL. Forget it.

HORACE. Come on!

MURIEL. Did a woman ever want to kill herself over you?

HORACE. When a woman says she wants to kill herself for a man, what she usually means is, she wants a man to kill himself for her.

MURIEL. That's cynical and that's French. German dogs and French cynicism. Jesus Christ. (*Pause.*) Oh, dear.

HORACE. What?

MURIEL. Nothing.

HORACE. You can do it.

MURIEL. Norwood Struther. Nicknamed Squeaky.

HORACE. What about him?

MURIEL. I'm not going to tell you.

HORACE. Yes, you are.

MURIEL. There was a woman who wanted to kill herself over you.

HORACE. My second wife.

MURIEL. The one you're still married to?

HORACE. Yes.

MURIEL. I don't want to hear this.

HORACE. Suit yourself.

MURIEL. What about her?

HORACE. She works for Southern Bell. Mother of three.

MURIEL. Your children?

HORACE. Yes. In 1964, she was a go-go dancer in a Baltimore strip joint. I was just out of the Army, passing through. I hung around. She got pregnant. I gave her four hundred dollars and left town.

MURIEL. That's when she said she'd kill herself?

HORACE. Yes. I forgot about her. I came back South. Freedom. One day she appeared at my doorstep, with a little boy. "Your son," she said. I took one look at him. He was mine. We got married.

MURIEL. Happy ending.

HORACE. Yes, except a year later, while she carried our second child, on the road, well, another woman. What was I supposed to do at a motel in Columbus, Ohio, read the Bible?

MURIEL. You could have done worse. It bothers you, what you do in motels?

HORACE. Yes.

MURIEL. Why don't you just stop it?

HORACE. Why don't you?

MURIEL. Jack Daniels, please. (HORACE *hands her the bottle. It goes back and forth.*) Suicide is more anger than sorrow.

HORACE. I have heard that.

MURIEL. I met Norwood Struther at a country club in Kitty Hawk called The Dunes. It went out of business, of course, without a golf course but that afternoon it opened, and my husband and I, we came from Elizabeth City to a party in the bar and he left me there.

HORACE. What for?

MURIEL. Work. He's very successful.

HORACE. I know he is.

MURIEL. He handed me a drink, kissed me and said, "Enjoy yourself," and was gone talking to a damned client. So there I was. Five o'clock on a Saturday afternoon, smiling at everyone, bored beyond description. Norwood Struther wore a blue linen blazer, a red and yellow tie, silly and snappy. He didn't say a word. Men liked him, slapped him on the back, called him Squeaky, kidded him about being a bachelor, fondly, but with some kind of something else about it, I couldn't tell what. Well, I was so sick and frustrated with my husband, mad at the world and my utterly asinine position at the country club, hello, there, Norwood, you squeaky bachelor, how are you, say something, and he did. He did have this stutter and high weird voice. I was desperate. "Bartender, tell my husband I've gone to the movies," and I was in Squeaky's bedroom in half an hour. He lived on the beach. We could hear the surf roaring and pounding. It took him ages to touch me. He was choking, face red as a lobster, mortified, in

215

his own home, in his own bed. He had a very small sexual organ. Tiny.

HORACE. Oh.

MURIEL. He tried to apologize. I hugged him and kissed him and said it didn't matter. Norwood wouldn't talk to me afterwards. Mumbled something I couldn't understand, stuck his head under a pillow. I had betrayed my husband — again — this time with a poor pitiful wretch lying next to me in misery. Outside on the beach, we could hear the surf pounding. The sea, powerful and potent, teeming with cruelty and life. There was moonlight, beautiful, gorgeous, ravishing, and me and Norwood. And my husband, off making money.

HORACE. We have to, you know.

MURIEL. I know. And you?

HORACE. And me what?

MURIEL. The first time you betrayed your wife.

HORACE. Which wife?

MURIEL. The one you're married to now!

HORACE. I told you.

MURIEL. Not in detail.

HORACE. Oh, that was ordinary. Later, there was this school-teacher. Very nice and proper.

MURIEL. Like me.

HORACE. Is that what you do?

MURIEL. I told you I teach school. You don't remember anything about me.

HORACE. Sorry. This — other schoolteacher and I — were in New York. I was at a convention, met her at a bar near her place. She took me home. I left about eleven. Three o'clock that morning, phone rings at my motel. She sounds terrible. Help, help. So I go back to her place and she is looking at me like I'm a demon from hell. "What's the matter?" "Did you call me on the phone?" "When?" "Last night, after you went home." "No." "You swear?"

"I swear." "Oh, my God, my God!" "What happened?" "What a
fool I am! What a *fool* I am!" *"What happened?"* "Well," she said,
"about eleven o'clock a man whose voice sounded like yours,
with that Southern accent, called me. You, I thought it was you,
said you had a way of making us both some money but you
needed two hundred dollars first, and couldn't get it since you
were out of town and would I lend it to you. Oh, I had such a
good time with you, I liked you so much, I could still feel you
inside me, so whether it was true or not I said yes, I have that,
come get it. You said, no, you wanted me to meet a man and
give it to him, with whatever else he asked for." "What?" I said.
"You told me to go to a children's playground off Central Park
West at midnight, and just sit in a swing and wait. You hoped I
would do this for you. I was speechless, and God help me, excited. I got the money and went. There were shadows of people
at the playground, coming and going in darkness, there for sex.
I was frightened and terribly alive. He was wearing a cowboy
hat. When he came up to me and I saw it wasn't you, I was
thrilled. . . . I gave him two hundred dollars and he opened his
pants and I knelt down and gave him sex. He thanked me and
was gone, leaving me there on my knees. I felt — I don't know —
delivered and debased. Then I thought, was that really like you?
What if it wasn't you who called me? Was it? Oh, tell me the
truth! We did meet in a bar but you were decent, weren't you?
You wouldn't do that to me, would you? But who else could
have? Nobody knew about us. It has to be you!" "No it doesn't,"
I said. "It could be somebody in the bar." "Oh," she said. "But I
don't go there often. I don't!" "Some, though?" "Yes, some." She
thought a minute. "That man could have heard us, heard I was
taking you home." "Right." "But that means it was somebody
who knows me, my phone number and everything." "That's the
only other possibility." "Oh, God," she said. "I don't know what
to believe. Was it some man who's been watching me in that
bar? Or was it you? Who did that to me?"

MURIEL. Do you expect me to believe this?

HORACE. It's true.

MURIEL. *Was* it you? You sent some man from that convention
to do that to her for two hundred dollars?

217

HORACE. No.

MURIEL. Then who did?

HORACE. She didn't know.

MURIEL. It was you.

HORACE. That's probable. But it wasn't.

MURIEL. It was.

HORACE. Did you keep up with Norwood?

MURIEL. I read about him, in the newspaper. In that beach house, with majestic surf and the ravishing moonlight, about a year later, with two big pistols, one at each side of his head, both at once. Paper said there was nothing left of his head but the top of his neck.

HORACE. Two years later?

MURIEL. Well, about.

HORACE. It was the day afterwards.

MURIEL. A week.

HORACE. I stole her money. You laughed at him. Is that it?

MURIEL. Both are probable.

HORACE. Both are.

MURIEL. God!

HORACE. Why are we here?

MURIEL. We just are.

HORACE. We want to be here.

MURIEL. We have to be here.

HORACE. Maybe it's the moon.

MURIEL. Or those stars. I'm shaking.

HORACE. I don't feel very good either.

MURIEL. Let's pull overselves together.

HORACE. If we can.

MURIEL. I'm really upset.

HORACE. Me, too.

MURIEL. I need a minute.

HORACE. OK.

MURIEL. Play something on that radio.

HORACE. Right. (*He turns on the transistor radio. Dials past rock music, talk show, finds a hymn: "Rock of Ages."*)

Rock of ages, cleft for me,
Let me hide myself in thee.

(HORACE *starts to dial past it.*)

MURIEL. Let's hear that.

HORACE. OK.

Let the water and the blood
From thy riven side which flowed —

MURIEL. Yes, I do want to be here.

Be of sin the double cure
Cleanse me from its guilt and power.
Not the labors of my hands
Can fulfill thy law's demands,
Could my zeal no respite know —
Could my tears forever flow —

MURIEL. So do you!

All for sin could not atone,
Thou must save and thou alone.
While I draw this fleeting breath,
While my eyelids close in death —

HORACE. Be quiet!

When I soar to worlds unknown,
See thee on thy judgement throne —
Rock of ages cleft for me
Let me hide myself in thee.

(HORACE *turns off the radio.*)

219

Romulus Linney

HORACE. Those stars.

MURIEL. They're so bright.

HORACE. And hard.

MURIEL. And cold.

HORACE. And still.

MURIEL. And they never change.

HORACE. And they never will.

> (HORACE *suddenly holds out his arms to* MURIEL, *who embraces him fiercely. They begin to make passionate love.*)

You Belong to Me
Keith Reddin

Characters:
JOYCE
GEORGETTE
LARRY
TED

(*A bar. Early evening.* JOYCE *and* GEORGETTE.)

JOYCE. Where'd you find this place?

GEORGETTE. See the jukebox?

JOYCE. Yeah.

GEORGETTE. All Patsy Cline.

JOYCE. The whole jukebox.

GEORGETTE. Just Patsy Cline.

JOYCE. Huh.

GEORGETTE. So how long ago did you kill him?

JOYCE. About half an hour.

GEORGETTE. OK. So good. So where's . . .

JOYCE. On the kitchen floor. With a cleaver sticking out of his head.

GEORGETTE. You wipe off the fingerprints?

JOYCE. Just like you told me.

GEORGETTE. So good. You want another drink?

JOYCE. How do I get away with this?

GEORGETTE. Unless you alert the media, you're okay.

221

JOYCE. There was so much blood.

GEORGETTE. Well there would be, wouldn't there. They make good margaritas here.

JOYCE. Very good.

GEORGETTE. Now listen to me, you listening?

JOYCE. Yes.

GEORGETTE. You and I are gonna sit here. We're gonna take my car, I'm gonna drive you home, we both . . . no okay wait, here's what we do. I drive you, on the way we go off the road, we hit some, have this accident, not a bad accident, but you know serious enough, they call an . . .

JOYCE. Who?

GEORGETTE. What?

JOYCE. Who calls?

GEORGETTE. Whoever. Some passing motorist. Somebody.

JOYCE. People don't stop for accidents.

GEORGETTE. Joyce, please, somebody will call an ambulance. They take us to the hospital. We wake up, we see the police are in the room. You go, what's going on? One moment you're having a drink with your friend and the cop says, I have terrible news, I'm sorry to tell you, we found your husband murdered. Lying on the kitchen floor we found Larry dead with a . . .

JOYCE. Meat cleaver.

GEORGETTE. Meat cleaver sticking out of his head.

JOYCE. Who called the police?

GEORGETTE. I don't know.

JOYCE. There's too many people calling other people. We can't get away with this.

GEORGETTE. Who's this we? I didn't kill him.

JOYCE. But you're aiding and abetting.

GEORGETTE. After the fact.

JOYCE. My alibi is that I was out drinking with you?

GEORGETTE. At least I'm coming up with something.

JOYCE. I would never get away with it.

(LARRY *enters.*)

LARRY. Sorry that call took so long.

(*He looks at them.* JOYCE *and* GEORGETTE *look at each other.*)

What? What did I miss?

GEORGETTE. Nothing, Larry. Nothing at all.

(*Lights fade.*)

(*The living room.* LARRY *and* JOYCE. LARRY *reading a news-paper.*)

LARRY. Huh.

JOYCE. What?

LARRY. That property on Wilshire is on sale. (*Goes back to reading paper.*)

JOYCE. Larry . . .

LARRY. Yeah?

JOYCE. You ever think about killing me?

LARRY. What?

JOYCE. I mean did you ever imagine killing me?

LARRY. No.

JOYCE. You ever think of how you would kill a person?

LARRY. You thinking of killing me? (*Pause.*)

JOYCE. No. (*Pause.*)

LARRY. You're talking about like after we have a big fight or some-thing. Like that?

JOYCE. Yes.

LARRY. No, I can't say that I have. (*Thinks.*) Uh no.

223

JOYCE. Not ever?

LARRY. (*Smiling.*) No, Joyce. Why would I want to kill you?

JOYCE. I mean imagining. Like if I took out a gun. (*She takes out a gun.*)

LARRY. Uh huh.

JOYCE. And I pointed it at you?

LARRY. Hey where'd you get that gun, Joyce?

JOYCE. You know, we're so close, it'd be kind of impossible to miss you.

LARRY. Is that a real gun?

JOYCE. It's loaded, I checked right after dinner.

LARRY. Okay, I don't get the joke, Joyce.

JOYCE. I want you to beg me not to kill you.

LARRY. Are you still mad at me about yelling at you about the American Express bill, is that what this is about?

JOYCE. Come on Lar, beg me. Beg for your life.

LARRY. I wasn't really mad.

JOYCE. I want you to crawl on your belly and say, don't kill me, Joyce. Come on, crawl.

LARRY. Okay, you don't have to pick me up after squash this week, I'll get Ted to drive.

JOYCE. Oooh, this gun is getting heavy. It's getting so heavy, Larry, I might have to make it lighter by emptying a few bullets out of it.

LARRY. Joyce . . .

JOYCE. Shut up, just shut your face.

LARRY. Joyce, stop this. Put the gun down. You don't want to shoot anybody.

JOYCE. Where'd you get that line, Larry, some repeat of *T. J. Hooker?*

LARRY. I'm your husband.

JOYCE. I bet you wish it was you holding the gun right now. You wish you had me in your sights, just a little pressure on the trigger and you blow me into next week. (*She starts waving the gun.*) Come on, start crawling.

LARRY. NO.

JOYCE. I'm serious.

LARRY. I'm not going to crawl.

JOYCE. NOW!

LARRY. I don't think you can really do it.

JOYCE. Oh no?

LARRY. I don't think so. Nope. (*Goes back to reading the paper.*)

JOYCE. Put that paper down.

LARRY. I haven't finished.

JOYCE. I said . . .

LARRY. I heard you.

JOYCE. Okay, you are dead.

> (*She fires the gun at* LARRY. *Pause. Then* JOYCE *sits and puts the gun away.* LARRY *lowers the newspaper.*)

LARRY. Anything the matter?

JOYCE. What?

LARRY. You got all quiet.

JOYCE. I was just thinking. (*Pause.*)

LARRY. I love you, Joyce.

JOYCE. I know.

LARRY. And? And?

JOYCE. (*Softly.*) I love you too.

> (LARRY *smiles. Lights fade.*)

> (*The bar.* GEORGETTE *and* JOYCE.)

JOYCE. The whole jukebox?

GEORGETTE. Just Patsy Cline.

> (LARRY *enters.*)

LARRY. Sorry that call took so long.

> (*He looks at* JOYCE *and* GEORGETTE.)

  What? What did I miss?

GEORGETTE. Nothing, Larry. Nothing at all.

LARRY. Ted had to change the squash time again.

JOYCE. Should we order another?

GEORGETTE. Let's go for it.

LARRY. Sure.

JOYCE. I'll be right back.

> (*She leaves. A beat.*)

GEORGETTE. I want to fuck you right now.

LARRY. Georgette.

GEORGETTE. Right now. Right on this table.

LARRY. Stop this.

GEORGETTE. I can't keep going on like this.

LARRY. What do you want me to say?

GEORGETTE. Say you'll do it. Like we planned. Say you'll kill her.

LARRY. I can't.

GEORGETTE. If you want me you have to do it. (*Takes a gun out.*) Here. Use this.

LARRY. Would you put that away.

GEORGETTE. I even got you a gun.

LARRY. People can see . . .

GEORGETTE. It's her or me, Larry, make up your mind.

LARRY. Georgette . . . you know how I feel.

GEORGETTE. Then take the gun and ice her.

LARRY. Ice her?

GEORGETTE. Take the gun. You know this is right. Otherwise you're living a lie. You've wanted to for years. So have I. All those years of pretending I was her friend. Listening to her boring stories. Looking at her disgusting haircut. I swear if you can't I will. I won't share you with her. You're mine for ever and ever. We're so close to making the dream come true. Take the gun. Take it. (*Pause.*)

LARRY. All right. (*He takes the gun.*)

(JOYCE *comes back with drinks.*)

JOYCE. What do we drink to?

GEORGETTE. Long life?

LARRY. To long life.

(*They drink.*)

JOYCE. You know, Larry, I've got to tell you. While you were on the phone before . . .

LARRY. Yeah?

JOYCE. I was thinking . . .

LARRY. What?

JOYCE. I imagined I'd killed you.

LARRY. Get out of here.

JOYCE. It's true. I imagined I was sitting here and you were dead. In the kitchen.

LARRY. How'd you do it?

JOYCE. With a meat cleaver.

LARRY. Ouch.

JOYCE. I was just joking around.

LARRY. I see. Well I'm not sure I find the joke so funny.

JOYCE. I shouldn't have told you.

LARRY. And you had no problem imagining me dead?

JOYCE. No.

LARRY. Did I put up some sort of a fight?

JOYCE. No, I got you when your back was turned.

LARRY. Meat cleaver, huh? Kind of messy.

GEORGETTE. Maybe you should have used a gun.

JOYCE. We don't have a gun.

GEORGETTE. You do have a meat cleaver.

JOYCE. And that's what I imagined I used.

GEORGETTE. I would have used a gun. Wouldn't you use a gun, Larry?

LARRY. I guess I would.

GEORGETTE. See Larry would have used a gun. Show her the gun, Larry.

JOYCE. What?

GEORGETTE. I gave Larry a gun.

JOYCE. You did?

GEORGETTE. Show her the gun.

LARRY. *(Takes out the gun.)* Here.

JOYCE. Why does . . . why did you give him a gun?

GEORGETTE. To kill you.

JOYCE. What are you talking about?

LARRY. The gun is to kill you. I'm going to kill you on the drive home. I'm going to pull over and shoot you and throw your body into a ditch and then Georgette and I can fuck our brains out.

GEORGETTE. That's it.

JOYCE. What about Jerry?

GEORGETTE. I'm going to kill Jerry. Larry will kill you. That was the deal.

JOYCE. No.

GEORGETTE. We've wanted this for a long time.

LARRY. So I'll settle up the tab and then I'll shoot you, Joyce.

JOYCE. But . . . why?

GEORGETTE. Tell her, Larry.

LARRY. Because we both hate your guts. And because you really bother me when I'm reading the paper.

JOYCE. I won't anymore.

LARRY. Too late. Say goodbye to Georgette. . . .

JOYCE. But . . .

GEORGETTE. Goodbye, Joyce.

JOYCE. But you love me, Larry. You know you do.

LARRY. Don't make it any harder. Let's go. (*Pulls her away from the table.*)

JOYCE. I haven't finished my drink yet . . .

GEORGETTE. Do it quick, Larry. I'll be waiting. I'll play some Patsy Cline on the jukebox and think of you shooting her in the head and then kicking her body into a ditch.

LARRY. I won't be long.

JOYCE. Wait . . . please . . .

LARRY. Don't beg, Joyce. Just get in the car. I promise it won't hurt. Much. (*He laughs.*) Ahahaha.

JOYCE. I thought you were my friend.

GEORGETTE. Bad call.

(LARRY *pulls* JOYCE *off.*)

GEORGETTE. Thank you, Larry.

(*Lights fade.*)

(*Lights up on the living room.* LARRY *in armchair reading paper.* JOYCE *sits in another chair.*)

LARRY. Huh.

JOYCE. What?

LARRY. Another interest rate hike.

JOYCE. Ah.

> (LARRY *lowers the paper.*)

LARRY. You know what to do when she gets here.

JOYCE. Of course, Larry.

LARRY. Just checking.

JOYCE. I still think poison is a bad idea.

LARRY. I don't know, it has a certain something . . .

JOYCE. A certain what?

LARRY. It's classy.

JOYCE. You think it's classy.

LARRY. Guns are so messy. Blood all over the walls and the carpet.

> (*Doorbell.*)

JOYCE. Okay, I'm going to get the door.

LARRY. Act natural.

JOYCE. I always do, Larry.

> (*She exits.* LARRY *pretends to read paper,* JOYCE *and* GEORGETTE *enter.*)

JOYCE. Look who's here, Larry.

> (LARRY *lowers the paper.*)

LARRY. Oh hi, Georgette, how are you?

GEORGETTE. Doing fine, Larry.

LARRY. That's good. Can I get you something to drink?

JOYCE. Georgette just got here.

LARRY. I was just being polite. Being a good host. You weren't offended, were you?

GEORGETTE. No. Although I should tell you I have stopped drinking.

JOYCE AND LARRY. You have?

GEORGETTE. Yes, I found I was drinking too much. I would get home from work and the first thing I did was walk in the door, walk straight to the liquor cabinet and pour myself a stiff drink. Then I would have about three or four more before dinner. A couple of times I had a few too many drinks and would pass out and the next thing I knew it was the next morning and Jerry would be shaking me awake and telling me it was time to wake up and get ready for work.

JOYCE. Wow.

GEORGETTE. Jerry would find me lying on the floor and at first he thought I was only pretending to be asleep, he thought it was some sort of game, Jerry and I sometimes pretend that . . . anyway he would gradually realize that I wasn't playing around, that I was actually passed out and he would put me on the couch and make dinner and finally he would go to bed. And it got to the point where we decided maybe I needed some help with this problem and I agreed he was right because I would never want the kids to see me like that and then Jerry reminded me that we don't have kids and I remembered that and said IF we ever had kids I would never want them to find their mother like that and so I've stopped drinking.

LARRY. How about a cranberry juice then?

GEORGETTE. No thank you.

JOYCE. Some coffee? Just made a fresh pot.

GEORGETTE. No, I can't really drink coffee this late, keeps me up all night.

LARRY. Herbal tea then?

GEORGETTE. No, I'm fine.

JOYCE. Mineral water? Diet Coke?

GEORGETTE. Nope.

LARRY. You really don't want anything to drink? Nothing?

GEORGETTE. No thanks.

JOYCE. Come on, how about some fresh-squeezed orange juice?

GEORGETTE. No.

LARRY. Tap water?

GEORGETTE. I'm not thirsty.

JOYCE. But you might get thirsty later. I'll just get you a glass of . . .

GEORGETTE. Hey I don't want anything to drink. Nothing. No liquids.

    (Pause.)

LARRY. Okay. Got it.

GEORGETTE. Look, maybe I better be going . . .

LARRY. Stay a minute, there's someting I wanted to talk to you about?

JOYCE. There is?

LARRY. Yes, Joyce I wanted to tell Georgette about that thing while you go into the kitchen and bring out those cookies you baked.

JOYCE. Right, the *thing*. Georgette, there's this *thing* Larry wanted to tell you.

GEORGETTE. Joyce, I'm not really hungry.

JOYCE. You are going to have one of my fucking cookies and that's it so sit there and shut up and listen to Larry. Make sure she doesn't go anywhere. (JOYCE *exits.*)

LARRY. Those cookies are great. We really want you to have one.

    (Pause.)

GEORGETTE. So, Larry, what did you want to talk about?

LARRY. Yeah, the thing I wanted to tell you. *(Rattle off in kitchen.)* Now you remember that little deal, that stock option thing you and Jerry got involved in? *(Banging of pots and pans off in kitchen.)*

GEORGETTE. The insider trading thing, Larry?

232

LARRY. If you want to put it in those terms, the information I gave you about the . . . Well, we all profited quite nicely from that little transaction.

GEORGETTE. Yes, we did.

LARRY. And we found out that there's going to be an investigation of that . . . you know . . .

GEORGETTE. Illegal insider trading move.

LARRY. I'd like to use the term preemptive nonloss of funds transaction.

GEORGETTE. So what, the SEC is looking into that deal?

LARRY. Yes they are. And I've already spoken to Jerry and he's happy to keep quiet about it. In fact he's fine with lying to the commission if necessary. But he says that there might be a problem with you.

GEORGETTE. Me?

LARRY. He told me that you've had this attack of conscience or something, that you kind of feel guilty about making all that money the way we did, maybe that had something to do with why you were drinking so much, and, well, the bottom line is we are all concerned, Jerry, Joyce and myself, we're concerned if you're gonna play ball with us on this.

GEORGETTE. Play ball?

LARRY. If you're on our team or not.

GEORGETTE. What we did was illegal, Larry.

LARRY. That's a very subjective response that I'm not financially at liberty to accept right now.

GEORGETTE. But it was wrong.

LARRY. Maybe to the losers who didn't make money on the merger it could be construed as morally bankrupt but to the rest of us who profited by it, including yourself, to the tune of that new car and the addition onto your house, it was a good thing.

GEORGETTE. You want me to lie about what I know about the illegal insider trading thing?

LARRY. If asked.

GEORGETTE. Well, I have to be honest and tell you I have a problem with that.

LARRY. (*Yelling into the kitchen.*) Honey?

(JOYCE *enters with plate of cookies.*)

JOYCE. Here we are, chocolate chip cookies.

LARRY. We want you to try one.

JOYCE. Go ahead. (JOYCE *offers plate,* GEORGETTE *takes one.*)

GEORGETTE. Aren't you two going to have any?

LARRY. We already ate a whole batch.

JOYCE. We're stuffed.

LARRY. But you go ahead.

GEORGETTE. No, I . . .

LARRY. Have a cookie.

JOYCE. *NOW.* (*Pause.*)

GEORGETTE. Just one. (*She bites into the cookie,* JOYCE *and* LARRY *watch intently.*)

LARRY. Pretty good, huh?

GEORGETTE. Yes.

JOYCE. THEN EAT THE WHOLE THING! EAT IT! EAT THE FUCKING COOKIE!

GEORGETTE. Okay. (*She eats the cookie.*) Thank you.

LARRY. She ate the whole thing, Joyce.

JOYCE. Yes she did. Have another. Now. (GEORGETTE *does.*)

GEORGETTE. That was . . . whoa, I feel a little . . .

LARRY. What? You feel what?

JOYCE. (*Very insincere.*) Are you okay, Georgette? Would you like to sit down?

GEORGETTE. Maybe I should. . . . (*She goes toward the chair.*) . . . Gosh, the room is spinning. . . .

JOYCE. I wonder what the matter is?

LARRY. Maybe she's sick

JOYCE. Maybe she's going to die.

GEORGETTE. What?

LARRY. Yeah, MAYBE SHE'S GOING TO DIE.

GEORGETTE. Wait a second . . .

JOYCE. Die, Georgette, die.

LARRY. Die, bitch.

(LARRY *and* JOYCE *laugh.*)

LARRY AND JOYCE. Ahahahaha.

GEORGETTE. What's happening?

LARRY. Bet you thought we'd never do a thing like this.

JOYCE. Bet you thought we weren't capable.

LARRY. Bet you thought we didn't have the guts.

GEORGETTE. I'm your friend!

LARRY AND JOYCE. Bad call.

(*Lights fade.*)

(*The bar.* JOYCE, GEORGETTE *and* LARRY.)

LARRY. Ted had to change his squash time again.

JOYCE. Should we order another?

GEORGETTE. Let's go for it.

LARRY. Sure.

GEORGETTE. I'll be right back. (*She leaves.*)

LARRY. I didn't want to tell you in front of Georgette.

JOYCE. What?

LARRY. It's about Ted.

JOYCE. About your squash game?

LARRY. No, I just made that up. Ted's wife left.

JOYCE. Where'd she go? To the mall for a white sale?

LARRY. No, Joyce, she left him. For good.

JOYCE. Beth left Ted?

LARRY. That's what he told me over the phone. He gets home from work, there's a note. He goes into the bedroom, her half of the closet is cleared out.

JOYCE. God.

LARRY. I told him to come over.

JOYCE. What, here? You told Ted to come here? Larry . . .

LARRY. His wife just left him, he's destroyed, Joyce. I told him to come over, have a few drinks, we'd listen to . . .

JOYCE. Oh Christ, just the way I want to spend my . . .

LARRY. He is my squash partner.

(GEORGETTE *reenters with drinks.*)

GEORGETTE. Here we go. What happened? What'd I miss?

LARRY. Nothing.

JOYCE. Everything's fine.

GEORGETTE. Come on, cheer up, people.

JOYCE. You're right.

LARRY. What do we drink to?

(TED *runs in.*)

TED. I'll kill her. I swear if I ever find her, and I will, I will find her, no matter where she's gone, I don't care if she's moved to the fucking South Pole, I will track her down and I will kill her, I will get a gun and shoot her or I'll stab her, or better yet I'll strangle her, I'll put my hands around her scrawny neck and squeeze the life out of her, or no no I'll stab her, I'll stab her in the microscopic muscle she calls her heart, I'll stab some butcher knife into the middle of her chest, let her bleed to death, then

236

I'll sit in some bar with a friend and have a drink and pretend like nothing's happened, the whole time her blood is pouring out of her, I'll be sitting in a bar like this and laughing, how could she do this, how could she pack her bags, leave some note and leave me, I'll poison her, I'll find her and tell her I just wanted her to know I understand why she had to do this, I'll say we can still be friends and then I'll say let's have one last drink and part friends, but all the time I'll be waiting for her to down her drink, which I mixed with poison, and then I'll watch her gag and shake and fall on the floor and I'll watch her die, I'll watch her look up at me and with her last breath ask why? Why did you do that? And I'll say because you can't leave me, nobody leaves me, you're mine, you understand, you belong to me, you're mine, how dare you leave me, you left and for that you have to die and I get to watch you die. So there's your answer. What's everybody drinking?

JOYCE. Margarita.

LARRY. Gin and tonic.

GEORGETTE. I was doing margaritas, but I think I'd like a scotch.

TED. Okay, round's on me. Mind if I play a little Patsy Cline? (TED *exits.*)

JOYCE. I don't think he's taking this well.

LARRY. He was crying on the phone.

GEORGETTE. Well, he had the car ride over here to get mad.

JOYCE. He is really mad.

LARRY. Yeah, I'd say he was really mad.

GEORGETTE. But to say he would kill her . . .

LARRY. He's not thinking right now.

JOYCE. He's overreacting.

GEORGETTE. I mean, that's not the solution.

JOYCE. No.

LARRY. No, violence doesn't solve anything.

GEORGETTE. I don't know the whole story, but I think we should make sure he cools down, doesn't do anything rash.

JOYCE. I agree.

LARRY. He's not thinking rationally.

JOYCE. He's not.

GEORGETTE. No he's not. . . .

> *(They look at one another and drink in silence. Lights fade as we hear Patsy Cline singing "You Belong to Me.")*

The Adoption
Joyce Carol Oates

Characters:
MR., a Caucasian man in his late thirties or early forties
MRS., a Caucasian woman of about the same age
X, male or female, of any mature age
NABBO, a child
NADBO, a "twin" of NABBO

(Setting: An adoption agency office. Sterile surroundings, merely functional furnishings. Prominent on the wall facing the audience is a large clock with a minute hand of the kind that visibly "jumps" from minute to minute. At the start, the clock measures real time; by subtle degrees, it begins to accelerate.

Time: The present.

Lights up. We have been hearing bright, cheery music ("It's a Lovely Day Today"), which now subsides. MR. and MRS. are seated side by side, gripping hands; they appear excited and apprehensive. They are conventionally well-dressed, as if for church, and do indeed exude a churchy aura. MR. has brought a briefcase; MRS., a "good" purse. A large bag (containing children's toys) close by.

To the left of MR. and MRS. is a door in the wall; to the right, behind them, is the clock. With lights up the clock begins its ticking, the time at 11:00.)

MRS. I'm so excited — *frightened!*

MR. It's the day we've been waiting for — I'm sure.

MRS. Oh, do you *think* — ? I don't dare to hope.

239

MR. They *were* encouraging, last time —

MRS. Yes, they were!

MR. They wouldn't send us away empty-handed again — would they?

MRS. Well, they did last time, and the time before last —

MR. But this *is* going to be different, I'm sure. They *hinted* —

MRS. No, they all but *said — promised —*

MR. — um, not a *promise* exactly, but —

MRS. It was, it was a promise! — almost. In all but words.

MR. Yes. They *hinted* — today is the day.

MRS. (*On her feet, too excited to remain seated.*) The day we've been awaiting — for so long!

MR. (*On his feet.*) So long!

MRS. I feel like a, a bride again! A — virgin! (*Giggles.*)

MR. (*Touching or embracing her.*) You *look* like a *madonna.*

MRS. It's a, a — delivery —

MR. (*Subtle correction.*) A *deliverance.*

MRS. (*Euphoric, intense.*) We can't just live for ourselves alone. A woman, a man —

MR. (*Emphatically.*) That's selfish.

MRS. That's — unnatural.

MR. Lonely.

MRS. (*Wistfully.*) So lonely.

MR. A home without —

MRS. — children —

MR. — is *empty.*

MRS. Not what you'd call a "home" —

MR. But we have means, we can afford to "extend our boundaries."

MRS. Thank God! (*Eyes uplifted, sincerely.*)

MR. (*Glance upward.*) Yes, indeed — thank you, God. (*Pause.*) Of course, um — we're not millionaires. Just, um — comfortable."

MRS. — "comfortable Americans" —

MR. — of the "educated" class — "middle class" —

MRS. Oh, dear — aren't we "upper-middle"? Your salary —

MR. (*Finger to lips, stern.*) We are *not* millionaires.

MRS. Well — we've "paid off our mortgage," we have a "tidy little nest egg," we've made "sensible, long-term investments" —

MR. (*Cautioning.*) We are what you'd call *medium comfortable.* We can afford to extend our boundaries, and begin a — family.

MRS. (*Almost tearful.*) A family! After twelve years of waiting!

MR. (*Counting rapidly on fingers.*) Um — thirteen, darling.

MRS. (*Belatedly realizing what she has said.*) I mean — twelve years of *marriage.* Not just *waiting.* (*Glances at* MR.) Oh — thirteen?

MR. (*Defensive.*) We've been happy, of course. Our marriage hasn't been merely *waiting* —

MRS. — for a, a baby —

MR. — a family —

MRS. (*Cradling gesture with her arms.*) — a darling little *baby* —

MR. — a strapping young *son* —

MRS. (*Emphatically.*) We've done plenty of other things!

MR. Certainly have! Hobbies, travel — (*A bit blank.*) — paying off our mortgage —

MRS. (*Grimly.*) We've been happy. We love each other, after all.

MR. Sure do! Sweetest gal in the world! (*Kisses* MRS.'s *cheek.*)

MRS. (*Repeating in same tone.*) We've been happy.

MR. Damned happy.

MRS. We have snapshots to prove it —

241

MR. Albums of snapshots to prove it!

> (*A pause.* MR. *and* MRS. *glance nervously at the clock.*)

MRS. (*A soft voice.*) Of course, every now and then —

MR. — in the interstices of happiness —

MRS. — between one heartbeat and the next —

MR. — in the early, insomniac hours of the morning, maybe —

MRS. — in the bright-lit maze of the food store —

MR. — like fissures of deep, sharp shadow at noon —

MRS. — we have sometimes, for maybe just a —

MR. — fleeting second —

MRS. — teensy-weensy fleeting *second* —

MR. — been a bit lonely. (*Pause.*)

MRS. (*Sad, clear voice.*) So lonely. (*Pause.*)

> (*The door opens, and* x *appears.* x *is a bureaucrat, in conventional office attire; may wear rimless glasses; carries a clipboard containing numerous documents. He/she is impersonally "friendly."*)

x. (*Bright smile, loud voice.*) Goooood morning! (*Consults clipboard.*) You are — Mr. and Mrs. — ?

MR., MRS. (*Excited, hopeful.*) That's right! (MRS. *quickly straightens* MR.*'s necktie, which has become crooked.*)

x. (*Making a production of shaking hands.*) Mr. —! Mrs. —! Soooo glad to meet you.

MRS. (*Flushed, hand to bosom.*) So g-glad to meet *you.*

MR. Is this the — (*Fearful of asking "Is this the day?"*) — the right time?

x. No time like the present! That's agency policy.

MRS. An — excellent policy.

MR. (*Nodding.*) Very excellent.

x. And you're punctual, Mr. and Mrs. —, I see. A good sign.

MR. Oh, we're very punctual.

MRS. (*Breathless.*) Always have been!

MR. We've been here since 7:45 A.M., actually. When the custodial staff unlocked the building.

MRS. We came to the c-city last night. We're staying in a hotel.

MR. —a medium-priced hotel! —

MRS. We were terrified of missing our appointment —

MR. (*Chiding* MRS.) We were not *terrified*, we were — vigilant.

MRS. Yes, vigilant —

X. It *is* wise to be punctual. Such details in prospective parents are meticulously noted. (*Mysteriously taps documents.*)

MR. (*A deep breath.*) And is today the d-day?

MRS. (*A hand on* MR.*'s arm, faintly echoing.*) — the d-day?

X. (*Beaming.*) Yes. Today *is* your day, Mr. and Mrs. —. Your application to adopt one of our orphans has been fully processed by our board of directors, and approved. Congratulations!

MRS. Oh —! Oh!

MR. Oh my God!

> (MR. *and* MRS. *clasp hands, thrilled.* X *strides to the door, opens it with a flourish and leads in* NABBO.)

X. Here he is, Mr. and Mrs. — your baby.

MR., MRS. (*Faintly.*) "Our baby!"

> (NABBO *is perhaps eight years old. He wears a mask to suggest deformity or disfigurement, but the mask should be extremely lifelike and not exaggerated. His skin is an ambiguous tone — dusky or mottled, not "black." He may be partly bald as well, as if his scalp has been burnt. He has a mild twitch or tremor.* MR. *and* MRS. *stare at* NABBO, *who stares impassively at them.*)

X. (*Rubbing hands together.*) So! Here we are! Here we have "Nabbo." (*Nudging him.*) Say hello to your new mother and father, Nabbo.

(NABBO *is silent.*)

MR., MRS. H-Hello!

X. (*A bit coercive.*) Say "hello" to your new mother and father, Nabbo. "Hel-lo."

(NABBO *is silent.*)

MR. (*Hesitantly.*) He isn't a, an actual — *baby* — is he?

X. (*Consulting document.*) Nabbo is eight months old. To the day.

MR. Eight *months* — ?

MRS. Oh but he's — so sweet. So —

X. Our records are impeccable.

MRS. — *childlike.* So —

MR. (*A bit doubtful, to* X.) What did you say his name is?

MRS. — *trusting.* So —

X. "Nabbo." "NAB-BO." (*Equal stress on both syllables.*)

MRS. — needful of our love!

(X *pushes* NABBO *toward* MR. *and* MRS. *He is weakly resistant.*)

MR., MRS. "Nab-bo" — ?

X. (*Brightly urging* NABBO.) "Hel-lo!"

(NABBO *remains silent. Visible tremor.*)

MR. Maybe he doesn't know — English?

MRS. Of course he doesn't, that's the problem. (*Speaking loudly, brightly.*) Hel-lo, Nab-bo! You've come a long distance to us, haven't you? Don't be frightened. We are your new Mommy and your Daddy — (*Points to herself and to* MR.) We'll teach you everything you need to know.

MR. We sure will!

(MR. *has taken a camera out of his briefcase and takes pictures of* MRS. *posing with* NABBO. NABBO *is rigid with terror of the flash.*)

244

MR. Beau-ti-ful! The first *minute* of our new life. (*Takes another picture.*)

MRS. This is a holy time. I feel God's presence here.

MR. (*To* X, *hesitantly.*) Excuse me, but is Nabbo a, um — little boy, or a little girl?

MRS. (*Gently poking* MR.) Dear, don't be crude!

MR. I'm only curious.

X. (*Checking document, frowning.*) You didn't specify, did you? You checked "either sex."

MRS. (*Eagerly.*) Oh yes, oh yes! "Either."

MR. (*Protesting.*) Hey, I was just curious. I'm Daddy, after all.

MRS. (*Fussing over* NABBO, *squatting beside him.*) He's "Daddy," dear, and I'm "Mommy." We've waited so long for you! Only for *you*, dear. Can you say "Daddy" — "Mommy"?

    (NABBO *remains silent, twitching slightly.*)

MR. (*As if* NABBO *is deaf.*) "DAD-DY" — "MOM-MY" —

MRS. (*Her ear to* NABBO's *mouth, but hears nothing.*) Of course, you're shy; you've come such a long distance.

MR. (*Solemnly.*) From the "dark side of the Earth."

MRS. (*To* MR., *chiding.*) Don't be so — grim, dear. That isn't the right tone. (*To* NABBO; *singing.*) "Little Baby Bunting! Daddy's gone a-hunting! Gone to get a new fur skin! To wrap the Baby Bunting in!"

MR. (*Joining in.*) " — wrap the Baby Bunting in!" (*Laughs, rubs hands happily together.*) I can't believe this is *real*.

MRS. (*To* NABBO.) Now, Naddo —

MR. "Nab-bo" —

MRS. That's what I said: "Nad-do."

MR. Dear, it's "Nab-bo."

MRS. "Nab-bo"? That's what I *said*. My goodness! (*She turns to the bag, removing a large doll from it.*) Look, Nabbo darling — just

245

for *you*. Isn't she lovely? (*Urging* NABBO *to take the doll, but* NABBO *is motionless, not lifting his/her arms.*)

MR. (*Taking a shiny toy firetruck out of the bag; in a hearty "masculine" voice.*) Nabbo, look what Daddy has for you. Cool, eh? (*Running the truck vigorously along the floor, making "engine" noises deep in his throat.*) RRRRRRRMMMMMMMM! Cool, Nabbo, eh?

X. (*Holding out the clipboard and a pen.*) Excuse me, "Mommy" and "Daddy"; please sign on the dotted line, and Nabbo is yours forever.

MRS. Oh, yes!

MR. Of course!

(*As* MR. *takes the pen to sign, however,* X *suddenly draws back. As if he/she has just remembered.*)

X. Um — one further detail.

MR., MRS. Yes? What?

X. It appears that — Nabbo has a twin.

MR., MRS. (*Blankly.*) A — twin?

X. From whom Nabbo is said to be inseparable.

MR., MRS. "Inseparable" — ?

X. They must be adopted together, you see.

MR., MRS. (*Trying to comprehend.*) Twin — ?

(*The minute hand of the clock continues to accelerate.*)

X. Yes. An identical twin.

MR. *Identical! Like our c-child?*

X. Frequently, our adoptees are from large lit- (*About to say "litter," changes his/her mind.*) — families. (*Pause.*) The term "twin" is merely generic.

MRS. I don't understand. Isn't our Nabbo one of a kind?

X. Nabbo is indeed one of a kind; we are all "one of a kind." But Nabbo also has a twin, from whom Nabbo is inseparable.

MR. But — what does that mean?

MRS. "Inseparable — "?

> (*Pause.* MR., MRS. *stare at each other.*)

MR. (*Suddenly, extravagant.*) Hell, I'm game! (*Throws arms wide.*)

MRS. (*Squeals with excitement, kneeling before* NABBO.) You have a *twin*, Nabbo? Another just like you?

MR. (*Recklessly.*) Two for the price of one, eh?

MRS. (*Faint, laughing, peering up at* MR.) Oh, but — "Daddy" — are we prepared? We've never had *one*, and now — *two*?

MR. Isn't that the way twins always come — in *twos*? Surprising Mommy and Daddy? (*Laughs.*)

MRS. (*Dazed, euphoric.*) Oh yes oh yes oh *yes*! (*Pause, voice drops.*) I'm afraid. (*Pause.*)

MR. *I'm* afraid. Gosh.

X. I regret to say, Mr. and Mrs. — , that our agency requires, in such a situation, that adoptive parents take in both siblings. For, given the fact of "identical twins," there can be no justification in adopting one instead of the other.

MRS. That's . . . so.

MR. (*Wiping face with handkerchief.*) You got us there . . . yes!

> (X *takes* NABBO's *arm as if to lead him back through the door.*)

X. (*Somber voice.*) There are so many deserving applicants registered with our agency, you see. Our waiting list is years long.

MRS. (*Desperate.*) Oh — oh, wait —

MR. Hey, wait —

MRS. (*Hugging* NABBO.) We want them both — of course.

MR. (*Wide, dazed grin.*) *I'm* game! — Did I say that?

X. (*Severely.*) You're certain, Mr. and Mrs. — ?

MR., MRS. Yes! Yes!

247

x. (*Goes to the door, opens it and leads in* NADBO, *with some ceremony.*) This, Mr. and Mrs. — , is "Nad-bo."

MR., MRS. (*A bit numbed.*) "NAD-BOO."

x. "NAD-BO."

MR., MRS. "NAD-*BO.*"

> (NABBO *and* NADBO, *twins, stand side by side. They exhibit identical twitches and tremors, cowering together.*)

MRS. (*Voice airy, strange.*) What a long long distance you have come to us — Nab-bo, Nad-bo! Yet we were fated.

MR. From "the dark side of the Earth" — from "the beginning of Time."

> (MR., MRS. *behave like doting parents, fussing over the twins.*)

MRS. We'll teach you the English language —

MR. *American* English language — greatest language on Earth!

MRS. We'll bring you to our home —

MR. *Your* home, now —

MRS. We'll love love love you so you forget whatever it is — (*Pause, a look of distaste.*) — you've escaped.

MR. *That's* for sure! No looking back.

MRS. No looking back, you'll be American children. *No* past!

MR. We're your new Mommy and Daddy — know what that means?

MRS. (*Pointing.*) He's "Daddy" — I'm "Mommy" —

MR. (*Overlapping, hearty.*) I'm "Mommy" — he's "Daddy" —

MRS. (*Lightly chiding.*) *I'm* "Mommy."

MR. (*Quickly.*) I mean — I'm "Daddy." Of course!

MRS. (*Taking out of the bag a cap with bells.*) I knitted this myself, for you! (*Pause.*) Oh dear — there's only one. (MRS. *fits the cap awkwardly on* NABBO's *head; takes out a sweater.*) Thank goodness, I knitted this, too —

(NADBO *takes the sweater from her, puts it over his head.*)

MR. You'll have to knit matching sets, dear. From now on everything must be in duplicate.

X. (*Smiling, but with authority.*) Hmmm! I do need your signatures, Mr. and Mrs. — , before the adoption procedure can continue.

> (MR. *wheels in a tricycle. Both children snatch at it, push at each other. The child who gets it, however, has no idea what it is, and struggles with it, knocking it over, attacking the wheels.* MR. *pulls in a wagon. Similar action.*)

MRS. Oh! — I nearly forgot. You must be starving — having come so far! (*Takes fudge out of bag.*) I made this chocolate-walnut fudge just yesterday!

> (NABBO, NADBO *take pieces of proffered fudge; taste it hesitantly; begin to eat, ravenously; spit mouthfuls out.*)

MRS. Oh, dear! (*With a handkerchief, dabbing at their faces.*) You mustn't be *greedy*, you know. There's plenty to eat here.

> (NABBO, NADBO *snatch at the rest of the fudge, shoving pieces into their mouths, though they are sickened by it, and soon spit it out again.* NADBO *has a minor choking fit.*)

MR. (*With camera.*) O.K., guys! Everybody smile! Say "MON KEE!"

> (MRS. *embraces the children, smiling radiantly at the camera. The children cringe at the flash.*)

MRS. This is the happiest day of my life. Thank you, God.

MR. This is the happiest day of *my* life. (MR. *hands* X *the camera so that he/she can take a picture of the new family.* MR., MRS. *smiling broadly,* NABBO *and* NADBO *cringing.* NADBO *tries to hide under the sweater, and* MRS. *gently removes it.*) Thanks!

X. (*Handing camera back to* MR.) Lovely. Now, we should complete our procedure. Your signatures, please —

MR., MRS. Yes, yes of course . . .

> (*Again,* X *draws the clipboard back out of their reach, at the crucial moment.*)

X. Ummm — just a moment. (*Peering at a document.*) I'm afraid — Nabbo and Nadbo have a third sibling.

> (MR. *has taken the pen from* X's *hand, and now drops it.*)

MRS. (*Faint, hand to bosom.*) A *third . . . ?*

MR. . . . another *twin?*

X. (*Hesitant.*) Not "twin" exactly. With these high-fertility races, the precise clinical term is — too clinical. Let's say "identical sibling."

MR. Tri-tri-triplets?

X. Not "triplets," exactly. (*Evasively.*) "Identical sibling" is preferred.

MRS. (*Vague, voice strange.*) Oooohhh another of you! — how, how — how *wonderful.* Your mother must be — must have been — (*Draws a blank.*) — if you had one, I mean. Nab-bo, Nab-do — I mean, Nad-do — ?

> (NABBO, NADBO *poke each other, but do not speak. Cap bells jingle. One shoves at the shiny firetruck, or the wagon. The other finds a piece of fudge and pops it into his mouth.*)

MR. (*Awkward, dazed, to* X.) B-But I'm afraid — we really *can't,* you know. Not three. We'd only prepared for *one.*

MRS. When we left home yesterday — to drive here — we'd only prepared — enough diapers, a single bassinet — (*Pause; a kind of wildness comes over her.*) A third? A third *baby?* Is it possible? I *did* always want a large family. . . .

MR. But, darling, not in five minutes!

MRS. We can buy a new house. More bedrooms! Bunk beds! A bigger family room! (*Pause, breathing quickly.*) I was so lonely in my parents' house — just the *one* of me. And everything done *for me.* Never a moment's want or deprivation . . . (*Pause.*) My mother was from a large family — eight children. Dozens of grandchildren.

MR. But not in five minutes!

MRS. (*Turning on him, cutting.*) What difference does that make? We've been infertile — *sterile* — for fourteen years. We've got a lot of catching up to do!

MR. (*Wincing.*) Thirteen years . . .

MRS. (*Laughing, trying to hug* NABBO *and* NADBO.) Here is our — deliverance! These "tragic orphans" — "from the dark side of the Earth." Human beings can't live for themselves alone. . . .

MR. (*Gripping* MRS. *by the shoulders.*) Darling, please! You're hysterical. You're not — yourself.

MRS. (*Shrilly.*) Who am I, then? Who am I, then?

MR. Darling! —

(NABBO *and* NADBO *have been cringing fearfully.*)

X. (*With authority.*) Mr. —, Mrs. —? I'm afraid your allotted time has nearly transpired. Even as you dally — (X *indicates the clock.*) — this past hour, 110,273 new "tragic orphans" have been, as it's said, "born."

MRS. (*Hand to bosom.*) How many? — My goodness!

MR. I think we've been cruelly misled here. I strongly object to being manipulated!

X. If you had troubled to read the agency's restrictions and guidelines handbook, Mr. —, more closely, you would not affect such surprise now.

MR. I did read it! I've practically memorized it! We've been on your damned waiting list for a decade!

MRS. (*Vague, intense, to* X.) There is a — a third sibling? — identical with our b-babies?

X. Identical DNA, chromosomes — identical faces and bodies. But, you know, not "identical" inwardly. In the soul.

MRS. "The soul —!" (*A strange expression on her face as of radiance, pain.*)

MR. (*Awkward, flush-faced.*) Darling, it's just that we — can't. We don't have *room* —

MRS. Of course we have room!

MR. We don't have resources —

MRS. Of course we have resources!

251

MR. (*Tugging at his necktie, panting.*) We're practically in *debt* — paupers —

MRS. (*Extravagantly, arms wide.*) We're wealthy! — We have infinite space — inwardly.

MR. Inwardly?

MRS. The soul is infinite, isn't it? *Mine* is, isn't *yours*?

MR. (*Baffled.*) My — soul? Where — ?

MRS. (*Tugging at* x*'s arm.*) *You* tell him! The soul is infinite, isn't it? "The Kingdom of God is within" — space that goes on forever!

> (MRS. *has been working herself up into an emotional state;* NABBO *and* NADBO *are frightened of her. They cast off the cap, sweater, etc., shove away the tricycle; begin to make mournful keening sounds and rock back and forth, their small bodies hunched.* x *scolds them inaudibly; they make a break for the closed door, and* x *grabs their arms to stop them.*)

MRS. What? — where are you going? Nab-bo — no, you're Nad-bo — I mean Nab-do — Nab-*boo* — come here! Be good! You're ours, aren't you? Mommy loves you *so much* — (*Tries to embrace children, who resist her.*)

MR. (*Blank, dazed smile.*) *Daddy* loves you so much! (*Pushes the tricycle back.*) Since the beginning of Time!

MRS. Since *before* the beginning of Time —

> (NABBO *and* NADBO *cower, hiding behind* x, *who is annoyed at the turn of events, surreptitiously slapping at the children or gripping their shoulders forcibly. The mourning-keening sounds seem to be coming from all over.*)

MRS. (*Hands to ears.*) Oh, what is that sound! It hurts my ears —

MR. Nab-boo! Nad-doo! Bad boys! *Stop that!*

x. (*Threatening children.*) It's just some village dirge — nothing! Pay no attention!

MRS. It's coming from here, too — (*Impulsively rushes to the door and opens it, steps through;* x *immediately pulls her back.*)

X. (*Furious.*) Mrs. —! This door can only be opened by authorized agency personnel! (x *shuts the door.*)

(MRS. *has recoiled back into the room. Hand over her mouth, she staggers forward as if about to collapse.*)

MR. (*Rushing to help her.*) Darling? What is it?

X. That door was *not* to be opened. I could call a security guard and have you arrested, Mrs. —! Taken out of here in handcuffs!

MRS. (*Eyes shut, nauseated.*) Oh . . . oh . . .

MR. Darling, what did you see?

X. (*Loudly.*) Mrs. — saw *nothing*. There was *nothing* to be seen.

MR. Darling — ?

MRS. (*Feeble whisper, leaning on* MR.'*s arm.*) Take them back. We don't want them.

MR. What did you see, darling? What's behind that door?

MRS. (*Trying to control rising hysteria.*) Take them back. We don't want them. Any of them. I want to go *home*.

X. Hmmm! I thought so. Poor risks for adoption.

MR. Darling, are you certain? We've waited so long . . . *prayed* so long . . .

MRS. (*A small scream.*) Take them away! All of them! (*Hides eyes.*) We're not strong enough —

X. (*Coldly.*) You're certain, Mr. and Mrs. — ? You can never again apply with our agency, you know.

MRS. Take them away!

MR. (*Trying to speak in normal voice.*) We're sorry — *so* sorry —

(x *marches* NABBO *and* NADBO *out, and the door is shut behind them.*)

MR. (*Weakly, belatedly calling after.*). Um — *so* sorry —

(*The mourning-keening sound grows louder.* MR. *and* MRS. *freeze; lights dim except on the clock face, where the minute hand continues its accelerated progress.*

253

Lights out. Mourning sound ceases.

Lights up on MR. *and* MRS., *who have come forward. Darkness elsewhere. (The clock is no longer visible.)* MR. *and* MRS. *speak in a duet of agitated rhythms, overlappings, a strange music that should suggest, though not too overtly mimic, the mourning-keening sound. This conclusion should be elegiac, a barely restrained hysteria; but it is restrained.)*

MRS. (*Hands to her face.*) What have we done! —

MR. It was a, a wise decision —

MRS. — necessary —

MR. — necessary decision —

MRS. Waited all our lives — Oh, what have we done —

MR. It was your decision —

MRS. Our day of birth — delivery —

MR. *Deliverance* —

MRS. — weren't strong enough —

MR. *You* weren't — *I* was — (*Pause.*) — *wasn't* —

MRS. What have we done! — not strong enough —

MR. Who the hell *is* strong enough I'd like to know —

MRS. God didn't make us strong enough —

MR. — rational decision, necessary —

MRS. — necessary — (*Clutching at her womb.*) Oh! Oh what have we done! My babies —

MR. (*Anguished, strikes chest with fist.*) I'm only human! What can I do! Who can forgive me? (*Pause, peers into audience.*) Who *isn't* human? You cast the first stone!

MRS. (*Hands framing face.*) That corridor! — that space! — to the horizon! — so many! And the *smell.* (*Nauseated.*)

MR. (*Reasoning.*) There isn't room in the heart — I mean the *home* — the *house*! no matter how many bunk beds. We're not paupers! — I mean, we're not millionaires. Who's been saying we *are*?

MRS. (*Confused.*) Bunk beds? — how many?

MR. How many? (*Rapidly counting on fingers, confused.*)

MRS. (*A soft cry.*) Our home — *house!* — empty! —

MR. (*Protesting.*) Hey: there's *us.*

MRS. So lonely! —

MR. Rational, necessary decision — no choice.

MRS. *So* lonely —

MR. Look, I refuse to be manipulated, to be made *guilty* —

MRS. So many years waiting, and so lonely —

MR. (*Pleading.*) Who the hell *isn't* human? I ask you!

MRS. (*Has found the knitted cap on the floor, picks it up lovingly, bells chime.*) God knows, God sees into the heart. Forgive us, God —

MR. We had no choice.

MRS. — no choice!

MR. And we're *not* millionaires!

 (*Lights begin to fade.*)

MRS. (*Waving, tearful and smiling.*) Goodbye Nabbo! — Nadbo! — Nabdo? — dear, innocent babies! Mommy loved you so!

MR. (*Waving, ghastly smile.*) Goodbye, boys! Sons! Your Daddy loved you so!

MRS. Don't think ill of us, don't forget us! Goodbye!

MR. Goodbye, sons! Be brave!

MRS. (*Blowing kisses.*) Mommy loved you so! Goodbye!

MR./MRS. Goodbye, goodbye, goodbye!

 (*Lights out.*)

255

Elegy for the House That Ruth Built
Arthur Kopit

(In the dark, we hear the opening music to Field of Dreams. *It's a soft, haunting sound.*

Lights slowly rise on JERRY DISIBIO, *early thirties, burly. He wears a NY Yankees satin jacket, which he clearly loves.*

He stares out, as if listening to the music. . . .)

JERRY D. The way it happened — I mean, *really* happened — was not even close to what you saw in the papers, or heard on CNN, or Howard Stern, or whatever you employ as your main source of information these days, the Internet maybe — it doesn't matter. The way it ended was just fuckin' weird.

(Pause.)

And none of us were prepared.

(Pause.)

Oh, we were prepared for the strike to end, I don't mean that. We may be lousy players but we aren't dumb. We knew what we were getting into. We knew our time was limited. We knew what we were . . .

(Long pause.)

We were trespassers on hallowed ground.

(Pause.)

Or anyway, *once* hallowed ground.

(Pause.)

Field of Dreams. You ever see that? Well, if you haven't, take my word, you should. Kevin Costner. It's a fantasy. Well . . . *sort* of. But then, what's baseball, right? I got twenty-five hundred bucks a week for living out my fantasy. That, plus this jacket. Not bad for a month's work, huh?

(He models it proudly.)

They gave this to us as we were leavin'. Speaking for myself, 'cause I don't know about the other guys, but I hadn't really expected it. I mean, for me, just to be out there, in right field, in Yankee Stadium, practicing for the opener. For that one amazing day . . .

256

(*Long pause.*)

I'll tell you something, don't quote me now, 'cause like I'll lose whatever meager reputation I have left, but I have gained, through this experience . . .

(*With difficulty.*)

I have gained respect for George Steinbrenner. Don't laugh! I mean it. 'Cause, first of all, I saw fear in his eyes. *Real* fear. On that day I just spoke of. When I ran in from right field to report on what I'd seen out there — seen and felt — me and my fellow outfielders . . .

(*Pause.*)

And later, when we'd *all* come in, 'cause we just couldn't play anymore, the infielders, everyone, you couldn't *pay* us enough to walk back out into the field. And Mr. Steinbrenner, bless his heart, he tried, he said, okay, how much more do you guys want? As if all we wanted was more money. And we said, no way, Jose — we are history.

(*Pause.*)

And he knew then that what I'd just reported was the truth. And he looked out into right field. A cold wind had come in. So cold he had to ask for something to put over him. From sixty degrees down to twenty in like minutes! *But only inside the stadium. . . .*

(*Pause.*)

Anyway, someone in the dugout threw 'm up a jacket and some towels to put around his head and Mr. Steinbrenner wrapped himself up. We could see him shivering. And not just from the cold. But from the fear. We all felt it.

(*Pause.*)

And I saw him look out into right field. I'd been the first to sense it — the movement, if you can call it that. It sort of went from right field to left. And he looked out into right field . . . And though *I* could see the Babe, with those famous bandy legs, and round jowly face, I wasn't sure if he could. But he could. 'Cause I could see the blood had drained from Mr. Steinbrenner's face.

(*Pause.*)

All the players had come out by then. To the steps of the dugout. It was like . . . so silent in the stadium. The wind had died. Never heard such a silence. And then, one by one, the players started pointing out to right field and saying, "I can see 'm! I CAN SEE 'M!" 'Cause at first, I guess only a few of us could.

(*Pause.*)

And then I saw DiMaggio. He was out in center, loping after these invisible fly balls like some great gazelle. Catching one and then another. And Mr. Steinbrenner saw the Jolter too, 'cause he said, "What the fuck's *he* doin' out there? He's not even dead!" I said, "They don't have to be dead to be out there, Mr. Steinbrenner. With all due respect, sir, I think they just have to be *worthy*."

(*Pause.*)

And then we saw this . . . *haze*. It had setled over the infield. And then . . . suddenly it cleared.

(*Pause.*)

And there was the Scooter! At short. And young. Like he used to be. And at first . . . Gehrig. I could see the fuckin' dimples in his cheeks! And he looked over at me. And he tipped his cap, and smiled. I turned to Mr. Steinbrenner. He could see it too. And there was a tear in his eye. He muttered something about there being a speck of dirt in his eye. And he started rubbin' at it. But I knew it wasn't dirt. We all knew.

(*Pause.*)

And then, suddenly the ball is whizzin' all around that infield — not the ball *we'd* been playing with but a pale, almost translucent kind of globe. Givin' off the most astounding light. Like moonlight. I'd never seen anything move so fast. None of us had. . . .

(*Pause.*)

And then, suddenly, Mr. Steinbrenner is angry. He points out at the Babe, and DiMag, and the Scooter. "These guys didn't even PLAY together! "So what the fuck are they doing here now?" He's *offended*! I couldn't fuckin' believe it! And then, all at once, I can see that Mr. Steinbrenner is thinkin'. 'Cause his brow is all knotted up. "Shit," he says. "Maybe I can sign 'em. HEY GUYS! COME IN HERE A SEC'!"

(*He smiles.*)

But they pay him no heed. He might as well be shouting at the wind.

(*Pause.*)

And then . . . as if this all wasn't weird enough already, one of the players on the bench — a replacement guy, like me, but older, in even worse shape, he has this Polaroid camera, he's been askin' guys to take pictures of him when he bats, well he comes out. He's just taken this snapshot of Gehrig smilin'. But the photo — it shows nothing but grass. And he shows us one he took of the outfield. Of the Babe, and DiMag. Same thing. Nothing in the photograph but grass. And empty stands. Mr. Steinbrenner, who, say what you will, is no dummy, says, "Fuck this. If they don't show up on Polaroids, they probably don't show up on TV either." And that ends his plans for signing 'em.

(*Pause.*)

And then — and I know you won't believe this — by the way, I've gotta tell you, you've done really well so far — but, on my word, may the Great Scorekeeper in the Sky scratch me from the lineup if this isn't true, but the sky suddenly darkens, I mean like THAT!

(*He snaps his fingers.*)

We look up. It's two in the afternoon. Why has this suddenly become a night game?

(*Pause.*)

And we see like this like cloud . . . only it's humming.

(*Pause.*)

And then we see what it is. It's fuckin' locusts. It's a plague of fuckin' LOCUSTS! And they're all coming down on us like kamikaze pilots. Only . . . it's not us they're after. It's Mr. Steinbrenner. Within seconds, you can hardly see 'm. His voice, muffled from being underneath five zillion bugs, is barely audible. But it's audible enough. "I'll settle the fuckin' strike!" he shouts. "I'll settle the fuckin' strike!"

(*Pause.*

He listens to the music.)

(*More calmly.*)

Anyhow, that was the last day we played. Mr. Steinbrenner called us into his office that night. He said he'd spoken to the other owners, and that those who had the older ballparks reported pretty much the same thing happening. Not with the Babe, of course. He was ours. But with guys like Ty Cobb, Tris Speaker, Lefty Gomez, Carl Hubbell.

(*Pause.*)

One of the owners, can't remember who, reported that a man in a long black coat had walked across the field to the box where he was sitting and announced that he was Abner Doubleday. And then spit this big black chunk of tobacco splat in the owner's face.

(*Long pause.*)

Anyway, that's how it came about — this sudden decision to settle. I figured they'd want us the hell out o' there as quick as possible. We all thought that. No more reminders, thank you very much.

259

But no. Mr. Steinbrenner said, "Hold up." And he turned to this old guy, he was in charge of equipment. Been with the Yanks for years. And he said, "Tommy. Give the boys some jackets."

(*Pause.*)

So I think that, Mr. Steinbrenner, underneath it all, is okay. 'Cause he didn't really have to do that, you know. Give us the jackets, I mean. . . .

(*Showing off the jacket.*)

It's the real McCoy. Not like you get in Herman's. The stitching's really fabulous. Real satin, too.

(*He stares out, smiling.*

The dreamy music of Field of Dreams *continues under for a moment.*

Then it fades.)

From Quills
a grand guignol
Doug Wright

> *Fanaticism in me is the product of the persecutions*
> *I have endured from my tyrants. The longer they*
> *continue their vexations, the deeper they root my*
> *principles in my heart.*
>
> — The Marquis de Sade in a Letter to His Wife

Characters:
DOCTOR ROYER-COLLARD, chief physician of the Charenton
   asylum
ABBE de COULMIER, administrator at the asylum
MADELEINE LeCLERC, the seamstress at Charenton; sixteen and
   quite lovely
THE MARQUIS, the asylum's most notorious inmate
A LUNATIC, a madman heard through a chink in the wall
THE VOICES OF THE INSANE, the tenants at Charenton

(Time: 1807.

Place: The office of DR. ROYER-COLLARD *and the quarters
of* THE MARQUIS, *at Charenton. The set may be quite simple,
represented by a few elegant pieces. The office requires only
a desk and chair, the cell may consist of a stool and a small
writing table and the bedchamber may be illustrated by
the mere presence of a cot.*

*A note on style: The play is written, I hope, with all the
fervor and self-consciousness of true melodrama. Events in
the play are not* cruel; *they are* diabolical. *Characters are
not* good or bad; *they are either* kissed by God or yoked in
Satan's merciless employ. *Similarly, the play should be
acted in a heightened, even archaic style. As grotesquerie*

261

mounts on grotesquerie, the play's passages should acquire an almost absurdist tone. The sensational stagecraft of the grand guignol — thunder sheets, blood packets, rubber body parts and sleight of hand — all might find a home in the text. Before appealing to the audience's hearts or minds, the play endeavors to appeal to forces far more primal.)

Scene 9

(Dr. Royer-Collard, Coulmier, Madeleine, The Marquis.)

DR. ROYER-COLLARD. It takes a dim man indeed to be outwitted by a lunatic.

COULMIER. To what do I owe this riposte?

DR. ROYER-COLLARD. Already this morning he has trumped you again.

COULMIER. But that's not possible. His cell is barren. No pen, no paper. His linens stripped, his carafe dry. He has nothing to fashion into pages.

DR. ROYER-COLLARD. That's what you think.

COULMIER. I don't dare ask . . .

DR. ROYER-COLLARD. Again, we have young Madeleine to thank for the discovery.

(Lights rise on MADELEINE, *a laundry basket in her arms.)*

MADELEINE. It's for Mother that I'm here. Cast me out upon the street, and I'd survive. But without her sight, and hardly a tooth in her head, she'd soon be dead. And who's to pay for burial? At least here we're guaranteed a pit alongside the morons.

DR. ROYER-COLLARD. Sit down, Miss LeClerc.

MADELEINE. If I hadn't come of my own free will, you'd have searched me out. You'd have forced me to confess, yes? Say it's so, Doctor. That I have no other choice.

DR. ROYER-COLLARD. That depends. What is it you've come to tell me?

MADELEINE. He's at it again. Pretended to leave some mending for me, outside his door. I reckon he meant it as a gift. (MADELEINE *sets the basket down, reaches into it and pulls out a shirt. It's decorated with cursive.*)

DR. ROYER-COLLARD. Where in God's name did he procure ink?

MADELEINE. Nowhere. He pricked the tips of his fingers with a carving knife. His latest fancies — they're scripted in blood.

(*Lights fade on* MADELEINE.)

COULMIER. Dear God, preserve us.

DR. ROYER-COLLARD. I decided to confront the Marquis myself. When I hoisted open the gates of the west wing, there he was, strolling about the corridor. His blouse and breeches were covered in script. He'd turned his very wardrobe into text! The idiot Giton was reading his leggings, while the hysteric Michete perused his vest.

(*Lights rise on* THE MARQUIS. *His clothes are awash with words.*)

THE MARQUIS. My latest masterwork begins at my right cuff, continues across my back and completes itself at the base of my left shoe.

COULMIER. Never was a wardrobe more vulgar in design!

THE MARQUIS. Monsieur Bouloir was a man whose sexual appetites might discreetly be described as "post-mortem." A habitué of cemeteries, his proudest conquest was that of a maid six decades his senior, deceased a dozen years. The vigor with which he frigged caused her bones to dislodge. Still he granted her the highest compliment he accorded any woman: "well worth the dig."

COULMIER. NOOOOOOOO!

Scene 10

(*Coulmier, The Marquis.*)

COULMIER. You! YOU! Such brazen defiance! Flouncing about like some demented peacock!

263

THE MARQUIS. Don't tell me. You've come to read my trousers. You'll note the longest sentence trails down the inseam.

COULMIER. How could you! Parading your decadence before the helpless and the sick!

THE MARQUIS. Piffle!

COULMIER. Your stories so aroused poor Michete, we've had to tie him to his bedposts.

THE MARQUIS. Lucky Michete. You tell him that there are some very reputable individuals, notable in French society, who pay good money to be tied to their bedposts.

COULMIER. What am I to do with you, Marquis? The more I forbid, the more you are provoked.

THE MARQUIS. My darling Coulmier. Here, in my dank quarters, I've had ample time to ruminate on our little tussle, And I've come to a conclusion you'll no doubt find deliriously satisfying.

COULMIER. I'm holding my breath.

THE MARQUIS. Headstrong though I may be, I could be convinced to abandon my writing. Quite voluntarily.

COULMIER. And what in God's name would that require? A thousand livres?

THE MARQUIS. Tsk, tsk, tsk. Much cheaper.

COULMIER. Your room, restored to its luster.

THE MARQUIS. Much simpler.

COULMIER. Your freedom. All we must do is swing the gates wide, and let loose the incubus from his untimely coffin.

THE MARQUIS. I wouldn't dream of it.

COULMIER. What then?

THE MARQUIS. A night, sugar-plum, spent with the partner of my choice.

COULMIER. Aha! What else?

THE MARQUIS. A lover who promises to yield everything to me. Whose body I might spread open to inspect as an entomologist probes his latest specimen. . . .

COULMIER. Poor soul!

THE MARQUIS. And this, above all else, is paramount. My choice must set all pride aside, and allow me to plumb with my lubricious engine the twin cheeks of delight.

COULMIER. Write countless unseemly tomes, Marquis. I will not pimp poor Madeleine!

THE MARQUIS. I wasn't talking about Madeleine.

COULMIER. Then who?

THE MARQUIS. *You, my precious.*

(COULMIER *turns a fiery red. He bellows:*)

COULMIER. OFF WITH YOUR CLOTHES!

THE MARQUIS. Coulmier, you rascal!

COULMIER. OFF, I SAY!

THE MARQUIS. Has my proposal so enflamed you?

COULMIER. I DO NOT MEAN TO *FLIRT*, MARQUIS!

THE MARQUIS. Oh, but you must! Sex without flirtation is merely rape, my pumpkin!

COULMIER. Damn you, Marquis! You are beyond villainy! You are the Devil! NOW STRIP!

(THE MARQUIS *begins to undress.*)

THE MARQUIS. My doublet?

COULMIER. Off!

THE MARQUIS. My collar?

COULMIER. Off!

THE MARQUIS. My shoes; they're naught but punctuation. . . .

COULMIER. Off!

THE MARQUIS. My chintz, my lace, my gabardine?

COULMIER. Off, off, off!

THE MARQUIS. Permit me to retain my gauzy underpinnings!

COULMIER. Every stitch!

THE MARQUIS. WON'T YOU JOIN ME, PONY-BOY?

COULMIER. You shall no longer leave your cell, understood? You'll lay your eyes on none but me from now on!

THE MARQUIS. Such abuse!

COULMIER. You will not render me a fool!

THE MARQUIS. I need not render you a fool!

COULMIER. At first, I thought you were to be pitied. But now I see you are to be feared, truly feared! I have been far too lax with you, Monsieur! Now you shall live as our Father intended — less like a man, and more like the beast you are! Naked, in a hollow pit!

THE MARQUIS. As lived the noble savages of Lescaux, where even today their glorious paintings remain, undimmed by time!

COULMIER. HOW DARE YOU DEFEND YOURSELF IN ART'S NAME! HOW DARE YOU RANK YOURSELF WITH THE LIKES OF VOLTAIRE, PASCAL AND RACINE! THEIR QUILLS ARE GUIDED BY THE HAND OF GOD, WHILE YOUR EVERY UTTERANCE IS MALIGNANCY UNMASKED! THEY SEEK TO ENNOBLE, TO ENLIGHTEN WHILE YOU ... HA! ... YOU! ... YOUR WORST STORIES REVOLT, WHILE YOUR BEST INDUCE VOMITING!

(THE MARQUIS *has stripped himself bare, save for his hair.*)

YOUR WIG! REMOVE YOUR WIG!

(THE MARQUIS *does.*)

THE MARQUIS. How prudent you are, Abbe. I'd planned to curl my locks in the shape of letters, and write a Paean to Buggery that would trail down my backside, and bob at my ass.

COULMIER. You will not spread your insidious gospel, where tyranny is the norm and goodness the last refuge of the weak! Where indifferent Nature rails, untempered by the presence of a God! Where art's magnitude is the breadth of its depravity! NO!

THE MARQUIS. No?

COULMIER. YOU WILL NOT EVEN WRITE YOUR OWN IG-NOMINIOUS NAME!

THE MARQUIS. Tsk, tsk, tsk. *Are your convictions so fragile that mine cannot stand in opposition to them? Is your God so illusory that the presence of my Devil reveals His insufficiency?* Oh, for shame!

COULMIER. May you spend eternity in the company of your beloved Anti-Christ, turning on his spit! (COULMIER *makes for the door.*)

THE MARQUIS. My suckling . . . my lip leech . . .

COULMIER. WHAT?

THE MARQUIS. My truest quill lies betwist my thighs. When it fills with ink and rises to the fore . . . Oh, the wondrous books it will write!

Scene 11

(*The Marquis, Madeleine.*)

THE MARQUIS. Madeleine!

MADELEINE. Marquis! Your every inch, exposed!

THE MARQUIS. This is how your employer chooses to keep me. Like a Roman sculpture, undraped!

MADELEINE. I'm ashamed to look!

THE MARQUIS. Surely you've seen a man naked?

MADELEINE. No, sir. It's only been described to me, in your books.

THE MARQUIS. Then you've had a most painstaking teacher. I've devoted many a page to the male form. Its rippling hillsides, its undulating prairies and its crested mount. . . .

MADELEINE. Is your body, then, somewhat . . . representative?

THE MARQUIS. For a man my age, and victim of my calumnies.

MADELEINE. I must say, sir, in your novels, you stoke the most unrealistic expectations.

267

THE MARQUIS. Oh, how you wound! What sure aim! What steady fire!

MADELEINE. I risk terrible danger, coming to see you this way.

THE MARQUIS. Your life, and your mother's besides.

MADELEINE. It was guilt which ushered me here, stronger than any commandment. How you must hate me.

THE MARQUIS. Never!

MADELEINE. But surely you know it's I who betrayed you to Dr. Royer-Collard. I gave him your soiled bed sheets, and your clothes besides. . . .

THE MARQUIS. And I love you the more for it.

MADELEINE. How can that be?

THE MARQUIS. I may be a scamp, a chancre and a blight, my blessed Madeleine, but I am not a hypocrite! Don't you see that by informing against me, you endorse my philosophy?

MADELEINE. I'm afraid I don't understand.

THE MARQUIS. You were willing to sacrifice me on the block to achieve your own gain. . . .

MADELEINE. Hence, my sorrow!

THE MARQUIS. In the animal kingdom, does the tiger spare his sister the doe? Not when he's hungry!

MADELEINE. Pity the poor faun!

THE MARQUIS. That, Madeleine, is natural order! A carefully orchestrated cycle of consumption which we all too often violate with our false codes of law and morality. But you! You rose above such petty constructs, and fed yourself upon my very carcass.

MADELEINE. And so I am endeared to you?

THE MARQUIS. I stand before you, not in rage, but awe.

MADELEINE. You're a queer one, all right.

THE MARQUIS. Can you smuggle a paper and quill to me?

MADELEINE. If only! Mother and I, we're weak with boredom, our evenings spent in silence. For a while, I read her the papers, with their accounts of the Terror. She found those too barbaric, and pined for your stories instead.

THE MARQUIS. Never fear, my angel. I have a plan.

MADELEINE. Let me be its agent, I beg you, as penance for my wrongs against you!

THE MARQUIS. Take note, beloved, of the chink in this wall. I'll whisper a new tale to my neighbor, the lunatic Cleante. He'll in turn whisper it to his neighbor, Dauphin. Dauphin will impart the tale to the retard Franval, and he will impart it likewise to the noisome Bouchon —

MADELEINE. Whose cell lies next to the linen cabinet!

THE MARQUIS. Precisely!

MADELEINE. And there, armed with a quill of my own, I'll receive your story through the wall, and commit it to paper!

THE MARQUIS. Voila!

MADELEINE. Oh, Marquis! How ingenious you are!

THE MARQUIS. Imagine! My scandalous stories, whipping through the halls of this mausoleum, like some mysterious breeze! A string of tongues, all wagging in service of my prose.

MADELEINE. But with men whose minds are so weak, will your art survive such a journey?

THE MARQUIS. My heinous vision, filtered through the minds of the insane. Who knows? They might improve it!

MADELEINE. I'll practice my hand, Marquis, and do your words justice.

THE MARQUIS. You can take them home to Mother, and on to my publisher besides!

MADELEINE. Only one thing troubles me . . .

THE MARQUIS. Fear of discovery?

MADELEINE. No. Fear of the inmate Bouchon, the agent closest to me in the line.

THE MARQUIS. Why him, more than any other?

MADELEINE. He holds a torch for me. Once, when I was darning his stockings, he pressed me hard against the wall, and his stinking breath caused my eyes to run. It was the Abbe de Coulmier who saved me.

THE MARQUIS. What of it?

MADELEINE. Well, sir, given the potency of your stories, and the fragility of his brain . . . it might cause a combustion, that's all.

THE MARQUIS. What are we to do, dearest? Shuffle the patients in their cells? That's not within our power. Now, accept the danger, or withdraw.

MADELEINE. I accept.

THE MARQUIS. Madeleine . . . ?

MADELEINE. Yes, Marquis?

THE MARQUIS. A kiss per page. The price holds.

MADELEINE. But how can I? We're forbidden to meet.

THE MARQUIS. Which is why this time, my pussy-willow, I must request payment in advance.

MADELEINE. You're a caution, you are!

THE MARQUIS. Quickly, before we are discovered!

(*They consume one another with kisses.*)

Scene 12

(*The Marquis, A Lunatic, The Voices of the Insane.*)

(*A crack of thunder. Rain begins to pelt the stone walls of Charenton. Alone,* THE MARQUIS *whispers into a crack in the wall.*)

THE MARQUIS. Psst . . . Cleante? Are you there?

(*A voice answers.*)

A LUNATIC. Marquis? Is that you?

270

THE MARQUIS. Who else would it be?

A LUNATIC. I've the most wonderful news, Marquis! I'm no longer a man! This morning, I awoke a bird!

THE MARQUIS. Quiet! Listen to what I say, and report it post-haste to your neighbor Dauphin.

A LUNATIC. I've huge, flapping wings, and a beak for scavenging! And I can warble, too! (*The* LUNATIC *begins to trill.*)

THE MARQUIS. CLEANTE!

A LUNATIC. Eh?

THE MARQUIS. I've news for you, too. This morning I awoke a cat.

A LUNATIC. No! It can't be!

THE MARQUIS. If you don't do what I tell you, I'll claw through this wall and eat you alive.

A LUNATIC. At your service, Count!

THE MARQUIS. Now. Are you ready?

A LUNATIC. Here, here!

THE MARQUIS. And so we begin. . . . Our story concerns the young heroine Fanchon, a harlot in a harem reputed to be the most varied in all Europe: there, you could plow a Prussian princess, sodomize twins or tickle the loins of a Hungarian dwarf.

> (*Down the corridor, faintly, we hear other voices pick up the tale.*)

THE VOICES OF THE INSANE. Tickle the loins of a Hungarian dwarf . . . tickle the loins . . . the loins . . . the loins . . . the loins . . .

THE MARQUIS. One day Fanchon was visited by a certain Monsieur De Curval, an accomplished surgeon, and an even more renowned Libertine. He had been barred from many of the city's finer brothels, so lethal were his exploits.

THE VOICES OF THE INSANE. So lethal were his exploits . . . so lethal . . . so lethal . . . lethal . . .

THE MARQUIS. Once they were secluded in her bedchamber, he bade Fanchon strip, and strip she did, with the speed of one

271

unaccustomed to clothing's confinement. As she stood naked before him, he ran his fingers across her skin, pulling apart folds of flesh, inspecting follicles.

THE VOICES OF THE INSANE. Pulling apart folds of flesh . . . folds of flesh . . . flesh . . . flesh . . .

THE MARQUIS. "What shall I ready, Monsieur?" asked Fanchon. "My mouth, my rounded ass or my Venus mound, my succulent oyster?"

THE VOICES OF THE INSANE. My Venus mound, my succulent oyster . . . succulent oyster . . . oyster . . . oyster . . .

THE MARQUIS. "None!" cried Monsieur De Curval, brandishing a scalpel he had hidden in his breast. "With my blade, I'll create new orifices, where there were none before! Once hewn, I can thrust my turgid member into regions unsullied by your previous suitors!"

THE VOICES OF THE INSANE. Unsullied suitors . . . suitors . . . suitors . . . suitors . . .

THE MARQUIS. With that, Fanchon expelled a scream so extravagantly pitched that the Libertine was obliged to tear out her tongue, cauterizing the wound with a poker from the fire. Next, he splayed her body across the mattress, and with the edge of his knife —

(*From off, in the distance, a sudden scream. It slices through the air, and echoes down the corridor.* THE MARQUIS *stops short. His face goes white. He recognize the howling voice. A bolt of lightning, as powerful as the zap that martyred poor Justine. We see — for a single, blistering moment — the body of* MADELEINE. *She's been hoisted from a rafter in the laundry room, and spins, wildly. Her body is a study in carnage. The face of* THE MARQUIS *contorts in pain. Blackness. The blowing of the wind. The curtain falls.*)

(*End of Act One.*)

Insurrection: Holding History
Robert O'*Hara*

Eight NEGROES *and One Cracker Play All of the Following Characters:*
RON
T. J.
MUTHA WIT / MUTHA
GERTHA / CLERK WIFE / MISTRESS MO'TEL
OCTAVIA / KATIE LYNN
NAT TURNER / OVA'SEEA' JONES
SYLVIA / CLERK SON / IZZIE MAE
REPORTER / COP / CLERK HUSBAND / BUCK NAKED
JORDAN / HAMMET / DETECTIVE

TIME: NOW AND THEN
PLACE: HERE AND THERE

THIS PLAY SHOULD BE DONE AS IF IT WERE
A BULLET THROUGH TIME

PROLOGUE

MUTHA WIT who is the ROOT, who is the FOUNDATION, who is the ROCK, who gives voice to **T. J.**; she **SINGS** of Going Home, of Renewing the soul, Re-defining our . . . ____ stories.

T. J. who is the GREAT-GREAT-GRANDFATHER, who is the SHINER, who is the 189-year-old man, who has inhabited a wheelchair for the last 100 years, who can move nothing on his body EXCEPT his left eye and the middle toe of his right foot; he **LISTENS.**

NAT TURNER who is the INSURRECTIONIST, who is the SLAVE, who is the PREACHA' MAN, who is the HATCHET MURDERER; **he FLEES into the** dark safety of the woods.

273

SONG — TROUBLE OF DE WORLD
(*Traditional.*)

MUTHA WIT:
soon we'll be done
trouble of de world(3x)
soon we'll be done
trouble of de world
goin' home
to live with my lord

no mo' weepin' and wailin'(3x)
goin' home
to live with my lord

i want to see my muther(3x)
goin' home
to live with my lord

i want to see my father(3x)
goin' home
to live with my lord

soon we'll be done
trouble of de world(3x)
soon we'll be done
trouble of de world
I'M GOIN HOME(5x)

YOU BETTA' WORK!

A BACKYARD.
MUSIC. DANCE. CONTEMPORARY. 1995.

FAMILY AND FRIENDS.(F&F)

F&F. **WORK OCTAVIA WORK. WORK OCTAVIA WORK. HEY!!
WORK THOSE BRAIDS OCTAVIA. WORK THOSE BRAIDS.
HEY!! SIDE TA' SIDE. UP N' DOWN. SIDE TA' SIDE. UP
N' DOWN. SIDE TA' SIDE. UP N' DOWN. SIDE TA' SIDE.
HEY!!** . . .

JORDAN. If she don't stop movin' so fast them things liable ta'
fall out.

SYLVIA. You know Octavia
she don't care.

JORDAN. She always movin' fast that's her nature.

SYLVIA. She'd probably drop to the flo' pick 'em up and weave 'em
ratt back in —

JORDAN. Without missin' a beat.

SYLVIA. You know it.

JORDAN. Just lak her mama.

F&F. **OWWWW. WORK GERTHA WORK. WORK GERTHA
WORK. SHAKE IT MAKE SHO' YOU DON'T BREAK IT SHAKE
IT MAKE SHO' YOU DON'T BREAK IT. OWWWW! . . .**

A WHITE REPORTER. How does it feel to know that your Great-
Great-Grandfather is still alive after all this time?

OCTAVIA. You ask the same question every year you come heah
you cain't think up nuthin' new?

REP. He must've seen so many amazing things over the course of
his life.

OCT. You know Gramps ain't said a word in 100 years . . . but you
should talk to Ronnie, he claims him and Gramps always havin'
conversations don't nobody believe him but he been claimin'
that ever since we was kids.

F&F. **FISHTAIL. FISHTAIL. FISHTAIL. HEY!!**

SYLVIA. If that reporter man see that boy actin' lak he and Gramps
talkin' ta' one another it'll be the one and only story they print.
I can guarantee you that.

JORDAN. That reporter man gon' print whateva' he wanna print.
Don't make no never mind what he sees or what we say.

SYLVIA. Hey, this my song, yall!! **THE ROACH** —

F&F. **THE ROACH THE ROACH IS ON THE WALL WE DON'T
NEED NO RAID LET THE MU1HAFUCKA CRAWL. HEY!
WORK!! . . .**

GERTHA. Git outta my face wit that paper and pen I tol' you I ain't
gat nuthin' new ta' tell you that you don't already know from last

275

year when you came he still shits and sleeps he don't talk he can't walk and today is his birthday the same day his birthday landed on last year.

REP. What about the reports that the Goverment wants to do some tests on Mr. T. J. to figure out if he's actually alive or just some dummy that you all got rigged up to get publicity every year?

GERTHA. He don't need no doctas messin' round wit his insides and if he was some dummy that we just gat propped up in heah then that'd make you a bigga jack-ass than the one you already is fo' comin' out heah ta' cover this story each and every year now wouldn't it?

REP. Well —

GERTHA. I hope that's not a camera I see ova there in them bushes.

REP. No —

GERTHA. I tol' you NO cameras 'llowed. This heah is a private party we don't want no TV cameras.

REP. I assure you that we don't —

GERTHA. Mr. Reporter man yo' assurances don't mean squat shit ta' me just stay outta my way.

REP. . . . Ok.

GERTHA. Good.

REP. . . . And thank you for allowing me exclusive coverage of this event.

GERTHA. You welcome, honey. Have fun.

F&F. **DO THE CRACK-BABY!! HEY. WORK THAT CRACK-BABY. WORK THAT CRACK-MAMA. WORK THAT CRACK-DADDY. HEY.** (*Deep voiced.*) **THE CRACK FAMILY. THE CRACK FAMILY. HEY!!**

NAT TURNER races through the woods, which are the dancing F&F.

No one sees him except MUTHA WIT, T. J. and RON.

TURNER huffs. He puffs. He HIDES/RESTS behind a few trees/ dancing F&F.

(Note: MUTHA WIT speaks for T. J. unless otherwise noted.)

RON. Did you see —

WIT. Yes . . .

REP. Mr. Porter may I ask you a few questions?

RON. . . Sure.

REP. How do you all know that Mr. T. J. is actually 189 years old and that his birthday is actually today I mean did any slave really know his date of birth in Africa didn't they go by the moons or something?

RON. He told me.

REP. But isn't it true that he hasn't actually spoken in this century.

RON. Yeah.

REP. Well —

RON. Well what?

F&F. **HEY!! RUFF-RUFF RUFF-RUFF BOW-WOW BOW-WOW RUFF-RUFF RUFF-RUFF BOW-WOW BOW-WOW RUFF-RUFF RUFF-RUFF!!**

NAT is Frightened out of the Woods/F&F by the BARKING.
HE Surrenders himself to a JAIL CELL.
Once again WIT, T. J. and RON are the only witnesses.

REP. I'm told that Mr. T. J. speaks to you on quite a regular basis . . .

RON. (*To* T. J.) Did you —

WIT. YES!

REP. Um, excuse me . . . um . . . Mr. Porter?

RON. What?!

REP. Your cousin Octavia told me that your Great-Great-Grandfather here speaks to you quite often and I was just curious as to how that was possible when he hasn't **spoken** in the last —

RON. He. shines.

REP. . . . . oh . . . . . .

277

F&F. **IF YOU DON'T WANNA PARTY TAKE YO' BLACK ASS HOME!!! HEY!...**

TURNER SUFFERS.
HE PRAYS.

T. J. AND RON WATCH. STUNNED. AS:

The REPORTER crosses to TURNER.

REP. Mr. Turner?

No Answer.

REP. Mr. Nat Turner? ... My name is Thomas R. Gray and I'm here to take your confession.

No Answer.

REP. Mr. Turner? ...

No Answer.

REP. Look you can give me your story or I can make it up and even if you do confess to me I'm probably gonna put in a little filler here and there so listen Nigga yo' silence will do you no benefit you dig? Because these country white folks ain't gonna let you breathe much longer after going out here with a hatchet and chopping up every white face you could find.

No Answer.

The REPORTER begins to WRITE.

REP. ... the CONFESSIONS of NAT TURNER ...
the leader of the late insurrection in Southhampton Virginia as fully and voluntarily —

NAT. ... Blood on the Corn ...

REP. That's better.
Speak.
Speak and although I'm a white slave-holding racist
Speak and you'll live forever on the pages I write.

NAT. ... The Sun turned Black ...

REP. SPEAK.
And Books about Books about you will be written.

278

NAT. . . . Figures Hieroglyphics Numbers . . .

REP. SPEAK.
And HIStory shall REVERBERATE with your name.

NAT. My name is Nat Turner.

REP. MAKE
HIS-
MY-
STORY

A Camera Crew converge on NAT.

NAT. And a Voice said unta' me —

OMNES. SPEAK.

REP. Is it true that your semen was found in the mouth and ears of several of the white children that you murdered Mr. Turner?

NAT. SUCH IS YOUR LUCK, SUCH YOU ARE CALLED TO SEE, LET IT COME ROUGH OR SMOOTH, YOU MUST BEAR IT ALL.

REP. What do you think the DNA tests on your Blood samples found in the corn fields will prove Mr. Turner and is it true that **you** yourself actually only killed **one** person?

A Police HELICOPTER appears above and drowns TURNER in Light.

NAT. The ALMIGHTY whispered to me —

OMNES. SPEAK!

REP. What about reports that all three major networks **and** TURNER NETWORK TELEVISION which many feel is owned by the distant relative of your former now dead slave master what about reports that they all offered you 6 figure deals for your story and film rights?

NAT. BEHOLD ME AS I STAND IN THE HEAVENS

REP. Is it true that Wesley Snipes and Denzel Washington have both been approached to portray you in the 8 hour mini-series that FOX TELEVISION wants to produce?

OMNES. SPEAK!

NAT. The HOLY GHOST sang—

REP. Spike Lee has called you his hero Mr. Turner any thoughts on that?

NAT. SEEK YE THE KINGDOM OF HEAVEN AND ALL THINGS SHALL BE ADDED UNTO YOU!

OMNES. SPEAK!

REP. Dead. Joseph Travers and wife and three children Mrs. Elizabeth Turner Hartwell Prebles Sarah Newsome

F&F. **FISHTAIL. FISHTAIL. FISHTAIL. HEY!**

NAT. BLACK AND WHITE SPIRITS IN BATTLE.

OMNES. SPEAK!

REP. Dead. Mrs. P. Reese and son William Trajan Doyle Harry Bryant and wife and child and wife's mother

F&F. **THE CRACK FAMILY! THE CRACK FAMILY!**

OMNES. SPEAK!

NAT. THE BLOOD OF CHRIST WAS ON THE CORN

REP. **Dead.** Mrs. Catherine Whitehead son Richard and four daughters and grandchild

F&F. **THE ROACH, THE ROACH, THE ROACH IS ON THE WALL**

OMNES. SPEAK!

NAT. FIGHT AGAINST THE SERPENT.

REP. **Dead.** Salathiel Francis Nathaniel Francis's overseer and two children John T. Brown George Vaughn Mrs. Levi Waller and ten children

NAT. THE NEGROES FOUND FAULT THEY MURMURED AGAINST ME.

F&F. **SHAKE IT MAKE SHO' YOU DON BREAK IT.**

OMNES. SPEAK!

NAT. THE DAY OF JUDGEMENT HAD COME!

REP. **Dead.** William Williams's wife two boys Mrs. Caswell Worrell and child Mrs. Rebecca Vaughn Anne Eliza Vaughn and son Arthur

OMNES. SPEAK!

F&F. **SIDE TA' SIDE UP N' DOWN SIDE TA' SIDE UP N' DOWN SIDE TA' SIDE HEY!**

NAT. THUNDER ROLLED IN THE HEAVENS.

OMNES. SPEAK!

REP. **Dead.** Mrs. John K. Williams and child Mrs. Jacob Williams and three children and Edwin Durry — amounting to fifty-five.

F&F. **BOW-WOW BOW-WOW**

OMNES. SPEAK!

NAT. the day was fast approaching —

F&F. **WORK NAT WORK!**

NAT. when the FIRST should be LAST and the LAST should be FIRST —

OMNES. SPEAK!

NAT. FIRST. LAST. LAST. FIRST.

F&F. **WORK PROPHET WORK!**

NAT. FIRST. LAST. LAST. FIRST.

OMNES. SPEAK!

F&F. **WORK NAT WORK!**

NAT. FIRST. LAST. LAST. FIRST.

SILENCE.

REP. The judgement of the court is that
you be taken hence to the jail from whence you came thence
to the place of execution and
on Friday next between
the hours of 10 A.M. and 2 P.M.

F&F. work prophet work

281

REP. be hung by the neck until you are

NAT. **FIRST.**

REP. **DEAD.**

NAT. **LAST.**

REP. **DEAD.**

NAT. **LAST.**

REP. **DEAD.**

NAT. **FIRST.**

(*Pause.*)

REP. and may the lord have mercy upon your soul.

F&F. **IF YOU DON'T WANNA PARTY TAKE YO' BLACK ASS HOME.**

A MIDNIGHT SHINE

RON massages T. J.'s left eye and the middle toe on his right foot.

(*Pause.*)

RON. . . . how ya' feelin'?

WIT. Old.

RON. Like your party?

WIT. Borin'.

RON. Huh?

WIT. Borin' people borin' party.

RON. . . . how that feel gramps?

WIT. Mo' eye.

RON. It's late. You should let me put you in bed before I leave.

WIT. Where you goin?

RON. I gotta go back to New York. Gotta go back to work, to school.

WIT. Ain't you don' wit that yet?

RON. Kinda, I just gotta do my thesis, then I'm really done that's why I gotta be gittin' back now research meetings . . .

WIT. What's a thesis?

RON. Fo' me it's a long paper I gotta write and lots of interviews I gotta do and books I gotta read.

WIT. Then what?

RON. Huh?

WIT. Then what you do after you don' wrote it?

RON. Then I gotta show it to a bunch of white folks who'll tell me whether or not I'm smart enough for them to let me stop paying them all my money every year.

WIT. Then what?

RON. Hopefully I can git a job and be like one of them white folks that look at other people's thesis.

WIT. Then what?

RON. . . . Gramps I think you're lil' tired and it's time for you to go to bed.

WIT. Then what?

RON. Then nuthin'. What you mean then what? Then I'm done. I git a job. I live, become fabulously rich and mildly famous.

WIT. Then what?

RON. Then I die I guess I don't know.

WIT. I didn't.

RON. You didn't what?

WIT. Die.

OCTAVIA appears in front of a mirror feeling her body.

After a moment, GERTHA enters.

GERTHA. What are you doing?

OCT. Mama take a look at my arm.

283

She does.

GERTHA. What about it?

OCT. Take a good look at it.

GERTHA. What?

OCT. Don't this arm look a lot longer than the otha' one?

GERTHA. . . . no.

OCT. Look here at my leg see how it bends out and away a lil' bit?

GERTHA. Octavia do you know what time it is?

OCT. I feel lak
I feel weird I don't know you know lak somethin' else or somebody else don' got into me inside me ain't that somethin' ain't
that weird?

(*Pause.*)

GERTHA. (*Through her teeth.*) Octavia are you pregnant?

OCT. Naw mama I ain't pregnant what you talkin' 'bout? . . . look
at my lips nah don't the bottom look a lil' bigger than the top?

RON. Gramps my plane leaves in two hours you need to git some
sleep you've had a big day I'm sure —

WIT. You a faggot ain't ya?

(*Beat.*)

WIT. When was you plannin' on tellin' me?

RON. Excuse me?

WIT. When was you plannin' on tellin' me? You tol' yo' cousins
didn't ya'?

RON. Yes.

WIT. Yo' Aint Gertha know don't she?

RON. Yes.

WIT. Everybody at that party today they know don't they?

RON. Yeah.

284

WIT. Even that reporter know don't he?

RON. Probably.

WIT. So when was you plannin' on tellin' me I'm not altogether blind . . . yet.

RON. . . . I didn't I didn't think I I I wasn't plannin' on telling you.

WIT. Why not?

RON. I—

WIT. You gat a special friend?

RON. . . . uh no.

WIT. **Why not?**

RON. This is somewhat of a surprise and I don't quite know if I feel completely comfortable talking to you about—

WIT. You think I been comfortable sittin' heah in this rolla' chair fo' the last 100 years you the only one of mine that could understand me I gat in this heah chair when I turned 89 years old most my friends was dead o' dyin' but I sat and I waited I waited 75 years sayin' nuthin' ta' nobody barely movin' even I waited 75 years fo' you to be born then I waited 25 mo' years fo' this moment fo' you ta' understand the favor I need ta' ask ya' 'n now you don' gat uncomfortable boy you know when I knew you was a faggot—

RON. What favor—

WIT. —22 hours I knew when you was just 22 hours old you popped outta Lillie and the next thang I knew she had you stuffed in my face cryin' 'bout how cute you was I knew then 22 hours was all it took not even a full day old.

RON. Did you say a favor you waited 100 years to ask me a favor what kind of favor Gramps?

WIT. I—

RON. Note I have a plane to catch Gramps so we may have to cut our little chat short and save it for your next birthday.

OCT. My butt look bigga to you?

285

GERTHA. You always had a big butt.

OCT. No you the one always had the big butt don't even try it.

They laugh.

GERTHA. I'm going to see if Ronnie gat Gramps in bed okay com' and let's wish 'im one last happy birthday.

OCT. Mama Gramps probably cain't even hear us he probably thought we was a bunch of crazy baboons this evenin' hoopin' and hollerin'.

GERTHA. Don't talk lak that 'bout yo' Gramps that man useta' be a slave.

OCT. And?

GERTHA. And that means somethin'.

OCT. What?

GERTHA. That you ain't suppose ta' talk 'bout 'im that's what nah let's go say goodnite.

OCT. Wait a minute let me look at one mo' thang.

She examines her belly gingerly as a pregnant woman would.

GERTHA. Don't play heifa.

They laugh.

WIT. Take me home Ronnie.

RON. **This** is the favor you waited a century to ask me?

WIT. Take me home.

(*Beat.*)

RON. Gramps you are at home yo' bed is right in the other room I'm gonna put you in it and guess what when you wake up you will still be at home believe me let's go.

WIT. **Drive** me.

RON. What.

WIT. **Carry** me. **Push** me. **Take. me. Home. Home. . . .**

RON. You. are. not. E. T. okay? Your. name. is. T. J. okay? You. live. here. Earth. Right here with Aint Gertha remember Aint Gertha you were passed to Aint Gertha after Aint Isabella died remember that I came to pick you up and brought you here now everybody already thinks that I'm crazy because I can speak to you and they cain't so I most certainly am not going to load you in a bicycle basket and try to peddle across the sky it ain't hap-penin' got it I love you but it ain't happenin' I gat a plane to catch and you obviously have sleep to catch Beddi-bye.

SILENCE.

WIT. **Slaves.**

RON. I know you were a slave the whole world knows you were a slave Gramps that's what we spent the day celebrating this whole day was devoted to your birthday the 189th birthday of a former slave my Great Great Grandfather **you.**

WIT. Prophet Nat.

OCTAVIA and GERTHA cross to RON and T. J.

OCT. Hi Gramps hi you?

GERTHA. Ronnie why ain't you don' put 'im in bed I know he must be knocked out.

RON. He ain't wanna go to bed yet he wanna ask me a favor.

OCT. What time is your plane?

RON. 5 A.M.

OCT. **Don't miss it.**

RON. Shut up.

GERTHA. Come on let's take 'im ta' bed.

RON. No no I got 'im we was just going he wanted to have a man to man talk.

OCT. With who?

RON. Funny.

GERTHA. I'll lay his p.j.s out on the bed Nite Gramps Happy Birthday.

OCT. Nite Old Man.

GERTHA. Octavia!?!

OCT. I just wanted to see if he'd move nite Gramps Happy Birthday.

GERTHA. Nite Ronnie have a safe trip baby I left you a lil' somethin' down in the kitchen fo' the plane ride.

RON. Thank you.

OCT. Nite Head.
I'm comin' up there next month ta' look at Columbia remember.

RON. Nite Aint Gertha
Octavia you call me before you show up I don't like surprises!

OCTAVIA and GERTHA disappear.

WIT. Prophet Nat.

RON. What about him.

WIT. Me.
We.
Slaves.
Prophet Nat.
Mama.

RON. Gramps, dear, you'll have to be a bit more clear with me.

WIT. Yo' story.

RON. My story?

WIT. Yo' story is at HOME.
Take me.

RON. Take you where?!

WIT. To Nat Turner?

RON. Nat Turner?

WIT. Prophet
They hung 'im
Prophet Nat.

RON. What we saw in the backyard tonight is that what you're
talking about is that —

WIT. INSURRECTION.

RON. (*Quiet.*) . . . oh my God . . . you were there.

WIT. JERUSALEM.

RON. Jer—
Jerusalem.
Nat Turner was on his way to Jerusalem from Southampton
Jerusalem, Virginia.

WIT. INSURRECTION.

RON. YES!
The Insurrection in Southampton.
Gramps remember my thesis remember that paper and books and
interviews I just told you about Gramps listen closely to me—
I need to know.
100 years.
100 years I never thought to ask you about Turner you

WIT. I. was. there.

(*Pause.*)

RON. Tell me!
Tell me Gramps unbelievable
100 years un. fucking. believable you were there
Wait
WAIT.
I'm going to git my tape recorder from my suitcase it's just
out in—
DON'T MOVE.

He exits.
He enters.

RON. Shit.
No one can hear but me in my head
Shit. Shit. Shit.
No problem no problem Ron calm down I'll remember I'll re-
member every single detail every word I'll remember
or I'll kill myself

He embraces T. J.

RON. Holding History.
I'm Holding History in my arms
Gramps
SPEAK.

ON THE ROAD

Hertz Rent-a-car.

RON. Where are we going Gramps?

WIT. Home.

RON. Gramps don't say that word again okay fo' your benefit don't say that again.

WIT. Don't ask then.

RON. Don't ask? We are in the middle of no-where we are on a road to no-where

WIT. turn here

RON. I am driving to no-where in a

WIT. left here

RON. Hertz Rent-a-car that is due back in two hours

WIT. along there

RON. a plane that has left a connection that I've missed

WIT. keep straight

RON. where are we going?!

(*Beat.*)

WIT/RON. Home.

RON. yes I forgot I asked didn't I?

Suddenly, WHITE SPIRITS and BLACK SPIRITS appear, BATTLING, around the car.

He swerves so as to not hit anyone.

RON. Gramps do you see what I —

WIT. Yes.

RON. Okay good just checkin' —

He swerves once more.

RON. If this car picks up and starts to fly I'll shit I swear I'll shit.

WIT. Don't swear.

POLICE sirens.
RON pulls over.
SPIRITS disappear.
COP appears.

COP. Let me see your license.

RON. uh okay uh it's an out of state license I've had a couple of drinks because of my Gramps' here birthday officer but I'm not drunk I just thought I was gonna hit those ghosts fighting that's all I was trying to
to not hit any of them.

COP. You saw ghosts?

RON. Yes.

COP. Fighting?

RON. Yes.

COP. And you were trying not to hit them?

RON. Yes.

COP. How many drinks have you had?

RON. I can't remember exactly it was a long time ago and they have I'm sure worn off by now I'm just taking my Gramps here home that's all officer he's had a big day.

COP. And where is his home?

RON. I don't know I mean I I

COP. Step outta the car please.

RON. Officer really I can explain kinda I'm a Ph.D. candidate at Columbia University

COP. Step outta the car please.

RON. my major is Slave History and my Gramps here was a slave so —

COP. I won't tell you again to step —

RON. he's 189 years old he can only move his left eye and his middle —

COP. Outta the car!

RON. okay.

WIT. Tell 'im we gats things ta' do.

RON. What?

WIT. Tell 'im we don't have no time fo' this mess.

RON. Are you outta your mind don't answer that.

WIT. Tell 'im.

The COP grabs RON.

COP. I tried to be nice but —

WIT. GET YO' HANDS OFFA MY GREAT. GREAT. GRANDSON.

(*Pause.*)

The COP looks at RON for a moment.
He backs up.
He disappears.

RON. He must've heard that how did he hear you he's going back to his car to call in the troops we're in the middle of no-where they're gonna lynch us they're he's leaving he's he's waving goodbye

WIT. Wave back.

RON does.

WIT. Smile.

RON does.

WIT. Now start this car up and let's go.

RON starts car and they pull off.

SILENCE.

WIT. Why ain't you talkin'?

RON. What would you like for me to talk about gramps I'm tired I don't know where we are —

WIT. I do —

RON. I don't know where or why I'm going to wherever I'm going I hate these dark country roads because they inevitably have white country people living near them all you can say is HOME HOME HOME so other than that I don't have too much else to contribute to this conversation you know I need to find out about Nat Turner I've just told you how important it is to my thesis but you seem unwilling to disclose any useful information so —

WIT. Let's talk 'bout Faggots first —

RON brakes car.

RON. Look.
Gramps.

WIT. What?

RON. I know you ain't been ALL here these past 100 years I know you've been busy waiting on me and everything BUT
Only Faggots are allowed to call each other Faggots.
No. body. else.

WIT. I heard lotsa folks that weren't no faggots callin' othas faggots some to they face even it started 'bout 60 years ago I reckon —

RON. Well they're not allowed to now.

WIT. Why not?

RON. Because.

WIT. Because what?

RON. BEcause because it's not it ain't P.C.

WIT. Who dat? He any kin ta' that E. T. you was talkin' 'bout a little while back?

RON. No. Hush.

He starts to drive again.

293

Robert O'Hara

(*Pause.*)

WIT. What you want I should call you then?

RON. "Ronnie" just like everybody else what you've always called me "Ronnie."

WIT. Okay.
    Turn heah.

(*Pause.*)

WIT. Ronnie?

RON. Yes Gramps.

WIT. You lak ta' have men lak that cop fella sit in yo' lap sometimes?

No Answer.

WIT. Huh?

RON. Hush.

WIT. Do ya'?

RON. I don't wanna discuss this with you.

WIT. Why not?

RON. Because I don't!

WIT. Why!?!

RON. Because I'm not —

BOTH. Comfortable.

RON. Yes.
    I'm not **comfortable**
    I'm happy you **know**
    Good
    Dandy
    but I don't wanna talk about my sex life

WIT. I didn't ask 'bout yo' sex life I was just wonderin' since you was a

RON. DON'T say it

WIT. I thought you wanted ta' know everythang?

294

RON. I do but —

WIT. So you want me ta' tell you everythang but you don't wanna tell me nuthin' you ain't comfortable.

RON. Gramps it's **not that** —

WIT. Then what is it then you go round tellin' everybody but me I thought we was buddies

RON. We are buddies, Gramps

WIT. Then why you left me out?

RON. I didn't leave you out —

WIT. You left me outta it Ronnie! Just lak all them other fools leave me outta it 'til it's time fo' 'em to sho' back up at my party.

RON. Those people care about you a whole lot.

WIT. Don't change the subject.

RON. I'm not changing the subject.

WIT. Then talk 'bout you bein' a faggot.

RON. I have nothing particularly interesting to say about it!

WIT. Is it fun?

RON. Is it fun?

WIT. Yeah. Is bein' a faggot fun?

RON. I don't really know what you mean.

WIT. How many years you been at that book learnin' and you don't know what fun mean? It mean lak havin' a nice time lak if you —

RON. I know what fun means Gramps.

WIT. Then why can't you just answer my question?

RON. Because it's not somethin' I'm use to being asked I've been asked a lot of different things but not ever is it fun
it is . . . fun . . . at times . . .

WIT. Then what?

RON. Huh?

WIT. Then what about the otha' times when it ain't fun?

(*Pause.*)

RON. It's not fun being alone, Gramps.

WIT. You ain't alone I'm wit ya'.

RON. I mean
at the times
when you're not with me Gramps
I'm alone
most of the time

WIT. Even when I'm not with ya' you ain't alone 'cos I'm still wit ya' even when you ain't 'round me.

RON smiles.

RON. . . . thanks Gramps

WIT. Fo' what
we ain't there yet.

RON. I know . . . nuthin'.

Silence.

WIT. You happy Ronnie?

RON. Happy is not quite the word I'd use.

WIT. Use anotha one then I know a few.

RON. . . . I keep myself busy, Gramps.

WIT. What busy gat ta' do wit happy?

RON. . . . sometimes busy makes you not need to be so happy
makes you not notice it so much
sometimes busy makes you forget happy

(*Pause.*)

WIT. Look at me Ronnie.

RON. Gramps I'm driving.

WIT. I don't care I said look at me boy.

RON does.

WIT. The worse thing you can do in this life is fo'git happy. . . .
now look at the road befo' we crash inta' that tree.

RON looks up just in time to swerve, yelling, out of harm's way.

WIT. There's too many folks out here that's gon' try ta' make you
fo'git you don't need to help 'em none
    all 'em folks that jumped in that water comin' ova' heah
    the othas that was pushed and even them ones that was thrown
ova' by they mamas they was neva' fo'gotten by us 'cos if we
would've fo'gotten 'em we wouldn't have been able to git through
de trouble
    them ones that was left on them boats after they gat heah they
could neva' fo'git them othas 'cos they learned the **power** behind
'memberin' they saw that **power** of **'memberin'** in each otha'
eyes as they passed one anotha' comin' and goin' up and down
off and on that **shoppin'** block they gave that **power** on ta' the
new birth the new life that's the **power** that made a nigga stand
up strong after he had his back and neck opened up by massa's
headman it made a niggra walk out her shack wit her head held
high after massa done visited her in the late night befo' and it
made **Turner** RISE up and shout out at the Heavens
    no don't you neva' ever fo'git Nuthin' / especially happy /
    'cos that **power** behind **'memberin'** is too **strong**
    it's in yo' blood

Silence.

WIT. You think we didn't have no fags —
I mean no people lak you on the plantation?

RON. Never thought about it frankly.

WIT. You should think 'bout it frankly once and a while you should
you didn't just happen ta' be that way ya' know it took a lotta
plannin' and organizin'.

RON stops car.

RON. What are you talking about?

WIT. Keep drivin'.

RON. What did you just say?

WIT. Keep. Drivin'. You deaf?

297

Robert O'Hara

(*Pause.*)

RON begins the car again.

(*Pause.*)

RON. Tell me.

WIT. Tell you what?

RON. Gramps don't play.

WIT. I don't wanna make you any more uncomfortable than you already is.

RON. Make me uncomfortable **tell me**!

WIT. Don't raise yo' voice Ronnie I'm sittin' ratt next ta' ya' I ain't in the grave just yet.

RON. I'm sorry who planned it?

WIT. Who you think?

RON. I don't know who I'm asking you who?

WIT. GAWD.

RON. Oh, God—

WIT. That's right.
GAWD
   created certain people a certain way and certain othas another way what you lak ain't necessarily what another person might go in fo' what I wanna do wit somebody may not be what another person wanna do wit somebody you understand?

RON. Kinda.

WIT. GAWD
   planned it
   planned you. me. my mama my daddy and so fo'th.

RON. You tellin' me there were Homosexual Slaves on the plantation?

WIT. What's dat?

RON. Faggots.

WIT. Yeah!
Ronnie there was white slaves on the plantation po' white trash
we useta call 'em —

RON. We still do.

WIT. — cos they was thought no betta than us niggas sometimes
they was treated worse than we was 'cos Massa thought the
white trash bein' white lak hisself should know betta than ta'
git po' in the first place there was Injuns too though we didn't
call 'em that to they face they lak ta' be called Apache Toma-
Toma this that and the otha thang but we didn't com' cross
"Injun" in they face 'cos they liable ta' cut the hair offa yo' head
   you think wit all them half-naked people out there up under
the sun pickin cotton sweatin' bendin ova that somebody wasn't
lookin' at somebody else's body that somebody wasn't givin' a
lil' wink-wink ta' somebody else I even had a few fellas give me
a lil look-see from time ta' time and it didn't do no harm ta' nobody to go behind a tree or cabin every nah and then and once
in a while grind up on one anotha —

RON. **WHAT!?!**

WIT. Don't you stop this car!
Everybody laked it
some just laked it mo' and did it much mo' than othas
women wit women
men wit men
women wit men
men with sheep
whateva'
   nah we did havta' keep it hush-hush 'cos if Massa found out
ain't no tellin' what he'd do 'cos what wit his bible teachin' and
everythang hell knowin' Massa he might've joined in but everybody knew it was happenin' even if they say they didn't some
folk nah try to say that white folks one that introduced us ta'
that stuff try ta' make folks think that niggas didn' know nuthin'
'bout such thangs just 'cos they don't wanna believe that if it
feels good somebody somewhere that they kin ta' was doin' it
befo' even in Africa you think oura people didn't lak ta' feel good
too don't you believe everythang you read in them history books
boy not even in them new ones they claim gat everythang in 'em
that was left outta the first ones some thangs ain't written out

fo' ya' on a piece of paper somethangs you 'memba lak you 'memba yo' mama's face or the smell of cane somethangs you just keep in yo' head 'tween yo' ears sometimes it safer that way you understand?

SILENCE

RON. I need to git some sleep.

Every Man Jack of You
Erik Ehn

Characters:
JULIUS CAESAR
JACK
CAESARETTE
EASTERN EUROPEAN WOMAN
CLAIR
KARL CASTLE
MARK ANTONY

1

(A twenty-three-year-old man drives a car on a winding road, late at night; an odometer reads out the miles in supertitle. The man eats crunchy food out of a cellophane bag. He is wearing black wool pants, a long-sleeved white shirt and a tightly knotted tie. His feet are bare. He sweats heavily. He listens to a magic NPR station — KARL CASTLE played backwards. The back seat is filled with neat cardboard boxes — this man is a travelling salesman. The ghost of JULIUS CAESAR appears in the road in front of him.)

CAESAR. The small actions of the pine branches are cat-cock fur roughed into midnight. And everything abrades to fluid. Pine acids, backwards radio, motor surging scratch against cruise control, and the wounds of Julius Caesar too.

(The driver opens his fly and starts to masturbate; he uses the cellophane bag to save his pants.)

Spanish fly flavored pork-rinds drill paprika cavities up into aluminum nerves. Coffee scratches fluid out the lower lids and from the soft female flesh at the inside pinches. Soda pops rub

301

two different weaves of rayon together inside your ear. Hair cut scratches your high starched collar sending static radio, and the boil of stations renders night to a shiny mass.

(*The crinkling bag and the radio static rise to a din. The car fax quickens. The man zips up; Caesar disappears. The man tries to send a fax and make a call at the same time.*)

JACK. Interference. Honey. Gone to — far away. Will make this the last leg, and then back again soon. The odometer puts me in mind of —

(*The odometer turns into a slot machine. The car goes away and* JACK *is playing the nickel slots obsessively, Caesar's Palace. A cocktail waitress enters; she wears a toga that doesn't quite cover her sex. She wears gartered stockings, shiny, translucent. Muzak plays: "In-A-Gadda-Da-Vida."*)

CAESARETTE. Cocktail?

JACK. The air in Tahoe —

CAESARETTE. Cocktail?

JACK. The air in Tahoe would be good for me —

CAESARETTE. Complimentary cocktail?

JACK. The air in Tahoe would be good for me if I ever breathed it. (*A surge of romantic music.* JACK *turns to face her.*) If you were the farmer's daughter we could be in the same joke together.

CAESARETTE. Cocktail?

(*Muzak resumes; they maintain eye contact.*)

JACK. I'll take a Rob Roy, a Manhattan and an Old-Fashioned, and kind of mix 'em all up together, okay? (*He slips a finger in her mouth; she doesn't resist.*) Tastes like nickels, I bet. (*He takes his fingers out.*)

CAESARETTE. Towelette? (*She hands him one. She crosses away;* JACK *goes to the bathroom.*)

JACK. The air in Tahoe is faraway.

(*The waitress tells this story to an old* EASTERN EUROPEAN WOMAN *playing at another machine.*)

302

CAESARETTE. In the bathroom, he used the towelette to clean his gender; it stings. He smashes a mirror and uses a fragment to flash a sequence into the electric eye of the auto-flush urinal. He faxes the towelette to his wife.

JACK. (*The area code:*) 918.

(*His magazine-beautiful eighteen-year-old wife,* CLAIR, *wears a tight blue shirt and heavy eye makeup. She's going to the bathroom in Tulsa — the fax comes up between her legs.*)

CLAIR. He has sores.

E.E. WOMAN. I don't speak English.

(*The wife finishes. Three martyrs broken on the wheels of the slot machine fall into alignment. Their chests are open and their hearts are cherries. Ten thousand nickels pour out of the machine — rats eat them before* JACK *can get back to them.* JACK *and his wife,* CLAIR, *wander outside, drunk. They stop at the same time, although they remain in separate worlds.*)

JACK. The fuchsia berries are pendulous.

CLAIR. (*Reading the fax.*) "Keno, Eggos and vinyl." (*She sits down, cross-legged.* JACK *falls; he put his head in her lap. She still doesn't see him.*)

CAESARETTE. (*Delivering a drink to the* EASTERN EUROPEAN WOMAN.) When he goes to the diner —

JACK. When she was wet, she was as soft as Irish moss, and tiny veined flowers dangled from the tops of her dewy hairs.

CAESARETTE. He has the waffles. He plays Keno with a big black crayon according to where the syrup collects in the grid of his breakfast. The wool of his pants crackles like cat-sex against the arched back of the night. But it is not night anymore.

JACK. (*Singing.*) I didn't get in for five years and then it's too dry to push/ A bird in hand is a flip-book — there's a better one in the bush.

(*The odometer says: "Five Years Pass."*)

CAESARETTE. When he goes back to his room at five in the morning, all he can get is the Keno channel, for five years. Pipes break and he has to live off air conditioner run-off for water, until rats eat through the wires. Then he's out, one spring, up a hill to fetch a coin bucket full of fresh. Poor Clair is his second wife and they are discalced.

> (JACK *starts to crawl up a snowy mountain: a mountain like in a beer commercial.*)

E.E. WOMAN. Caesarette, take a break.

> (*She does.* E.E. WOMAN *takes over as narrator — playing two slot machines at once now.*)

Caesarette cleans herself in the breakroom. The breakroom is filled with precious jewels and clean cotton towels warm from the dryer. A massive pearl comes out of her mouth. He read a story like this in the track locker room in his Catholic high school.

CLAIR. There is an extra set of footprints in the snow. The big guns are starting in the hills.

> (CAESARETTE *walks backwards in front of* JACK, KARL CASTLE *crawls backwards, talks backwards, away. Distant guns.*)

E.E. WOMAN. The pearl is slick and iridescent; the waitress has been chewing black licorice. She rubs the pearl on her privacy, lubrication and two fingers of pressure, outside, in, a 360-degree tongue. Hips rock forward, rider to the pommel, and the pearl sluices up her vagina, held there, controlled back and forth by the muscles inside. Lips demurring open, shut, with a slight viscous click. Pearl's an eyeball. It sees the sun that morning, her head goes back, and she's blind.

CLAIR. He comes to the ice legs of Caesarette. He falls asleep as ice water comes to body temperature in his mouth.

> (*Blackout.*)

2

(In JACK*'s motel room — the blinds drawn. The TV shows Keno.* JACK *has taped a waffle iron to the ceiling. He stands on the bed, his left hand forced against the iron's live surface. On his right hand, a catcher's mitt. He masturbates into the mitt. Meanwhile, elsewhere, a still-drunk* CLAIR *uses a combination pay phone/slot machine.)*

CLAIR. Jack? Ja — Jack?

(Jackpot. Nickels galore. JACK *gets off. The* CAESARETTE *comes by the phone booth with a bucket and collects the nickels, the rats in her wake nibbling coins and toes.)*

CAESARETTE. He's down to a dollar. Five years. He's in a dollar motel in the desert between Tahoe and Reno.

(A recorded voice comes over the phone.)

VOICE. We're sorry.

*(*CLAIR *is suddenly alone on stage. She sits in* JACK*'s motel room and smokes. In the distance, at a fair,* JACK *stands next to a large clown-face with an open mouth. Baseballs are fast-pitched into the mouth;* JACK *feels each impact in his chest.)*

CLAIR. Neon serpents, diamond backs, abstract themselves through sand, motile and repetitive. The catcher's mitt into which he cashed out gets pregnant the way a horseshoe crab does, tight in its shell, and gives birth to baseballs. The balls are hum-babied against Jack's chest until he comes up cherry.

(The pitches stop, and JACK *shows the sacred heart.)*

The last one unravels — the string is DNA — the serpent string leads Jack out into the desert. The line follows an extra set of footprints in the sand. There's a ball of putty in the center. Jack picks it up and takes an impression of his teeth.

(The clown's gone; JACK *is crawling across the desert floor, chasing a ball of putty. He makes an impression of his grimace and lays it down.)*

The desert floor speaks in Caesarette's voice.

CAESARETTE. He puts his hand to his face — the waffle grid transfers. His features are under the control of this pattern. The other baseballs fasten in the sand and come to maturity. They move forward through the heat waves. Their faces are baseball-kid; kid gloves. Tongues between the fingers. The kids finish the crossword on Dad's face with invisible ink off their tongues. The action of these tongues is contagious.

(*A hand puppet rises from the sand and licks* JACK*'s face until* JACK*'s tongue is moving too. The hand goes away.*)

CLAIR. The desert fantasizes about Marine World USA. The seals: licorice tongues, multiple, moving in one mouth of clear water.

CAESARETTE. He moves his own tongue. He puts his mouth down on the labia of the desert, and kippers fly to seals.

(*The sound of women suffering in the distance.*)

CLAIR. Suffering women under the maguey on the sides. Left there.

CAESARETTE. You will never forget this.

(*Blackout.*)

3

(*A tree;* JACK *stage left and the* E.E. WOMAN *stage right. The* E.E. WOMAN *is young now — appears about twenty, is fifteen; her clothes are the same she wore when she was old.* JACK *reaches around the trunk and unbuttons her orange sweater.* CAESAR *and* MARK ANTONY *lean down from the branches with nooses — an electric cord for the woman, a belt for the man.* CLAIR *reads a series of postcards.*)

CLAIR. "Dear Clair. I die of autoerotic asphyxia at age twenty-eight in Kansas City, Kansas. The radio is playing." I don't hear any radio, Jack.

(*The nooses tighten.*)

"In the Lutheran church nearby it is crayfish time — the Swedes are singing and the red shells cry buzzbomb harmonies."

(*Whistle, pop — bombs.*)

"They are putting on a play and white cheesecloth is blowing. The Lawyer and the Levite and the Samaritan. Altar girl and the massive candle. Wax on my chest. This heart is sacred. The veins in the eyes crackle to flame. Pearl expensed.

(*The* E.E. WOMAN *and* JACK *are off the floor.* CLAIR *speaks for herself.*)

The object of his attachment is on the other side of a tree in the cool forest in Tuzla . . . I mean Tulsa. (*Looking at the woman.*) I would rather hang from the tree with her than cut her down and dig, Jack.

(*The wife cuts the woman down; buttons her sweater and buries her. The sound of tigers moving through the forest.*)

JACK. (*His eyes bugged large.*) Crayfish eyeball. Pop.

Moon Under Miami

Scenes From a Play

John Guare

Characters:

OTIS

MERMAIDS

VOICE

FRAN FARKUS

REGGIE KAYAK

OSVALDO MUNOZ

WALT WILCOX

BELDEN

SHELLEY SLUTSKY

GISELLE ST. JUST

WAYNE BENTINE

(A man — is it an Eskimo? — appears in a parka, mukluks. Snow falls on him. Wind. He lowers his binoculars.)

OTIS. *(To us.)* I love the way Alaska feels. You have all the dark at once. And then you have all the daylight at the same time. It's neater. The hard part of it is it is harder to shadow people. First of all, there are no shadows. Fashion wise, it's harder to trail people because everyone looks the same. But that's all democratic and good. In the Inuit — the Eskimo language — Alaska is the word for Great Land. And it is a great land. Look! A caribou leaping! I sit on an ice floe here at Point Hope and watch Russia on the horizon across the Bering Strait. To see your enemy that close. Oh, I know, I know. The evil empire is gone, but the Russians are still over there, nabbing our whale blubber, and the Federal Bureau of Investigation of which I'm an agent — Hello — Special Agent Otis Presby here — accept no substitutes — the bureau is nothing if not vigilant. The lesson of the caribou, mountain goats, fur seals. They are peaceful because they're vigilant. They know who their enemies are. I like an enemy. Some people say the lonely quiet must drive you crazy, but No! I have all these icebergs for company. I look at my icebergs sailing by, all grand lumbering innocence like great thoughts as yet

308

unthought. Yes. All great ideas started out as icebergs. The wheel. Language. Love. Democracy. The Federal Bureau of Investigation. America. Each great idea began as an iceberg floating down to us, tilting, calving, melting until those ideas become part of our souls. (*Ominous music.*) And then one day an Eskimo floated by on an ice floe. Dead. And another. And another. And another. Their faces blue. Bloated. I know the Eskimos put their dead on ice floes and send them out to become part of the great — the Great Idea — but this one. I rake it in. This Eskimo is clutching in his dead fist two things. A hypodermic needle and a campaign button. "Time for a change. Vote for Reggie Kayak." He's the Congressman from Eek. Is there any connection? I hold up the empty bag that had contained Chinese cut heroin. (OTIS *looks at the label.*) I can't read the label in this light. Only the chlorine blue light of the iceberg. Wait. The death-dealing snow has a label. A street name. It says "Moon Under Miami."

    (*A trio of mermaid voices sing.*)

MERMAIDS. (*O.S.*) "A new kind of moon . . ."

OTIS. (*To us.*) It's Friday afternoon. I follow the Congressman from Eek. He's in a panic. I call his office, pretending to be the telephone repair man. "Is the Congressman from Eek there? He's making an emergency trip out of town? Thank you." Hmmm. Won't let him out of my sight. I have frequent flyer miles. Be back at my post on Monday. Nobody will know I'm gone. What can go wrong?

    (*A voice booms out:*)

VOICE. "The important thing in life is to have a great aim and to possess the aptitude and perseverance to follow it."

OTIS. Yes! Thank you, sir. Mr. Hoover said that. (*He begins — well, it's not a strip tease, but he starts to take off his clothes. He gives new meaning to the layered look.*) I had planned to stay in Alaska forever but sometimes you have to leave town. The trail leads me south. I mean, up here, anything's south. No. I mean, south. (*He pulls off his mukluks.* OTIS *is stripped down to a Hawaiian shirt and Bermuda shorts. He puts on sunglasses. The iceberg recedes into darkness as a trio of* MERMAIDS *appear behind* OTIS *and take him into the darkness.*)

309

MERMAIDS. (*Sing.*) "Follow me down
  Down to Miami
  It's Paradise
  To dream on the sand.
  The Bay of Biscayne
  Will simply drive you insane
  Its breezes calm you
  And then embalm you."

> (*All sound is drowned out by bongos. The* MERMAIDS *lead* OTIS *into a nightclub, all South Sea grandeur, and seat him at a table.* OTIS *looks in wonder at the giant Easter Island statues, bamboo thatching, zebra-skin banquettes, ancient signed photos of ancient celebrities on the red walls. Some of the guests enjoying their evening are simply painted behind those banquettes. The* MERMAIDS *make sure* OTIS *sees the man seated at the other table. The man is the Congressman from Alaska, waiting nervously. The* MERMAIDS *join the painted guests. The bongos play wildly. Suddenly a spotlight swings around the room.*)

VOICE. The Boom Boom Room of the Fountaine Moon Hotel proudly presents the one, the only, Fran Farkus.

> (*The spotlight comes up on* FRAN FARKUS, *an aged, ageless platinum blond.*)

FRAN. (*Sings.*) "I go to Hawaii
  When I want a good lei
  Now we're in Miami
  Going down at the Moon!
  I keep a big heart on
  My sleeve so I can say
  I'm loving Miami
  Going down at the Moon!
  Miami's romance
  Knocks you off of your feet
  I'll show you my pants
  Can you stand the heat?
  So stay in Hawaii
  If all you want's a lei
  Or else come to Miami
  And park your carcass

On top of Fran Farkus
And let's all go down to the Moon!!!"
Good evening, ladies and gentlemen. Welcome to Miami's own
Boom Boom Room, where the elite meet to eat — anything. Any-
one. The food here is shit. Let me see that menu. Stone crabs?
Thirty-five dollars! Christ, I'm sitting on a fortune. Let me intro-
duce to you the man who tickles my ivories every night and
anything else he can get his hands on. Mr. Bobby Devine! (*Sings.*)
"I'll be down to get you in a taxi, honey.
You better be ready about half past eight
We're going to dance off both our shoes
When they play those jelly roll blues
Tomorrow night at the — "
Tomorrow night? Tomorrow night! Oh, shit, I can't go tomor-
row night. Bobby, can you go? Tomorrow. I want to go tonight!
(*To us.*) How are you? Huh? How are you? This section looks
like shit. Do we have any celebrities here tonight? Let me see
the list. Oh, we have Francis the Talking Mule who's co-starring
with me in my latest film *On Golden Blonde*. Oh, seriously,
we have the Congressman from Alaska. Where are you?

> (*The spotlight finds* REGGIE KAYAK, *the Congressman from
> Alaska, who waves nervously.* FRAN *sits on* REGGIE's *lap.*)

FRAN. (*Continuing.*) Oh, he's got little snow balls.

> (OTIS, *sitting at another table, lowers a menu.*)

OTIS. (*To us.*) Who is he waiting for? Whoever sits at that table is
the source of all the drugs swarming into Alaska.

FRAN. Do I smell whale blubber? Is it true you all live in igloos
and rub each other down with whale sperm? Fabulous. Bobby,
play me some Eskimo songs. "Love To Keep Me Warm"? No.
"Winter Wonderland"? That gets too wild. "Baby, It's Cold Outside"? I wish I was frigid. It'd make life easier for the band. We
get all the politicians in here. Reagan was in here. He's a doll.
We danced. He kept circling to the right. He sang in my ear.
(*Sings.*) "Seventy-six hormones did the trick for me
Nancy's feeling just like a bride to be."

OTIS. (*To us.*) Who is the Congressman waiting for? I faxed ahead
for backup. Where are they?

(OSVALDO MUNOZ *enters, all smiles. His lapels are covered with campaign buttons.*)

FRAN. Look who we got here! Up for re-election! The Honorable Osvaldo S. Munoz, our own Congressman from Hialeah! Talk about hung like a horse.

(OSVALDO MUNOZ *takes* FRAN'S *mike.*)

OSVALDO. (*To us.*) The friendship between the Jewish community and the Cuban world of Miami warms the cockles of my heart. Of all the candidates, I ask you, who else has got a Jewish mother and a Cuban father? I am proud to say to the people of Miami — *I am a Juban.* Miami, I love you. Please re-elect me! Vaya con Dios! Shalom! For a change Vote for Munoz.

FRAN. Gracias and mazel. Time for a change. Is that a hint? Thank God I got legs. Or else the floor would smell like tuna fish. A big hand for Congressman Osvaldo Munoz. You may be nowhere in the polls but we love you.

(OSVALDO *is out of the room, waving, passing out campaign buttons.*)

You believe these erections. I mean, elections. I'll vote for the first candidate to get me laid. Nothing personal, Bobby.

(WILCOX, *a harried man in his fifties, wrinkled suit, enters the Boom Boom Room, looking for someone.* BELDEN *follows.* WILCOX *and* BELDEN *examine each table. They reach* OTIS's *table, stop and stare at him.* BELDEN *takes out a gun.* OTIS *lowers his menu.*)

OTIS. Four score.

WILCOX. Seven years.

OTIS. Hold these truths.

WILCOX. Self evident.

OTIS. Oh beautiful.

WILCOX. Spacious skies.

OTIS. Amber waves. Agent Presby down from Alaska. Thank God you're here.

(BELDEN *puts away his gun. The three shake hands.*)

WILCOX. Special Agent Walt Wilcox. Deputy Agent Belden. Welcome to Florida.

OTIS. There he is over there. The Congressman from Eek. Don't look. He mustn't suspect. We have to catch him in the act of buying.

WILCOX. What is this place? My wife would love it here.

BELDEN. Would you stop talking about your wife!

(SHELLEY SLUTSKY *and* GISELLE ST. JUST *come into the Boom Boom Room and walk to their table. He is a large powerful force in a tropic shirt, gold chains and linen jacket.* GISELLE *is terminally chic.*)

FRAN. Oh, it's not all politics. We have our regulars. A hand for Shelley Slutsky who gets more ass than a toilet seat. He's with his french pastry — what's your name, honey? Giselle. Isn't that a classy name? If she had every dick that's been stuck in her sticking out of her, she'd look like a porcupine. (*Sings.*) "Say there, you with the scars on your thighs."

(SHELLEY *is not pleased to see* REGGIE *sitting at his table.* REGGIE, *grovelling, stands up and shakes* SHELLEY's *hand as* SHELLEY *and* GISELLE *sit.* GISELLE *takes out a cellular phone and dials.* REGGIE *leans into* SHELLEY *urgently. We don't hear.*)

OTIS. There he is. This is the evil empire. Look at him. The source.

BELDEN. Oh, I know this guy.

OTIS. You know him!

BELDEN. Sheldon S. Slutsky. Continental Investors.

WILCOX. Investments, loan-sharking, laundering money, general extortion. They're harmless.

OTIS. Harmless? Like piranhas, they're harmless.

BELDEN. In Miami, these two are Little Bo-Peep and Tom Thumb.

(REGGIE *stands up from the table.*)

REGGIE. Shelley, you can't cut me off!

313

John Guare

SHELLEY. Who do you have to fuck to get a drink in this joint?

REGGIE. Thanks to me, you got into Alaska. I betrayed my own tribe, my own people, to do business with you.

SHELLEY. Waiter!

OTIS. Excuse me, sir. I'm about to become a waiter.

WILCOX. You can't moonlight.

(OTIS *goes off as* WAYNE BENTINE, *a distinguished Congressman in his sixties, enters.*)

FRAN. Look who's just come in! We are very honored to have the Congressman from my favorite state — that is if you like them small. At my age, I like them any way I can get them — Rhode Island's own Congressman Wayne Bentine!

(*Drum roll. The follow spot finds* WAYNE BENTINE. *He does not look amused. He's trapped in the light and bows.*)

So what brings the Chairman of the House Ethics Committee to the Boom Boom Room, doll-face? Don't be shy.

BENTINE. (*To us.*) We're here in Miami holding the first annual World Hunger Conference asking the question: When does foreign aid become a crippling device designed to control countries that cannot afford freedom. Which brings up the issue of can we afford democracy?

FRAN. Sounds fucking fabulous. You'll make a real difference. (*Sings.*) "What a difference a douche made."

BENTINE. Excuse me. I came in here thinking this was a supper place. (*He tries to escape.* FRAN *keeps him in the spotlight.*)

FRAN. I saw Congressman Bentine before the show. Wayne, I'm going to tell them this, and he said to me, "Fran, do you know anything about real estate?" "Well, sure." Then he whipped out his shlong and said, "Is this a lot?" "Oh, my God, that is the ugliest dick I have ever seen. Quick put that in my mouth before someone else sees it."

BENTINE. I'm obviously in the wrong —

FRAN. Seriously, Cupcake. I want to wish you the best of luck on the World Hunger Conference. World Hunger. And God knows

314

when I look at you I get hungry. So, (*Sings.*) "Eat me, Daddy, 8 to the bar."

(BENTINE, *aghast, turns to* SHELLEY.)

BENTINE.   Who is this creature? She is absolutely disgusting.

SHELLEY.   Listen, you fuck. You want your knees broken?

(BENTINE *flees.*)

FRAN.   My next song might be a little bit risqué. (*Sings.*)
"Missed the toilet last night
Shit all over the floor
Cleaned it up with my toothbrush
Don't brush my teeth much anymore."

(OTIS *appears as a Boom Boom Room waiter wearing a sarong, leis and headdress. He wheels a food trolley with a video camera under a lobster. He stops by* WILCOX*'s table.*)

WILCOX.   Waiter! Which is better? The Cajun shrimp or the lobster Bali Hai?

OTIS.   Sir. Four score.

WILCOX.   Amber waves. First, bring me a Mai-tai, no a Suffering Bastard. No, a Samoan Fogcutter in the hula girl glass.

OTIS.   Sir! I've got the videocam under the lobster. I'm wired. We are moving in. Cover me.

WILCOX.   Can't we do it after the show?

Wish Technology
Mark O'Donnell

Characters:
PUDGE, a thirty-five-year-old man
POTS, his thirty-nine-year-old sister
GEMMA, her six-year-old daughter
DAD, almost eighty

(*The setting is a pretty garden party in a bohemian suburb,
though in fact the undertone is more somber. As far as the
audience knows, though, it's a pleasant family get-together.
A trellis may suffice to suggest the garden. A fanciful modern garden chair of fifties vintage, wrought metal with a
very high, pointed back, is at the yard's rear wall — seen or
not — a few yards away from the party itself. The chair
is only borderline comfortable and resembles, slightly, a
broadcast tower. The edgy, headache-causing noise of bottle
rockets is heard, but blessedly, just distant enough not to
grate.* PUDGE — *officially, Paul, and, contrary to his childhood nickname, trim — thirty-five years old, wanders on as
if a little tired of socializing, and sits. He rubs his aching
temples and then momentarily amuses himself by wearily
pretending he's a psychic "broadcasting."*)

PUDGE. Whew! . . . "Air to tower! Do you receive? May Day! May
Day!"

(*More bottle rockets, reinforcing the warfare joke. His sister*
POTS — *derived from Patricia — and her six-year-old daughter,*
GEMMA, *are heard from offstage.*)

POTS. Gemma! Careful now!

GEMMA. (*Off.*) Uncle Paul! Tolliver's letting me dance with him!

316

PUDGE. I see! (*Then, to himself.*) Oh, that's gotta hurt.

(POTS *enters, also nicer-looking than her nickname. She's almost forty.*)

POTS. That poor cat. (*She calls offstage.*) Don't go anywhere near those rockets, Gemma! (*Now, back to* PUDGE.) Howard has really gone over the bend, bringing bottle rockets. (*She calls offstage again.*) Howard, playing with fireworks! You're forty-two years old! (*Now, back to* PUDGE.) Sparklers I don't mind.

PUDGE. I think Howard still secretly aspires to kill one of us.

POTS. . . . Uhhh! (*She stands behind* PUDGE *and rubs his weary shoulders.*) . . . Speaking of death . . .

PUDGE. Pots! Don't be creepy!

POTS. I'm sorry. I was trying to be funny. I just wondered if you heard what Dad said to Howard, about how he knew Mom had died, but that she just wouldn't admit it?

PUDGE. I kind of get what he's saying, though. He knows how furious she must be about it. —Er— How she would be. Oh, you know what I mean. (*Pause.*) . . . George . . . well, he babbled like that near the end, too. (*Suddenly ashamed of his word choice.*) Except, I, I don't mean it's near the end for Dad. You know what I mean —

POTS. I know, Pudge, but come on. We know it is. It's not awful of us to know that.

PUDGE. Well, it just makes me feel helpless, like I'm watching myself in a horror movie. . . . (*Sighs.*) Gemma is certainly in love with that cat.

POTS. I told you, she refers to this as Tolliver's House. And the Frazers' is The Big Dog Duke's House.

PUDGE. Of course, now that makes me jealous of Tolliver. I want Gemma to say, "Let's go to Uncle Paul's house!"

POTS. Oh, she loves you, too. Animals are just easier for her to comprehend. Or to carry, anyhow. (*Pause.*)

PUDGE. I wish I could be a father, if there were some honest way. . .

317

POTS. I know. I remember you said that once. You'd make a good father. I wish you'd give the Sperm Bank another thought.

PUDGE. Ehhhhhh . . . Without love? All that paperwork . . . It would be like a tax audit. (*Pause.*) George's antiques were his babies. I'm surprised he could bear to sell them. He used to stay friendly with the buyers just so he could go and *covertly* visit the furniture.

(GEMMA *has wandered back on.*)

POTS. (*Tenderly touches* PUDGE's *arm.*) Oh, you miss him, I know. Pudgy . . .

GEMMA. Why do you call him Pudgy? He's not pudgy.

POTS. I told you, Gemma . . .

PUDGE. I used to be fat, Gemma! No, I did!

POTS. Oh, you were never that fat.

PUDGE. The word "*that*" proves I was.

POTS. For heaven's sake. Howard just started it to torture you. (*To* GEMMA.) And your Uncle Howard called me Pots because I was always stuck with the pots after dinner.

PUDGE. Oh come on, you volunteered.

POTS. Well, I was a good little Catholic. Sugar but no spice.

(GEMMA's *not interested in this grown-up abstract talk.*)

GEMMA. Can I go see Big Dog Duke?

POTS. Okay, honey, just don't step on any of Mrs. Frazer's flowers, okay?

(GEMMA *wanders off again.*)

Careful! . . . No . . . I wanted Jesus to raise me out of the pew at St. Colman's and announce to everyone how good I was! I was bucking for sainthood. So were you.

PUDGE. (*Sighs.*) Well, we sure aren't now. (*Pause.*) We may get it unwittingly.

POTS. Well, unwillingly, more like it. (*Pause. She mentally reviews her own romantic history.*) Anyway, some of those saints were

318

just model dishrags. . . . Burn me, behead me, I can handle it! My role models! Suffer the drunkard to come unto me! Saint Patricia of Fairview!

(*Pause.* PUDGE *basically reads her mind. She's in a better relationship now.*)

PUDGE. Well, we got burned and beheaded all right . . . Keith is looking good. Er — I don't mean that to sound hubba-hubba or anything — you know what I mean. I really am impressed with him, that's what I mean. Honestly, I was always nervous about Mack, and I am so relieved with Keith!

POTS. Oh thanks, Pudge! You know, I was so scared! I mean, I was pretty sure he was falling in love with me, but at the same time I was scared about how he and Gemma would connect, and I wanted him to love her too!

PUDGE. And he is? I mean, he does?

POTS. I think so, I really do! I mean, so far, so good, at least! Look at him over there, tolerating Howard's pointless stories. I keep thinking, When is this all going to come crashing down? I keep thinking, Yikes! I am so precariously lucky!

PUDGE. No, you deserve it, Pots! (*He hugs her. We hear* DAD *off-stage.*)

DAD. Louise? Howard, where's your mother got to?

(*The two roll their eyes at their father calling their dead mother's name.*)

POTS. You know what's weird? I keep catching myself thinking, why isn't Mom answering? She must be doing laundry. And then — *Duh!*

PUDGE. (*Shrugging.*) Well . . . like father, like son. I keep thinking George is in Europe on one of his antique hunts.

POTS. I know. Maybe that's good . . . Maybe he is!

PUDGE. Oh no, old-movie metaphysics! (*Pause.*) I mean, I put articles aside for him to read. Stuff like that. Double *duh!*

(GEMMA *wanders back on.*)

GEMMA. Momma! Duke isn't home. The stupid people took him somewhere.

PUDGE. Awww.

POTS. He'll be back, Gemma. You just have to come back another day.

GEMMA. (*Impatiently.*) Another day!

PUDGE. Gemma! Last time I saw you, you were in love with a little pink pony with a mermaid's tail.

POTS. Remember, honey? You had a doll like that? You still have it somewhere.

GEMMA. (*Suspiciously.*) Yes.

PUDGE. (*Grinning.*) And how is it?

GEMMA. How is it? It's a doll. It isn't any way. But I guess it's okay.

POTS. She's gone on to Barbie, God help us.

PUDGE. (*Playfully.*) You could sit in the wishing chair over there and wish for Big Dog Duke to come back.

GEMMA. (*Doubtfully.*) Ohh! That's just a regular chair. It just looks weird.

PUDGE. (*Improvising.*) See, well, that's part of it. That high pointy back there points right up to heaven, and you just make your wish, and it goes up the back and bang, straight into outer space. Very high tech. Like a lightning rod. Or the reverse of a lightning rod. It sends lightning out! (*He's entertaining* POTS *more than* GEMMA *now.*) "Air to tower! Do you read me?" Wait a second. Maybe it's "Tower to air!" I guess it depends on whether you think the earth is in the air or not.

POTS. I think you're in over your head.

> (GEMMA *looks blank; this is just nonsense. She turns and goes.*)

Well, *she* didn't buy it, anyway. (*Beat.*) Did you just dream that up?

PUDGE. Actually, no. . . . George said it looked liked a broadcasting tower, and he, uh, used to sit and complain to God in it.

(*More bottle rockets are heard.*)

Gemma! She's determined to blow herself up. Come here!

(DAD *enters, looking back carefully to avoid any errant bottle rockets. He's nearing eighty; a nice, modest man, frustrated by his own senility. He wears a ratty old sweater.*)

PUDGE. Whoa, Dad! Ka-boom! Anzio all over again! How's our veteran birthday boy?

DAD. Movin' kinda slow, but, uh . . . I'm doin' all right, Howard.

PUDGE. I'm Paul, Dad.

DAD. Oh, sorry, Paul! . . . I get so confused now. . . .

PUDGE. It's all right, Dad. All dads mix up their kids. . . . Their kids' names, I mean. . . .

POTS. Dad, that bunch of holes! Why not the new sweater I got you?

DAD. Mm, your mother wouldn't like it. She likes to keep the gifts packed away.

(*What can they do? The "kids" trade tiny furtive shrugs.*)

PUDGE. So! What a birthday wing-ding! What next? Disney World?

DAD. (*Half-coughs as a bitter joke.*) Huh! How about Purgatory?

(*All three laugh together.*)

PUDGE. Oh, Dad! . . . We're already *in* Purgatory!

DAD. (*Joking, or disoriented again?*) Huh? Oh. Yeah . . . I hear the explosions. . . .

POTS. (*Makes to lead* DAD *inside.*) Dad, I know Mom would want you to look swanky at your own party, though! Come on . . . let's put on that birthday sweater I got you. (*She steps offstage briefly to fetch the new sweater.*)

DAD. She could pinch those pennies, boy, she got us through some real scrapes. We ate rice and lard that winter after . . . well, after one of you was born. . . . Her and her coupons . . . she shoulda been foreman where I worked! That was it. She was smart, boy!

321

PUDGE. No, Dad, so were you! I mean, you *are*! What about you? You worked so hard for us! I could never work as hard as you did!

DAD. Well, I'm stupid now! Couldn't even remember where I was going yesterday! Drove around for an hour. Good thing I finally recognized the house and just went home.

PUDGE. Well, see, that's all right!

DAD. Whatever it was I went out to get, I still don't have it.

PUDGE. But at least you understand what . . . that it is happening. It's not your fault, you're fine, it's just your body you have to contend with. . . . We're so proud of you!

DAD. *(Makes a surprisingly smart joke of this not-quite-patronizing compliment.)* Gee! Thanks, *Dad!*

(Slight laugh.)

PUDGE. I didn't mean to be patronizing, Dad. I'm just grateful. I'm just . . . trying to be here for you.

DAD. *(Again, is he joking or confused?)* Well . . . you are here. I can see you. *(Pause. He remembers to ask after Pudge's lover, forgetting he's dead.)* How's uh . . . uh . . . your friend . . . uh . . . George?

(Confused pause: Ouch! POTS *reenters to the rescue.* GEMMA *wanders back on.)*

POTS. . . . Come on, Daddy, let's gussy you up. Anyway, Keith is ready to take your picture. There! No holes! Will you watch Gemma, Paul?

DAD. Take my picture! I'm no pin-up!

*(*POTS *leads* DAD *off.)*

Your mother should be in the picture, not me. . . . Someone has to go downstairs and get her. She's been down in the basement doing laundry for . . . for a long time — And — I can't go down there — It's dangerous! . . .

POTS. We're not at home, Daddy, this is Paul's house. . . .

DAD. We're not at home?

POTS. No, Daddy. We're not. . . .

(GEMMA *has carefully approached* PUDGE.)

GEMMA. Can I try the high-tech wishing chair?

PUDGE. I thought you didn't believe in it.

GEMMA. Well . . . just in case.

PUDGE. Well, sure! Or just for fun, how about that? . . . It's so high-tech you don't have to do a thing but sit and wish. We simply place the niece unit within the wishing field . . . (*He seats her ceremoniously. She looks to him for instructions.*) It's voice activated.

GEMMA. (*Confidentially.*) I'm going to wish for California Hair Barbie and her Hawaiian Dream Beach Buggy!

PUDGE. How shocking! That's so materialistic.

GEMMA. (*Afraid she's being disqualified.*) What do you mean?

PUDGE. Shouldn't you wish for peace on earth?

(*Her lip trembles. She feels her wish is being taken away.*)

GEMMA. Couldn't somebody else wish for peace on earth?

PUDGE. (*Regrets teasing her.*) Oh, of course! — And I wish they would! Awwww — Don't cry, Gemma. I'm only teasing. You wish for whatever you want to wish for.

GEMMA. How many wishes do I get?

PUDGE. As many as you want. But remember, even with special high-tech wish technology, there's still no absolute guarantee you'll get what you wish for.

GEMMA. (*Thoughtfully.*) Okay.

PUDGE. You're willing to run that risk?

GEMMA. (*Seriously.*) Yes.

PUDGE. Then . . . fire away!

(GEMMA *takes a deep breath. She knows it's a game, but can't help hectically imagining what she'd wish for if she could.*)

GEMMA. Okay! . . . I wish for . . . California Hair Barbie and her Hawaiian Dream Beach Buggy and her Dream Soda Fountain and any Barbie stuff I don't know about from now on forever and ever amen, and Magic Flower Maker, and the pretend-you're-having-a-baby costume I saw during *Tiny Toons* . . . and . . . (*She runs out of steam momentarily and grasps for straws, like she's on a supermarket sweep.*) . . . Peace on earth, okay? . . . And, and all the ice cream I want, but not all at once, because I don't know where to put it, it might melt, so have a gallon delivered every day, no, every couple days! I'm not crazy, I don't want to eat a whole gallon a day! I'd get sick! And fat!

PUDGE. You could wish that you could eat all you want and not get fat or sick.

GEMMA. (*Impressed.*) Can I do that?

PUDGE. Sure.

GEMMA. Okay. And I wish nobody else would get sick or fat either!

PUDGE. Ohh! You are so good.

GEMMA. (*Playing along with the silliness.*) Except the devil. I wish *he* would get sick! *And* fat!! (*Getting excited at her own joke.*) And all monsters should get really fat so everyone hates them and then they get really sick and die!

PUDGE. This is getting violent. And what about ghosts? Do you want them to get fat and sick and die?

GEMMA. Ha ha! No! Ghosts can't die! They're already dead! And they aren't allowed to be fat. Ghosts are skinny. And besides, some ghosts are good ghosts.

PUDGE. You're right. Like Casper! (*Thinks of George and Mom.*) Or even . . . well, never mind.

GEMMA. But there are bad ghosts, huh—like in the movie *Polterghost!* Yes, they should die. Or whatever it is ghosts do. They should just stop it.

(*This would appear to conclude the wishes. Pause.*)

PUDGE. Okay. "Wish Central, do you read us?" . . . (*Pause.*)

GEMMA. (*Starts up again unexpectedly and excitedly.*) And some plastigoop! . . . And the Magic Flower Maker! I know I asked for that already, but Correen has one and it broke, so in case mine breaks I should get another one — Or no, wait! Make it one that doesn't ever ever break! And make all the Barbie stuff unbreakable too! Except she should still be able to bend! (*She suddenly gets a brilliant idea.*) Oh! Oh!! Make everything unbreakable! Everything in the world! Except food, we have to eat that! We have to break it into pieces! And . . . ooo . . . What else? Make it so Keith is my real father! . . .

> (*Lights begin to fade slowly. Faintly, we hear a few more bottle rockets going off.*)

And . . . um . . .What about fireworks? Is that them breaking when they go off? Or not? Anyway, leave fireworks the way they are. And . . . Oh, what else? . . . What else? . . . (*Pause.*) What else, Uncle Pudge? . . .

> (*Fadeout.*)

Saved or Destroyed
Harry Kondoleon

Characters:
KARIN
VINCENT
ANNE
IVAN

(*Set: Whatever's available—a theater, an auditorium, a room, a studio. . . . I don't really want a set or, rather, I want the set to be the stage the play is performed on. The back wall, if distracting, can be neutralized with a drawn curtain or one large screen, anything blank. (Eventually, as noted in the script, there are six chairs and a pile of mattresses.) All the characters are to be played by any age group of actors, any race or color, or a mixed group. I don't care. It isn't the kind of play where one must present a nearing verisimilitude to parent-child age differences. These are simply the best actors available at this time and place. If the play is being done in a theater that keeps a company of actors, so much the better, they can be culled quickly from the lot. I'm interest in agile actors with intense emotions.*)

(*Lights up on:*)

KARIN. I'm pregnant again.

VINCENT. How do you know?

KARIN. I know because it's the truth.

VINCENT. But you've been certain before.

KARIN. But now I'm very certain.

VINCENT. You've been very certain before.

KARIN. Oh, stop! I have some good news that I'm enthusiastic about and you're characteristically negative. Do you realize how often this happens? Look in the mirror, see what you find there! I only have positive feelings about having this baby, this child, and your negativity won't root it out, these feelings won't abort me, not again.

VINCENT. You never had an abortion. You had a miscarriage, early in the pregnancy.

KARIN. It might as well have been an abortion. Your nihilistic vibrations could provide murder enough!

VINCENT. Karin, calm down. Must this start with hysteria and recrimination? Can't we embark on this joy if it is to be a joy with some measure of care and consideration as to have some humanity to mete out to our potential offspring?

KARIN. I need to buy a little tape recorder, one of those little ones you can hide in your pocket. That way I can record your little speeches and I can replay them for you. And you'll be flabbergasted, Vincent, to hear your vacuous syntax, your shaky tentative emotions and choiceless stuttering.

VINCENT. As usual you've jumped ahead.

KARIN. Oh I'm sorry. Gee, you know, I have to pee. I should've gone before we started but there it is.

VINCENT. Go, please, take your time.

KARIN. I may in fact take some time. To be terribly frank, I'm getting over a touch of diarrhea.

VINCENT. Aren't we all, darling, aren't we all? Enjoy the flush.

(*She exits in a hurry.* VINCENT *addresses the audience directly.*)

Then it's just us, isn't it? Unless of course you too choose to visit the ladies' room or the gentlemen's room or the more canine choice of the curb. Alas, if I haven't frightened you off already I'll introduce myself to you as your host — one of your hosts for the evening. This is the evening, isn't it? Or is it just very late afternoon, extremely late afternoon. All's well that ends well. Tra-la-la. Where was I?

327

Oh yes, I've been sent to warn you that the hellish melodrama you've come to expect won't be played out to satisfaction this late afternoon. In lieu of the saber fight and usual mud wrestling we are to have introductions to a cluster of dissatisfied actors. Exciting! That's why people come to the theater anyway, don't they, to see actors and measure their own dissatisfactions against those of the characters? Breathless enjoyment! But, fear not, these dissatisfactions will outweigh yours and you will return from this mucky-muck refreshed and readapted. (*Shouting suddenly toward offstage.*) We're going to need those mattresses out here after all. Yeah, a few of them. And set up some chairs. Regular normal chairs. And adjust the lights. Now, before we go any further I want to introduce myself more personally. You can call me Vincent. Our creator has granted us the liberty of our real names. I am your average sometimes-working actor. You have probably not seen me in undistinguished productions in regional theaters across the country — lots of Shakespeare because he-can-handle-the-rhetoric-of-it. You have also possibly not seen me on TV, I was almost nobody in an episode of an episodic murder mystery. I was the cuckolded husband on a daytime soap opera — yes, you don't remember too! — but then they forgettably had me sawed-off in a train wreck. Movie roles you might have missed? Two or three or five or ten a long while ago and so briefly that amassed they would not sustain two fistfuls of popcorn. I am not, good ladies and gentlemen, one of the stars. (*He shouts.*) Now! And be prompt. Now.

> (*Stagehands enter dragging mattresses. These mattresses have no cover and are piled haphazardly, three or four of them. The stagehands all drag out six chairs, loosely put in a semicircle, much in the manner of a play reading. The chairs are upstage of the mattresses. When the stagehands have exited and the mattresses are in place,* VINCENT *reclines on the top one.*)

I should rest now, perchance to dream.

> (*Enter* KARIN, *as before. But she is very young now, they are both adolescents. She sits on the edge of the mattress, excited, restrained, lovely.* VINCENT *is very young, shy, with nearly no traces of the* VINCENT *we've seen.*)

KARIN. Vincent, are you sleeping? Are you? Come on, I saw your eyes flinch — you're not sleeping!

VINCENT. As your mother would say: I'm resting.

KARIN. Well, Buster, can I rest here with you?

VINCENT. Free country.

KARIN. Your dad's having a fit outside because he says they paid too much for the rental.

VINCENT. My father always has fits, that's his thing. My mother calls them his temper tantrums and says I'm to ignore them.

KARIN. He scares me when he yells but mine yells too.

VINCENT. Two screamers.

KARIN. My mother was mad yesterday about the movie we all went to see. She said it was too adult. She said she disapproved of the nudity.

VINCENT. Nudity? What nudity?

KARIN. The *implicit* nudity, she said.

VINCENT. Implicit? Well, just tell her we all have implicit nudity.

KARIN. (*Trying to sound more adult.*) She just meant it was *risqué*.

VINCENT. Why are you sitting so close to me?

KARIN. You know why.

VINCENT. Well, it's too hot and sticky and we just arrived and do you wanna get caught or what?

KARIN. Oh, Vincent. You know you like it as much as I do, more even, or as much.

VINCENT. Like what?

KARIN. Poking and feeling.

VINCENT. Just so long as you know it.

KARIN. Nothing wrong with it.

VINCENT. Just so it stays there, doesn't go any further.

KARIN. Because we're first cousins?

329

VINCENT. Yeah, because we're first cousins! Darn right. We don't want to end up with an unexpected child all distorted and contorted like Quasimodo.

KARIN. No, no. But don't they all come out that way?

VINCENT. They may look that way but they don't stay that way. Ours would stay that way.

KARIN. Are you sure?

VINCENT. Yes I'm sure.

KARIN. (*Readjusting her position on the bed, seductively.*) I don't find it hot and sticky at all. I feel the cool breezes from the ocean. I can taste the salt on my lips. Can you? Let me taste the salt on your lips.

> (KARIN *kisses* VINCENT. *He recoils and looks up guardedly to see no one is coming in and then kisses her, strokes her, "dry petting" furiously, they make touching little sighs and groans as they furtively watch that no one observes them.*)

VINCENT. We have to stop!

KARIN. Why!

VINCENT. Because this can only lead to intercourse.

KARIN. Is that such a bad thing?

VINCENT. Yes! My mother says intercourse except right before and during marriage is a very bad thing.

KARIN. Do your parents have intercourse?

VINCENT. I think so. I saw in my father's attaché case hundreds of them, condoms, in boxes, tan boxes.

KARIN. I guess they're not reusable.

VINCENT. Guess not.

KARIN. I've never seen one. It's hard for me to imagine what one looks like.

VINCENT. I have one.

KARIN. You do? Where?!

VINCENT. In my wallet. Carry it everywhere.

KARIN. You do? How come?

VINCENT. In case of an emergency, silly.

KARIN. Can't this be an emergency?

VINCENT. No.

KARIN. Can't it be an emergency one day this summer? I think an emergency might be coming.

VINCENT. We have to be very careful.

KARIN. A careful emergency, very careful.

(*Lights fade, the sound of the ocean, waves coming in and out. In darkness* VINCENT *exits and* ANNE *enters. As the ocean sounds fade and the lights come up* ANNE *is sitting on the edge of the mattress.* KARIN *is rigidly poised on the mattress.*)

ANNE. Karin, there's something I want to talk to you about. Don't interrupt me!

KARIN. (*Baffled, hurt.*) Mommy, I haven't said a word.

ANNE. No, no, you haven't but you could. I encourage you to interrupt me, to voice your thoughts.

KARIN. The movie we saw at the beginning of the summer, there was nothing wrong with it. You went on about it like it wasn't normal. It was perfectly normal, Mommy. I've been meaning to say so.

ANNE. You and Vincent spend entirely too much time together. For the last three weeks you've been virtually glued to one another. There are hundreds of boys and girls on the beach, you couldn't find one to make friends with?

KARIN. Vincent is my friend.

ANNE. He's your cousin. He's a boy. Don't you need a friend who's a girl to confide in? You know, Karin, you can always confide in me. You know that, don't you? Oh, it was a mistake to take a share with them. Your father has nothing but contempt for his brother — it's depressing to watch. And your aunt, although she

331

tries, she's intolerable! I had such high hopes for my nephew. I so much wanted him to be a homosexual but it doesn't seem to be happening.

KARIN. (*Incredulous.*) What?

ANNE. Homosexuals, and you'll find this to be true as you grow older, as a group they tend to be more sensitive, more talented, even to possess a higher intelligence.

KARIN. That's crazy, completely crazy!

ANNE. I had such high hopes for Vincent. When he was named head of the school newspaper and literary magazine on the same day, I thought —

KARIN. I was appointed the head of the literary magazine, not Vincent!

ANNE. Yes? What movie? What movie are you referring to? With the two people fornicating in the Rolls-Royce, is that the movie?

KARIN. I can assure you, Mother, Vincent is definitely, definitely *not* gay. You have my sacred word on it.

ANNE. (*Electrified.*) I knew it! I bloody knew it! You cunt, you precocious bloody little cunt! How dare you defy me — how dare you? After all I've done for you! If you only knew. You belligerent child, you cow, you . . . you . . . you cunt. (ANNE *slaps* KARIN *hard against her head.* KARIN *falls to the ground crying.*)

KARIN. Stop it! Stop saying that to me. Stop!

ANNE. Your sacred word! I have your "sacred word on it." I have the sacred word on you too! Where did you even pick up that word "sacred," from your psychotic Uncle Maurice? Now what are we going to do, Karin, tell me *what are we going to do?* You're knocked up, I know it. A knocked-up adolescent. The most fertile are the underaged. Knocked up by your own cousin.

KARIN. Stop saying that!

ANNE. I hope you get a black and blue from that smack, Karin. To learn a lesson, to remember a lesson.

KARIN. I hate you!

ANNE. Hate me all you like but we're in a bloody difficult scene here, Karin. Acknowledge that much and when your father learns of this he's liable to cut your head off. (*Breaking out of character.*) I need to break here.

    (*Enter* VINCENT.)

VINCENT. Go ahead, Anne.

ANNE. Go ahead, he says. I have to sit down. (*She sits in one of the chairs. She puts her head down into her hands.*) The doctor says I have cancer. Cancer, just like that, all general. I have this swelling in my abdomen, you can't see it with what I'm wearing but oh you can feel it! Doctor says when he figures out which cancer it is we're to begin chemotherapy. Don't you see? I'm living on borrowed time. I can't afford to sit here and play-act, my cancer is real, ladies and gents. There's no time. (*She lets out a sharp cry of pain. She has had an attack, this is not the first.*)

VINCENT AND ANNE. (*They speak in perfect syncopation, taking exactly the same breaths and pauses. The actors must rehearse this with furious precision; it is not a pas de deux but a solo with two voices.*) But I can't afford to quit. I need the money. I need the money. I have expenses just the way you do. I'm not trained at much else. I need the money. I wouldn't be much good waiting tables, I'd break everything and insult the tippers. I'd end up homeless or sleeping on a cot in my sister's house. I need the money. Acting stupid is the only thing I'm good at. Hey! How'd you get that way? Life made me this way. Colored hat with bells, a baton-rattle, rouged cheeks, a startled smile. (*Pause.*) And somehow it would all make sense if I should become a star. It could still happen. One of the networks might require my type, whatever type that is, a regular spot on a situation comedy can bring big bucks and amusing fan mail and moderate to excellent coverage providing the publicist isn't sitting on his duff. (*Pause.*) But that seems more a realistic dream for the young pretties. If you're not young and pretty, well, then you'd better be pretty darn brilliant! I mean drop-dead brilliant! (*Arch tone of grandiosity.*) And then you can meet the scintillating people. Oh yes, good chap, all the scintillators radiating their multifarious charms — no, I don't mean multifarious. I mean multifaceted, yes, multifaceted. Lalique, Baccarat, me! And then after you have the scintillating people you have love affairs, oodles

333

of them and you fly to Rio and you fly to Ibiza and you fly to Puerto Vallarta and you fly to the goddamn moon! You are adored. And if you decide to have children, they adore you too and if you choose to treat them like shit that's okay too because when you croak they can go write their bitter revenge memoir about you and live happily ever after on the royalties, to say nothing of your residuals. It's a happy story, a Las Vegas story, told over craps, hunched over slot machines and siphoned of all serenity.

KARIN. Sit down, Anne, you must be exhausted.

(ANNE, *who has been standing facing* VINCENT, *sits down.*)

I don't even know what you're doing here. You should be home in bed with someone taking care of you.

VINCENT. She doesn't look exhausted.

ANNE. I don't?

VINCENT. No, not at all. You look good, in full clear voice, an artist.

ANNE. You're a gent, Vinnie.

VINCENT. I just tell the truth.

ANNE. Did I hurt you, Karin? With the slap?

KARIN. Not at all, not in the least. It was too expertly done. You're a pro.

ANNE. But you fell so abruptly.

KARIN. (*Her secret.*) Knee pads.

ANNE. Oh, all right. Let's go on.

KARIN. It isn't necessary, we can break.

ANNE. No, Ivan has to come on, let's just get through that. It's all déjà vu anyway; if we don't do it I'll just go home and believe we did it anyway.

VINCENT. You're not here to kill yourself, Anne.

ANNE. No, that job's already taken, leave your résumé and photo at the front desk.

(KARIN *without a pause regains her place on the floor — a strange eagerness to begin again. She is crying as before, so convincingly and so young again it seems to instantly disqualify nearly all that has preceded it.*)

ANNE. (*In character.*) And when your father learns of this he's liable to cut your head off.

(*Enter* IVAN.)

This opening scene of Harry Kondoleon's play is, tragically for us as well as for the American theater, his last play. This brilliant young writer died in 1994 and is mourned by all who knew him. — J.G.

Degas, C'est Moi
David Ives

Characters:

ED
DORIS
DRIVER
DRY CLEANER
NEWSGUY
WORKER
UNEMPLOYMENT WORKER

OTB WORKER
LIBRARIAN
YOUNG WOMAN
HOT DOG VENDOR
MUSEUM GUARD
MUSEUMGOER
WAITER

(ED, *on a bed. Morning light. A gray wall behind him.*)

ED. I decided to be Degas for a day. Why Degas? Why *not* Degas? Pourquoi pas Degas? Maybe it was the creamy white light on my walls as I lay in bed that morning . . .

(*Creamy white light overspreads the gray wall.*)

Or the prismatic bars of light in the ceiling.

(*Prismatic bars appear at the top of the wall.*)

Maybe it was all the cheap French wine I'd been drinking. It's true, I didn't know much about Degas.

(*A slide of Degas is projected on the wall.*)

Dead French impressionist painter of ballerinas . . .

(*Slide: a Degas dance scene.*)

. . . jockeys . . .

(*Slide: a Degas racetrack scene.*)

. . . that kind of thing. And it's true, I wasn't dead, French or a painter of any kind. And yet — were Edgar Degas and I not united by our shared humanity?

(*Slide of Degas again.*)

By our common need for love?

(*Slide: Doisneau's photo "The Kiss."*)

Coffee?

(*Slide: a cup of coffee.*)

Deodorant?

(*Slide: a naked armpit. That disappears as* DORIS *enters.*)

DORIS. Have you seen my glasses?

ED. Doris — I said — I'm going to be Degas today.

DORIS. I left them here someplace —

ED. — she said, not noticing the brilliance of the idea.

DORIS. He's gonna kill me if I'm late again.

ED. I am Degas!

DORIS. Don't forget the dry cleaning. (*She kisses him, and exits.*)

ED. Doris was distracted by the banal, as usual. No matter. I started my day immediately and brushed my teeth as Degas. (ED *hops out of bed and produces a green toothbrush. The bed disappears.*) Everything seemed different, yet nothing had changed. The very sink seemed transfigured. The porcelain pullulated with possibilities. And will you look at the light on that green plastic . . . ! This thing is revolting. (*Tosses it away.*) In the shower — (*We hear the sound of shower running as he sudses himself.*) — it felt strange, lathering an immortal. What was even stranger, the immortal was lathering back. How had I become such a genius? I, who flunked wood shop in high school? Had it been my traumatic childhood?

(*Slide: a boy of five.*)

My lost pencilbox?

(*Slide: a pencilbox, marked "Lost Pencilbox."*)

Uncle Stosh's unfortunate party trick with the parakeet?

(*Slide: a parakeet.*)

I was great. I was brilliant. My name would live forever! (*He considers that a second.*) No. It's too big. I started breakfast.

(*Slide: two fried eggs. Sound of frying.* ED *shakes a frying pan.*)

Frying my eggs I got fascinated by the lustrous yellow of the yolks. (*Sniffs the air.*) Something burning? My muffin. (*Produces a completely blackened muffin and considers it.*) Being Degas was going to take some practice. (*Tosses the muffin away.*) I went out into the world with dry cleaning.

(*Some clothing on a hanger slides out on a line as we hear city noises, cars honking, etcetera. The light changes and a slide of a city skyline appears.*)

O glorious polychromatic city, saturated with light! Gone the dreary daily déjà vu. Today — *Degas* vu.

(*A car driver enters at a run, holding a steering wheel, headed right for* ED. *Loud car horn and screeching brakes heard as* ED *dodges aside.*)

Idiot!

DRIVER. *Moron!* Watch where you're going!

ED. Jerk! Do you know who you almost killed?

DRIVER. *Asshole!* (DRIVER *exits.*)

ED. Another inch, and the world would've lost a hundred masterpieces.

(DRY CLEANER *enters, writing on a pad.*)

But then at the dry cleaners' I noticed something strange . . .

DRY CLEANER. Pair of pants, jacket and a skirt.

ED. My dry cleaner acted exactly the same.

DRY CLEANER. Name?

ED. Degas.

DRY CLEANER. Tomorrow. (*He tears the slip from the pad, gives it to* ED *and pushes the clothing back out on the line.*)

ED. Then the newsguy on the corner sold me my paper just like always.

(NEWSGUY *enters.*)

NEWSGUY. *Daily news.*

ED. Merci.

NEWSGUY. Change. (NEWSGUY *exits.*)

ED. As I headed down Broadway, people passed me by without a second glance.

(*People enter and pass him.*)

I, Edgar Degas!

(*More people pass him.*)

And then it was that I realized with a shock: *It made no difference to be Degas.* I might as well have been invisible. I could be anyone.

(*More people pass him.*)

And yet — and yet — maybe the other Degas had walked this invisibly through Paris.

(*Slide: a Degas street scene of Paris, as we hear a French accordion and the clip-clopping of horses.*)

Bumped into by the bourgeoisie . . .

(*A pedestrian bumps into him as a* WORKER *enters pushing a two-wheeler.*)

Shouted at by workers at the Left Bank Key Food . . .

WORKER. Watch your back! (WORKER *exits.*)

ED. There was a kind of comfort in this. Nobody recognized me, but nobody hounded me either. Completely anonymous, I was free to appreciate the gray blur of pigeons . . .

(*Slide: flying pigeons.*)

The impasto at Ray's Pizza . . .

(*Slide: pizza window.*)

The chiaroscuro of the M7 bus.

(*Slide: a city bus. An* UNEMPLOYMENT WORKER *enters.*)

UNEMPLOYMENT WORKER. Next!

ED. My delicious anonymity continued at Unemployment.

> (*Accordion and horses stop as a sign descends which says, "Line forms here."*)

UNEMPLOYMENT WORKER. Sign your claim at the bottom, please.

ED. Do you notice the name I signed in the bottom right corner?

UNEMPLOYMENT WORKER. "Edgar Degas."

ED. Edgar Degas. And — ?

UNEMPLOYMENT WORKER. And — ?

ED. *Edgar. Degas.*

> (*Small pause.*)

UNEMPLOYMENT WORKER. Next! (UNEMPLOYMENT WORKER *exits and the sign goes away.*)

ED. Recalling my lifelong interest in racetracks, I stopped off at OTB.

> (*Slide: a Degas racetrack scene, as another sign descends which also says, "Line forms here."* OTB WORKER *enters.*)

OTB WORKER. Next!

ED. Ten francs on Windmill in the third.

OTB WORKER. Mais oui, monsieur.

ED. Windmill — I said to him — because the jockey wears brilliant silks of crimson and gold.

OTB WORKER. (*Handing over the betting slip.*) Windmill —

ED. — he said —

OTB WORKER. — always comes in last.

ED. And Windmill did. But who cares? (*Tears up the betting slip.*) I was Degas.

> (OTB WORKER *exits and the sign goes away. Slide: the city library.*)

Oh. The library. Maybe I should read up on myself.

(*A sign descends: "Silence." A* LIBRARIAN *enters.*)

LIBRARIAN. Section D, aisle 2.

(*A book descends.* ED *opens it.*)

ED. Hilaire Germain Edgar Degas. So my first name is *Hilaire*. Hilarious.

LIBRARIAN. *Shhhhh.*

ED. But who needs the lies of academics? I know who I am.

(*The book flies out.*)

Famished by creativity, I stopped at Twin Donut.

(*Slide: a donut, as two tables appear. A* YOUNG WOMAN *sits at one, writing in a journal.* ED *sits at the other.*)

TWIN DONUT WORKER. Vanilla cruller!

ED. Here! (*Takes the plate.*) There I was, scribbling a priceless doodle on my napkin when I noticed someone staring at me.

(*The* YOUNG WOMAN *stops writing and, pausing for thought, looks at* ED.)

A young woman writing in a journal. Had she recognized me? She smiled slightly. Yes. She knew I was Degas. Not only that. (*He looks again.*) She *loved* Degas. That one look redeemed all my years of effort. My work had given meaning to someone's life. Should I seduce her? It would be traditional. But no. I'd only leave her, hurt her, go back to Doris. Not to mention what it would do to Doris. But isn't it my duty as an artist to seduce this girl? Experience life to the fullest?

(*The* YOUNG WOMAN *goes back to writing.*)

Too late.

YOUNG WOMAN. (*Writing.*) "April six. Twin Donut. Just saw Edgar Degas two tables over. So he likes vanilla crullers too! Suddenly this day is glorious and memorable. Would love to lie in bed all afternoon and make love with Degas. Should I tell Dwayne?" (*She rises.*)

ED. Adieu.

341

YOUNG WOMAN. Adieu. (*She exits and the tables disappear. Afternoon light. Street sounds and a slide of a city street again.*)

ED. On Fifth Avenue, a mysterious figure passed me, leading a Doberman. Or vice versa.

> (*A figure in a raincoat, hat and sunglasses, holding a stiffened leash, as if a dog were on it, crosses.*)

Somebody famous. But who? Kissinger? Woody Allen? Roseanne? Other things distracted me, too. Money . . .

> (*Slide: a dollar bill.*)

Job . . .

> (*Slide: the want ads.*)

Athlete's foot . . .

> (*Slide: a naked foot.*)

Had the itching, pain and discomfort fed my artistry? But wait a minute. I just remembered. I am *Degas!*

> (*Slide: photo of Degas. A* HOT DOG VENDOR *enters.*)

HOT DOG VENDOR. Hot dogs!

ED. The labor of hanging onto one's identity amidst the daily dreck.

HOT DOG VENDOR. Pretzels!

ED. It's too much.

HOT DOG VENDOR. Good Humor!

> (*Empty picture frames descend, as the* HOT DOG VENDOR *exits and a* MUSEUM GUARD *enters.*)

ED. At the museum, I toured the rooms of my work. Amazing how much I accomplished — even without television.

> (*Slide: a Degas self-portrait.*)

A self-portrait. Not a great likeness, maybe. But so full of . . . what? . . . *feeling.* I stared into my fathomless eyes.

> (*A* MUSEUMGOER *enters and stands beside him looking at the self-portrait.*)

MUSEUMGOER. Mmm.

ED. Mmmm.

MUSEUMGOER. Mmmmm. Bit smudgy, isn't it?

ED. "Smudgy"?

MUSEUMGOER. This area. Something not quite realized.

ED. Okay. So I had an off day.

MUSEUMGOER. Excuse me?

ED. Not everything I did was perfect. Can you do better?

MUSEUMGOER. Indeed . . . (*The* MUSEUMGOER *slips away.*)

ED. Probably headed for Van Gogh. To kneel in adoration at the sunflowers — of course. If these philistines only knew what a pain in the ass Vincent was.

(*Slide: "Woman With Chrysanthemums."*)

What's this . . . "Woman With Chrysanthemums." Ah, yes. A personal favorite among my masterworks. When I remember that morning over a century ago — can it be that long now? — when this was an empty canvas and I stood in front of it paralyzed by its whiteness. Intimidated by its nothingness, so pregnant with possibilities. Any mark I made might be a mistake. Any stroke might ruin its purity — and my career along with it. I'd be a laughingstock. A failure. Then I reached for my brush — (*He produces a paintbrush.*) — and it all crystallized. I saw it all. This pensive woman, oblivious of the transcendent burst of color right at her shoulder. The natural exuberance of the flowers — alongside her human sorrow. Yes. Yes! Our blindness to the beautiful! Our insensibility to the splendor right there within our reach! When I finished, I was exalted. Will I ever have a day that inspired again . . . ?

MUSEUM GUARD. Step back, please.

ED. Excuse me?

MUSEUM GUARD. You have to step back, sir. You're too close to the painting.

ED. I'm too close to this painting . . . ?

MUSEUM GUARD. You copy?

ED. I copy. I *am* this painting!

MUSEUM GUARD. Sir?

ED. I stepped back.

> (*He does so, and the slide fades out and the picture frames fly up out of sight. The* MUSEUM GUARD *exits.*)

But the glow of my exaltation stayed with me all the way to the Akropolis Diner, where Doris met me for dinner.

> (*Two tables again.* DORIS *at one, where* ED *sits with her. A man sits at the other. Slide: an empty diner.*)

DORIS. Oh God, what a day.

ED. What a fabulous day. Epic!

DORIS. Six hours of xeroxing.

ED. No, but listen. Degas. Remember?

DORIS. Degas . . .?

ED. I've been Degas all day. Since morning.

DORIS. The toilets backed up again.

ED. I've been Degas.

DORIS. Can you believe it?

ED. I *am* Degas.

> (WAITER *enters.*)

WAITER. Help you?

ED. Cherie, what will you have?

DORIS. Alka-Seltzer.

WAITER. One Bromo.

DORIS. Make it a double.

WAITER. And you?

ED. I'll have a Reuben.

WAITER. *Gimme a Rube! (Exits.)*

DORIS. They said they were going to fix those toilets a week ago.

ED. As she spoke, I began to feel Degas slip away a little . . .

DORIS. Waiter!

ED. . . . like a second skin I was shedding . . .

DORIS. Waiter!

ED. . . . leaving nothing behind.

DORIS. Where is that guy?

ED. Then I noticed a man at another table, staring at me. Looking at me with such pity in his eyes. Such unalloyed human sympathy.

DORIS. I found my glasses.

ED. Then I realized.

DORIS. They were in my purse all the time.

ED. The man at the other table was Renoir.

> (*The man gets up and leaves.*)

By now, Degas was completely gone.

> (*Light changes to night light, the rear wall darkens to black, as* ED *and* DORIS *rise from the tables, and the tables disappear.*)

Doris and I walked home in silence.

> (DORIS *exits.* ED *alone, as the lights darken further around him, to a single spot.*)

People say they have a voice inside their heads. The voice that tells themselves the story of their lives. Now I'm walking up the street, now I'm putting the key in my door, is there a meaning to all this, who's that person on the stairway coming down, now I'm taking out my door key, now I do this, now I do that. The facts of our lives. Yes, I'd always had a voice like that in my head. But now, tonight, no one was hearing it anymore. That presence that always listened in the back of my mind was no longer there, listening in. Nor was there a presence behind

that presence listening in. Nor a presence behind that, nor behind that, nor behind that. All the way back to the back of my
mind, no one was listening in. The story of my life was going
on unwatched. I was alone. (*The bed reappears.* ED *sprawls on
it, his forearm over his eyes.*) When we got upstairs I sprawled
on the bed while Doris ran the bathwater. Degas was dust.
All my glory, all my fame, all my achievements were utterly
forgotten. Immortality? A cruel joke. I had done nothing. Absolutely nothing . . .

(*A light comes up on* DORIS, *naked, drying herself with a
towel.*)

Then I looked through the doorway into the bathroom and saw
Doris standing naked with her foot up on the edge of the old
lion-footed tub, drying herself. The overhead light was dim, but
Doris was fluorescent, luminous, with pinks and lavenders and
vermillions playing over her skin. The frayed towel in her hand
gleamed like a rose. She turned and looked back at me and
smiled.

(DORIS *turns and looks over her shoulder at* ED.)

DORIS. Bon soir, Degas.

ED. Degas? Who needs him? (*He holds his hand out to her across
the intervening space, and she holds hers out to him.*)

(*Lights fade.*)

PERMISSIONS

Professionals and amateurs are hereby warned that these plays, being fully protected under the Copyright Laws of the United States of America and all other countries of the Berne and Universal Copyright Conventions, are subject to a royalty. All rights including, but not limited to, professional, amateur, recording, motion picture, recitation, lecturing, public reading, radio and television broadcasting and the rights of translation into foreign languages are expressly reserved. Particular emphasis is placed on the question of readings and all uses of these plays by educational institutions, permissions for which must be secured from the authors' representatives.

For all inquiries regarding the plays published in *Conjunctions: 25,* contact the following agents:

Creative Artists Agency
9830 Wilshire Blvd.
Beverly Hills, CA 90212
(Wendy Wasserstein, Jonathan Marc Sherman)

Amy Freed
2255 35th Ave.
San Francisco, CA 94116

John Hawkins and Associates, Inc.
Sharon Friedman
71 W. 23rd St.
New York, NY 10010
(Joyce Carol Oates)

ICM
40 W. 57th St.
New York, NY 10019
(John Guare, Doug Wright, Han Ong, Mac Wellman)

Joyce Ketay
1501 Broadway
Suite 1910
New York, NY 10036
(Tony Kushner, Ellen McLaughlin)

Helen Merrill Ltd.
435 W. 23rd St., #1A
New York, NY 10011
(Erik Ehn, Christopher Durang)

William Morris Agency
1325 Avenue of the Americas
New York, NY 10019
(Paula Vogel, Eric Overmyer, Jon Robin Baitz, Keith Reddin, Nicky Silver, Suzan-Lori Parks, Harry Kondoleon)

Howard Rosenstone
Rosenstone/Wender
3 E. 48th St.
New York, NY 10017
(Robert O'Hara, Donald Margulies)

Tantleff Office
375 Greenwich St.
Suite 700
New York, NY 10013
(Arthur Kopit, Mark O'Donnell)

Writers & Artists
19 W. 44th St.
Suite 1000
New York, NY 10036
(David Ives, Romulus Linney)

NOTES ON CONTRIBUTORS

JON ROBIN BAITZ is the author of *The Film Society, The Substance of Fire, The End of the Day* and *Three Hotels*. His new play, *A Fair Country*, will be presented at Lincoln Center Theatre in January. *Amphibians* will be produced at the Seattle Repertory Theatre sometime next season.

CHRISTOPHER DURANG is a playwright and actor. His plays include *Sister Mary Ignatius Explains It All for You* and *The Marriage of Bette and Boo.* A new play, *Sex and Longing*, is scheduled for Lincoln Center in the fall of 1996.

ERIK EHN's *Beginner*, written for Undermain Theater in Dallas, has just been published by Sun & Moon Press. *Erotic Curtsies* will be produced by Bottom's Dream, Los Angeles, this fall. *Every Man Jack of You* was originally written for ACT Writers Group, founded and led by Mac Wellman.

AMY FREED's plays include *Still Warm, Claustrophilia* and *The Ghoul of Amherst.* The excerpt from *The Psychic Life of Savages* published in this issue is taken from a full-length play that was produced in the spring of 1995 at the Woolly Mammoth Theatre.

RED GROOMS, artist, has designed sets since 1964. His most recent show of installations was held this fall at Marlborough Gallery in New York City.

JOHN GUARE, guest editor of this issue, has written many plays, including *House of Blue Leaves, Six Degrees of Separation* and *Lydie Breeze*, as well as the screenplay for Louis Malle's *Atlantic City.* He was elected to the American Academy of Arts and Letters in 1989 and is a council member of the Dramatists Guild.

DAVID IVES is the author of "All in the Timing," an evening of six short comedies that recently completed an eighteen-month run off-Broadway in New York.

HARRY KONDOLEON (1955–1994) was the author of the novels *Diary of a Lost Boy* and *The Whore of Tjampuan*, a book of poems, *The Death of Understanding*, and many plays, among them *Love Diatribe, Zero Positive, Anteroom, Christmas on Mars* and *Self Torture and Strenuous Exercise.* He was included in the anthologies *The Way We Live Now* and *Best Short Plays 1984.*

ARTHUR KOPIT is a playwright and screenwriter. *Elegy for the House That Ruth Built* was commissioned by Bay Package Productions in San Francisco for an evening of one-act plays dealing with baseball, the overall evening called "Hitting for the Cycle."

TONY KUSHNER's plays include *A Bright Room Called Day*; his adaptation of Pierre Corneille's *The Illusion; Angels in America: A Gay Fantasia on National Themes, Part One: Millennium Approaches* and *Part Two: Perestroika;* and *Slavs!, or Thinking About the Longstanding Problems of Virtue and Happiness,* which will be published in a collection of his recent writing by Theatre Communications Group this fall.

ROMULUS LINNEY is the author of three novels and many plays, including *The Sorrows of Frederick, Holy Ghosts, Childe Byron, Three Poets* and *2*, produced throughout the United States and abroad. He is professor of the arts at Columbia University.

DONALD MARGULIES's plays include *Sight Unseen, The Loman Family Picnic, The Model Apartment, What's Wrong With This Picture?* and *Found a Peanut*, all of which will be published in a collection by Theatre Communications Group. "Kibbutz" is a scene from an abandoned work called *Heartbreaker*.

ELLEN McLAUGHLIN's plays include *Days and Nights Within, A Narrow Bed* and *Infinity's House*, all of which have received American and international productions. The two plays included in this publication serve as prologue and epilogue to a full-length work entitled *Iphigenia and Other Daughters*, which was produced Off-Broadway at Classic Stage Company this year.

JOYCE CAROL OATES is the author most recently of the novel *Zombie* (Dutton). Plays of hers have been performed in New York, London, Paris and Vienna. Her plays have been collected in *The Perfectionist and Other Plays* (Ecco, 1995) and *Twelve Plays* (Dutton, 1991). Her forthcoming play *Cry Me a River* will be performed at the Preview Theater of the University of North Carolina School of the Arts in Winston-Salem (January 1996).

MARK O'DONNELL's plays include *That's It, Folks!, Fables for Friends* and *The Nice and the Nasty* (all produced at Playwrights Horizons), *Strangers on Earth* and *Vertigo Park*. Knopf has published two books of his stories and will publish his novel, *Getting Over Homer*, next spring.

ROBERT O'HARA is a director/playwright and is currently artist-in-residence at the New York Shakespeare Festival. He recently completed the M.F.A. directing program at Columbia University, where he directed his award-winning new play, *Insurrection*, for his final thesis production. He is at work adapting his new play, *Brave Brood*, for the screen.

HAN ONG is the author of *The L.A. Plays, Reasons to Live* and *Swoony Planet*. They have been presented at the American Repertory Theatre, the Mark Taper Forum, the Magic Theatre and the Almeida Theatre in London. *The Chang Fragments*, of which *Mrs. Chang* is "Fragment Two," will be produced in the spring of 1996 at the Joseph Papp Public Theatre.

ERIC OVERMYER's latest play is *Dark Rapture. The Dalai Lama Goes Three for Four* was produced in June 1995 at the Magic Theatre (San Francisco) as part of an evening of baseball plays, "Hitting for the Cycle."

SUZAN-LORI PARKS's new play, *Venus*, directed by Richard Foreman, will co-premiere at The Yale Repertory Theatre and The Public Theatre next spring. Her first feature film, *Girl 6*, directed by Spike Lee, will open next spring at a theatre near you.

KEITH REDDIN's plays include *Life and Limb, Rum and Coke, Nebraska, Life During Wartime, Big Time* and *Brutality of Fact*.

JONATHAN MARC SHERMAN's plays include *Women and Wallace, Veins and Some Tacks, Sons and Fathers, Sophistry* and *Wonderful Time.* The scene published in this issue of *Conjunctions* is from his new play *Evolution.*

NICKY SILVER is the author of *Pterodactyls* (Oppenheimer Award, Kesselring Award), *Raised in Captivity, Free Will & Wanton Lust* (Helen Hayes Award, Best New Play 1994) and *The Food Chain.*

PAULA VOGEL's anthology, *The Baltimore Waltz and Other Plays,* will be published this fall (Theatre Communications Group). Other plays include *Hot 'N' Throbbing, Desdemona, The Oldest Profession* and *And Baby Makes Seven.* The excerpt published in this issue of *Conjunctions* is from a work in progress that will be produced at The American Repertory Theatre in spring 1996.

WENDY WASSERSTEIN's *Antonia and Jane* was adapted from Marcia Kahan's screenplay for Laurence Mark Productions. It is an American version of Ms. Kahan's British film. Ms. Wasserstein also adapted Stephen MacCauley's novel *The Object of My Affection* for film and her plays *The Heidi Chronicles* and *Uncommon Women* for television.

MAC WELLMAN's recent plays are *The Hyacinth Macaw* (Primary Stages), *Swoop* and *Tallahassee* (Workhouse). His novel, *Annie Salem,* is forthcoming from Sun & Moon Press. *The Sandalwood Box,* which appears in this issue of *Conjunctions,* was originally commissioned and produced by the McCarter Theater, Princeton, New Jersey.

DOUG WRIGHT's plays include *The Stonewater Rapture, Interrogating the Nude, Dinosaurs, Buzzsaw Berkeley* and *Lot 13: The Bone Violin.* He is a past recipient of the William L. Bradley Fellowship at Yale University and the Alfred Hodder Fellowship at Princeton.

DAVID MAMET SOCIETY

An organization for the study of David Mamet's work and of performances of it on stage, film and television has been launched.

The Society has published two annual newsletters and will begin publication of a hard-cover annual review in 1996. We invite submissions of critical essays, performance and book reviews, and interviews for an inaugural issue.

For inquiries, membership information, or to submit essays, reviews, or other materials, write:

Leslie Kane
Department of English
Westfield State College
Westfield, MA 01086
- or -
Christopher C. Hudgins
Department of English
University of Nevada
Las Vegas, NV 89154-5011

Thinking About the Longstanding Problems of Virtue and Happiness

(Essays, a Play, Two Poems and a Prayer)

TONY KUSHNER

The first collection of writings by the Pulitzer Prize-winning author of *Angels in America*, including Kushner's latest play, the Obie Award-winning *Slavs!*

Paper $13.95

Angels in America

Parts One and Two, boxed set

TONY KUSHNER

Contains both *Millenium Approaches* and *Perestroika*, winners of consecutive Tony Awards for Best Play.

"The most ambitious American play of our time."

–Jack Kroll, *Newsweek*

$22.95, Paperbacks in slipcase

Approaching Zanzibar

and Other Plays

TINA HOWE

"Plays that can best be characterized as poetic farces, as antic elegies."

–Ross Wetzsteon
New York Magazine

Paper $13.95

Passion

STEPHEN SONDHEIM
and JAMES LAPINE

Winner of the 1994 Tony Award for Best Musical, this tale of an Italian woman's unrequited love for a young army officer explores Eros and its implications.

Paper $10.95

subUrbia

ERIC BOGOSIAN

Bogosian's first full-length play since the acclaimed *Talk Radio*.

"As ferocious as Mr. Bogosian's own one-man shows."

–*New York Times*

Paper $10.95

The America Play

and Other Works

SUZAN-LORI PARKS

Includes six of this innovative young writers works as well as essays which provide insight into her provocative theatrical style and innovative vision.

Paper $14.95

TCG is pleased to announce forthcoming play collections by
Donald Margulies, Nicky Silver and Paula Vogel.

PLEASE HELP SUPPORT *CONJUNCTIONS*

The generosity of many individuals and organizations helps make it possible for *Conjunctions* to continue to publish the best in new writing, from fiction to drama to poetry to interviews to work that defies categorizing.

If you would like to join those below who have contributed toward future issues of *Conjunctions*, please contact us at (914) 758-1539, or write Michael Bergstein, *Conjunctions*, Bard College, Annandale-on-Hudson, NY 12504.

All donations are tax-deductible, and greatly appreciated.